"Do you mind if I get undressed while we talk?"

"Not at all," Rebecca replied softly, sinking down to the edge of the bed and watching as the gunslinger's fingers methodically unfastened the buttons of her black shirt. When she peeled it off to reveal her shoulders and her creamy breasts, Rebecca was unable to take her eyes away from the beautiful spectacle. Josie's breasts fairly glowed in the dancing candle flame, and Rebecca ached to reach out and touch them. Transfixed by the tantalizing beauty in front of her, Rebecca suddenly found herself tongue-tied and blushing. She could not even think of what it was she wanted to say, and she simply sat like a schoolgirl admiring her first real crush.

Josie could not help but notice where Rebecca's eyes were fastened, and she smiled at the mix of emotions revealed in that simple look. If she had ever wondered whether there was a chance the little blonde was attracted to her, she wondered no more. Blatant desire was written on Rebecca's young face, but there was uncertainty as well. Josie knew she must be patient with Rebecca and give her all the time she needed to sort out her feelings without her influence. Much as she wanted to take the smaller woman in her arms and smother her with kisses, she knew Rebecca was not ready for that. She would allow Rebecca to set the pace, taking her cues from her.

Josie reached down and clasped Rebecca by her wrists and pulled her up to where she could place a kiss on her forehead. Then she whirled her around and sat her down on the edge of the bed facing the other side of the room, and at the same time she rose and unbuckled her belt and dropped her pants to the floor. "Don't turn around. I'm naked," she said as she grabbed her long johns from the back of a chair and quickly stepped into them. By the time Rebecca did turn around, Josie was slipping her arms into the sleeves and all but covered up. "I'm going to blow out this candle now so you can get undressed. Unless you want to tease me by getting naked in front of me," Josie said with a raised eyebrow and a sly smile.

"Blow it out," Rebecca said shyly.

Another Book by BL Miller

Accidental Love
BL Miller

Other Books by Justice House Publishing

Tropical Storm
Melissa Good

Lucifer Rising
Sharon Bowers

Gun Shy
Lori L. Lake
[Coming soon]

Silent Legacy
Cìaràn Llachlan Leavitt
[Coming soon]

Josie and Rebecca

THE WESTERN CHRONICLES

BL Miller and Vada Foster

JUSTICE HOUSE PUBLISHING

Tacoma, Washington

www.justicehouse.com

JOSIE AND REBECCA:
THE WESTERN CHRONICLES

Copyright © 1999 by BL Miller & Vada Foster

JHP book No. 4

JHP books are distributed by BookMasters.

Cover by Chrissy David
Book design by Robin Paterson

This book is printed on acid-free paper.
The type face is Times New Roman, 11 point.
The paper is Book Opaque.

ISBN: 0-9677687-3-X
First Edition, January 2000
1 2 3 4 5 6 7 8 9

PRINTED IN CANADA.

TO: PAULETTE AND JEAN

HOPE YOU GUYS ENJOY THE BOOK!!
PLEASE WRITE AND LET ME KNOW
WHAT YOU THINK. HRHVADA @ AOL. COM
LOVED HAVING YOU HERE!! (TROUBLE MAKER!)

Love Val

Dedication

There is no doubt in either of our minds that this story wouldn't have been completed if it wasn't for the never-ending dedication of swqVerda Foster. She believed in this story from the first sentence and never gave up on it. It is through her efforts as much as ours that this story made its way to the light of day and we dedicate "Josie And Rebecca: The Western Chronicles" to her.

BL Miller

B L was raised in New York but now lives in central Maine with her two cats. A self-described romantic mushball, she spends her free time writing lesbian fiction and playing handywoman around the house.

Vada Foster

Vada has always had a passion for the written and spoken word. She been a writer, director, singer and actor since her school days where she was bitten by the acting bug. She has been involved in dozens of theatrical productions - both in front of and behind the scenes- primarily in Long Beach, California, where she has also served on the Board of Directors of Lambda Players .

She has paid the bills with a variety of different jobs ranging from production artist to switchboard operator, and for more years than you can count on all your fingers and toes, as an Operations Planner for a large toy company. "Josie and Rebecca: The Western Chronicles" is her first novel, but she is also known as a "bard" in the "Xena-verse." She lives in southern California with her twin sister and an assortment of dogs and cats.

Acknowledgements

"Josie and Rebecca: The Western Chronicles" has been through several incarnations. It began as an Uber Xena story under the title "The Western Chronicles" written by BL Miller. BL's muse called her to other things, and at that point Vada Foster became involved. She revised the beginning of the story somewhat (Xena had to go) and finished writing it. The story was subsequently posted on the internet in installments as a first draft.

Debbie Cassetta asked if a copy of the story could be donated to Sword and Staff for a charity auction (thanks for your great work with that, Mist!) so the draft needed to be polished up. For the copy that was donated, the authors wish to gratefully acknowledge Angelique for the original artwork she created. We also owe a big thanks to Jené Geller for the graphics design on the cover. Lori Buck spent simply hours editing, and taught me a lot about things grammatical, and should get a medal for that.

For the incarnation you hold in your hands, we are indebted to Chrissy David for all the work she did on the cover. We want to thank Stephanie Elliot for additional editing, and Angelique for once again allowing us to use the art she created.

Finally and always, we owe thanks and more to Verda for pushing us both in the direction of our computers when we had other things to do. Without her, this book would never have been finished.

1: Alone

The late afternoon sun set across the wind-ravaged canyon, turning the rock into a brilliant tapestry of orange and brown. The lone rider sat atop her golden mare, her raven hair flowing loose over her shoulders. The wide brim of her black Stetson kept the sunlight from blinding her as she looked around for a safe place to sleep. Spotting a cave off in the distance, she leaned down to whisper into the horse's ear. "Come on, Phoenix. Just a little bit longer and we'll rest." Urging the horse up a narrow slope, Josie kept watch over the surrounding area.

It had been only six weeks since her gang had been ambushed while trying to rob a train in Missouri. It was only her quick thinking and fast gun that had kept her alive. She hoped that Henry and Jonah had also escaped; she had seen them take off in separate directions to draw the posse away from her. Deep inside, she knew the ambush had been orchestrated by one of her men in an attempt to kill her, no doubt to collect the bounty on her head. To be sold out for one thousand dollars by one of the men with whom she had been riding for two years stuck in her craw. When they had set out on what was to be their last train robbery, she could not have foreseen that before the day was out she would be riding for her life with a fully armed posse on her heels. Even now, she knew nothing about the fate of her two trusted comrades.

Reaching the cave entrance, Josie dismounted and removed the saddle and saddlebags from Phoenix's back. She looped the reins loosely over a low branch, allowing the bay horse to crop grass in the dappled shade.

Josie carried her belongings into the cool interior of the cave. Not that there was much in the saddlebags; most of her supplies were left at the main camp when she had embarked on her ill-fated trip to the railway siding. Once settled into the cave with a small fire to keep her warm, Josie took stock of her inventory, starting with her clothes. She had her black boots, complete with silver tips and spurs. Filthy black cotton trousers covered her legs and a thin, black, long-sleeved shirt and brown leather vest covered her upper torso. She wore a black leather belt that was more than just for keeping her pants up; a hidden pocket sewn into the inside concealed a small knife. If her hands were tied behind her back, the pocket was within easy reach. That little secret had saved her life more than once. The vest also had a secret compartment. A dingy gray kerchief was wrapped around her neck. Her black Stetson was resting nearby. These were the only clothes she owned now.

Her weapons were the only other things she still had in her possession. Two Colt Peacemakers were strapped to her legs by bullet-rimmed gun belts crisscrossed over her slender hips. There were less than six cartridges for the Winchester 73 strapped to the saddle. The rest had been expended escaping from the posse. Each boot contained one Bowie knife and she still had her whip, albeit a bit shorter than when it was new.

Rummaging through the saddlebags again, she found no money, no dried meat, nothing she could use. Only a small bottle of ink and a broken pen resided in one pouch, while a fork and spoon took up another. There were no pots or pans, nothing in which to cook a meal. "Not even a piece of jerky," she growled, shoving the saddlebags away. Putting the canteen to her lips, Josie took several sips of the precious water. She wished she had more than one canteen; the days were too hot to ride without draining the flask at least twice. Josie was trying her best to follow the river, knowing that a town would eventually appear. As much as she hated taking the chance of being recognized from the wanted posters, she had no choice but to get more supplies. Using the scratchy saddle blanket to cover herself, Josie laid her head against the saddle and settled in for a light sleep.

2: The Rescue

Josie urged Phoenix along, following the sounds of a woman's screams. Soundlessly, she slid from the horse's back, and with the grace of a cat, crept to the edge of the clearing from which the sounds emanated. Her eyes narrowed when she saw two scruffy men holding a young woman while a third pawed her body.

"Why don't you pick on someone your own size, boys?" Her voice startled the pawing man, who turned and began to reach for his gun. Josie's hands were quicker and she fired two shots into him before his gun was halfway out of his holster. The other two let go of the girl and reached for their weapons. The sharp-shooting woman took them down with only one bullet each. Truth be told, she could have killed the first man with only one bullet, but she felt that he deserved two for trying to rape the frightened woman.

The blonde woman sank to the ground and huddled into a small ball. Josie could not see the girl's face since it was buried in her arms, but the shaking shoulders and sniffles told her the girl was crying. With a shrug, the gunslinger turned away and walked to where the men lay in pools of their own blood. She stripped the gun belts from their bodies and searched their pockets for coins or anything else that might be usable. The one who had been trying to tear the clothes off the young girl had a pocket full of Confederate currency and even more stuffed into the band inside his gray uniform cap. With a shake of her head, Josie dropped the bills on top of his prostrate form. "The South won't rise again...and neither will you, Johnny." She straightened up and gave a sharp whistle. Phoenix stopped munching grass on the edge of the clearing and trotted obediently to her mistress's side. Josie draped the three gun belts around the saddle horn and stuffed the coins and two knives she had taken off the dead men into the saddlebags. After securing the leather straps on the saddlebags, she put her foot in the stirrup and smoothly vaulted into the saddle. She made a clicking noise with her tongue and the horse broke into a trot. The sound of the hoof beats penetrated the girl's stupor.

"Wait!" the girl cried as she struggled to her feet. "You can't leave me here." She looked around at the blood-soaked dead men and the look in her eyes was that of a frightened child. "Please," she added quietly.

Josie's keen hearing picked up on the absolute fear and helplessness in the girl's voice. Cursing under her breath, she reined in her horse and urged her closer to the girl. "What's your name, girl?" she asked in her most intimidating voice.

"Re-Rebecca," she stammered. She looked up at the woman who had saved her. Dressed all in black save for the vest and scarf, the tall woman looked like death itself to the inexperienced farm girl. The only humanity she could see in the finely chiseled face was the piercing blue eyes.

"Do you have a home around here?" The gunslinger asked.

"N-No. I live in Chancetown." Josie groaned inwardly. Chancetown was a couple hours ride in the opposite direction. Looking around, the outlaw saw no signs of horses.

"Where are their horses?" she demanded.

"Uh..." Rebecca shook her head. "They had a wagon...I don't...."

"I'm going to go have a look for it. Stay here!" Josie barked as she urged Phoenix out of the clearing.

When Josie returned, she found Rebecca sitting, curled up in a ball, as far away from the dead men as she could get. She stopped the horse in front of the girl. Rebecca looked up at her but said nothing.

"I found the wagon. It had gone over the edge of a cliff. I had to shoot the horses." She had only been able to salvage a few of the drifter's' goods, since most of them had been smashed beyond use in the fall down the hill, but she saw no need to share this information with the young woman.

"How do I get back home?" Rebecca asked softly, her voice on the verge of breaking. She had never been away from home before and now she was with a woman who had just killed three men.

Josie pointed in the direction of the town. "Go that way. On foot, it'll take you no more than half a day." The girl nodded and slowly rose to walk away, her shoulders slumped. The kidnapping and near rape had shaken Rebecca to the core, and the thought of walking all that way alone was almost more than she could bear. Josie debated and argued with herself for a few moments before nudging Phoenix forward to catch the girl.

"Get up here. I'll drop you off outside of town," she said as she dismounted. Rebecca looked up at the tall horse, her eyes widening.

"She's awfully big."

"She's a horse!" Josie snarled. "They're supposed to be big."

Rebecca moved to put her foot in the stirrup but paused. "I'd rather walk beside you."

"I don't have time for this, girl. Either get on the horse now or I leave."

"But I can't ride in this dress."

"Suit yourself," Josie growled, gathering the reins in her hand and preparing to mount the horse.

"No, please don't leave me," Rebecca pleaded. "I'll ride, but I can't do it with my dress around my waist. I'd be...exposed."

Josie shook her head and sighed. "Stand still and spread your legs." Rebecca looked at her, horrified. Josie forced the young woman's legs apart by nudging her ankles with her booted foot. Ignoring the yelp of protest, she pulled a bowie knife out of her boot and stabbed through the material, halfway between the girl's hips and knees. After putting the knife back, she grabbed the torn material with both hands and ripped it the rest of the way down to the hem. "Mount up," she snarled. Rebecca put her foot in the stirrup and Josie boosted her into the saddle. When the young woman was settled, Josie vaulted smoothly up behind her.

The torn ends of Rebecca's dress flapped in the wind as they made their way to Chancetown. Rebecca gripped the saddle horn with both hands as the large horse's hooves ate up the ground beneath them. Josie's hands rested on her own thighs, her left hand holding the reins. She was never comfortable with physical contact, unless she was fighting. This frightened child needed comforting, but that was not something the outlaw was willing to do. All she wanted was to get the blonde safely home so she could get back to her own business.

"Um...can I ask you something?" Rebecca said timidly.

"You just did," Josie answered wryly.

"Oh, well, I guess I did. I-I was just wondering what your name was. So I could thank you properly for saving my life."

"You sure you want to know, little girl?" Josie taunted. The woman sitting in front of her nodded. "The name is Josie Hunter."

Rebecca stiffened and gripped the horn even tighter. "Josie Hunter, the outlaw? Terror of the Railway?" She stopped when she realized that the names might not go over so well with the heavily armed woman behind her.

"The same," Josie replied. "Any more questions?"

"What? Oh, no, Jo-I mean...."

"You mean to keep quiet and not bother me or I'll kill you without a thought." Rebecca pressed her lips together tightly and vowed to do just that.

3:   Chancetown

The outlaw pulled up the reins the instant she saw the first signs of civilization. Wordlessly, she dismounted and waited for the young woman to get off her horse so she could be on her way. Rebecca's knuckles were white from holding onto the saddlehorn, and it took a moment for her to disengage her fingers and lower herself to the ground. Josie climbed back into the saddle.

"Wait, you're not going to leave me here all alone, are you?"

"Chancetown is right over there." Josie nudged Phoenix and took off, leaving the blonde woman standing there. Rebecca turned and headed home, not as excited as she should have been, although not really knowing why.

As Rebecca walked through the main street in town, she could not help but notice that several people stopped and blatantly gawked at her. The wife of the man who ran the feed and grain store recognized the girl and, draping a horse blanket over her shoulders, she escorted the shaken young woman to the doctor's office. The doctor sent his son to tell Rebecca's family that she was in town. While waiting for the doctor to examine her, she got a look at herself in a mirror, and she understood why everyone was so worried. She was a mess. Her dress was completely ruined from the outlaw's knife and stained by the men's blood. Her hair was loosely scattered about her head, with bits of grass and dirt tangled up in it. It took vigorous protesting by Rebecca to convince the doctor that she was not in need of a personal examination. The sheriff arrived at the same time as her parents. Her mother took one look at the torn dress and burst into tears. Her father scowled at her.

"How could you let somethin' like this happen to you!" he roared as he stepped closer to her, his hand upraised. Sheriff Wellman stepped between them.

"Now, just hold on there, Caleb. We don't know what happened yet. No sense beating the girl for something she ain't done yet." The beefy sheriff waited until the angry man lowered his hand before turning to look at Rebecca, who was being held in a death-lock hug by her mother. "Girl, what happened?" he asked.

It took a moment for Rebecca to get Sarah to release her. "I was out in the fields when three men in a wagon stopped and asked if I could tell them how to get to Chancetown. While I was telling one of them, the other two came up from behind and grabbed me. They threw me into the wagon and took off. I…" She was cut off by her father's angry voice.

"And you let them?" he growled as he took a step forward. The sheriff turned his head and gave Caleb a warning glare.

"I didn't let them!" she cried. "I tried to get away from them but there were three of them, and…."

"Did they hurt you, child?" Sarah asked her daughter, with genuine concern in her voice.

"No. They were going to, but I was rescued."

"Rescued?" her father asked incredulously. "And just who'd be the one that rescued you?"

"Josie Hunt…" She started to say the outlaw's full name, but stopped herself out of fear for what the gunslinger would do to her if she were caught because she told the sheriff she was in the area. Quickly she added, "I-I think that's what she said her name was. I was so upset I might have misheard."

"You tryin' to say Josie Hunter saved you?" Caleb said angrily. "Drag me out of the fields for this nonsense!" He glared at his wife. "This is all your fault for lettin' her daydream all the time and read them books. Nothin' good ever came from readin' no books. She should be learnin' how to be some man's wife 'stead of all the time havin' her nose buried in some damn book."

"But Daddy, I…." A strong slap across the face silenced her. Sarah cried out, but made no effort to stop him.

"You always did talk too much fer your own good, girl. Look at you!" He looked at her disheveled hair and clothes. "Why, you ain't much better than them bitches and whores over to the saloon." He grabbed Rebecca by the upper arm, squeezing it painfully. "You git yourself out to the wagon right now, girl! You hear me?"

"Y-yes, you're hurting me," she cried as his fingers tightened. Sarah knew better than to interfere. She stepped back a few feet and silently prayed that he would not beat their daughter in front of the sheriff.

"You ain't seen hurt like you're gonna see it when I git you back home," he hissed under his breath so only Rebecca could hear him. Visions of her father's ideas of punishment flashed through her mind. She started to shake her head back and forth.

"No, Daddy, please. I didn't do anything wrong."

"You're lyin', girl! Makin' up stories 'bout that outlaw rescuin' you. Why, even I know that murderin' bitch died a while back with her gang. 'Sides, she's purely evil; ain't no way she'd risk her own neck to go and save your worthless hide." He smacked her once more before dragging her out to their wagon and roughly pushing her into the back. He did not bother to help Sarah up. Sheriff Wellman came over and silently assisted her. Caleb climbed up on his side and grabbed the reins, unmindful of his daughter's tears.

Sheriff Wellman watched them drive away. His eyes locked on the sad, green eyes in the back of the wagon. Doctor Thompson stood next to him.

"Think she's tellin' the truth?" The sheriff asked.

"Hard to say. But if she is, she'd be better off with the outlaw than her father right now." Dr. Thompson decided not to mention the numerous faded bruises he saw when he examined her.

"You may very well be right about that, Doc." The sheriff knew all too well just how violent Caleb's temper was. He had pulled the man out of enough barroom brawls over the years to know just how badly alcohol affected the farmer. It was obvious that Caleb had already started his daily drinking binge and the sheriff had no doubt that it would be several days before the young woman showed her face around town.

Rebecca lay awake, tears streaming down her face. She was in too much pain to sleep anyway. Upon arriving at the farm, her father had dragged her into the barn and beaten her severely with a leather strap until, in desperation, she made up a story that he believed. She told him that she had met up with a young man from town who tried to have his way with her. When she refused, the boy slapped her around and left her miles from home. She said she tore her dress on barbed wire while crawling under a fence. He smiled and accepted that story, giving her a fresh beating for lying about the outlaw and the men, and another series of lashes for running away in the first place. Only when his massive arm ached from raising the strap did he finally drop the leather and leave the barn. Rebecca slumped to the earthen floor; the last sound she heard was him cursing her as he headed to the house. Only when she was certain that he had drunk himself into a stupor did she dare leave the barn and enter the house. Her sister, Kate, and her mother helped her get cleaned up and put ointment on the multitude of lashes and cuts on her back and legs. Her thin dress and corset did nothing to ease the severity of the blows from the strap. Her mother had long ago run out of words to comfort her oldest daughter. For some reason, Caleb visited his wrath on Rebecca more than on any of his other women. Sarah suspected it was because no matter how much he beat her, he could not break Rebecca's spirit.

Now, lying in bed, her body in agony, Rebecca wondered just why she had bothered to return. She tried to roll over and winced in pain as her thin nightshirt rubbed against her tender skin. A loud crash downstairs told her that her father was now awake from his drunken slumber. Fear of another beating gripped her. *This is no way to live*, she thought. As he lumbered up the stairs, she heard him mumbling about his troublesome daughter and how he could only hope that "this damn foolishness" did not ruin her chances of finding a husband.

Rebecca waited until she heard the snores coming from her parents' room before climbing out of her bed. She walked carefully around the floorboards she knew creaked to avoid waking Kate, who was sleeping soundly on the other side of the room. Pulling one peasant dress from the pile of dirty clothes and grabbing her shoes, she quietly left their room and headed downstairs. After dressing quickly, she found a pen and ink and wrote a short note telling her mother and sister that she loved them and would send word soon.

Once away from the farm, Rebecca realized that she had no idea which direction to take. Other than the farm, Chancetown was really the only place she knew. Without consciously thinking about where she was going, she found herself walking down the main street of town. Sheriff Wellman stepped out of the saloon at the same moment she walked by.

"Hold up, girl. Where you goin'?" Rebecca looked at him fearfully. Her eyes reminded the lawman of a frightened deer.

"I-I...." She was not sure what to say to him. Would he let her go? Would he tell her father? "Please don't say anything," she finally asked in fear.

"Come here." He gently grabbed her arm, mentally cursing himself as he watched her flinch. Letting go, he motioned for her to follow him over to the jail.

He's going to send me back there. "No, please...I can't go back...please," she begged. "I'll do anything, please!"

"Quiet down, child," he said softly as he opened the door to the jailhouse. Lighting a lantern, he motioned for her to sit down in a nearby chair before walking behind the desk and settling into his wooden chair. "Do you have any money?"

"No."

He reached into a drawer and pulled out a small strongbox. Opening it, he pulled out two dollars and held them out to her. "I know it's only sixteen bits, but you can't go out there with nothing."

Rebecca looked at him in shock, not knowing what to say. "I...I..." Never in her life had she held two bits, much less two dollars. "I don't know how to thank you." The sheriff cut her off with a wave of his hand.

"Don't thank me, child. I know your father." He folded up the bills and stuffed them into her boot. "I should have stopped him a long time ago. Now you better get goin' before the sun comes up and he discovers you missing." Rebecca stood up to leave. "Where you goin' to, anyway?"

"West," she said as she opened the door.

4:   Snakes

Rebecca tried to follow the tracks of the outlaw but the half moon was not cooperative. Several times she strayed off course, ending up almost a mile off by the time daylight started to help her. The relentless heat threatened to drain her completely, but fear of her father put life into her steps as she finally picked up the trail and started to follow it.

Her peasant dress was stuck to her skin by the time evening mercifully set in. Rebecca's stomach was growling and her throat was parched worse than she could ever remember. Her legs felt like iron weights as she trudged along, no longer sure if the hoof-prints belonged to the bay-colored horse or not. A vulture flew overhead, screeching his arrival. The tired woman quickened her pace to somewhere between a crawl and a walk. The burning orange of the setting sun was in her eyes, blinding her to the danger so close by. Only the telltale rattle gave her any warning.

Rebecca came to a total stop, her eyes wide in terror. It was not just one rattlesnake; she had inadvertently stepped into a nest of the deadly creatures. A snake to the left of her started to move in no particular direction, merely uncoiling and recoiling. Her heart was pounding in her chest so hard she was certain it was going to break through her ribs. She willed her legs to move, but they were frozen in place by her fear. The rattler slithered along the ground, its forked tongue slipping in and out of its mouth. Out of the corner of her eye, Rebecca saw several other snakes also starting to uncoil. A bloodcurdling scream pierced the evening air as her legs found life and started to run back away from the venomous snakes. Relocating the trail, Rebecca ran as fast as she could, her lungs burning with the effort. In the far distance, she swore she heard the sound of a horse running hard, or was it just the blood pounding in her ears? Stumbling over a large stone, she fell face first onto the dusty ground.

In the twilight, the large horse almost did not see her lying there. Only at the last second did Phoenix rear her head and move to the right to avoid trampling the girl. "Whoa," Josie said, pulling hard on the reins. She looked around for signs of any other people before dismounting. The grime-covered face looked up at her. In her sternest voice she asked, "Are you the one who let out that horrid scream?"

"Y-Yes. There were these snakes, lots of them, and...."

"You screamed like that for a few snakes?" Josie asked incredulously. "I heard you from miles away."

"I was scared. There were so many of them." Rebecca slowly rose to her feet, groaning at the ache in her muscles. Josie reached out quickly to help steady the still shaky woman.

"You shouldn't be out here." She took another look at the girl before her. *Not as young as I thought, definitely old enough to marry.* The girl was certainly pretty enough beneath the caked-on dust. She released her grip and leaned her arm against Phoenix's saddle. "What are you doing out here? I left you in that town."

"I couldn't stay there anymore."

Without a word, Josie vaulted effortlessly onto Phoenix. *No. I'm not taking on some sniveling girl who can't take care of herself.* "Don't follow me, girl!" she warned before urging the horse into a gallop. *Damn it to tarnation,* Josie mentally cursed. She had left dinner on the spit when she heard the scream echoing through the canyon and it was certain to be ruined by now. The hungry outlaw guided Phoenix back to the campsite. *I swear if I ever see that annoying little brat again, I'm gonna shoot her.*

5:   Dinner

In her anger at the blackened lump that was supposed to be dinner, Josie kicked the spit, sending the burnt food and wood flying. Grabbing her knife from her boot, she set off to catch another rabbit. Darkness had already settled, making the task more difficult.

Two hours later, a large jackrabbit was skewered on a new spit and set to cook. Josie settled down against a large rock and started to disassemble and clean one of her guns. For safety's sake, she always had one fully loaded at all times. The firelight bounced off the gleaming metal as she slowly and methodically polished the weapon, glancing up from time to time to make sure the meat didn't burn. After both guns were perfectly cleaned and polished, she reached for her Winchester.

Josie had just opened the breech of the rifle when she heard the clear sounds of someone moving closer to her. Whoever it was made too much noise to be of any danger, but the outlaw put her hand on her Peacemaker just in case. A branch must have hit the girl because Josie heard a yelp from what was quickly becoming a familiar voice. She released her grip on the handle of her gun. "You'd better come out here before I start shooting," she yelled, smirking when she heard the girl yelp again.

Rebecca stumbled through the brush and into the small clearing. "I told you not to follow me," Josie scowled, knowing the flames illuminated the frown on her face. "You'd do well to do what your elders tell you to."

"I'm sorry. It's just that I'm cold and hungry and I smelled your food, and well I guess I just followed my nose." Rebecca started to ramble on, then thought better of it when the outlaw glared at her. Josie said nothing, turning her attention back to the food. Unsure of what to do, Rebecca backed up a few steps and sat down, her face barely visible in the campfire. *You think I don't know you're there?* the outlaw thought to herself. She settled back against the saddle and reached for her rifle. Josie gave the Winchester a thorough cleaning, oblivious to the burning food.

"You're going to ruin it." Josie glared at the source of the interruption. "I mean the rabbit," Rebecca said nervously. "It's burning."

"Damn!" Josie reached over and turned the spit, relieved to see only slight charring. Most of the meat was still good. Without saying a word, she sat back and returned to the task of cleaning her weapon. This time, however, she kept one eye on her dinner.

Josie was aware of the eyes watching her as she cut the meat off the carcass and laid it on a flat piece of bark. She deftly sliced the hunks of meat into smaller pieces, eating half the meat while the hungry woman watched. When she had eaten her fill, she looked down at the remaining food. *Guess I'll catch another rabbit for jerky tomorrow.* "Here." She held out the piece of bark holding the meat. "Come on, I know you're hungry. Your stomach makes almost as much noise as your mouth." Josie did not bother to admit that it was only the girl's interruption that kept the rabbit from being burnt to a crisp.

Rebecca timidly walked over to take the makeshift plate from the outlaw. Once the plate was in her hand, however, the smell of the cooked meat overwhelmed her fear. She sat right down, only a few feet from Josie, and proceeded to eat the rabbit greedily. "Mmm, oh this is so good. Mmm, I haven't eaten since...oh thank you, by the way. I didn't know if you were going to, mm, give me any, even though you should have, since...I saved your dinner." Josie's eyebrow arched prominently as the rest of her face remained stoic and unreadable. Rebecca decided that perhaps she had said too much. She ate another bite in silence as her eyes settled on the canteen.

"Here," Josie said in an exasperated tone as she handed her the water. "Try not to drink it all." Rebecca heard the words and took only a few small swallows before handing it back. Her thirst was barely touched but she dared not take any more. Josie knew by the weight of the flask that the girl had taken very little. The green eyes still stared at the container. Cursing herself inwardly, Josie passed the canteen back. Rebecca smiled and drained the flask.

Rebecca set the now empty piece of bark down and stared at the ground. "Did you want something else?" Josie growled, keeping her focus on the rifle.

"Sorry, it's just that it's warmer by the fire." She looked around. "And there are no snakes."

"Make your own damned fire," the outlaw muttered in a voice clear enough for the young woman to hear. Rebecca nodded and slowly rose to her feet. She faced away from the taller woman, her head hung low.

"Thank you for the food and water," she said as she slowly walked away. Josie knew the young woman wanted her to ask her to stay but no such words would be forthcoming from her mouth.

Rebecca walked until she could just make out the campsite through the brush. She sat down on the ground and leaned her back against a tree, her focus fixed on the woman near the fire. She fell asleep to the sight of Josie stoking the fire with logs, banking it for the night.

Josie silently crept over to where she knew the girl was sleeping. The pale moonlight pierced through the leaves and shone upon the sleeping face. She now saw bruises that had not been there the day before. *No wonder you're running away*, Josie thought. *But I'm not going to be your caretaker.*

6: The Shadow

Rebecca woke to a bright sun beating down on her. She quickly scrambled to her feet, wincing at the soreness. The outlaw was gone. She moved into the campsite and placed her hand over the now dead fire. It was cold. Ignoring the pain in her legs and feet, Rebecca set out to follow Josie. As she walked, she wondered if the outlaw knew she had slept only a few feet away. She tried to remember the stories she had heard about Josie.

The details were sketchy to her, but the general information was clear. Josie was wanted in more than half the states for one thing or another. She led gangs on raids of wagons and stagecoaches. Rebecca thought that she had read that train robberies were the dark-clothed woman's specialty. Rumor was that the "Terror of the Railway" was responsible for no less than one hundred deaths, and even more shootings and robberies. Rebecca tried to merge the image of the outlaw that she had read about with the image that she had seen. Josie Hunter was featured in several of the dime novels Rebecca had read in bits and pieces sitting on a barrel in the back of the mercantile while her mother shopped. But the woman described in those stories bore no resemblance — other than in name — to the exotic creature who had grudgingly shared a meal with her last night. Her father had said that Josie was pure evil, but that was not what she saw. Why would someone who was purely evil bother to rescue her from bandits or give her food to eat? Surely she would have just let her go to her fate, perhaps even killed her herself. No, the tall woman in black was not purely evil. There was some good in her heart, of that Rebecca was sure. She wondered what had happened to make the blue-eyed woman become one of the most feared criminals in the west.

She followed the trail all day, resting only for a few minutes at a small creek to wash her face and drink as much water as she could without choking. She did not know how much of a head start Josie had on her, and she did not want to add to the distance. Her feet protested every step, and her legs screamed with every stride. Rebecca did not know why she felt so compelled to follow the outlaw, she just knew she had to.

Cresting a short rise, Josie noted the signs of a small camp. A quick look at the horses and tents told her that there were at least five men. At the moment, three were engaged in a card game. She did not see any others. Urging Phoenix to go back down the rise, Josie thought about the blonde girl. The outlaw was certain that the young woman was following her. Josie dismounted and hid herself and Phoenix within the cover of nearby trees. Sure enough, within an hour, the blonde woman appeared in the distance.

Josie was not the only one to notice the girl walking in the dirty dress. One of the men from the camp had climbed up the rise to relieve himself and whistled. "Hey boys! Guess what's headin' our way?" Five other men climbed up the rise and looked to see what all the fuss was about. Josie cursed silently and took a small step backward to hide herself more.

"Thomas..." the first man said quietly, although Josie's keen hearing picked up every word, "You and John head over that way." He turned to face the other men. "Mike and Sam, you two go over there. Rich and I will stay here. We'll surround her." The men laughed lecherously.

If there was one thing that Josie hated, it was a bunch of men trying to pick on a small girl. Putting her hands on her guns, she stepped out from the cover of the trees. "Why don't you pick on someone your own size? Or are little girls all you can handle?" Two men reached for their side arms. Josie's bullets flew, cutting them both down. "Anyone else?"

Rebecca heard the gunshots and panicked; she dove under the nearest bush and prayed no part of her clothing was showing. There were several more exchanges of gunfire before there was a long period of silence.

"You can come out now, girl," Josie said in an annoyed tone. Rebecca slowly climbed out from the bushes and looked at the outlaw. Josie gracefully slid from her saddle. In three long strides, she was within arm's reach of Rebecca. "You don't listen very well. I had to kill six men to keep them from raping you. That makes a total of nine men's deaths on my hands because of you." Rebecca did not know what to say. She felt bad for the men who died.

"I'm sorry," she said meekly. In an instant, Josie's gun was against her nose. She heard the unmistakable sound of the hammer cocking.

"Don't be sorry, just improve. Figure out a way to save your own hide; I'm sick of doing it for you." She looked at the blonde thoughtfully. "I should kill you now to make sure you don't bother me anymore." Rebecca said nothing as she looked down at the cool steel pressed against her nose. Deciding that her point had been made, Josie pulled her gun back, releasing the hammer gently before sliding it into her holster. She mounted Phoenix and turned back to the men's camp.

7: Divvying Up The Booty

Josie rode back to the campsite and took inventory of the supplies. The men were well-stocked, with full complements of weapons and supplies. The guns were useless to her, being of inferior quality to her own. She stuffed some bullets into a pouch and tied it to her saddle horn. Never can have too many bullets, she mused. She was about to search the tents for the best bedroll when she heard the sound of Rebecca vomiting in the bushes. Cursing herself mentally, Josie went to check on the young woman.

Rebecca was just wiping her mouth when Josie walked up to her. "I told you not to follow. What part of that don't you understand?" the outlaw said angrily, although she was slightly concerned about the pallor of the girl's face. The paleness only served to accent the bruises more.

"I understood you perfectly," Rebecca replied angrily. She was embarrassed to be seen in such a state, after all, the dead men were bandits. But the sight of their dead bodies still made the innocent girl sad for the loss of life. "You can't take all their stuff, so I see no reason why I can't pick through it, too. After all, I could use some of these things as well."

"Suit yourself, little girl," Josie said evenly.

"My name is Rebecca!" she retorted. "And I'm not a little girl."

"Makes no difference to me," Josie replied as she headed back to rummage through the men's belongings.

Exiting a tent with her new bedroll in hand, Josie noticed the scent of fresh meat cooking. Looking at the fire, she saw that Rebecca had thrown more logs on and was cooking up some of the food the dead men left behind. The outlaw's stomach growled as the pleasant odor conjured up memories of long ago meals. One thing that Josie had no skill at was cooking.

"There's plenty for both of us," Rebecca said as she continued to turn the cooking beef. She kept her eyes on the food, fearful of the possible angry look that might be coming from the outlaw. "I mean, there's no sense wasting it. The meat won't travel well and if we don't eat it, then the vultures will." Josie conceded the point, making her stomach rumble again with joy at the thought of decent food. Without saying a word, Josie continued to search the camp for useful items. She came up with a small folding shovel, several pieces of flint, a few dollars and coins, two more canteens, and spare clothes. Her saddlebags were full of the much-needed supplies by the time Rebecca announced that the food was ready to eat.

Rebecca waited a few minutes for the outlaw to come over and pick up the plate of beef and beans before making a plate of her own. Without a sound, Josie sat down on the other side of the fire and started to eat her food. Rebecca quietly passed her the canteen of water. Josie made no effort to take it, concentrating solely on eating the tasty food. Setting the water flask on the ground between them, Rebecca turned her attention back to her dinner. She was spooning some more beans on her plate when she saw Josie reach out toward her, plate in hand. Rebecca suppressed a smile as she scooped more food onto the outlaw's plate.

After wiping her plate with the last of the bread, Josie set the dirty dish and utensils down on the ground. Without so much as a thank you, she rose to her feet and wandered off. Rebecca sat quietly by the dying fire, afraid to leave and afraid to stay. The big horse was munching on some grass nearby, so she knew the outlaw would be back. Deciding between the unknown and the murderer who had already threatened to kill her, Rebecca maintained her position by the fire.

Rebecca had used up most of the loose kindling while trying to keep the fire going. It was now twilight and she was beginning to wonder if Josie really was going to come back, despite the evidence of Phoenix standing nearby.

"You still here?" Rebecca jumped at the sound of the outlaw's voice just behind her. Josie continued to walk past her until she reached the opposite side of the fire. She dropped an armful of wood onto the ground.

Reaching for a nearby hatchet, Josie cut the branches into usable lengths, throwing several directly into the fire.

"I-I didn't know if I should leave or not. I mean, I wouldn't want you to have to kill anyone else or anything," Rebecca said nervously. Josie said nothing as she continued to chop the wood. Uncertain of what else to do, the young woman got up and started to walk around the camp, heading for the still-tethered horses of the dead men. Rifling through the saddlebags, she found a pen and a small bottle of ink. She did not find any paper or parchment. A more thorough search revealed only small scraps of paper and a pocket-sized bible. There was a blank page preceding the beginning of the familiar book, but Rebecca did not dare use it. She had once bent the corner of a page in her father's bible and received a sound whipping for it. Putting the bible back in the saddlebag, she returned to the fireside.

Josie had finished cutting the wood and was now intently cleaning one of her guns. Positioning herself so she could watch the outlaw but not be too close, Rebecca sat down. The long fingers moved gracefully across the smooth steel, polishing it with an old, stained piece of cloth. Rebecca heard the soft click as Josie opened the barrel to clean it. Hours seemed to fly by as the outlaw cleaned all of her weapons and the young woman watched.

The warm fire, the filling meal, and the hypnotic rhythm of Josie's hand rubbing the polishing cloth across the steel all served to lull Rebecca to sleep. The outlaw watched her for a few moments before covering her with one of the blankets. Hours later, Josie still sat there, wondering why this young girl seemed so intent on following her.

8:   Mason's Gulch

"Get up." Josie roughly nudged the sleeping woman with her silver-tipped boot.

"Hrrummphhh." The sleeping form snuggled deeper under the covers.

"Get up now or I leave you behind," Josie snarled. Rebecca quickly sat up and tried to bring herself to wakefulness. "You've got one minute to make a trip to the woods, then I'm leaving."

"No breakfast?" she whined as she stood up and stretched. Josie looked at her and frowned.

"You can't travel around dressed like that," Josie said as she looked at the long peasant dress and soft-soled shoes.

"What am I supposed to wear?" she called as she headed into the woods. Josie walked into one of the tents and selected two shirts and two pairs of britches.

Tossing them in a pile on top of Rebecca's blanket, the outlaw set out to find the small man who had been the previous owner of the clothes.

"Put these on." Josie pointed at the clothes pile, which now included a pair of pointed-toed boots and a beige Stetson. Rebecca picked up the clothes and looked at her, then at the tent, then back to her. "I'm not waiting all day," Josie said as she crossed her arms and arched an eyebrow at the young woman.

"Sorry," Rebecca murmured. She reached up to undo the first button, then looked at the outlaw. Josie scowled and muttered a curse before turning around to double-check the cinch of Phoenix's saddle. Rebecca quickly undressed and slipped into the britches. They were a little loose and slightly too long for the small woman.

"What about the corset?" she asked as she reached behind her for the laces.

"You'll be more comfortable without it" was the reply. Rebecca quickly removed the corset and slipped on the loose-fitting shirt.

"I'll saddle up one of these horses for you," Josie offered.

Rebecca was tugging on the boots when Josie started toward the string of horses and the young woman hopped after her, pulling on the last boot.

"I can't...ride alone," she protested even as the gunslinger tightened the girth on the smallest of the horses. "I'm afraid of horses. One kicked me when I was a little girl, and since then I can't bear to be on a horse by myself. Please, can't I just ride with you? I feel safe when you're up there with me." Josie looked into the innocent green eyes of the young blonde and saw that she was most sincere about her fear of horses. Even so, it was not practical for them to ride double over a prolonged period of time; it would be hard on the horse, not to mention uncomfortable for Josie. Only in bed did she like to be close to a woman. When the loving was over, she wanted her space. With a shrug, Josie draped the usable supplies on the back of the horse she had saddled and untied the rest. She had planned to keep two of the men's horses, but if Rebecca would not ride, there was no point. She led the little horse to where Phoenix stood waiting for her and effortlessly vaulted into the saddle. She looked down at the younger woman whose expectant face was turned toward her.

"You'll have to walk," she said emotionlessly. "I can't put the extra weight on Phoenix in this heat." She made a clicking sound with her tongue, and the big bay mare started moving, the smaller horse following obediently behind. With a sigh, the blonde fell in with the parade.

As the morning wore on, Rebecca fell further and further behind. Her feet hurt too much from walking the previous day to keep up with the well-rested mare. Her stomach grumbled from lack of food, and her normally sunny disposition was turning noticeably cloudy. "Josie," she called to the woman far ahead. "Josie, please wait!" The young woman watched as the horse stopped. When it was obvious that Josie was not going to come back to see what she wanted, Rebecca broke into a trot to catch up to the outlaw before she changed her mind and decided to ride on. She drew alongside the horse and rider and gasped as she fought to catch her breath.

"I can hardly walk anymore," she said petulantly. "My feet are killing me, and I'm starving. Don't outlaws eat?" The tone in Rebecca's voice and the little girl pout on her face almost made Josie laugh out loud. She turned away and managed to put a serious scowl on her face.

"Yes. We eat little blonde farm girls for breakfast. How nice for me there's one so handy."

Rebecca raised her hand to slap the gunslinger on the thigh, but the look in the ice blue eyes made her think twice. She dropped her hand and grumbled, "I'm serious. Please, can't we stop and eat?"

"Oh, all right." Josie slid from the back of the horse and, looking around for a shady spot, saw a small grove of trees over a small rise. "Can you walk that far?" she asked, pointing to the oasis in the distance. Rebecca nodded and eagerly began trekking up the hill. Josie watched as the blonde walked away, and a smile came to her face. She gave her head a little shake wondering, not for the first time, what had possessed her to allow this slip of a girl to talk her way along for the ride.

Rebecca threw herself down in the shade of a large oak tree and pulled the boots from her aching feet. Blisters had formed and many had broken already, leaving her feet oozing and raw. Having her feet bare so she could feel a cooling breeze on them felt wonderful. Josie tethered the horses a few feet away but still in the shade, and rummaged in her saddlebag for some jerky. She unwound the strap of the canteen from the saddle horn and walked to where the younger woman was lying in the grass. Her eyes widened as she saw the condition of Rebecca's feet, and she mentally kicked herself for insisting that the poor woman walk. *And she didn't complain once, not really.* She dropped down beside the little blonde, placing the canteen into one of her hands and a hunk of jerky into the other. Rebecca had been almost dozing with her eyes closed, but when she felt the canteen against her hand, she opened her eyes and smiled at the outlaw.

"Thanks," she said gratefully, tipping the canteen to her dry lips and taking a large swallow. She coughed as a bit of the liquid went down the wrong pipe.

"Easy does it," Josie admonished her. "Won't do you much good if you choke yourself to death." From where she sat, Josie could see the dark smudges that marred the pretty face of the innocent girl. Beneath the purple bruises was evidence of earlier beatings. Josie put her finger under Rebecca's chin and turned her head up to get a better look. "Who did this?" she asked softly. Rebecca's eyes began to glisten with tears as she watched the outlaw's examination of her discolored cheek. She lowered her head when Josie finally let go.

"My father."

"Somebody should give him a taste of his own medicine," Josie whispered through clenched teeth. She silently promised herself that if she should ever encounter the man she would gladly do just that.

Rebecca shook her head, and the tears that were pooled in her eyes slipped down her cheeks. "He's not a bad man, really," she protested. "He was a good father; very strict with us children, but usually fair. When my brother was killed in the war, he sort of...snapped. Then he started drinking, and when he drinks...."

"You don't have to tell me. I've been around plenty of that type of man. But you shouldn't excuse him. What happened to your brother had nothing to do with you."

"I know, but...."

"No," Josie said sternly. She thought of her own father, the kindest, most gentle man she had ever known, and wished that the innocent girl beside her could have grown up in such a safe and caring environment. "A father should never hurt his children, no matter what." Feeling emotions so close to the surface was awkward for Josie. Standing up, she let her eyes roam around the surrounding countryside as if she was looking for something. "I'll be right back," she said abruptly. She walked toward a clump of bushes in the distance and within a few minutes was out of Rebecca's sight.

Rebecca watched the tall black-clad woman walk away. She could not imagine what had caused her to leave so suddenly unless she was looking for a place to relieve herself. With a sigh, Rebecca started to chew on the dry jerky. Her appetite seemed to have deserted her and she thought about tossing the jerky away, but realized she would undoubtedly want it later. She slid the piece of dried meat into her pocket and lay down in the cool grass to wait for the gunslinger to return.

Josie stood gazing down at the still form under the tree. Rebecca's face was relaxed in sleep, her lips slightly parted. She seemed so child-like to the toughened older woman. Yet she was not a child. Josie reckoned she must be about eighteen, which was considerably older than she herself had been when she set out on her own. She found herself wanting to protect her from any further abuse. "Hey, wake up lazy bones," she said softly. Rebecca still breathed with sleep, so the gunslinger knelt down beside her and said a little louder, "I brought dessert." The green eyes flew open and focused on Josie who held her vest in her hands with a large bulge hanging down.

"Dessert?" Rebecca yawned and stretched. Josie laid the vest on the ground to reveal a mound of plump, ripe blackberries. A huge grin spread across Rebecca's face. Her appetite returned with a vengeance at the sight of those juicy berries. She grabbed one and popped it in her mouth, pushing her tongue against the roof of her mouth to squeeze the juice throughout. "Ohhh, that's heaven," she breathed as she reached for another. Josie watched as one after another of the berries disappeared into the ravenous girl. Suddenly it occurred to Rebecca that she had eaten all the fruit and Josie had none.

"Oh, I'm sorry. I didn't mean to eat them all. I'll go pick you some more." She started to rise, but Josie put her hand on her shoulder.

"Not necessary. I ate a bunch while I was picking them. Sit back and let me have a look at your feet." She sat on the ground and brought Rebecca's feet to her lap. They looked too tender to attempt to put footwear on without allowing the blisters some healing time. "I'm afraid you won't be able to wear those boots again any time soon."

"Oh, tarnation. I was just beginning to like them," she said sarcastically.

"Stay here," Josie said, rising and crossing to her saddlebags, where she found a roll of gauze. She returned to where Rebecca sat and once again took her feet in her hands. Gently, she wrapped the gauze around each foot in turn and then tied it loosely around Rebecca's ankles.

"Not very fashionable, but it should keep the dirt out of those blisters until they heal a bit." Josie stood up and held out her hand to the young woman, who grasped it in both of hers. Josie tugged her to her feet and then swept her into her arms. She walked to Phoenix and stood Rebecca on her feet briefly so she could grasp her waist. She lifted her up and boosted her onto the horse's rump.

"Looks like you get your wish after all," she said as she swung up into the saddle. "Put your arms around my waist and hold on," Josie said as she urged Phoenix into a trot. Both women were left to their own thoughts as they rode west. Rebecca held on tight as she bounced up and down with each step of the massive horse's hooves, her thoughts on the painful past she was leaving behind.

"Whoa." Josie pulled Phoenix to a stop just before the edge of a town. "Get down." She watched as Rebecca slid down off the horse.

"What's wrong?" the runaway asked as she watched the outlaw reach into the saddlebags and pull out her dress.

"Put this on," Josie said as she handed her the garment. "You don't want to be seen with me. It'll be easier for you if you're in your own clothes. You'll be safe there."

"Wait. Aren't you coming?" Rebecca reached up and touched the outlaw's thigh as Josie climbed back into the saddle.

"No. It's not safe for me to go there. There's a price on my head, you know." She looked down at the hand and arched an eyebrow. Rebecca gulped and moved her hand.

"Sorry. Just a habit, I guess. I like to touch people while I'm talking to them." A momentary silence fell between them. "Do you want me to get anything for you? I mean, I can go and bring it back."

"You expect me to trust you with my money?" Josie asked incredulously.

"I haven't lied to you yet. I didn't have to offer, you know." Rebecca was hurt by her distrust. Josie's blue eyes bore down on her, trying to search for signs of deceit. The young woman's face showed pure innocence and honesty. Although cautious, Josie decided to take a chance. There were too many things she needed that could not be found on the prairie.

"All right. I'll trust you," Josie said as she dismounted. Quicker than Rebecca could react, the outlaw's hands were on her upper arms, squeezing painfully. "But if you cross me, I'll send you to your maker without a thought." Her words were firm and full of threat.

"Y-yes. Please, you're hurting me." She looked at the hands gripping her arms as tears started to blur her eyes. Josie let go and turned to open the saddlebag.

"Do you know how to read?"

"Of course I know how to read. I can write too. Actually I'm a very good writer, if I do say so myself. I do mostly poems and children's tales, but I'd really like to become a pulp writer, you know, writing stories about famous people and places and..."

"I only asked you if you could read," Josie said, annoyed. She pulled out the ink, pen, and paper, then wrote out a short list of necessary supplies. The total was less than six bits. She could afford to lose that if it was a trick. Handing Rebecca the note, she said, "Don't tell anyone who this is for, and don't mention my name to anyone. When you have everything, come back here."

"All right." Rebecca maintained a straight face, but inside she was jumping for joy at the chance to do something to help the woman who had saved her life twice.

Mason's Gulch was a typical western town. Several small buildings formed the only street. A large stable occupied the far end of town. The standard businesses were there: telegraph office, jail, saloon, smithy, bank, hotel, general store, and doctor's office. Rebecca quickly set out to find the items on the short list.

She was in the general store picking up the last item on Josie's list, a spool of fine thread for stitching. As she approached the counter, she heard the owner and another man talking. She stopped at the end of the aisle and listened. Judging from the star on the other man's vest, he had to be the sheriff.

"...I'm telling ya, there ain't no way we're gonna be able to hang onto our skins and our belongings both. I say we hand over what they demand and ask them to spare our lives."

"Mike, what makes you think they gonna just take the money and git? If'n we give up, they gonna just kill us all anyway. I say we fight 'em," the sheriff replied. "If we can get enough men up on the roofs we can ambush 'em. We can't just sit here and wait for 'em to slaughter us like cattle."

Rebecca moved forward and placed the purchases on the counter. The sheriff put his fingers to the brim of his hat and tipped it slightly in acknowledgment of the young lady. Mike smiled as he wrapped up her order. "Two bits, miss."

"Who are you talking about?" she asked as she handed him the coins.

"You're not from 'round here, are ya?" Mike asked.

"No, I'm just passing through."

"Well, I hope your husband is well-armed. The Caram gang is heading this way." The name was well-known to Rebecca. This gang of thieves was famous for their brutality and their skill at eluding capture. As far as she knew none of them had ever been apprehended, and their numbers increased constantly.

"Are you going to fight them?"

"There're too many of 'em. We're mostly farmers. We don't got the skills or the know-how to fight 'em." He looked at the storeowner, then back at her. "I suggest you head back 't' where you be comin' from 'n warn 'em. A farmer from just over the ridge said he saw their camp yesterday, about a day's ride from here. I reckon they'll be riding through here at first light t'morrow."

As Rebecca headed back to the edge of town, she noticed the multitude of women and small children. She had heard the stories about the Caram gang. Even children were not safe from those murdering cutthroats. She quickened her pace, and her feet protested the abuse. Her shoes were better than the boots, but they still pained her quite a bit.

Josie came out from behind some trees after making certain that Rebecca was alone. "Did you get everything?" she asked as the young woman approached.

"Yes. Josie, have you heard of the Caram gang?"

"Not a decent one in the lot from what I hear," she said as she took the goods out of Rebecca's hands and began to stash the things in her saddlebags.

"They're going to ride into Mason's Gulch tomorrow."

"Then I think we'd better put some distance between us and Mason's Gulch before the sun goes down," the gunslinger said as she tightened the strap on the saddlebag. Rebecca stared at her thunderstruck, unable to believe any woman could be so callous about the lives of innocent people. Josie stared back until the younger woman at last looked away. Rebecca turned on her heel and marched off toward town.

"Where are you going?" the outlaw asked.

Without turning back Rebecca replied, "I'm going to do what I can to help those people."

"You'll just get yourself killed, and that's no help to anyone," Josie said sharply.

Rebecca paused and said over her shoulder, "Maybe so. But at least I will have tried." She started up again and had gone several yards down the road when Josie called after her.

"What are their defenses?" Josie could not see the smile that lit up Rebecca's face because she looked very serious by the time she turned around and came back to where the gunslinger stood.

"I heard the sheriff say they don't think they can stand up to the gang. Josie, there're children in that town. Those killers won't care."

"What makes you think I do?"

"I don't know." Rebecca stared into the blue eyes of the outlaw. This time it was Josie who broke the eye contact; it was too unnerving. "I guess I just don't think you would let small children die."

"If I go into that town, they'll hang me from a rope before sundown."

"No, they won't. Josie, you're their only hope. Come into town with me. We'll meet with the townsfolk. I'm sure they'll want your help."

"I can't go into town, Rebecca. It's too dangerous. Do you know what they'll do to you if they find out you're with me?"

"If the Caram gang destroys this town, Chancetown is next. They have to listen to me. I have an idea. Stay here." Rebecca turned and ran back to town, ignoring the still burning ache in her overused leg muscles and the sting of her blistered feet.

"This had better be good," Josie muttered to herself as she went back into the cover of the trees. A thin smile crept to her lips as she realized that her clever companion had once again bamboozled her.

If there was one thing the outlaw hated, it was waiting. Almost an hour passed before she heard the sound of a jingling harness and crept out of the cover of the trees to see who it was. Rebecca was directing the driver of the buckboard toward the clump of trees where Josie waited, and a second man rode in the bed of the wagon. Josie remained in the bushes, although her senses told her that the trio was more likely to be in fear of her than to pose any threat. Neither man was armed; the one with the badge pinned to his chest wore a holster, but it was empty. The older man looked as if he had never handled a gun in his life.

"Josie?" Rebecca called as she peered at the thick brush, looking for the dark-clad woman. Several nervous seconds passed before the gunslinger stepped out into the open, her hands resting on the handles of her guns. "Good, I knew you'd wait. This is Mayor McGregor," she motioned toward the portly man on her left. He nodded nervously. "And this is Tom Glance, the sheriff of Mason's Gulch."

"Ma'am," Tom acknowledged her with a tip of his hat. Josie nodded at each of the men. The sheriff had taken a great chance coming out here unarmed to meet a known killer, and to top it off was also polite and respectful. *Well, I reckon it's time to see what they want.*

"Sheriff, I understand that you require assistance in keeping the Caram gang out of your town." Josie tipped the brim of her hat back, allowing both men a better look at her intimidating gaze. "I'm willing to do what I can to help, but I need certain assurances before I do."

"Anything," the mayor said. "We ain't rich or nothin', but we kin give ya whatever we got."

"All I need is oats for my horse and some salt pork."

"That's all?" Tom looked at her incredulously. It made no sense to him that this outlaw did not mention money. Of course he was not about to bring it up. Josie realized what he was thinking and gave a feral grin.

"Little man, if what I wanted was your town's money there'd be nothing left for that band of killers tomorrow." She fingered the butt of her gun. Satisfied that they had reached an understanding of sorts, Josie whistled for Phoenix.

Despite grumbling from some of the townsfolk about "That damned fool woman's harebrained plan," Josie was able to get them into position before daybreak. At both ends of the main street leading into and out of town, men waited with wagons positioned, ready to move them to prevent the gang's escape. On the rooftops overlooking the street the younger men and women who did not know how to use guns were stationed with bottles filled with coal oil and sulfur matches. If Josie and the other armed people could not stop them, the plan was to toss the flaming bottles into their midst. Josie hoped it did not come to that, since the flames could just as easily consume the buildings that were dry as tinder. Once the preparations were in order, all they could do was wait. Josie remained perched on top of a building, her eyes constantly scanning both the street below and the vast expanse of land beyond the edge of town. Rebecca willingly agreed to stay back in the jailhouse and wait for her. Josie did not trust the town's only saloon to be a safe place for the young prairie girl.

Two hours after sunup, a small cloud of dust on the horizon heralded the approach of the Caram gang. Josie gave the hand signal for the others to be ready. As she expected, the gang moved casually, expecting easy pickings from the small, isolated town.

The townsfolk remained hidden as the twenty men rode into town. Josie kept the leader within the sight of her Winchester. Once the last outlaw was past the wagons, Josie let out a piercing Cherokee war cry. The sound had the desired effect. The Caram gang was momentarily confused as they looked for the source of the sound. At the same time, the townsfolk moved the wagons, blocking the exits. Rifle barrels protruded from the windows of every shop in town, effectively surrounding the gang. John Caram, the leader of the group, glared at Josie as he realized the trap.

"Woman! You've made a mistake. You think we're going to let a handful of farmers and a squaw stop us?" He reached for his sidearm; Josie fired once, striking him cleanly in the right shoulder. His gun flew from his hand as he howled in rage and pain.

"Anyone else want some lead plums?" she taunted as she took aim again, this time at Caram's head. "I suggest you have your men lower their weapons unless you all want to shake hands with Saint Peter before nightfall."

Rebecca watched the entire proceedings from the safety of the sheriff's office. She had been standing in the doorway until the sound of the rifle fire sent her scurrying under the desk. She only came out when she heard the joyous cheers of the townspeople. Stepping out of the building, she was startled by a strong hand clamping around her mouth and pulling her into the alley. Rebecca struggled briefly before she realized it was Josie who grabbed her.

"Rebecca, I need you to get the supplies promised me and bring them to the glen about a mile west of here," Josie said as she released the girl from her grasp.

"But..."

"You think that sheriff is really going to let me go? There's a one thousand dollar price on my head."

"But you helped to save the town...." she protested.

Josie shook her head. "They don't care about that now. I served a purpose for them; now they'll think of the money. I have to get out of here. If you don't want to get it for me, that's fine." She turned to walk away, but Rebecca reached up and grabbed her arm.

"Josie, I'll be there. Leave me the horse we got from those men to carry it with and I'll get the things you were promised." Rebecca watched the stoic face, looking for any kind of acknowledgment that her words had been heard. The outlaw walked away, not certain whether she would ever see the runaway again.

9: A Good Deed Rewarded

Josie heard her approaching. Moving from her cover in the trees, she reached the young woman and took the reins of the heavily laden horse. She counted the sacks of grain and salt pork and realized there was quite a bit more than she had expected.

"Where did you get all this? This is twice what I asked for."

"They wanted you to have it as their way of saying thanks."

"You're lying." The blue eyes narrowed as her hand reached for her sidearm. Rebecca's eyes went wide with fear.

"N-no, I swear. They wanted me to take some money and other supplies, but I thought you would be mad, so I refused. I told them that all you wanted were the oats and pork, so they insisted on giving more than the original agreement," Rebecca said as she silently prayed the outlaw would believe her.

Josie searched the face in the pale moonlight. As always, there was no hint of deception or betrayal. "Did anyone follow you?"

"No. I left town heading east, then doubled back."

"Good." Josie removed the supplies from the back of the horse and opened one of the sacks of grain. She filled a feedbag for her mare, and put a heap on the ground for the little horse who worked so hard to carry it. With her back turned, the outlaw could not see the beaming smile on the young woman's face.

"Josie?" Rebecca asked as she settled into her bedroll.

"What?"

"I'm glad you didn't get hurt today. That was a very brave thing you did."

"All I did was shoot a man who deserved it," Josie said dismissively.

"No." Rebecca sat up and looked across the fire at the tall woman. "Today you did the right thing. You stood up with people that you didn't know, and protected them from a gang of outlaws bent on destroying their town. Josie, if you hadn't left, they would have told you themselves how thankful they were."

"Rebecca, it's not that simple."

"Yes...it is just that simple, Josie. Today you did the right thing. How long has it been since you've done that? Each day it will get a little easier."

"Go to sleep...before I shoot you," Josie growled as she rolled away from the fire.

"Good night, Josie," she said softly before laying back down. She refused to take the gruff threat as anything more than her newfound friend being grouchy.

10: The Wrong Place at the Wrong Time

After a breakfast of salt pork and coffee, they set out southwest, away from their pasts and toward an uncertain future. With her blistered feet still healing, Rebecca rode upon Phoenix while Josie walked alongside leading the little mare. Hoping to help pass the time, the young blonde began telling tales of life on the plains. The outlaw listened half-heartedly, her senses trained to listen and look for signs of trouble. Josie's intuition had never failed her before and the sudden prickling of the hairs on her neck made her pull the horse to a stop and motion for the prairie girl to be silent. Her ice blue eyes scanned the horizon, catching the almost imperceptible sight of a rifle barrel poking out from behind a rock. Josie extracted her Winchester from its scabbard and jerked Rebecca off the saddle.

"Behind that rock. Now!" she ordered, keeping her rifle focused on the sniper. Rebecca had just made it behind the rock when a single shot rang out. She kept her head down out of fear.

"Josie?"

"I'm here. Stay where you are," she hollered back. She looked down at her injured leg. The bullet had entered at mid-thigh and there was no sign of an exit wound. Using her elbow and her uninjured leg, Josie scrabbled around the rock and collapsed at Rebecca's side.

"You're hurt!" the young woman exclaimed. Without warning, Josie twisted and brought the rifle up, aiming slightly above the head of the distant gunman, causing the small pile of rocks above him to shake violently. The hammer clicked on an empty chamber and Josie ducked back down behind the rock, pulling shells from her gun belt as she did.

"We have to get out of here," Rebecca said

"If we move now, we'll be dead before we can reach Phoenix." She looked down at the blood that soaked her pant leg and had begun to pool on the ground. "But you're right, we can't stay here much longer." She opened the chamber of the rifle and filled it with bullets. A flip of the lever and the rifle was ready to go. Josie spared a quick look at her new friend. "If anything happens, I want you to take the horses and get out of here."

"Josie, nothing."

"If anything does, take the horses and go." The tone in her voice made it clear this was not open for discussion. Rebecca nodded mutely. The outlaw gave her one last look before pivoting and firing at the potential rockslide. Her left index finger worked the trigger as her right hand pulled the lever again and again. The quick succession of bullets freed the rocks, sending them tumbling. The man let out a bloodcurdling scream as the granite rained down on him, and then all was silence.

"Get the gauze from the saddlebag," Josie said to the girl, and Rebecca ran to do her bidding. The outlaw untied the bandanna around her neck and when Rebecca returned, she handed it to her. "Tie this around my leg above the wound. It'll slow the flow of blood." Rebecca did as she asked, but the sight of so much blood made her feel queasy. "Now put the gauze over the wound..." she broke off at the look on Rebecca's face. It looked as though the girl was about to faint.

"Josie, we have to get you to a doctor!" Rebecca said frantically as she tried to help the outlaw to her feet. Using the smaller woman for leverage, she climbed on top of the boulder that moments before had been their hiding place and whistled for Phoenix. The mare trotted to her side and, using her powerful arms, Josie pulled herself into the saddle.

"Climb up on that rock and then get up behind me," Josie said to Rebecca, whose face was still unnaturally white. Rebecca did as she was told and a moment later was settled behind the wounded gunslinger. "Hold tight to my waist. If it seems like I'm about to pass out, give me a good squeeze so I don't fall out of the saddle."

"But I'm not strong enough to keep you..."

"Don't worry; you won't have to keep me up here. I'm just afraid I might forget where I am or let go, and you can keep me focused." Rebecca tightened her grip so much she thought her arms would fall off from the pressure, but it was enough to keep the gunslinger fairly upright in the saddle.

They rode the rest of the day and night, stopping only long enough to give the horses a much-needed drink and a few minutes of rest. They arrived just before daybreak at a small ranch. Smoke already curled from the chimney so Josie did not need to rouse the house. Sure enough, before they had even come to a stop, a small woman with dark hair came out of the house holding a rather menacing rifle. The scowl on her face dissolved into a huge grin when she recognized her visitor. "Josie!" she boomed.

"Hello, Belle. It's been a long time," the outlaw said as she nudged Phoenix to a stop just beyond the porch rail.   Without waiting for an introduction, Rebecca slid off the horse as if she had been doing it all her life and said to the woman with the rifle, "She's wounded. Help me get her down from there." In her excitement at seeing her old friend, Belle had not even noticed the pallor of her cheeks or that Josie's left pant leg was completely soaked with blood, as was Phoenix's left flank. Rebecca's words galvanized her into action, and she jumped off the porch and ran to Josie's side.

"Put your arms around my neck," she instructed the gunslinger. "And you, blondie, carefully lift her leg over the saddle, and then take hold of both her legs." Josie leaned down as instructed and wrapped her arms around the stout woman's neck. Rebecca was almost afraid to touch Josie's wounded leg, but she did not want to rile the feisty Belle so she did as she was told. In a few moments they had Josie on the ground between them, her arms draped over their shoulders. They hobbled into the house and, with a nod, Belle said, "Bring her to that room over there."

Unwilling to let go of the injured woman to grasp the doorknob, Belle simply gave the door a kick. It opened to reveal a plain bedroom with a bureau, a washbasin, and a pitcher. The two women maneuvered Josie to the side of the bed and laid her down as gently as they could. Josie's teeth were clenched against the pain, and tears welled up in her eyes as Belle worked the boot off her foot. Belle glanced up at the young blonde who stood frozen at the head of the bed. "There's whiskey in a jug in the kitchen. Fetch that and a glass." With a nod, Rebecca made her way across the room. Before she was out of earshot, Belle added, "Oh, and some cloth. Enough to clean her up and to use for a bandage. It's in a chest in the kitchen. And when you're through with that, draw some water from the well and put it on to boil." She took a pair of scissors from a sewing box on top of the bureau and proceeded to cut the ruined trousers off the wounded gunslinger.

"Those are my best drawers," Josie complained.

Belle guffawed. "Not any more, they ain't." Rebecca came into the room with her arms full of white cloth, a whiskey jug and glass in her hands. She was just in time to see Belle peel back the fabric she had cut from around the wound, which had begun to bleed afresh.

"Oh!" Rebecca gasped and turned away from the sight of the blood. When she and Josie were on the way to Belle's she was able to deal with the gore because she had to, but now that someone else was there to take care of her friend, Rebecca seemed to lose her nerve. Her face paled, and she thought for a moment she would be sick. "I can't...I don't think...I'm sorry, I think I'm going to be sick."

"Well then, take it out of here, girl," Belle said, a bit more gruffly than she had intended. "Just leave the things, and go do something useful." She poured a healthy dollop of whiskey in the glass and handed it to Josie, who swigged half of it in one gulp.

"Take care of the horses," Josie said to Rebecca's retreating back. "And don't worry, this old harridan will take good care of me."

"I know. But I wish I could help...." She hazarded a glance at Josie, making sure to look only at her face and not at the bloody mess of her leg. Josie gave her a wan smile and tipped her glass toward the little blonde before finishing off her whiskey.

"Bring me that water when it's hot and leave it outside the door," Belle asked.

By the time Rebecca finished brushing down and settling the horses, Belle had managed to dig out the bullet and dress the wound. She dressed Josie in a long shirt, and the outlaw was finally resting comfortably. Before attempting to remove the slug, Belle had given her enough liquor to ensure she would rest for quite a while. She came out of the bedroom to find the young blonde in the kitchen feeding wood to the stove.

"Fire was dying," she said by way of explanation. She should not have presumed it was all right to work in someone else's kitchen without asking first, but she could not bring herself to go back into the room Josie occupied.

Belle simply nodded. "What's your name, child?" she asked as she closed the door to Josie's room.

"Rebecca. Is she going to be all right?" Her intense concern and fear were evident on her young face. The older woman placed a strong hand on her shoulder.

"She'll be fine in a few weeks. She lost quite a bit of blood and the muscles need some time to heal. Come on; let's rustle up something for you to eat. Then you can tell me what happened."

"I'm sorry, I never caught your name."

The older woman smiled warmly. "Belle," she said as she held out her hand. "Belle Shirley." Her firm grip surprised Rebecca. The woman appeared to be the same general age as Josie, but significantly shorter. "This is my home."

She showed Rebecca around the small but neat ranch house. There were three rooms, all made up for sleeping. One was obviously Belle's; the other two appeared to have no occupants. There was nothing of a personal nature in either room. It was one of those rooms that now housed the injured outlaw. A small eating area doubled as the main room. "Excuse me for asking, but if you live here alone, why so many sleeping rooms?"

Belle let out a deep belly laugh that shook her whole body. "It's not because I enjoy company, girl. Many persons who have...shall we say...run afoul of the law have found a need to hide out here for a while." She looked over at the door to Josie's room. "Many have come here for the same reason as her. We can't always trust a local doctor to tend to our wounds properly, especially once he finds out that we're wanted. Many of them would just as soon poison us as heal us. We've had to learn how to take care of our own injuries."

"And you keep this place so they have a place to go."

"Yes. So far the law hasn't found us out." She went into the small kitchen and heated up some stewed beef in an enameled tin pot. "Only a few of us know this place. Josie must really trust you to bring you along here." She looked at the young woman again, appraising her from head to toe. "What do you do for her, girl? You don't look like a gunfighter and you're too innocent to be something else."

"Well, we've only been traveling together a few days," Rebecca said, not understanding the latter remark. "So far I haven't done anything for her except get her into trouble."

Belle smiled warmly and put her arm around the younger woman. "It's been many a year since this place has had any laughter. Tell me a funny story while I make us some fresh buttermilk biscuits to go with this stew."

"Mmm!" she licked her lips unconsciously. "For fresh biscuits I'll tell you every story I know." She sat down on a high stool and proceeded to rattle off several fanciful tales of Ethan Allen and the Green Mountain Boys, Paul Revere, and other heroes of the Revolutionary War. Belle listened intently, learning more than she ever knew about that period of American history. Rebecca's voice was animated, every word full of emotion. Her hands moved in tune with her mouth, illustrating different points within her stories.

"You tell your stories very well, child," Belle said as she served up a bowl of stew for each of them.

"Oh, if you don't mind, I'd like to feed Josie first, then eat."

"Rebecca, she's not going to know if you eat first."

"But I'll know," she said quietly. Belle looked at her inquisitively for a moment before turning back to the pot and ladling out another bowl of stew.

11: The Calm Port

Rebecca helped Josie sit up and eat, filling the air with a constant chatter the whole time. She discovered quickly that the outlaw was quite interested in history and proceeded to tell the story of the Boston Tea Party. When she noticed the blue eyes fighting to stay awake, she moved closer and spoke in lower tones. The soft voice had the desired effect. Within minutes, Josie was sound asleep. Rebecca lingered a while longer, enjoying the opportunity to see the outlaw unguarded and vulnerable. She brushed a stray lock of black hair away from the older woman's face.

"She'd break your hand if she saw that." Rebecca jumped out of her seat and turned to see Belle standing in the doorway.

"I didn't...I mean I..."

"Relax, child. Just giving you a warning. I've known Josie for many years now and touching just isn't something she's good at."

"What do you know about her? I mean, it's not like she's much for girl talk or anything." They both chuckled quietly.

"I think whatever Josie wants you to know about her, she'll tell. I make it a point not to talk about other people, especially when they can shoot as well as she can." She waited until Rebecca nodded in understanding. "Now, she ain't gonna be able to help out around here for a while, so you're going to help out for her. Right now I think we should get some rest. Tomorrow will be a busy day."

And tomorrow was a busy day, as were the days after that. Belle put the young woman to work mending fences and tending to the horses. In the evening, Rebecca would pull buckets of water from the well to use for cooking and cleaning. At night, she would eat dinner with Josie and tell her more stories about the War of Independence.

"...and then General Arnold moved his troops north...."

"Why did you stay?" Josie interrupted. Rebecca looked at her for a moment, as if not understanding the question.

"I stayed because you're my friend. Friends do that for one another, you know."

There was a long silence as Josie turned her head to stare at a knot on the wall. Rebecca sat there silently, unsure of what to say or if she should leave or not. "Thank you," the outlaw finally said quietly. Her face was an unreadable mask.

"Well, um...." Rebecca stood up and rubbed her hands on the front of her dress as she tried not to let her happiness at the thanks show. "Guess it's time to turn in. Tomorrow's gonna be a busy day," she unconsciously rubbed her aching forearms.

"If you rub liniment into them, they won't hurt as much," Josie said. She received a warm smile for her efforts.

"Thanks." Without thinking about it, Rebecca leaned forward and gave the outlaw a quick hug. "Good night." She felt Josie stiffen and make no effort to return the embrace. "Sorry."

"It's all right, Rebecca. I'm just not a touchy-feely kind of person, that's all." She fixed her blue eyes on a knot on the wall for a moment. "Don't forget to rub liniment on those muscles," she added softly.

"I won't forget. Good night." As she left the room Rebecca smiled from ear to ear. They had actually spoken kind words to one another. She had called Josie a friend and the outlaw had looked for a moment as if she were going to respond in kind. The young woman took it as a very good sign indeed.

12:   Lessons

"If you're gonna ride with Josie, you need to learn some things. You do want to be helpful, don't you?" Belle asked as she handed the young woman a mug of coffee.

"Anything, name it. I'll learn anything," Rebecca said enthusiastically.

"How are you at sewing?" She almost laughed at the stricken look on the blonde girl's face.

"I can't sew to save my soul."

"Well, you're gonna learn, my dear. Wounds need to be stitched, not to mention clothing. A neat row of small, tight stitches helps to prevent infection and disease. You wouldn't want Josie to go through life with a jagged scar 'cause you didn't stitch it right, now would you?" Belle said as she rose and pulled out a small sewing basket from under the counter.

"No, of course not." She looked at the materials being laid out in front of her with trepidation. "But you mean I'd have to actually do that...put a needle...into her skin?" She paled at the thought.

"Just think of it as soft leather." She placed a needle in Rebecca's hand. "Now let's get started."

An hour later, Rebecca held up a two small pieces of leather sewn together. Belle took it from her and held it up to the light. She shook her head. "Does that seam look straight to you?" Before Rebecca could even reply the older woman pulled a small knife from her belt and cut the threads apart. "Try again, and this time pay attention to the seam, not just the stitches."

Hours later an extremely frustrated Rebecca handed Belle her latest effort, fully expecting it to be pulled apart again. The older woman went through her usual routine to inspect it. "Not bad. Quite an improvement over when we began, now, wouldn't you say?" she added as she handed it back to the young woman. Rebecca turned it over in her hands, noting that it did indeed look better than her first attempts. Belle collected the loose materials and put them back in the basket. "Starting tomorrow, you practice your stitching for one hour each morning and one hour each night. Work on straight seams and jagged ones. Mend your clothing to fit you properly. If I see one seam out of line, I'll tear the whole thing apart and make you start over."

After a week, Josie was up on her feet and starting to feel a bit anxious to leave. With the aid of a cane, she walked over to her window and looked out. Rebecca was sitting under a tree, taking advantage of the afternoon shade. The outlaw's keen eyes picked out that the young woman was sewing, all of her attention on her task. A soft knock on the door interrupted her. "Come in, Belle." Belle was pleased to see Josie on her feet. She could not help but notice that the gunslinger's eyes were riveted on the attractive, young blonde out in the yard.

"She's pretty spunky, that one," Belle said with a chuckle. "Been practicing her stitching all the time." She walked up behind the outlaw and joined her in watching the young woman. "She's trying to impress you."

"She's afraid I'm going to leave her behind somewhere," the outlaw said quietly, her focus remaining on Rebecca.

"Are you?" Hearing no answer, Belle continued. "How long has she been traveling with you?"

"Not long. This isn't a permanent arrangement."

"Well, it don't hurt none for her to know how to stitch people up."

Josie moved from the window back to the bed. "Nope, I don't suppose it does."

Even though Belle offered her the use of the other unoccupied bedroom, Rebecca preferred to sleep on a pallet on the floor in Josie's room, explaining that she wanted to be close in case Josie needed something. She was awakened one night by the sounds of the tall woman thrashing about in her bed. When Josie cried out as if in pain, Rebecca leapt to her feet and groped her way to the bed in the darkness.

"Nooo," Josie moaned as she violently shook her head from side to side. Without hesitation, Rebecca climbed up onto the bed with the outlaw. She slid her arm under her shoulder and pulled Josie's head to her chest.

Gently she ran her hand over Josie's sweat-drenched forehead and hair, and softly she began to sing.

Belle was also wakened by the sounds of the gunslinger, but she immediately recognized it for the nightmare it was. Josie had always been plagued by nightmares, oftentimes calling out in remembered pain long into the night. Belle considered going to see if there was something she could do, when she heard the sweet strains of "Beautiful Dreamer" in a clear and beautiful voice. The sounds of Josie's nightmare were no longer audible. With a smile Belle relaxed back onto her own bed, listening to the young girl sing.

When Josie's breathing was once again deep and even, and her brow no longer furrowed, Rebecca eased herself out from under the sleeping woman. She actually hated to leave the comforting warmth of Josie's body, but she was afraid she would fall asleep herself, and the thought of what Josie would do if she found her there was enough to send her back to her pallet on the floor.

After healing from her gunshot wound, Josie helped Belle mend the roof and do other repairs around the small ranch. Every so often Rebecca would come into view, usually caring for one of the horses or hauling buckets of water. The outlaw noted that not once had she heard her young companion complain about all the hard labor.

Rebecca worked as hard as she could, trying to prove to both women that she was capable of pulling her own weight. Belle was more forthcoming with the compliments, but it was the rare look of approval in Josie's face that encouraged her to continue on when her limbs ached and her muscles screamed. The liberal amounts of liniment helped, but only slightly.

The extra time devoted to practicing her stitches showed in Rebecca's newly tailored clothes. Knowing that she would be expected to wear pants if she wanted to ride double with Josie, she determined to make the clothes they had taken from the dead man fit her as well as Josie's fit her. She succeeded more than she would have imagined. She no longer had to push her sleeves up just to see her hands. Her britches were now the right length and no longer required a belt to stay up. There was no mistaking the pride in her face when she showed off her outfit for the first time.

"Wonderful, Rebecca," Belle said as she inspected the seams. "When you first picked up the needle you couldn't stitch a straight line. Now look what you've done. Child, you can do anything you set your mind to if you only try."

Rebecca looked over to Josie. "Better," was all the outlaw said, but the small smile on her face spoke much more. The smile that swept across the young blonde woman's face remained there for the rest of the day as she went about her chores.

13:   Parting

"Where are you headed?" Belle asked as she watched Josie saddle Phoenix. The early morning heat hung in the air, promising a scorcher of a day ahead. The gunslinger wiped her brow with her bandanna.

"Tombstone. You know that little mining town not far from here." Belle nodded. Josie looked around to make sure Rebecca was not nearby then leaned in close and spoke quietly. "She'll be safe enough there."

"She's been getting stronger, ya know. Working so hard here and all. She's a good talker, unlike someone we know," her eyes twinkled at the scowl from Josie. "That little sprite's got a strong heart."

"I'm not changing my mind, Belle." Josie turned her attention back to tightening straps and checking the fit of the bridle. Belle looked out and caught sight of the young blonde heading their way. "She's coming, Josie." She turned to look at her dark-headed friend. "That girl has worked her rear off trying to impress you while you healed and now you're just gonna dump her like a sack of mealy flour?"

"Belle," she sighed, "just how safe do you think it would be for a young, innocent girl like that to be following me all over the place? All it'll mean to her is an early death...or worse." She took the reins and led the horse out of the stall. She had already packed their supplies on the smaller horse and she gathered up her lead rope as well, as she walked from the stable. She turned back to Belle and said, "Don't say anything to her." Belle nodded.

She knew Josie would do what she thought was best, regardless of anything she might say or do.

"Ready?" Rebecca asked expectantly as she watched the outlaw exit the stable, Belle close behind her. Josie mounted and held her hand out, pulling the young woman up effortlessly behind her.

"Hang on," she said before nudging Phoenix into a trot, giving a short wave to the sharpshooter as they pulled out of sight. Rebecca turned her head and caught a sad look on Belle's face. As she waved, the prairie girl swore she saw the sharpshooter's lips form the words… "Take care of her."

14:   Girl Talk

They rode in silence for five hours before Josie decided to take a break. Finding a shady area, she pulled Phoenix to a stop and helped Rebecca down before dismounting herself. Removing the saddlebag that held the stash of food Belle had packed for them, Josie walked over and sat down with her back supported by a large tree. "She packed enough food for an army," she quipped as Rebecca sat across from her and took the offered piece of jerky. She looked at the eagerness with which the young woman was eating the dried strip of meat. Rebecca looked up and saw a twinkle in the light blue eyes and a slight smile tugging at the gunslinger's lips. She rolled her eyes and Josie chuckled, dissipating the tension that always seemed to be present around them. *Perhaps it won't be so bad having her around,* the gunslinger thought as she passed the canteen of water to her. A momentary pang of lost innocence tugged at her and Josie let the thought pass from her mind. *Once we get to Tombstone, Rebecca will just have to find someone else to take care of her, that's all there is to it,* she thought. Oblivious to the outlaw's internal struggle, Rebecca chattered away while she ate. "You know," she said as she shoved a piece of bread in her mouth, "you could always become a bounty hunter."

"A bounty hunter?" Josie spat contemptuously. "They're the lowest form of life on the earth. Nothing but money-hungry murderers who'd kill ya as soon as look at ya." She pulled a hunk of bread off the loaf and put it in her mouth.

"It's a perfectly 'legal' profession," Rebecca urged, pulling her head back slightly when she saw Josie's eyes narrow at her inflection of 'legal.' "I mean, uh, that you could make money that way, and you'd probably be able to get pardons if you catch someone big enough."

Too fast for Rebecca to react, Josie moved forward, closing the distance between them until all that the young woman could see was the deepness of her blue eyes, which were flaring. "You want me to hunt down people that I used to ride with? To help the law when all they want to do is see me hanging from a noose?"

"And why would they want to do that to you, Josie?" She took a deep breath in fear of going too far for the temperamental outlaw. "Perhaps if you tried to help make the world a little better, like you did in Mason's Gulch, maybe they wouldn't be so quick to wrap a rope around your neck."

A long silence passed between them before Josie leaned back against the tree. "It's easier to rob trains," she said casually, not realizing that she had fallen into the trap set by the young woman.

"Uh huh, but think about this...people don't usually shoot at you when you bring another criminal into town. They look at you as a hero, not a villain. Besides, think of how much fun it would be to put some of your enemies behind bars." The faraway look in the outlaw's eyes told her she had found an opening. "All those who betrayed you, who hurt women and children and are still running around; wouldn't you like to see them get what they deserve?"

Just when Rebecca thought she had Josie right where she wanted her, the outlaw looked at her and spoke calmly. "I don't care. As long as they stay out of my way, I'll stay out of theirs." She shrugged her shoulders and continued to eat. Josie's features hid her amusement at the scowl on the younger woman's face. Rebecca decided that the rest of the meal would be a silent affair while she thought up a new plan. No matter how hard the outlaw tried to be rough and mean, the young woman knew deep down inside she was a kind and gentle person who could and would do the right thing if given the chance. As the day wore on and they were once again on their way, Rebecca's mind filled with questions that she wanted to ask but did not dare. What caused Josie to become a criminal in the first place? Did she have a family? Time passed quickly as both women remained lost in their own thoughts. Josie concentrated on the words exchanged during dinner.

When darkness settled across the land, Josie pulled off the dirt trail and found a suitable area for bunking down for the night. The gunslinger concentrated on cleaning her weapons and sharpening her knives, and Rebecca tried out her sewing skills by mending a tear in her blanket while reciting more of her story about Benedict Arnold before moving on to Ethan Allen and the Green Mountain Boys. Josie half-listened, nodding occasionally but doing nothing to discourage the conversation. When it came time for sleep, the women laid their blankets out on the ground on opposite sides of the fire. "Good night, Josie," Rebecca said before letting out a long yawn. She closed her eyes, not expecting an answer.

"Good night, Rebecca," the outlaw answered softly.

15: Tombstone

Josie left Phoenix at the OK Corral and the pair walked over to the saloon. Rebecca had wisely changed into her dress. Despite its battered appearance, it would certainly raise fewer questions than her britches would. Josie, of course, remained in her dark outfit, looking every bit the outlaw. She grabbed the younger woman's upper arm and pulled her close to speak before entering the saloon. "Listen to me carefully. Don't talk to anyone, don't look at anyone, and never leave my side." The look in her blue eyes and the tone in her voice made it clear that this was not any kind of request. Rebecca nodded, noting somewhere in the back of her mind that at least the outlaw was bringing her in instead of leaving her somewhere else to wait for her.

Pushing open the swinging half doors, Josie strode in and took an all-encompassing look around. A long bar took up the wall on the left, while stairs and a piano took up the wall at the far end. The right side of the saloon consisted of several small, green, felt-covered, round tables surrounded by chairs, some of which looked ready to fall apart. Josie kept Rebecca between her and the door as they walked over to the bar. "Whiskey," she ordered, and as an afterthought she added, "and sarsaparilla."

There was no question as to which drink belonged to whom. The portly barkeep placed the shot glass and bottle in front of the tall woman and handed the smaller woman the nonalcoholic drink. "Two bits for the whiskey and twenty cents for the soda."

Josie tossed the coins on the bar and turned to watch the goings on. Her eyes fell on a table of three men playing poker. With one gulp, she drained her drink and set the glass on the bar. "Stay here," she said before walking over to the trio.

"Hello boys." They looked up from their battered cards to see the imposing woman towering over them. "You seem to be short. Is my money any good at this table?"

The biggest of the men, a large, burly fellow with a scraggly beard and a long, jagged scar across his face looked at the meager pot in front of him. The potential benefit from letting this woman into the game was appealing. Despite the six guns slung low on her hips, she was still a woman, and he had no doubt that he could handle himself well enough with any woman alive. He grinned to reveal uneven rows of brown teeth and tipped his hat to the gunslinger. "Why, sure, there's always room for a pretty gal at our table, right boys?" The others were not as certain as their large friend of their ability to handle themselves with someone as formidable as this woman appeared to be. But they silently agreed that there was safety in numbers and did nothing to dissuade her from sitting down. She pulled a chair out and dropped into it.

"Deal," she said with a smile that did not do anything to remove the icy glint from her eyes.

Two hours later, the burly man threw his cards down in disgust and slowly rose, making sure to keep his hands away from his sidearm. "You've broke me, Miss. I'm done." Josie nodded with satisfaction as she pulled the last pot closer. No sooner had she gotten the notes and coins into her pocket than the skinny man sitting across from her narrowed his gaze and lowered his hand below the table. He would be damned if a woman was going to walk away with his money. Before he could get his hand on his gun, the table suddenly flipped upwards at him, blocking his vision before slamming into him with enough force to send him backward, his chair splintering upon contact with the wooden floor. The third man in the group had similar thoughts and made a move for his gun. A roundhouse kick sent Josie's heel into the side of his face, and the fight was on. None of the patrons seemed to care what the fight was about as they began scrapping with each other.

Rebecca worked her way closer and closer to the swinging doors, ducking once as part of a chair came flying at her. She tried to locate Josie in the mass pandemonium of flying bodies and smashing bottles. She found her only when two men tossed the dark-clad woman down the length of the bar. With a gleeful yelp, Josie stood up on the bar and looked for the best place to jump back into the fray. She somersaulted off the bar and landed with her feet against the chest of a very surprised patron. After a couple of minutes the barkeep sighed, threw his towel down on the bar, and buried his face in his hands while shaking his head in disbelief. A few minutes later Josie appeared at Rebecca's side apparently no worse for wear, although her shirtsleeve was almost completely torn off. "Having fun?" she asked breathlessly before grabbing two men and knocking their heads together.

"Not as much as you seem to be having," Rebecca quipped as she jumped back to avoid another flying body.

"Nothing like a good fight to get my juices flowing," Josie replied with a feral smile still on her face as she looked around at the roiling battle. The sound of a shotgun being fired several times into the ceiling brought the bedlam to a standstill as everyone turned to see the source of the shots. The barkeep was standing there, gun in hand, covered with dust from the ceiling that he had shot. He looked up at the holes and sighed again.

"Every time a woman comes in, there's trouble," he muttered, his gaze leveled at the pair near the doorway. Josie reached in her pocket and pulled out several bills then put them on the bar before turning and leaving. The barkeep looked at the retreating form in surprise as he picked up the notes from the counter.

"What happened in there?" Rebecca asked as they headed up the street to the boarding house.

"The pipsqueak across from me didn't like losing to a woman," she said casually as she inspected the torn shirt. "Looks like you'll be doing some sewing tonight."

"I don't mind," Rebecca answered as she looked at the jagged tear. The shirt was not much to begin with; the elbows were worn almost through, the collar was frayed, and two buttons hung loosely by their threads. "Although the best thing to do would be to get you a new shirt." The look she received told her that was out of the question. "Or I could sew this one up," she said with a tone of defeat in her voice.

"Ten dollars?" The muscles in Josie's jaw tensed noticeably. "No way in tarnation am I going to pay that much!" She turned and stomped over to the door assuming that Rebecca would follow. The young woman had other ideas, however.

"Look, you have to admit that ten dollars is a lot to ask for such a..." she paused and looked around the parlor as if to pick just the right word.

"...quaint little place. After all, the flophouse near the corral only charges four dollars a week for both of us."

"I include one meal a day with my price," the boarding house owner protested. "Eight dollars."

"Six and you throw in a bath for tonight," the young woman countered. Josie watched the debate carefully. Clearly Rebecca had the knowledge of words and the wit to haggle efficiently.

"Seven and the bath."

She started to say "six," but the look on the proprietress's face told her she would not go any lower. Rebecca knew that seven was more than fair for two people. She decided to quit before she talked them into sleeping in the corral with the horses. "All right, seven, but that had better include the bath."

"I said it did, didn't I," the woman said irritably. "Take the room at the end of the hall. Outhouse is in back."

Rebecca turned to Josie, a bit fearful the outlaw would be mad at her for stepping in. Instead, the tall woman nodded and handed over the required funds. While it was not a smile or words of praise, the young woman still somehow understood the silent message that was conveyed.

Rebecca stood nervously at the side of the bed, looking at it as if there were sharp razors waiting for her. "What's the problem?" Josie asked as she removed her clothes. "Haven't you ever slept with another woman before?"

"No! Why..." she stopped when she realized what the outlaw meant. Blushing hotly, she continued. "I mean, well, with my sister and occasionally a cousin, but..." She turned away from the now naked woman. "I guess I'm just a bit shy."

"So it would seem," Josie replied as she pulled a nightshirt over her head and down her body. Although designed for a full-grown man, it only came to mid-thigh on her tall frame. "Are you going to sleep in your dress?"

"What? Oh no, of course not." She turned and walked behind the privacy screen, not seeing the way Josie rolled her eyes and smiled.

They each lay on an edge of the bed trying to stay as far apart as possible to leave room for the other. Always a deep sleeper, Rebecca was out quickly. Josie, however, was easily awakened by the slightest noise and found the young woman's light snoring to be distracting. Several times she adjusted her pillow to try to muffle the sounds, but with no success. Her keen hearing would not allow it. She lay awake as hour after hour passed. In the darkness of the night, the loner reflected back on her life. She saw visions of the crimes she had committed over the years, the looks of abject terror on the faces of her victims. Years of running, robbing, and hard drinking had blocked all those sights from her mind. As dawn settled across the land, she thought about how she had helped the town of Mason's Gulch and the sense of accomplishment she felt when she had stopped the band of thieves. It was time for her to make a decision, one that would forever alter her life one way or another. She had never consciously made a choice to be a criminal; it had happened by accident. For the first time in years, she believed she actually had a choice between being good or evil. The full sun was visible before she gathered the courage to make the only choice with which she could live.

16: Careers

After a quick breakfast consisting of the remains of their rations, Josie wrote a note telling Rebecca to stay put and then left the boarding house. With purposeful strides she crossed the street and entered the jail.

"What can I do for you today, young fella?" the sheriff asked without looking up from his solitaire hand.

"I want to look at the wanted list," she said in a commanding tone. His head popped up at the unexpected gender.

"Uh...yes, of course." He reached over and retrieved a stack of wanted posters piled haphazardly on the corner of his desk. As he passed the pile to her, he realized that he was using his gun hand and was defenseless should this tall woman in black choose to send him to Saint Peter. To his relief, she simply took the pile of papers and sat down in a nearby chair, apparently uninterested in him. "Uh...somethin' you're looking for...uh...Miss?"

Josie smiled inwardly at the sheriff's fear of her. "Just seeing who's worth what," she replied, her eyes poring over the wanted posters. She studied every name, what they were wanted for, and where. She studied each likeness and tried to commit each characteristic to memory. She smiled at the sight of the familiar name. Looking over to make sure the sheriff wasn't paying attention, she folded the paper and stuffed it in her pocket. *Doesn't even look like me. Still, it won't do for him to see it so soon after meeting me. He looks dumb but not that dumb.* After several minutes, she stood up and put the pile back on the corner of his desk. "I suggest you double check the locks on your cells. I have a feeling you'll be filling up soon," she said as she walked out the door, leaving a confused and nervous sheriff behind.

She reviewed the list of wanted men in her mind, discarding some as not being worth the bother and making mental notes on others. Horse thieves were not on her list of those to turn in for justice. Although she had bought and paid for Phoenix, she herself had stolen a number of horses in her day. Deciding that no man should die for stealing an animal, she moved on in her mental list to concentrate on those for whom she would look. Men who raped or murdered women and children were highest on her list. Her eyes narrowed when she saw the familiar blonde woman exiting the doctor's office. Her long legs quickly ate up the distance between them.

"What are you doing here? Are you sick?" She began a visual inspection of Rebecca.

"No, I thought I could learn something about healing while you were off doing whatever it is that you were doing." It was then that Josie noticed the two small jars that were in the young woman's hands. "Oh, one is for cleaning a wound and the other is to help with pain."

"How much did those cost?" Josie asked warily, her mind already trying to calculate the amount.

"Nothing. He gave me these small bottles for helping him."

"Helping him?" Her eyes narrowed. "Helping him do what?"

"A young boy came in with a broken arm. I told him a story while the doctor put on a splint. You should have seen him, Josie. His name was Timothy and he didn't cry, not one bit. He just sat there and listened to my story." The smile on her face and tone of pride in her voice were infectious and Josie reluctantly allowed a small smile. As they walked back to the boarding house together, Rebecca recounted all she had learned in the short time she was with the doctor and spoke of going back later to learn more. Josie did not miss the hopeful "see I'm trying to learn something so I can help" tone in the young woman's voice, although her face remained impassive.

After a quick supper that was barely edible, the pair retired to their room. The gunslinger sat on the floor, bracing her back against a wall while the young woman sat on the bed, using the headboard as a backrest. Josie went through her usual routine of cleaning and inspecting her weapons while Rebecca read by lamplight. Doc Jackson had loaned her a beginner's medical text and she was voraciously reading it, absorbing as many details as she could about different emergency treatments for wounds and illness. She skipped over rare or unusual injuries, concentrating mostly on things she perceived could happen on the road: snake bites, bullet wounds, scorpion stings, and more. Josie watched out of the corner of her eye as page after page was turned in Rebecca's quest for knowledge. *I'll give you one thing, Sprite, you have determination,* Josie thought to herself as she turned her attention back to the task at hand, that being the polishing of her guns.

When Rebecca rubbed her eyes for the third time in an hour, Josie set her rifle down and stood. "I think that's enough reading for one night." Taking the book from the reluctant girl, she set it down on the table and prepared for bed. When she turned to get into bed, she found that Rebecca had simply lain down across the bed, not bothering to undress. "Hey girl, get yourself ready for bed." She took a step closer and found that the young woman had already fallen asleep. Sighing, Josie sat down and jerked Rebecca's foot onto her lap. It was the first time she really noticed the soft-soled shoes worn with the dress. *Looks like you'll need new shoes soon.* She removed first one, then the other before using her control over the young woman's legs to maneuver Rebecca into the proper position on the bed. She lay down in the small space remaining to her, her body forced to curl around the sleeping form to avoid falling off the bed. Exhaustion got the best of the outlaw and she fell asleep soon after her head hit the pillow.

17:   Nightmares and Understandings

It was after two when Rebecca woke to her bedmate thrashing about in the throes of another vicious nightmare. She reached out to stop the arms flailing about, missing more than once and having to back up quickly to avoid being struck in the face. Once again Rebecca took the outlaw in her arms and began to sing softly. "It's just a dream. Everything's gonna be all right now," she whispered between verses. In the darkness of the night, she heard the older woman whimper softly before falling into a more dreamless state. She continued to sing and stroke Josie's hair gently until she was certain the other woman was past the nightmare. "That's right, you rest now." She would be wakened twice more during the night by the outlaw's demons and, both times, she would calm Josie back to restful sleep. While waiting for the sandman to arrive, Rebecca allowed herself to feel the mixed emotions of wishing that the nightmares did not happen and the pleasure in being able to soothe Josie's troubled sleep.

Rebecca awoke to find herself alone in the room, the sun shining brightly. With a groan, she buried her head under the pillow to block out the light and tried for a few more minutes of sleep. The sound of the door opening caused her to poke her head up from under the pillow, look at the bright-eyed and wide-awake gunslinger, groan, and put her head back down. "Five more minutes," she mumbled.

"Rebecca, it's after nine already. I've been up for at least three hours. Let's go." Josie set the two mugs of coffee down on the table. "I mean it."

"I'm up, I'm up," she grumbled before sitting up and stretching. She plodded over to the table and flopped down in the chair, muttering her thanks as she took her mug.

"You're not a morning person, are you?" Josie asked before taking a gulp of her coffee and grimacing. "Damn, this is strong. Miss Patricia must be trying to kill us so she can rent this room out to someone else."

Rebecca chuckled and took a sip from hers. "Ugh, I think you're right," she said as she forced the bitter brew down her throat. In the moment of silence, she decided to broach the subject of the nightmares. "Josie, do you remember the nightmares you had last night?" She watched the gunslinger stiffen noticeably. "It's all right if you don't want to talk about it, but I know that it helps sometimes to talk about them."

"There's nothing to talk about, Rebecca. I don't remember it," she lied. Even in the light of day, her mind replayed the visions that tormented her during the night.

"Well, if you wanted to talk about it, I just wanted you to know that you could...with me, I mean," she said before drinking the rest of her coffee and standing up. Josie nodded noncommittally. Rebecca stepped behind the privacy screen and started to get dressed. "So where did you go?"

"I had to get some information. You know, what you said about being a bounty hunter does make sense."

"Well yeah, you can get into places where regular bounty hunters couldn't. You know how these men think, how they act." She tried to tighten the laces on her corset, but this particular one tied in the back. "Josie, can you help me with this?" Seconds later she felt strong fingers pulling the laces into place and tying them off. "Thanks." She turned around and looked up at the tall woman. "You know, I really do hate corsets."

"Me too, that's why I don't wear them," Josie said, allowing a small smile to come to her lips. "Now, I have a list of names of men that would bring in a fair amount of money with little effort." They went back to the table and sat down. Rebecca busied herself with brushing her shoulder length hair. Josie took another gulp of coffee and continued. "Cletus Wilson is a no-good bully with a bounty of a hundred dollars on his head here in Tombstone. I went to the watering hole this morning and found out where he's hiding."

"How did...?" Rebecca smiled and shook her head. "After seeing you in action yesterday, I'm sure I don't want to know."

Josie flashed a smile full of teeth, quite proud of her intimidation tactics. "You probably don't, Sprite. Now I want you to stay here or at the Doc's place until I return."

"All right," she nodded. "But promise you'll be careful?"

"Rebecca...."

"Sorry, but I do worry about you," she protested. "Someone has to."

"Well, I think you worry enough about me for the both of us. Now don't go anywhere until I return." Josie rose to her feet, intent on walking out the door and taking care of business. Before her hand could touch the doorknob, however, she turned around and gave Rebecca one of her most serious looks. "I mean it, Sprite. This isn't Chancetown. Don't wander off by yourself."

18: First Bounty

Josie crouched down in the bushes, concealing herself from the man hiding in the bunkhouse. Wilson was not worth much but it would be enough for her to leave with Rebecca and move on. He was wanted for armed robbery and was known to drink far too much in the evenings. All she had to do was wait for him to pass out and then she could tie him up and bring him back to town. Unfortunately it was still early in the day. Her eyes fell on a buckboard nearby. *At least I have an easy way to haul your ass in, Cletus.* She stole over to the barn and found one strapping horse, albeit a bit smaller than Phoenix, who was still safely tucked away at the OK Corral. Still, he would do the job. Pulling the brim of her Stetson down to shade her eyes, Josie settled back in the bushes to wait for night-fall to come.

Rebecca returned the book to Doc Jackson and looked around at the stores that littered the sides of the main street. Her eyes fell upon the saloon and her mouth watered for something tastier than stale water and bad coffee. *No reason I can't go in there and have a sarsaparilla or two, maybe even a beer.* Slipping two of the dollars Josie gave her into her bodice, Rebecca glanced at the boarding house briefly before heading up the street to the watering hole.

Signs of yesterday's activities were still apparent throughout the room. The tinderbox was overflowing with former chairs and table legs. The remaining tables were spread out along the edges, surrounding broken glass swept into a pile in the middle of the floor. Rebecca noted that two of the large mirrors on the wall showed cracks that she had not noticed there before. The barkeep looked up from polishing the bar and spotted her. He frowned and looked around for her trouble-making friend before walking up to her. "I don't want another fight in here today, Miss. Now you look like a nice child, you shouldn't be hangin' out in a place like this."

"I'd like a sarsaparilla, please," she said firmly, trying to sound every bit like her taller companion. The barkeep shook his head in defeat and handed her the bottle of soda. No sooner did she place her hand around the glass than his eyes widened and she heard footsteps behind her.

"Well now, lookie what we have here? If it ain't the purty little thing that was with that bitch in black yesterday," the deep male voice said as a grimy hand landed on Rebecca's shoulder. Looking into the mirror behind the bar, she recognized him as the lanky man who sat across from Josie during the card game.

"Uh oh," she said softly, instantly regretting that she had disobeyed Josie's instructions.

Josie rubbed the back of her neck as she climbed the stairs. It had been nearly daybreak when she pulled into town with her captive securely tied up in the back of the buckboard. What she hoped would be a quick 'drop 'em off and pick up the money' became a severe testing of her patience. A distrusting teller refused to honor the draft note given to her by the sheriff, forcing her to go and return with the lawman in tow to retrieve her cash. *I suppose having it made out to bearer didn't help either,* she thought to herself. Reaching the top landing, Josie turned and quickly reached their room. *You better not be sprawled all over the bed, Sprite,* she thought to herself. After a long day of waiting, all she wanted to do was crawl into bed and sleep and the thought of fighting with Rebecca for space was not something she was in the mood for.

"Rebecca, it's me." She entered the room, only to find herself alone. To her surprise, the two mugs from yesterday's coffee were still sitting on the table. Frowning, she checked around to make sure that all their belongings were still there. *What's going on?* She went downstairs and found the woman who ran the boarding house.

"Where's Rebecca?" The look she received from Miss Patricia chilled her to the bone. "What? Where is she?"

"I-I thought she was with you," the round woman stammered. "I haven't seen her since yesterday. She left shortly after you did." There was fear in her eyes, but no sign of deceit. Josie turned on her heels and headed to the doctor's office.

Two hours later, Josie was leaning on a hitching post, looking around and trying to figure out where Rebecca could have gone. Lifting her hat and wiping her brow, her eyes fell upon the slatted doors of the saloon. It was one of the few places she had yet to check. *Well, it won't hurt to wet my whistle*, she thought. *Maybe someone even saw her.*

The barkeep gave her a terrified look that went beyond the activities of two days past. "Whiskey," she barked as she leaned against the bar. She noted that his hands were shaking as he set the small glass in front of her. *He knows something.* "I'm looking for my friend, the one that was with me the other day. Have you seen her?" Her tone made it clear that a lie would not be tolerated. Sweat began to form on his brow and he backed up slowly. Quick as a cat, Josie reached over the bar and grabbed his shirt at the throat. She jerked him forward, slamming his gut against the wooden bar, and stared menacingly at him, her face mere inches from his. "Now you listen here, little man. Put those hands up here and away from the gun I know you got hidden under there and tell me what I want to know. Girl, blonde, a head smaller than me. Where is she?"

"Ah...she...well...." She jerked him one more time, making sure that bruises would be left behind. "Ugh...he took her."

"Who?" She cocked her gun and placed it against his nose. Her anger was at a frightening level and she knew it would be easy to pull the trigger. She suspected he knew it too. "I want answers and I want them...now," she nudged the cool steel against his face to punctuate her point.

"Smith. Tom Smith...he took her." At her questioning look he added, "He's the one from the poker game."

"Where?" she growled.

"Ah...." Beads of sweat were rolling down his face, which was turning red from her grip on his collar. "Small ranch 'bout an hour due north of here. The Double S."

Without another word, she shoved him back and left the bar. It only took a few minutes to saddle Phoenix and tear off in search of her young friend. *Hurt her and I'll kill you*, she vowed. *No way in hell's half-acre am I gonna leave her here with these people.* She decided Tombstone was too dangerous for Rebecca. *I'll just have to find someplace else for her, that's all.*

Rebecca pounded on the door again, sending more dust scattering. "Please let me out. It stinks in here. Let me out," she bellowed, knowing no one could hear her. The outhouse was too far away from the main house. She shoved at the door again, finding the ropes used to hold the door closed showed no signs of budging. "Of all the places to stick me," she muttered before resuming her pounding. "My friend is Josie Hunter and if you don't let me out well...well you'll be sorry when she gets hold of you. Let me out!" She sighed and pressed her head against the wood. "Please."

Josie looked down from her perch on the hillside at the lone ranch. The area was too wide open and flat for her to attempt anything during the day. If she made a run at the ranch, Rebecca would be dead before she could reach her. Being out of earshot, she was unable to hear the young woman's calls for help from the small building set so far behind the main house. The gunslinger forced herself not to think about the possibilities of what could be happening to her young friend while she waited. It was hard enough not to go blazing in there with guns drawn without having to think of Rebecca's innocence being threatened. She impatiently waited for the second day in a row for darkness to fall.

Two lamps burned brightly inside the ranch as Josie crept up alongside the small building. She needed to know how many men she was dealing with, and exactly where Rebecca was before she could make a move. Looking through the small window partially obscured by a dirty piece of cloth being used as a makeshift curtain, she could only make out some of the room, noting that there were two rooms off the main room that she could not see into. She watched as the lanky man she fought with at the saloon rose and headed to the door. She quietly slipped around the side as he stepped off the porch and walked several paces away from the house. She watched as he pulled down his britches, squatted, and relieved himself. Her brow furrowed. *Why is he doing that there instead of in the outhouse?* He went back inside and she headed behind the house. She grinned when she saw the ropes wrapped around the small wooden structure.

"Rebecca," she whispered.

"Josie? Oh Josie, please let me out of here."

"Shh." She quickly cut the ropes, reaching out and grabbing the young woman as she fell through the now open door. "Whoa there, little one." She helped Rebecca to her knees where she gulped in long draughts of fresh air. Rebecca went to speak but Josie's hand was quicker, covering her mouth and pulling her behind the side of the outhouse. "Stay quiet. I don't want them to hear you. Are you all right?" In the dim moonlight, she tried to visually inspect Rebecca for any signs that would confirm her fears. To her great relief, the dress appeared intact and the young woman showed no evidence of being violated.

"I'm fine. I'm just glad you're here."

Me too. Now that she had saved Rebecca, the next task was protecting her. "Come on, I want to be long gone before he realizes that you're missing." *I'll come back later and take care of that pile of dung.*

It was at that time that Smith decided to go check on his captive. He was really disappointed that the tall bitch in black had not decided to pay him a visit. He was looking forward to getting her back for his black eye. He chuckled to himself as he thought of other things he could be looking forward to. It did not make a difference to him if that girl lived or died; she was only good as bait for the bitch. Perhaps a little fun with her was called for, a payback to her friend for besting him in cards. He froze when he saw the partially open door to the outhouse. He never heard Josie come up behind him. One sharp contact with the butt of her gun on his skull was all it took to send him bonelessly to the ground.

"What are you going to do with him?" Rebecca asked as she watched Josie tie his hands and feet together.

"Take him back to town to answer for his crime." She double-checked her knots before stepping away from him. "He's lucky I didn't just kill him." She gave the unconscious man a not so gentle shove with her foot.

"Josie, I wasn't hurt. Just shaken up a bit."

"But you could have been," Josie snapped, taking a step closer to her. "What in tarnation did you think you were doing going into that saloon alone? You could have been killed." She grabbed the smaller woman's chin and forced her gaze upward to look at her. "Or worse, Rebecca. When I tell you to stay somewhere, stay there."

"I-I'm sorry," she stammered. Josie released her grip and took a step back.

"Don't be sorry, Rebecca. Just do as I say. I'm tired of rescuing you." There was anger in her voice, but something else as well, a touch of concern. She turned to pick up her quarry and placed him across the back of his horse.

"Thank you for saving me...again," Rebecca said softly. She was certain that Josie heard her but chose to ignore her.

Josie looked at Rebecca's dirty dress, then at the horse, then back to her. "How did he get you here?"

"He, uh, kinda threw me over the saddle. That horn really hurts when it's pressed against your ribs, you know."

"No, Rebecca, I've never had that pleasure," she sighed. "You'll just have to ride side-saddle. We can't keep cutting your dresses every time you need to ride."

The ride back to town took longer than it should have because Josie had to make certain Smith did not fall off the horse, although she was tempted to shove him off a few times just to see him fall to the ground. He woke up once and tried to wiggle off the saddle only to have Josie knock him back into dreamland. She was actually disappointed that he failed to wake up again. Her nerves were still frazzled from the whole ordeal and a good fight was just what she needed to take the edge off. Rebecca was pressed hard against her back, her arms tightly gripped around Josie's waist. She looked over at the form slumped over the smaller horse. *You are so lucky, you know that? If you had hurt her...* There was no need to finish the thought. It would not have been the first time she killed a rapist.

Rebecca watched as Tombstone came into view. Josie had been even more tight-lipped than usual. She therefore was not surprised when they stopped in front of the sheriff's office and she was pulled down from the saddle. "Go inside and wait for me."

"Josie, I..."

The outlaw pointed at the building. "We'll talk later. Right now get in there and don't talk to anyone in the cells."

Effectively silenced, Rebecca did her best to smooth her rumpled dress and stepped inside the jail. The sheriff looked up from his solitaire game and almost knocked his chair over in his haste to stand up. "Good evening, Miss..."

"Cameron. Rebecca Cameron."

"What can I do to help you, Miss Cameron?"

"My friend, um...well...she's bringing in a man who kidnapped me and locked me in his outhouse all night." There was a scuffling sound outside and a firm boot opened the door. "I believe that's her right now."

Josie dragged the bound man in and dumped him unceremoniously on the floor. Rebecca noticed her would be kidnapper now sported a split and bloody lip. "Well, um...as I said, Sir. He kidnapped me and locked me up in his outhouse."

"Did he try to hurt you in any way?"

"He threw me over his horse, ruined my best dress and locked me in the vilest outhouse I've ever had to suffer in. Isn't that enough?"

"Well Miss, now there's just some things we can't keep a man locked up for. Now you don't look like he hurt you none. Why don't you and your..." He bit his lip and eyed the Colts resting on the dark woman's hips. "…uh friend go have yourselves a nice dinner up at the Horseshoe and just forget all about it. I'll make sure he don't bother you none no more." The sheriff found himself taking a step back as Josie suddenly appeared just inches from his face.

"We're leaving tomorrow," the outlaw said, moving so close that the brim of her hat pressed against the lawman's forehead. "If I see him, he sees Saint Peter, got it?"

He held his hands out, making it clear he wasn't reaching for a weapon. "I'm sure we can come to an understanding, Miss." He still did not know the name of the intimidating woman he was dealing with but he knew enough to realize she was not one to be taken lightly. "I suppose spending a day in there won't hurt Tom none."

"It won't hurt him nearly as much as my Peacemaker," Josie replied. Stepping back and nodding at him, she reached out and took hold of Rebecca's arm. "Let's go."

Rather than dropping Rebecca off at the boarding house, the gunslinger made her come along to the corral to drop off the horses. Josie was brooding and attempts to start a conversation were met with silence. Walking back to the boarding house, the only sound heard was the rhythmic clicking of boots against wood. Rebecca decided to try one more time. "Josie, I'm sorry."

"We'll talk inside." They were the first words spoken by the outlaw since they left the sheriff's office.

Once in their room, Josie pointed at the privacy screen. "Get ready for bed." Rebecca did as she was told, grabbing her nightdress and stepping behind the barrier. She heard the sound of a sulfur match being struck followed by an increase in light that told her Josie had lit the oil lamp on the table. *Wonder if she does that when she's mad.* The silent treatment was unnerving enough but being unsure of Josie's mood was even worse.

"Will you talk to me?" she ventured.

"I told you to stay put," Josie said firmly. "You didn't do what you were told and you know what happened."

Rebecca pulled the nightdress over her head. "I didn't realize…" she began.

"That's right, Rebecca." The outlaw stormed across the room and jerked the privacy screen back. "You didn't realize but I did. It's too dangerous for you to be alone." The young woman winced at the pressure on her shoulder from Josie's firm grip. "You need to promise me, and I mean right now, you'll listen to what I tell you."

Rebecca nodded her head shakily. "I-I promise. Josie please, you're hurting me." The words had the desired effect as the gunslinger's hand drew back. "I was thirsty and wanted a sarsaparilla. I didn't think anything would happen."

"Well, you were wrong." Josie walked away and flopped down on the bed. "Do you have any idea what I've been through today looking for you?" She undid the top two buttons of her shirt and loosened her bandana.

"I'm sorry. I didn't mean to worry you." Rebecca hesitantly crossed the room and sat down beside Josie. "I won't do it again."

The Stetson sailed onto the table. "I was up all night dealing with a drunken slob who was too stupid to realize he was being taken to jail and then when I want to get some sleep what happens? You end up needing rescuing...again."

Rebecca fought to keep her lower lip from quivering. *She's going to send me back.* "Josie?"

The gunslinger laid back, her feet dangling over the side of the bed. "Mmm?"

"Thank you...again. I know you're mad at me but I'll be good from now on, I promise."

"You'd better get some rest, we're..." Josie paused to let out a long yawn. "We're heading out as soon as I wake up."

We're heading out? "Josie? Which way are we headed?" *Anywhere but east, anywhere but east. Please don't take me back to Chancetown.* "Josie? Josie, are you awake?" She touched the sleeping woman's shoulder. "Wait, you still have your boots on."

Two days without sleep had taken its toll on the gunslinger. Rebecca turned up the wick on the lantern, seeing now that in addition to the boots, Josie was still wearing her holsters. *Well, maybe if I do it nice and slow.* Her hands unsteady, she reached for the leather thong that held the holster against Josie's leg. The simple knot came loose easily and she repeated the procedure on the other leg. *Now comes the tricky part.* She reached for the belt buckle only to find her hand caught in an iron grasp.

"What?" the sleepy voice grumbled.

"I was trying to get your holsters off."

Josie grunted and experienced hands undid the buckles with ease. A jerk of the hips and the belts came out from around her body. Rebecca reached out and took the holsters. "I'll put them around the bedpost like you do."

The gunslinger made another unintelligible noise and shifted until she was in the right direction, her hands blindly grasping for the pillow. The lamplight reflected off the silver tips of the black boots, reminding Rebecca of the danger her shins were in. Deciding that it was a good idea to protect herself, she donned her own boots and climbed into bed next to the slumbering woman. "Good night, Josie."

"Grumph." The grip on the pillow tightened.

Rebecca lay there for several minutes listening to the deep and even breathing next to her before speaking again. "Thank you," she whispered before letting sleep claim her as well.

19:   Moving On

After a quick breakfast and a cup of coffee, the pair headed over to the corral to retrieve the horses and put Tombstone behind them. Since they were going to be on the road again, Rebecca wore her britches and shirt. Once at the corral, Josie went to pay the owner while Rebecca went in to feed the horses a few apples. She was still intimidated by the bay's sheer size, but was bound and determined to make friends with the horse. A snort and firm nudge drew Rebecca's attention away from Phoenix to the gray mare in the adjoining stall. "Howdy. I don't remember you being this friendly before." The little horse had a gentle, sweet expression, and Rebecca could almost swear she was smiling. "Now stop pushing me," she squealed as she backed up out of reach. "Oh, you're a cute one." She held out an apple, giggling at the tickling feeling of the little mare's lips on her hand. Taking advantage of the busy mouth, Rebecca stroked the mare's nose. "Oh, you like that, don't you?" she cooed. Phoenix nickered in protest and she complied with another apple. "Now don't be jealous, Phoenix." She used both hands to scratch and rub the smaller horse, smiling when she received a snort of enjoyment in return. She did not hear Josie enter the stable and lean up against one of the supports.

"Do you like her?" Her voice caused Rebecca to jump slightly.

"Well, as far as horses go, she's fine." She almost added a comment about the mare being friendlier than Phoenix but decided against it.

"Do you want her?" Josie said. Rebecca turned around and eyed her with a look of confusion.

"I...I guess I have been thinking of her as mine ever since..."

Josie laughed and shook her head. "Rebecca, this isn't the horse we picked up outside Mason's Gulch." She pointed to a stall on the opposite end of the stable. "That's the horse we had." Rebecca looked from one horse to the other and could not imagine how she had mistaken this sweet little mare for that one.

"Really?" *I like this one better.* The young woman used her nails to give the friendly horse a healthy scratching behind the ear. "Oh. Well it was nice meeting you," she said to the mare.

"Rebecca, she's yours if you want her."

"Wha..." She looked from the gunslinger to the horse and back, now realizing why it was in the stall next to Phoenix. "Oh Josie." Without thought she moved forward and wrapped her arms around the taller woman's waist. "Thank you."

"You're welcome," Josie answered as she extricated herself from the arms wrapped around her body. "Rebecca, I don't like to be hugged," she said, looking around to make sure there were no witnesses.

"Oh, sorry," the young woman said, the twinkle never leaving her eyes. "How did you come by this horse?"

Josie shrugged as if it was no big deal. "Remember the man I told you I brought in for the bounty? I found her and the buckboard with him. Since her disposition seemed more...suitable for you, I decided to sell the other horse and keep this one for you."

"Buckboard? You mean I won't have to walk everywhere or ride behind you?" She gave a look up at Phoenix, her eyes showing her dislike of riding upon the massive steed.

"It would seem that way." With the look of happiness in Rebecca's eyes, Josie did not have the heart to mention that it was still a short-term arrangement. "Let's get them ready." The gunslinger busied herself with Phoenix's tack, not wanting to think about the day when she would leave a town alone.

An hour later they were on the road again. Riding on the flat wagon, Josie handled the reins for the mare while Phoenix walked behind, tethered to the back of the buckboard. The rising sun threatened to make the day unbearably hot and the swirling dust made the need to take a drink from the canteens frequent. Rebecca sat next to the gunslinger, holding the Winchester in case it was needed. Trying to help pass the time, the young woman entertained with stories about the Texas-Mexican war and the bravery of Jim Bowie. Josie nodded from time to time to indicate she was listening, but her eyes never left their constant scan of the surrounding landscape looking for any sign of trouble.

Eventually, the heat and dust made it impossible for Rebecca to continue talking. She tipped her head back and held the canteen to her mouth, hoping the remaining drops would be enough to quench her thirst. "I can't believe how hot it is today." She removed her hat and fanned her face. "How do you think the horses stand it?" The gray mare continued to plod along, oblivious to the conversation going on behind her.

"They drink lots of water, Sprite," Josie said, reaching for her own canteen. She took a long swallow, her face twisting with distaste for the warm water. "Ugh. I think we need to head toward the river soon. I don't think our water is going to last otherwise." She tugged on the reins, guiding the mare off the beaten path and through the sparse underbrush.

"The river?" Rebecca smiled broadly. "Oh yes, won't that be wonderful?" Absently reaching up and wiping the perspiration from her face, she continued. "I'm sure the horses will appreciate the water too."

"Speaking of which," Josie began. "You still have to name this one, you know."

"Name her? You didn't ask the man what her name was before you took her?"

"He was so drunk he wouldn't have known his own name much less that of a horse. Name her whatever you want."

"Anything?" Rebecca looked at the horse. "So what do you want to be called? Let's see…" She tapped her fingers on her chin as she pondered the problem. A smile broke across her face. "I've got it. Flossy."

"Flossy?" Josie gave her a look. "You've got to be kidding."

"Nope. I like it. Do you like it, Flossy?" To the gunslinger's dismay, the mare whinnied in agreement with the new name from the honey-voiced woman. "Flossy it is then," Rebecca said triumphantly.

Josie rolled her eyes. "Flossy."

"Hey, be nice. I could have named her Petunia."

"Flossy is fine."

"I thought you'd see it my way," Rebecca said smugly, proud to have won the argument. Josie smirked.

"Just remember that you are responsible for 'Flossy.' You have to feed and brush her, and take care of her gear."

"Oh sure, Josie. I'll do a good job too, you just watch."

"Uh huh," the gunslinger said in a knowing tone. There was no doubt in her mind that Rebecca would do everything in her power to please her or prove that she should stay with her. What Josie did not want to admit to herself was that it was working. After taking care of Smith, there really was no reason Rebecca could not remain in Tombstone, except that Josie would not be able to keep an eye on her then.

After refilling the canteens, they traveled northeast with the hope of reaching Wilcox by nightfall. The insignificant town would not have been worth stopping in at all except it was the last place they could get supplies before reaching the Oxbow Route. The hot summer sun beat down on them unmercifully, making Josie regret her choice in clothing. The black, long-sleeved shirt and britches only served to absorb the heat, not to mention her Stetson, which, while providing much needed shade for her eyes, acted like an oven on her head. Before long the top three buttons on her shirt were open in a futile attempt to cool off. "Damn, it's hot," Josie muttered as she wiped her brow again. The gray bandanna, usually wrapped around her neck, was now soaked with sweat and grime as she used it to keep the perspiration from running down her face. The dust from the road stuck to her skin, only serving to add to her discomfort. She rubbed her hands down the front of her thighs. "Damn, my legs feel like they're on fire." Josie laid her duster over her lap, hoping the lighter color would absorb less heat than her dark britches. Rebecca handed her the canteen of water.

"Do you still think we'll make it to Wilcox by nightfall?" the young woman asked.

Josie tipped the canteen up and took a large swallow before making a face and handing it back. "Ugh, that water's hot enough to make coffee," she grumbled. She shook her head at the jerky offered. "If I eat that, I'll have to drink more of that rancid water. No thanks." Pouring some of the water on her bandanna, Josie wiped her face and looked at the horizon. "I suppose if we don't die from the heat, we might make it there by then." She handed the canteen back to Rebecca, who looked equally as hot despite wearing lighter colored clothes. "Try to save as much water as you can. We're not going back to the river and it's gonna get hotter than blazes before it starts to cool off again." After giving Phoenix a quick glance, Josie snapped the reins. "Let's go, 'Flossy'," she said, stressing the silly-sounding name. .

Rebecca was never happier to see the sun setting before in her life. By mid-afternoon, Josie's mood was decidedly foul from being overheated, and the young woman was afraid to say a word for fear of getting her head bitten off. When they passed a small ranch both let out a sigh of relief. Wilcox could not be much further. "We'll rest in town for the night," Josie said, keeping her eyes straight ahead. "The horses need to rest and I need a bath."

"Yes you do," Rebecca agreed, wrinkling her nose.

Josie turned and looked at her. "Hey..." she said, feigning hurt. "You don't smell so good yourself."

Rebecca thought the gunslinger was being serious until she saw a twinkle in the blue eyes. She smiled and let out a soft laugh. Josie turned her attention back to the dusty road. "We'll get cleaned up and let someone else cook dinner," she said. Now that the sun was setting and she was beginning to cool off, Josie felt bad about the way she had snapped at the young woman she was beginning to consider a friend. Her brow furrowed. *When was the last time I cared about someone else's feelings?* It took only a few seconds to decide that it had been far too long. She craned her neck and looked in at the carpetbag in the back of the buckboard. Rebecca's corset and dress, her only dress, were stuffed inside. "That dress of yours is getting mighty worn."

"I suppose," the young woman answered. "I keep mending it."

"You can only mend something so long before it's time to turn it into rags." Josie looked down at the reins in her hands. "Reckon we'll have to pick up a new dress for you while we're in town." She shot a quick glare at Rebecca, silently warning her not to even think of giving her a hug. "After all, I can't have you go wandering 'bout town, looking like a raga-muffin."

Since they were only staying the one night, Josie decided to splurge and get two rooms at the hotel instead of settling for a flophouse. After bathing, they went downstairs to the combination saloon/restaurant. Josie ordered a hearty meal of stew and cornbread for both of them.

"Name your poison," the busty waitress said.

"Beer and whiskey."

"Sarsaparilla," Rebecca answered, looking forward to something other than water to quench her thirst. The waitress walked away, leaving the women alone. Looking around, the young woman noticed the looks and stares directed at them.

"Don't worry 'bout them," Josie said, reaching into her vest pocket to get her tobacco pouch. "I reckon they never saw two women eating dinner before." She said the last part loud enough for several nearby tables to hear. Heads immediately lowered and focused on their own plates.

Rebecca leaned over the table. "You didn't have to be so loud," she whispered. Josie smirked and leaned over as well until her lips were only inches away from the young woman's ear.

"But how else were they going to hear me?" the gunslinger whispered back. Sitting back, Josie allowed herself a satisfied grin. The beer, whiskey, and sarsaparilla arrived, much to the thirsty women's delight. The hot day had drained any energy they had and the conversation died to nothingness. By mutual agreement, dinner was a quiet affair followed by an early retirement to their rooms.

Josie awoke in the middle of the night, her dreams too much to bear. Again and again she saw the face of a young girl looking up at her, the young woman's chest completely covered with blood. Knowing sleep would not be possible, Josie got out of bed and splashed water from the basin on her face. Sliding her britches on and grabbing her sidearms, she settled into a chair and waited for the sun to rise.

Rebecca was sleeping soundly when Josie entered her room with two cups of coffee. "Time to get up, Sprite," she said as she set the cups on the small table. Seeing no movement from the young woman, she lightly kicked the bed with her booted foot.

"Grmphf."

"Rebecca, let's go. I want to get our supplies and get on the road early." She waited another moment, then jerked the blanket off the sleeping girl. She never expected what happened next.

The young woman screamed and curled up into a ball, covering her face with her arms and pressing herself against the wall. "No, please!" she said in a quavering voice, her whole body shaking with fear.

Stepping back, Josie tried to make sense of what she was seeing. "Rebecca?" Slowly the young woman moved her arms and looked up at her.

"I'm sorry," she mumbled. "Guess you just surprised me." Crawling off the bed, Rebecca headed for the chamber pot in the corner. Josie studied a knot on the wall until she heard the scraping of the chair against the floor, then turned around and sat down at the table. There was an awkward silence as each woman remained deep in her own thoughts. Josie watched Rebecca out of the corner of her eye. *What's got you so scared, Sprite?* she silently asked herself. Rebecca's face and body betrayed every emotion as she fought to regain some kind of composure. Unsure what to say, Josie chose to remain quiet and wait for her to speak. Rebecca drained half of her coffee before speaking. When she did, her voice still carried a bit of shakiness to it. "Please don't wake me up like that again."

"I won't," Josie said. She wanted to ask what it was that had frightened the young woman so, but comforting and personal conversations were foreign to her and she was not sure she could handle all the emotions that went with caring that much about someone else.

"I um..." Rebecca began, her eyes fixed upon the battered tin cup in her hands. "I'm sorry about before. I didn't mean to react like that."

"It's all right," Josie shrugged. "I startled you."

"No, it's not that, it's just that…" Rebecca gripped the mug so tightly that her knuckles turned white. "My father used to wake me up like that." Her voice lowered to a whisper. "Sometimes I didn't wake up even then and he…he'd…." She shuddered at the memory.

"Rebecca…" Josie fidgeted with her own mug. *I'm not an animal like him. I'd never hurt you like that.* Unsure of how to put her feelings into words, she finished her coffee and stood up. "I'm not him," she said as she reached for her Stetson, hoping Rebecca understood the unspoken meaning. "I'll meet you outside."

Rebecca changed into her dress, frowning at the way it looked. At dinner last night she was embarrassed to wear such a tattered thing in such a nice place but, unlike Josie, she could not walk around town in britches. No one dared question someone as tall and well-armed as the gunslinger, but a small thing like herself would only bring about trouble wandering around like that.

Josie was leaning against a post when Rebecca finally exited the hotel. The gunslinger looked at the faded and slightly tattered dress and grimaced. "The first thing we're doing is moseying over to the dressmaker's and getting you a new dress."

Rebecca thought about offering to make a dress herself, but something inside told her Josie wanted to buy this dress for her. She nodded and allowed herself to be led to the dressmaker.

The dressmaker was a large woman, easily twice the weight of Josie and three times the girth. The top of her dress barely held her more than ample bosom as she walked over to talk to them. "I'm Rita, owner and seamstress. And just what'll ye be looking for today, missies?"

"She needs a new dress," Josie said. "Something simple and easy to care for." She looked quickly at the wide expanse of skin showing from the front of the seamstress's dress. "And not revealing."

Rita wondered if she should have been insulted, but answered. "Aye, a simple traveling dress, perhaps? Something in a calico?" She moved over to a rack containing several simple dresses of varying colors and sizes. Removing one from the rack, she held it up so both women could see it. It was a light green, checkered pattern with long sleeves and a high lace neck that Rebecca was sure would choke her. She was just about to voice her opposition to it when Josie nodded.

"That'll be fine." She turned to Rebecca. "You stay here and wait for the dress. I'll go get the supplies." She strode to the door and grasped the knob, then turned back. "And Rebecca…."

"Yes?"

"Don't leave." There was something about the tone in Josie's voice that made the young blonde swear it was less of a statement and more of a question.

"I won't," she promised. Josie nodded and left in search of the rest of their supplies. Resigning herself to her fate, Rebecca let the large woman fit her for the dress. *As soon as we're out of town I'm changing back into my britches,* she thought as she was turned and pinned. A devilish smile came to her face as she imagined what Josie would look like wearing a dress. The mental image was so amusing that Rebecca chuckled, causing an errant pin to poke her in the hip. "Ouch."

"Then hold still," the seamstress admonished.

Josie returned almost two hours later; the wagon loaded down with a variety of supplies and staples. A small washboard was securely tied to the side of the wagon, while the back area contained as many supplies as Josie could afford. She was not the least bit happy with the cost. A large sack containing oats for the horses sat in the middle of the cargo area. Unwilling to ask for assistance, Josie had hefted the sack herself, pulling a muscle in her lower back in the process. She was glad when Rebecca bounded out of the shop, new dress in hand, and climbed up into the wagon without assistance. Waiting until the new garment was carefully placed in the small trunk under the seat, Josie clicked Flossy into motion. The forward jerk reverberated through her sore muscle, causing her to take a sharp breath.

"Josie? Are you all right?" Thinking that the outlaw had been in another saloon fight, Rebecca looked for any sign of injury.

"I'm fine," she replied, her eyes never leaving the road ahead as they pulled out of town.

"You sure?"

"Rebecca..." she snapped.

"Sorry." Several minutes passed before she spoke again. "Josie, have I told you the story about Daniel Boone? No? Well…." She burst into her tale, knowing full well the gunslinger was only half-listening, but preferring to hear her own voice over the howls of the coyotes in the distance. Several hours and tales later, Josie pulled the wagon off the trail and chose a spot to set up camp for the night.

Pulling the horse to a stop, Josie waited for Rebecca to get down before slowly getting down herself. The sore muscle, aggravated by hours of sitting on the wooden bench, made itself known as soon as she tried to straighten out and stretch. Rebecca had just walked around to that side of the wagon and saw the unmasked look of pain on her face. "Josie, you're hurt!"

"No," she said softly. "Just a sore back, that's all."

"I could rub it for you. I mean, I still have some liniment and I got pretty good at rubbing my own muscles when they were sore."

Josie looked at her. "I'm not helpless," she said, pressing her thumb against the protesting muscle. She hissed at the sharp pain it caused. *Stop it, Josie. It won't kill you to let her give you a backrub,* she told herself. "All right," she said, watching a smile break out on Rebecca's face.

"Great. I'll move this stuff out of the wagon and you can...."

"No. That sack..." she said pointing to the oats, "...is what gave me this. We'll have to sleep on the ground tonight. You should be used to it by now."

"Sure, no problem." Rebecca turned and started to remove the items they would need to camp on the ground. "No problem..." she whispered to herself. "I should be used to sleeping on the hard ground, uh huh, sure. Much more comfortable than, oh, say a padded wagon back, yup."

"Quit bellyaching or I will make you empty out the entire wagon, including the sack of oats," Josie threatened, but her tone made it clear she was not being serious. Both chuckled at the thought of Rebecca trying to lift the large, heavy sack.

Using Phoenix's saddle as a backrest, Josie sat back and let Rebecca deal with setting up the small camp. As the sun set, they ate a hearty stew, washed down by Josie with a mug of ale from the small keg on the wagon, while her companion settled for tepid water from the larger keg. Rebecca insisted on cleaning up after dinner, leaving only the pot and two mugs out for the morning coffee. At Josie's instruction she retrieved the shotgun from the wagon. "Are you ready for that backrub now?" she asked as she handed over the Winchester.

"Really, Sprite, I'll be fine. Just a good night's rest and..." The stubborn woman groaned as a sharp pain shot through her back. "Damn that hurts."

"I'll get the liniment," Rebecca said as she ran to the wagon. Resigning herself to the backrub, Josie removed her vest and shirt, exposing her upper torso to the cooling night air. She couldn't resist a smirk when the young woman turned around and saw her.

"You need to get over this modesty of yours, Sprite." She settled on her stomach while Rebecca knelt down next to her and opened the bottle. Gentle hands rested near her spine.

"Where exactly?"

"Lower...all right, over to the left...ow, right there..."

"Like this?"

"Yeah...just like that..." Josie closed her eyes and rested her cheek against her forearms as she relaxed under the gentle touch.

"I'll tell you a story..." Rebecca spoke softly as her hands continued to massage the sore muscles. Josie groaned as those hands moved against her back, finding the tightness and slowly forcing her muscles to relax.

"That reminds me of one my mother used to tell me when I was a little girl," Josie murmured when the story was finished. She made no effort to stop Rebecca's massaging hands from moving up her back. "You do that good, you know?"

"Thank you," the young woman replied. "Would you like me to tell another story?"

"Mmm, sure." Josie kept her eyes closed, feeling months of tension drain from her body. She let the melodic voice lull her into a light doze until eventually it came to an end.

"How was that?"

Josie turned her head and looked at her young companion before sitting up. Rolling her head and twisting her back, she allowed a small smile to come to her lips. "It feels better," she said before reaching over and grabbing her sleeping shirt.

"Good. Well, I guess I'll go to bed. Goodnight." She rose and headed to the other side of the fire, trying hard not to let her disappointment show. Her fingers and forearms ached from the lengthy massage and she had hoped for a better compliment.

"'Night," Josie replied, watching the young woman settle into her blankets. She arched her back one more time, relishing the limberness. "Thank you, Rebecca," she said just loud enough for Rebecca to hear before turning over and facing away from her, but not before seeing the smile on the young woman's face. Josie made a mental note to compliment her more often.

20: Bite

Two days later they felt no closer to their destination. The dusty ruts in the ground led endlessly into the distance, slicing the landscape in two. Only the occasional brush or collection of rocks gave any indication of progress. The excessive heat had not dissipated, forcing both the women and horses to use more water than had been planned. Josie took pains to use only minimal amounts for herself, knowing they were still a distance away from the nearest watering hole. Aware of the bounty hunter's reluctance to take any water for herself, Rebecca decided to limit her own use, an action that was not lost on Josie.

The reds and oranges of sunset filled the horizon. Josie led the wagon off the trail and to a small outcropping of brush and rocks. They fed and cared for the horses, the younger woman mimicking every move the bounty hunter made. Once Flossy and Phoenix were settled, they set about getting their camp set up. Although several pounds of oats had been used, the idea of hefting the sack out of the wagon every night and back in the morning was unappealing to Josie. So as they had been doing, bedrolls were set on opposite sides of the fire. The gunslinger worked to get the fire going while Rebecca gathered from the wagon the items they would need for the night. As the deep red ball of fire disappeared over the horizon and the dark gray of twilight settled in, all the gear was set up for the evening. A small pot of coffee warmed in the fire. "I'm going to go look around," Rebecca said as she stood up. "I won't go far."

Josie nodded and went back to cleaning her gun. "Be careful," she said softly, as the young blonde disappeared from sight.

Rebecca wove her way through the pillars of stone, mentally making note of the twists and turns so she could find her way back. The moon was not yet high enough in the sky to cast any useful illumination on the area. As her thigh grazed the thin branches of a small bush, she heard the unmistakable rattle. Fear gripped her now racing heart and all thoughts of direction left her mind. Taking a small step backwards she heard it again, this time even closer than before. In the very dim light her eyes were unable to pinpoint the location of the deadly snakes. Whether it was her eyes playing tricks on her or a real snake moving closer, she never knew. Rebecca let out a loud shriek and turned to run away. Frightened and disoriented, she tripped over the same bush that she had scraped against before and landed too close for the rattler's comfort. It struck with blinding speed, sinking its curved fangs deep into the back of her left calf before slithering back and coiling up in a defensive posture.

Before the scream had died, Josie was racing toward her, shotgun in hand. "Rebecca!" she called as she made her way through the darkness, bumping into the stone pillars of granite in her haste.

"Josie? Josie!" Rebecca cried, her eyes wide as she tried to see any more snakes. Paralyzed by fear, she was unable to move. "Josie!" she cried again, her voice barely above a whisper.

"Rebecca!" She stopped just short of stepping on the young blonde as her keen eyes made out her form on the ground.

"S-ssnakes." Tears rolled freely down Rebecca's face as she felt the burning pain in her leg. Her protector's presence gave her the strength she needed to move. She turned and wrapped her arms tight around the gunslinger's leg. Josie's keen eyes picked out three snakes coiled up in the darkness. All seemed to be a safe enough distance away. She set the Winchester down on the ground and turned her attention to the terrified Rebecca.

With a firm grip, she extricated the frightened woman from her leg. "Were you bit?"

"Y-yesss," Rebecca bawled as she reached for her lower leg. Josie released her grip long enough to remove her bandanna and tear it in half. She quickly tied one piece just below Rebecca's knee and the other right above the ankle. Scooping the sobbing woman up in her arms, Josie raced back to camp.

Knowing time was of the essence, she set her wounded charge down on the blanket and pulled a knife out of her boot. "How many times were you bit?" she asked while rolling Rebecca onto her stomach.

"I-I think once," came the hoarse reply.

"All right, lie still now." Using one hand to hold Rebecca's leg down, she cut the pant leg open, exposing two angry-looking puncture marks against the creamy white skin. *Damn, those are deep,* she thought to herself. "This will hurt," she said, unsure if the young woman heard her over her sobbing. Already the affected area was puffing up. Quickly checking to make sure the restricting bands of cloth were not so tight they cut off circulation, she placed the blade against Rebecca's skin and made quick incisions across both wounds. The young woman's cries and screams were enough to wake the dead as she tried to pull her leg away. Josie's powerful arms held her down forcefully. "Rebecca, we don't have time for you to be fighting with me. You need to calm down." She contemplated cold cocking the young woman, but the hysterical sobs gave way to sniffles. "Concentrate on your breathing. Take deep, slow breaths." Her long fingers worked to squeeze out as much blood and venom as possible. Rebecca buried her face in her hands and let out a series of ragged sobs. Josie stretched her body out along the ground, bringing her mouth closer to the bloodied leg. "I have to suck the poison out."

"No!" the young woman wailed, but she was powerless to stop it. "It burns, my whole leg burns," she cried. Josie adjusted her position to maintain her hold. Pressing her lips against Rebecca's calf, she began sucking as hard as she could. The vile taste made her stomach turn but she refused to let it impede her progress. Again and again she drew as much of the fluid into her mouth as she could, turned her head, and spit it out before repeating the process. Already the fluid was changing from a watery substance mixed with blood to mostly blood, but Josie knew that the first fifteen minutes were all there was to remove the venom. After that, they would just have to wait for the remainder to run its course. She continued to suck as hard as she could, her ears tuning out the wails and cries of her companion. When all she could taste was the blood, the gunslinger stopped sucking and reached for the saddlebag.

"N-now what?" Rebecca asked. She was still crying but had stopped the hysterical sobs. "It still hurts so much."

"I know it does," Josie replied, removing a small roll of cloth and several pieces of gauze from the saddlebag. "The fangs sank into the muscle." She put the pads over the bleeding wounds and wrapped the calf securely. "Roll over," she said as she rose and headed for the wagon. She pulled out Phoenix's saddle and returned to Rebecca's side. "I'm going to put this under your leg. It's important to keep it elevated, you understand?" The dim firelight allowed her to see the nod in reply. Josie placed the saddle under her leg then covered her with the blanket, tucking it in around the young woman to keep her warm and to hopefully stave off shock.

The bounty hunter kept vigil over her all night, changing the bandage frequently. She grimly noted that the soaked bandage still showed traces of yellow, indicating that she had not gotten out all the venom. The fangs had penetrated deeper than she thought but it was too late. There was nothing Josie could do now but wait and let the snake bite run its course. She took some comfort in knowing that no matter how deep the wound, it was not life threatening. It would be painful, however, and most likely would swell up for a time before it got better.

Using her leather glove as a makeshift potholder, Josie removed the pot from the edge of the fire and poured more coffee into her half empty cup. *What am I going to do with you?* she asked herself while looking down at the sleeping woman. *I can't leave you alone for a minute, can I?* Rebecca stirred, groaning softly. "Shh, go back to sleep." She was answered with an unintelligible mumble. "That's right, sleep now." She brought the cup to her lips and took a healthy swallow of the strong brew. Morning was still a long way off.

Rebecca woke up to the smells of coffee brewing and meat sizzling on the fire. Josie was sitting next to her, mug in hand. "Morning, Sprite. How's the leg feel?" the gunslinger asked as she took a sip of coffee, trying hard not to grimace.

"It burns and my skin feels...tight." She tried to roll onto her side, finding herself trapped by the leg elevated above the saddle. To her surprise, Josie reached out and pushed her back down.

"Don't move around so darn much. You have to keep it up until the swelling goes down." Josie said as she handed her the cup. Propping herself up on one elbow, she gratefully accepted the coffee.

"Thanks." Rebecca took a sip, crinkled her face, and looked at Josie. "How much coffee did you use? This stuff is really strong."

"It is, isn't it?" the gunslinger responded as she looked down at the blackness in her mug. "Well, since you do it so well, you can be in charge of making the coffee from now on." She set her mug down on the ground and stood up. "I'll be back in a minute. Stay here."

Rebecca forced herself to drink the vile brew while waiting for the bounty hunter to return. Three shots rang out, breaking the silence of the morning. Josie returned moments later with her shotgun and three lifeless snakes in her hand. The sight of the rattlers, even dead, was enough to start the young woman's heart racing. Seeing the panicked expression on Rebecca's face, Josie tossed the snakes on the far side of the fire. "Dinner," she said simply. The blonde nodded, her eyes never leaving the pile of serpents. With a sense of pride, the bounty hunter pulled out her knife and began to skin and clean the snakes. She did not know which one had bitten her friend, but it did not matter now. All three would make a fine stew. "We're going to be here for another day or so. I want to make sure there's no infection."

Rebecca nodded, grateful for the chance to rest. Her leg throbbed from the bite and any thought of walking on it was out of the question. Fortunately the rock formations helped provide some shade from the burning sun, allowing her to settle back and daydream about a valiant knight slaying dragons to protect a princess. It was her favorite fantasy, one that provided hours of relief from the horrors of her former home life. Today it provided the same relief, this time from the pain in her left leg. From time to time she looked over to find Josie making stew or cleaning her guns. Rebecca dozed on and off all day, comforted in the knowledge that there was more than a fantasy hero to protect her.

By nightfall, the swelling had diminished enough for Rebecca to move about. She found herself unable to eat the stew containing chunks of rattler meat; the memory of being bitten was just too strong. Contenting herself with some warmed over jerky, she watched Josie enjoy the stew. Both washed their dinners down with ale. Despite her dislike for the taste, Rebecca worried about the effect the extra day would have on their still dwindling water supply.

After dinner, Josie changed the bandage on Rebecca's leg and saw that the wound was no longer oozing anything but blood. The long night of watching over the young woman caught up with her and the bounty hunter settled into bed early, leaving Rebecca alone with her thoughts. *She's been so good to me. Didn't yell at me once about getting bit.* Deep inside she knew it never would have happened if she had just remained calm. *Josie can't be worrying about me all the time.* Staring at the twinkling stars, she vowed to get over her fear of snakes.

21: Night Demons

Rebecca woke in the middle of the night to answer nature's call. When she finished her business and returned to the camp, she noticed Josie thrashing about in the midst of an obvious nightmare.

Genie moved up next to her, gun drawn. "Do you think they'll come?" she asked quietly. Josie did not offer a glance in her direction, preferring to keep her eyes on the door.

"If they do, we'll be ready for them," she replied. Her hands gripped her Peacemakers nervously. Ten horses had been stolen from the ranch in the past two weeks and they were certain that the Double Bar was responsible. Genie's father refused to stand up to the bullies, knowing full well that the McCann's controlled not only the local sheriff, but the district judge as well. Genie and Josie figured the only way to stop the horse thievery was to stand watch over the herd.

The telltale creak of the barn door being opened drew their attention. Three men entered quietly, taking careful looks at the main house to see if they had been detected. They did not notice the two teenagers hiding in the loft, guns drawn and aimed at them. Genie's youthful voice filled the air, "Don't move!"

John McCann, the youngest son of the Double Bar's owner, panicked immediately and started firing his gun in the direction of the loft. Reacting quickly, Josie began firing both guns in return. Within seconds it was over.

Smoke from the guns hung in the air as both sides inspected the damage. John lay on the ground, bleeding profusely from a mortal wound. She felt a warm stickiness against her arm and turned to see Genie lying lifelessly next to her, the girl's chest covered with blood.

"Well if that don't beat all," the stocky man said as he raised his gun in her direction. "Looks like we done caught ourselves a little gal horse thief. Ah bet old man Sanders will be real pleased to see we done protected his horses from a stinkin' half-breed." He moved closer, knowing full well that her guns were empty. He looked up at the still body next to her. "Done gone and kilt his daughter too. Tsk tsk. Shame she couldn't tell 'em what really happened." He glanced over at the other man, who was busy removing anything of value from McCann's body. "Ain't that right, Bill?"

Josie recognized Bill as one of the Sanders's ranch hands. "Ayup, that'd be right, Tom. I saw it all with my own eyes, I did. That damn injun done come in here and tried to take off with the horses. Poor Genie come in to stop her and got a wooden overcoat for her trouble. Done killed Johnny too, damn horse thief."

Tom raised his gun again. "You gonna hang, half-breed."

With speed born out of desperation, Josie jerked the gun from Genie's still hand and fired, catching Tom in the chest. Her second shot struck Bill in the cheek, sending him backward against a wooden post and knocking him out cold. The sounds of approaching ranchers and the elder Sander filled the air. She knew Genie's father hated her for her parentage and had forbidden his daughter to see her. It came down to her word against Bill's, and she knew who would be believed. She got up and ran to the far side of the loft, kicked open the doors, and jumped to the ground below. She heard the shouts of the men as she was spotted. There was no choice for her now. Josie ran for the woods, never looking back. The men fired blindly, missing with every shot. "It's that half-breed friend of Genie's," she heard one of them say. She heard the crack of the rifle just as a burning pain seared through her upper arm.

"Josie? Josie, wake up," Rebecca said as she shook her gently. The blue eyes popped open as the gunslinger bolted to a sitting position, momentarily disoriented. Her hand reached instinctively to her left bicep, fully expecting it to be bleeding. Rebecca put her hand on Josie's right shoulder. "Hey, are you all right?"

The bounty hunter took in her surroundings and let out a loud sigh. Pulling herself into a cross-legged position, she rested her arms on her knees. Rebecca moved and fetched the canteen. It was only then that Josie realized the young woman had been touching her. When she returned,

Rebecca made no move to resume her position, merely handing the gunslinger the canteen and leaning back on her heels. "Another nightmare?" she asked softly. Josie took a deep swallow of water and nodded slightly, her gaze settling on the red embers of the fire. "Do you want to talk about it?" Rebecca ventured again. "Sometimes it helps. I mean I know it does for me."

There was a long silence while the gunslinger internally debated the question. "Make coffee." She twisted sideways and grabbed a branch to stir the fire. She knew that sleep would elude her for the rest of the night. Rebecca set the pot in the fire to heat up, then settled down an arm's length away from Josie.

"When I was seventeen, I had a best friend...Genie." She said it so softly that Rebecca had to lean forward to hear. "When I first went back to live with my mother, she was the only person who didn't see me as being different just because my father was Cherokee. We became the best of friends; we were inseparable. Genie's father owned a small horse ranch and he found out that a neighboring ranch was stealing the horses, but he was too scared of them to do anything about it." She leaned forward and stirred the fire some more as she collected her thoughts. "Genie and I, we were young, we thought if we just caught them in the act that justice would be done." She snorted lightly. "Instead, Genie was killed, and I became wanted."

"What happened?" Rebecca prodded gently as she poured coffee for Josie and herself. The gunslinger took the mug and stared at the wisps of steam that rose from the black abyss.

"One of the thieves worked for Genie's father. He was helping them steal the horses. It would have been his word against mine." Her voice rang with bitterness. "I had no choice but to run."

Rebecca started to ask a question, but the gunslinger's look made her think twice. They sat there quietly, staring at the fire as time passed. The young woman tried to fight off sleep but before long her head bobbed. "Go to bed, Rebecca." Josie said, startling her. "Go on, get some sleep."

Josie sat there long after Rebecca fell asleep, remembering her brief friendship with Genie and the end of her innocence.

22: A Bad Day

The morning sun shone down brightly on the small camp. Josie had already packed their belongings back into the wagon and had breakfast done, at which time she felt she had waited long enough for Rebecca to wake up on her own. The gunslinger felt a bit guilty for having awakened her with the nightmare last night. She had hoped that the smell of coffee and sizzling meat would have roused her companion, but the young woman continued to snore softly, her head buried under her blanket in an unconscious attempt to keep the sun out. Josie reached over with the butt of her shotgun and gently poked at the sleeping form. "Rebecca....Rebecca, get up."

A low groan came from under the blanket. Josie poked again, this time getting the result she wanted. Rebecca slowly pulled the blanket off her face and squinted at the brightness. She groggily took the tin cup from the bounty hunter and took a sip, immediately grimacing. She looked over at Josie quickly, afraid she would be angered, but the gunslinger arched an eyebrow and her face took on a crooked grin. "Coffin varnish?"

"Ugh, coffin varnish is right," Rebecca replied as she drank some more down. "Try using a little less coffee," she said with a friendly smile. "This stuff will put hair on your chest." She swallowed the last of the drink in her mug and rose to her feet. "I have to make a trip; I'll be right back."

"Try not to run into another nest of snakes," Josie warned half-jokingly. Rebecca smiled, but heeded the warning and looked around carefully before choosing her spot. The last thing she wanted to do was to squat near a rattler.

Rebecca returned to the camp a minute later and rummaged around in the saddlebag until she found the rags she needed. Although Josie said nothing, the young woman blushed furiously as she headed back to the privacy of the bush. Of all the things she hated, the monthly menace was the worst. Rebecca knew it would only be a matter of hours before she started getting the painful cramps that accompanied it. The pain in her still healing leg was nothing compared to the headache and cramps that hit by mid-day. As nonchalantly as possible, Rebecca folded her arms against her abdomen and pressed down, trying to ease the discomfort. The constant jostling from the ride did nothing to help and she clenched her eyes tight against the pain. A particularly bad cramp hit, forcing a low moan from her mouth. "Want some laudanum?" Josie asked without taking her eyes off the road.

"I don't know," Rebecca replied, slowly opening her eyes and looking over at the gunslinger. "I've never taken anything for it before," she added in a smaller voice.

"Why?" Josie asked evenly as the muscles in her jaw tightened. "Didn't your family know you were in pain?" The touch of anger and indignation in her voice was almost imperceptible, but Rebecca noticed it and, instead of flinching, felt a sense of comfort that she did not understand.

"I started getting these really painful cramps and the headaches when I was fourteen. I told my mother, but..." She turned away, unable to look at her raven-headed companion. The wagon stopped as Josie jerked the reins. Rebecca felt strong fingers cup her chin and found herself staring into ice blue eyes.

"But what, Rebecca?" Her tone softened slightly, but inside the gunslinger's anger was churning into a steady boil. "But what?"

"Medicine costs money...money we didn't have." Her voice was barely above a whisper, but Josie heard the lie all the same.

"Didn't have, Rebecca? Or were you afraid to tell your father?" The visible flinching gave the bounty hunter her answer. Releasing her hold on the young woman, she reached over the seat for the saddlebag that contained their bottle of laudanum. "Take some," she said as she handed Rebecca the nearly full container.

"Thank you." She put the bottle to her lips and took a small swallow. Another cramp hit, forcing her to bend slightly while pressing against her midriff with her free arm. She took a bigger swallow. Satisfied that Rebecca had drunk enough to ease the pain, Josie put the stopper in the bottle and put it back in the saddlebags. Without another word, she clucked her tongue and sent Flossy into motion.

They passed the time in an amiable silence until breaking for lunch and to rest the horses, then continued on for several hours. The deep ruts in the road made the ride even more bumpy than usual, and Josie began to notice a slight change in the feel of the ride.

She was about to pull Flossy to a stop when the right front wheel passed over a small rock. The force of the landing was enough to snap the rusty pin that held the spoke wheel to the axle. In a split second the wagon lurched, tipping violently to the right. With lightning reflexes, Josie released the reins and reached out to grab Rebecca before she could topple off of the bench. The added weight of the young woman caused the gunslinger to slide on the bench, imbedding several splinters into her rear on her way down.

"Damn," Josie swore as she climbed out of the wagon and unbuttoned her britches. Her gun belts dropped loosely to the ground, dragging the britches down with them. Rebecca stood up and inspected the damage to the buckboard. The wheel was lying on its side on the ground, firmly wedged under the corner of the wagon. Their belongings were scattered about and both the barrel of coal oil and the box of soap had opened, mixing and spilling their contents all over the bedding materials and clothes. Josie's britches were down around her ankles along with her drawers while she tried unsuccessfully to remove the offending pieces of wood. She turned to look at the wagon and scowled. "Of all the...." She shuffled closer to the wagon. "I can't believe this." A soapy mix of oil and soap formed a puddle on the dusty ground.

"Josie, why are you like that?"

"Because I have a baker's dozen worth of splinters up my ass, Rebecca!" she growled. She tried again in vain to remove one of them. Bending to reach the cuff of her boot, Josie pulled out the bowie knife and held it out. "I can't reach," she said sourly before turning around. Rebecca tried hard to suppress the urge to giggle at the gunslinger's fate but the embarrassing position was just too much.

"Land sakes, Josie. Didn't your mamma ever tell you not to take your bloomers off in public?"

Josie turned her head and leveled a glare at the grinning blonde. "And didn't your mamma tell you it's not a good idea to rile someone who's all horns and rattlers?" The pain from the splinters wasn't as great as the embarrassment at having to have another person pluck them out. She leaned her hands against the side of the tilted wagon and pushed her bottom out.

"I'll be gentle," Rebecca said, still grinning.

"I'm so glad you're enjoying yourself."

"You have to admit that it is rather funny. Hold still."

"You're really in a hurry to chat with Saint Peter, aren't you? Ouch!"

"Sorry," the young woman said, pulling out the largest offender. "This is going to take a while."

A continuous stream of ouches and curses filled the air as Rebecca diligently removed every splinter. The none-too-happy Josie refastened her clothing the instant the last splinter was removed.

"Can you fix it?" Rebecca asked, looking at the wheel trapped beneath the wagon.

"I don't know." The gunslinger pressed her shoulder against the rail and pushed, hoping to right the wagon. "Ungh. Damn it." Looking around, Josie gauged her surroundings. Wide open flatland speckled with upcroppings of cottonwood trees and brush was all that could be seen. The wagon provided little protection should it be needed. Still it was the best they could do under the circumstances and Josie knew it. She could only hope that no one else was thinking of taking the same trail. "Start unpacking the wagon."

Rebecca did as she was told, separating the clothes and bedding from the rest of the oily, soapy mess. The gunslinger knelt down next to the axle. "The damn pin broke." The smell of coal oil and soap mixed together penetrated her senses, furthering her aggravation. Without thinking, Josie rose and kicked the axle with all her anger.

Rebecca spun around at the groan of pain in time to see the intimidating bounty hunter grab her foot and hop around in a circle before falling to the ground, cursing the entire time. "Josie? What happened?" she asked as she rushed to her side.

"Oh, I kicked the stupid, damned axle," Josie said through gritted teeth as she held her booted foot with both hands. She let loose a deep breath and closed her eyes. "I think I broke my foot."

Despite Rebecca's best efforts to make the boot removal as gentle as possible, Josie's foot was still bumped and jarred, causing her to clench her jaw and take deep breaths to avoid yelping at the pain. Her suspicions were confirmed when her toes finally came free of the leather. The big toe was already a deep purple, the bruising extending all the way to the foot. Rebecca tsked at the broken toe and looked around. "I guess we're making camp early tonight."

"Guess so," Josie said dejectedly.

23: Helping Out & Fixing Up

"Are you sure you'll be all right?" Rebecca asked. Josie looked down at her from atop Phoenix. Her toe throbbed within the black leather boot. Sleeping the night without blankets to protect from the desert chill had not helped.

"I'll be fine, Rebecca. The stream should only be a couple hours away, and a town not much further than that." She handed over one of her Colts. "Just in case. Don't hurt yourself with it."

Rebecca took the weapon, her fingertips rolling over the pearl handle. "How long do you think you'll be gone?" she asked quietly, trying not to let her fear show.

"I'll get the pins for the wagon and then I'll be back late tonight, or early tomorrow." She adjusted the fit of her Winchester in its sheath before realizing that she was stalling. "Be careful," Josie said gruffly before kicking Phoenix into a gallop, taking her away from her young friend. Rebecca watched her ride away in a billowing cloud of dust.

"You too, Josie," she said softly. She thought about what the bounty hunter had said about the stream being only a few hours away. *Surely Josie won't mind if I washed the clothes and blankets?* Smiling to herself at the idea, Rebecca looked for something with which to hold the remainder of the soap.

As expected, the edge of the stream appeared within two hours. Josie gratefully dumped out the remainder of the stale water from her canteen and filled it with the cool liquid. Both woman and horse took advantage of their respite. Phoenix drank her fill from the stream while Josie stepped in, clothes and all, to cool her overheated body down. The gunslinger waited until she was sure Phoenix was refreshed before saddling up and putting her abused bottom in the saddle again. "Let's go, girl," she said to the bay mare. "We have to get that pin and get back. Yeah, I know," she said to Phoenix's snort. "We wouldn't need the buckboard if it wasn't for her." The constant bumping against the saddle continued to remind Josie of her trip sideways on the wagon bench. "She's not staying, I can promise you that." The horse plodded along, a lone audience for her mistress's ramblings. "You know I couldn't leave her in Tombstone, and Wilcox wasn't much better either." She wiped her soaked bandanna over her face. "As soon as I find a town where I know she'll be safe, that's where I'll leave her." Phoenix gave another snort, earning a frown from the gunslinger. "I didn't ask for your two bits," she grumbled.

The sun had been down more than an hour when Josie found a small ranch. The clinking and clanging of metal against metal filled her ears as she headed to a large barn. All the doors were open in a feeble attempt to disperse the heat from the roaring fire. A large, burly man swung a hammer again and again, striking a horseshoe braced against the anvil. His face was covered with sweat and soot, matching his black leather apron. "You a cartwright?" she asked as she stepped into the doorway.

He never looked up from his work, apparently unaffected by a strange woman showing up at his ranch. "Cartwright, smith, whatever needs being done, I guess," he said in a deep voice that matched his build. Josie guessed that he could easily lift a small horse.

"I need cotter pins," she said as she stepped closer, stopping a couple of feet from him. She did her best not to limp and was grateful that he did not look up. He stopped pounding the shoe and looked up at her. "Over there," he said, pointing to a small box sitting on a nearby bench. "Find the ones ya need; the damn wagons are all different."

It took several minutes for Josie to find four cotter pins that would fit the axles on the wagon. She would be damned if she was going to buy one, go back, and discover that another one was rusted. A quick mental check of her funds allowed her to grab a few more, just in case. "Six bits," he said when she showed him the pins. Josie put the coins on the bench and headed for the door, again trying not to allow the pain in her toe to affect her gait. She stopped and turned around, her eyes catching a large expanse of sheepskin hanging on the wall. Her thoughts immediately went from the pain in her foot to a pain somewhere else.

It was a sweat-soaked Rebecca that reached the stream two hours after Josie had visited it. With no saddle, the young woman was forced to lay all the clothes across the back of the horse. She carried the sack containing the soap in one hand and the washboard and the reins in the other. Flossy went to the edge of the water and nickered contentedly as she drew the cool liquid into her mouth. Removing her boots, Rebecca stepped into the water, letting the cool mud slip between her toes and the water soothe her hot aching feet. She let out a sigh of relief and flopped down into the water, giggling slightly. "Oh, isn't this wonderful, Flossy?" The stream was shallow enough that Rebecca had to tuck her knees up in order to submerge herself but she didn't mind. The cool water was a godsend on the blazing hot day and she was in no hurry to make the long trek back to the wagon. "I think I'll wash myself before I get started on the blankets and clothes." Only after a refreshing swim did she begin her chore, not returning to the wagon until nearly sunset. The length of time required for accomplishing the task had just as much to do with her constant swim breaks as with the stubbornness of the coal oil within the clothes. It was after dark by the time she managed to get the fire started, the still wet clothes, and blankets were draped over the sides of the wagon. Those that didn't fit there were scattered over nearby bushes and rocks. The evening air was still dry and hot, allowing the blankets to dry in time for bed.

As night settled on the land, two women laid awake staring at the stars above. Rebecca snuggled under her now clean blanket using the gunslinger's blanket as a pillow. Josie rested her head against her saddle with Phoenix's saddle blanket covering her. The last waking thoughts both women had were of each other, both silently hoping the other was safe and well.

Rebecca drank the last of her coffee and stared into the fire. She was proud of how clean she had gotten the clothes and blankets. She used several rags to try and clean up the soapy, flammable mixture from the rest of the items and was pleased with the amount of progress she had made. Almost all of their belongings were clean and only the sacks of sugar, salt, and flour had to be discarded. Thankfully, the jerky and the rest of their staples had been spared from damage. The fire burned low, and her thoughts turned to Josie. *Please be safe, Josie. I miss you. Come back soon.*

It was mid-afternoon when Josie returned to the damaged wagon and her friend. Rebecca let out a yelp of joy and ran over to her, stopping just short and regaining her composure. "How are you?" she asked simply, her hand covering her eye to block out the sun as she looked up at the tall gunslinger sitting atop the equally tall steed.

"Fine," Josie answered as she dismounted, making sure her right foot hit the ground first to minimize the jolt to her injured left one. She smiled slightly, happy to see that Rebecca was fine. Her eyes settled on the neat pile of folded clothes and neatly packed piles of supplies. "Rebecca... you cleaned up everything?"

"Well, most everything. I couldn't clean the sugar, salt, or flour, but most all the rest I was able to save."

"Where did you get the water?" Josie asked. Her eyes narrowed when the answer came to her. "Rebecca, did you go all the way to the stream?"

She took a step back before answering the gunslinger. "Well...yeah. I took Flossy with me." She decided not to mention that she had left the gun with the wagon. Josie walked slowly over to the pile of clothes and blankets. Her hand glided over the material as a smile came to her lips. Holding her spare shirt to her nose, she inhaled the clean scent of lye. Any trace of coal oil had been removed, a task Josie thought impossible. "You did a good job, Rebecca." The smile that came to the young woman's face reminded her of a child getting exactly what they wanted for their birthday. She walked over and tended to Phoenix, tossing the sheepskin on the bench of the wagon as she passed.

"What's that for? Oh," Rebecca chuckled. "What's the matter, Josie? Don't like the way the bench bites?" She was rewarded with an arched eyebrow before Josie rolled her eyes and shook her head. The pair shared a pleasant evening and slept peacefully knowing the other was just on the other side of the fire.

Josie uttered yet another curse as the board slid off the stone when she tried to use it as a lever to lift the wagon. "We need something...wider," she said, looking around for something to fit the need.

"Josie, this is the widest stone we could find out here in the middle of nowhere," Rebecca muttered as she wiped the sweat off her brow. "Are you sure there's no other way to do this?"

"What do you want me to do, Rebecca? Climb under the wagon and lift it with my back?" she growled. Three hours of no progress had brought out her foul mood. Every time she got enough weight down to move the wagon upward, the board would shift off the curved stone. None of their supplies could take the strain of holding the weight. She looked down at the wheel stuck under the wagon again and cursed. "You know all these ranches with the wagon wheels out front? Well, they didn't settle there because they liked the area. That's where their damned wagon broke down!" Josie growled and smacked her hand against the side of the wagon as she walked around looking once again at their belongings.

"Want a broken hand to go with the toe?" Rebecca mumbled as she repositioned the stone and board. Josie appeared next to her and knelt down, holding the cracked barrel that once held the coal oil.

"I heard that, Rebecca," she said as she placed the barrel under the board. "Let's try this again."

With much grunting and straining, Josie managed to force the corner of the wagon up enough for Rebecca to pull the wheel out from under it. It was not high enough for her to fit it to the axle, however. Without thinking, the young woman ducked her shoulder under the corner and pushed up with her legs, helping lift it the final inch or so needed to place the wheel in position.

"Get out from there!" Josie yelled, pressing down on the board with all her might.

"Just do it," Rebecca grunted, her arms shaking from the effort. "Do it!"

Josie quickly positioned the wheel and shoved the pin through the hole as far as she could by hand. "All right, get out from under there."
Josie used the butt of her revolver to pound the pin in the rest of the way before twisting it into place. "Whew." She wiped the sweat off her face with the remains of her torn bandanna. She looked at Rebecca, who was brushing the dust off her britches. "You shouldn't have done that," she admonished.

"I'm all right," the blonde answered. "I told you I could help."

"Help doesn't include breaking your back trying to lift a wagon." Josie threw her hat angrily. "Do you have any idea how hurt you could have been?"

"But..."

"No buts. You shouldn't be taking chances like that!" She reached out and gripped the smaller woman's shoulders. "What if that board slipped again? You would have broken your back."

"Josie, please." Rebecca struggled to get out of her grasp. It was then that the gunslinger realized just how strong her grip was. Letting go quickly, Josie turned and walked over to where her hat rested on the ground. Silence fell between them as both women struggled to get their emotions under control. It was Rebecca who finally spoke.

"I was just trying to do my share a-and help."

"Aw, Sprite..." Josie heard the hitch in the younger woman's voice and turned to face her. "I know you meant well, but you shouldn't take chances like that." Turning around, she walked over and put a firm hand on Rebecca's shoulder. "You could have been really hurt and what would I have been able to do out here alone?"

"I had to help. I didn't mean to scare you."

"You didn't sca-..." Josie stopped when she realized that was exactly what had happened. Like it or not, she cared about the naive girl from Chancetown. "Hrumph." Tugging the brim of her Stetson, she turned toward the wagon. "Well since you're feeling mightier than a mule, let's get the wagon loaded up." She didn't see the knowing smile on Rebecca's face.

"Sure, Josie."

24: An Old Friend

The next month on the road was rather uneventful; there were no more accidents and Josie managed to apprehend two more men on her list. The monies were meager but were still enough to allow them to head northeast to the Black Hills.

"How much longer before we reach Deadwood?" Rebecca asked, taking her hat off and rubbing her forehead on her sleeve for what felt like the hundredth time that day.

"At least four more hours. Think of the nice cool bath you can have once we get there," Josie said, as she wiped her brow with her already soaked bandanna.

"Are you sure it's safe there? What if someone recognizes you?" Josie's lip twitched into a small grin.

"Trust me, Sprite. The codgers that live in Deadwood aren't worried about me." She stared off into the distance as her mind relived memories of her last trip to the mining town. She was so lost in thought that she missed the next question. "Huh?"

"I said..." Rebecca's voice conveyed her annoyance at her words being ignored...again. "If they're not worried about you, then who are they worried about?"

"You'll see," Josie answered with a knowing smirk. "Come on, Flossy. You're moving slower than molasses uphill in the middle of winter."

"I'm a telling ya, Sprite. I don't care how much it costs, we're having ourselves a nice meal," the gunslinger said as she guided the buckboard onto the main street. "I'm looking forward..." Pulling hard on the reins, Josie looked from one side of the street to the other, noting every building and possible ambush point. "That isn't right."

"What?" Rebecca asked. Josie's gaze settled on one building.

"The assayer's office is closed," she said as she climbed down from the buckboard.

"So? Maybe he drank too much laudanum."

"No. This is a mining town, Rebecca. Even if the regular assayer were sick, there would be someone else to take his place. Look around...do you see anyone? It's the middle of the day...where is everyone?" Lowering her hand to her side, Josie rested her thumb on the hammer of her Colt. Putting her free hand on Rebecca's shoulder, she spoke quietly. "Listen to me. I want you to be quiet and stay right behind me. If I start shooting, get on Phoenix and get out of here as fast as you can." She shook Rebecca's shoulder for emphasis. "Do you understand me?" She waited until the smaller woman nodded before releasing her grip. Hitching the reins to the post, she pointed at the saloon. "Good. Let's go. We'll get some answers there."

They entered the dim saloon and headed for the bar. "Whiskey and a sarsaparilla," Josie said as her eyes moved about the room.

"Four bits." The gruff looking man behind the bar sized up the well-armed woman. The outlaw gave him a dirty look as she fished out two quarters.

"Where is everyone?"

"Dead, mostly. Those that ain't will prob'ly be there soon."

"What happened?" Rebecca asked, drawing a look from Josie. The barkeep set the drinks down, placing the whiskey in front of the more dangerous looking of the two.

"Mostly 'cause-a them damn injuns. Savages always attacking us." He took an involuntary step back when he saw the tall woman's eyes narrow at him. Rebecca gave him a similar look, though not as effective, before placing her small hand on the outlaw's forearm. The touch was enough to break through and keep Josie's anger in check.

"Just tell me where I can find Jane," Josie said through gritted teeth. Every part of her body wanted to reach over the bar and grab him by the throat. She dimly realized that it was only because Rebecca was standing next to her that she did not act on her impulses.

"Sure, sure." He put his hands up in a placating gesture. "She's at the boarding house. Only place big enough to hold all of 'em."

Josie allowed herself one more withering gaze at him before turning. "Let's go." She did not look to see if the young woman followed her. Once outside, she jerked the reins free and jumped onto the seat of the buckboard. She slapped the reins against the horse's rump even before Rebecca was seated, nearly pitching her from the wagon.

"Josie, are you all right?" She did not miss the whiteness of the outlaw's knuckles as she held the reins in a death grip.

"The boarding house must be that big one at the end of the street," Josie said, refusing to meet Rebecca's gaze. She was not ready to let go of her anger.

"Josie..." Rebecca covered Josie's hand with her own. "He's just ignorant. Come on, let's go find your friend." The outlaw nodded slightly and released a deep breath.

Entering the boarding house, they were shocked at what they saw. The parlor held no furniture, and the floor was covered with sick and injured people. Several men still had arrows sticking out of their bodies. Josie reached behind her back and retrieved the small knife from its secret place in her belt. Blue eyes quickly assessed the situation. Looking for someone healthy enough to help her move some of the patients, Josie spotted a young man kneeling next to one of the sick women. "You, come here and help." He looked up at her but made no effort to move. Glaring at him, she spoke in a tone that brooked no argument. "We need to separate the sick from the injured and start treating them. You don't look like you're sick or injured..." she lowered her tone to a growl, "...so get to it."

"B-but my mother...what would she think if I left her alone at a time like this?"

"What do you think your mother would say if you sat there and made no effort to help others?" Rebecca asked in a tone that filled him with guilt. He bent down and gave his mother a kiss on her sweaty forehead.

"I'll be back soon, Mother."

He rose and moved over toward them. "My name is Michael. What can I do to help?" He was close to Rebecca's age, with dark curly hair that refused to be tamed.

Josie moved over and knelt next to a man with an arrow sticking out of his upper chest. She carefully removed his shirt while giving instructions. "Rebecca, get as many clean rags as you can. Tear some into long strips. Get water and throw a poker in the fire. Michael, I need you to hold him still while I push the arrow through." The young man swallowed and grimaced as he grabbed hold of the injured man's shoulder. "All right, now I'm going to rotate him onto his side." As she did, she thought how grateful she was that the man was unconscious. She hoped he was out enough not to feel the pain, but she was not that lucky. He woke and let out a bloodcurdling scream when she pushed the arrow through and broke off the point. Rebecca ran over and knelt at his head.

"What's your name?" she asked as she stroked his temples.

"W-William." His voice was hoarse from screaming.

"My name is Rebecca. That's my friend Josie and that's Michael. We're here to help you, all right? Now, I want you to lie back and let me tell you a story."

"It hurts," he gasped. Josie rose to check on the poker.

"Shh, it's all right. I know it hurts," Rebecca spoke in soothing tones, encouraging William to relax. "There once was a beautiful young woman..." She continued to weave her tale, completely hypnotizing both him and Michael. Josie reached down and, in one fluid motion, grabbed the shaft and pulled it from the man's body. Rebecca had been watching the outlaw and had her hands on William's shoulders just as Josie reached down. William screamed and continued to scream as Josie cauterized the entry and exit wounds before he mercifully passed out from the pain.

"Now just what in tarnation is going on down here?" The voice was female, albeit a bit deep, but Rebecca would have sworn she was looking at a man. Short, dark hair framed a slightly rounded face, weathered from years of hard living and harder drinking. The woman focused on Josie. "You! Damn, I thought you was dead as a can of corned beef, killed back there with your gang."

"Henry and Jonah aren't dead, Jane; neither am I." Josie rose and gestured at the young blonde woman. "This is my friend Rebecca. Rebecca, this disreputable polecat is Martha Jane Canary, better known as Calamity Jane."

"Mighty nice to meet you, Miss Rebecca. Josie, 'bout time I saw you. Could use some help here."

"So I see." The gunslinger took control. "Rebecca, Michael, take the ones that are sick upstairs. If there's any injured up there, get them down here if it's not too serious." Rolling up her sleeves, she looked at Jane. "So where do we start?"

Rebecca and Michael worked together trying to cool down the feverish patients or warm up the ones suffering from chills. "Michael, do you know what these hard, red lumps are?" she asked, pointing to a rash of rapidly forming lumps on the victim's arm.

"No," he said as he shook his head. "I've never seen anything like that before." He rubbed his temples. "Ah, I wish there was some laudanum. I swear it feels like there's a herd of cattle stampeding in my head." His hands moved to completely cover his temples as he fell to his knees.

"Michael!" Rebecca exclaimed as she knelt by his side.

"It hurts, oh it hurts," he cried as tears started to leak out from his tightly shut lids. Rebecca moved his hands out of the way and started to gently massage his temples. She moved her thumbs down to massage his upper neck, relieving the tension as she hummed a gentle melody.

"Just relax and think of a time when you were happy. Close your eyes and think of that time. Tell me about that time."

"I was ten, back when we stilled lived in Virginia. Papa had just bought me a horse of my very own," he smiled and leaned back against Rebecca's chest. She continued to massage his temples. "I was a small boy. I couldn't get up in the saddle."

"I know that feeling," she said with a laugh in her voice. "I'm sorry, go on."

"You have a beautiful voice, Rebecca. It goes well with your beautiful face." They exchanged soft smiles of nervousness. "What was I...oh, the horse. I couldn't get up on my own. I remember Papa coming over and lifting me up in his arms to put me on the saddle. I never felt more safe, or more loved."

"That's a very sweet story," Rebecca said looking down at him. Michael's head was now resting in her lap. She noticed beads of perspiration on his forehead. "You're warm," she said with concern in her voice. "I mean really warm. I'll get Josie."

"Rebecca, I'm fine." He forced himself into a sitting position, facing her. "Why don't you go see if Josie needs anything and I'll get back to looking after these people."

"Are you the only one caring for all these people?" Josie asked as she continued to stitch up a nasty gash in her patient's abdomen. Jane removed a small flask from her belt and took a long pull. "I do what I can. It seems like there's more sick and injured everyday. I can't keep up with 'em all." She held out the flask. Seeing the shake of the outlaw's head, she said, "Suit yerself. You go help someone else; I've got this one."

Josie nodded and moved off to tend to another man felled by arrows. This time the wound was mortal and she knew it. The outlaw found she could not meet the young man's eyes as she passed him by in search of someone she could help. She saw Rebecca come down the stairs and waved her over.

"I thought I'd come down and see if you needed any help."

Josie put her to work cleaning soiled rags and blood-soaked knives. Rebecca estimated there were at least twenty men with wounds from fighting, and thirty men and women who were sick. She had seen at least a dozen of them upstairs while she was looking for rags. Many of them had the hard, red lumps on their arms and legs. Some complained to her of pain, and she shared what laudanum they had with the ones who seemed to be in the most pain until there was none left. After that all she could do was provide them with a gentle touch and a soft voice for a few moments of peace. Night had fallen while the women moved among the sick and injured, not stopping themselves to rest or eat. Rebecca was so exhausted by the time Josie found a place for them to lay down that she fell asleep immediately, not even taking the time to ask the outlaw about the skin rashes.

Josie removed her gun belts and lay down next to the sleeping form. In a short time she too was asleep. For the first time in almost a month, she was blessed with no nightmares. The gunslinger's dreams were filled with peaceful visions of her life when she was young, just before the War Between the States broke out. Swirling images of her mother and her friends sitting in the parlor, speaking of great changes to come, of laughter and warmth, and of love and safety. Josie smiled in her sleep and remained that way all night long.

The next three days were spent in much the same fashion. Whenever Josie thought she was gaining on the injured, soldiers from the nearby fort poured in with various arrow and hatchet wounds from their raids on the Indians. Rebecca continued to care for the rapidly worsening sick people while Josie tended to the wounded. Calamity Jane alternated between the two floors, doing her best to calm and comfort as many as she could while keeping the two women separated. She realized the young girl did not know the people they were treating were suffering from smallpox and deliberately kept the information from Josie as well. With all the wounded soldiers coming in, it was easy to keep the outlaw busy downstairs, usually until long after Rebecca went to sleep. With the young woman spending most of her time upstairs, there had been little time for conversation and Jane hoped to keep it that way for a while longer.

Rebecca made her way over to where Michael was standing, staring out the window. Placing a gentle hand on his shoulder, she asked "Michael? Are you all right?"

He turned his tear-streaked face to see her. "Oh Rebecca. It's Mother...she, she..." He broke into sobs as he pressed his face against her and wrapped his arms around her in a fierce embrace. Rebecca guided him to the floor. "We...we were just supposed to stop in Deadwood for supplies, that's all," he choked. "Then the stagecoach driver took sick and then, then..." Rebecca rocked him in her arms as he desperately sought comfort from the pain in his heart. Feeling the heat against her chest, she reached down and pressed her hand against his forehead. "Michael, you're on fire." Turning one of his hands in hers, Rebecca gasped at the multitude of bright red lumps on his wrist and lower arm. "Michael, stay here, all right?"

Josie was changing a soldier's bandages when Rebecca came up behind her. "Josie, I need to talk to you."

"I'm busy right..." The concerned look on the young woman's face stopped her protest.

"Josie, the sick people upstairs...they've got something contagious." Rebecca lowered her head. "I meant to tell you sooner."

The sickening feeling Josie felt when Rebecca was bitten by the rattler returned in full force. She bounded up the stairs two at a time, her worst fears confirmed when she saw Michael crying over the dead body of his mother. His bare arms clearly showed the signs of the pox. She heard footsteps behind her and put her arm out to stop Rebecca from entering the room. "No."

"Josie, I have to check on Michael." She tried to move past the outlaw.

"Rebecca, it's too dangerous." Josie grabbed the young woman's upper arms. "Don't you understand? It's smallpox, Rebecca." Her grip relaxed when she saw the shocked expression on her friend's face.

"No...." She looked up at Josie with disbelief. "But Michael, he's so young."

"Smallpox doesn't care how old you are, Sprite." She allowed a brief flash of concern to cross her normally stoic face as she pressed her hand against Rebecca's cheek. "How do you feel?"

The young woman smiled at the gesture. "I'm fine, Josie. Look, if I was going to get it, I would have it already," she said, feigning a confidence she did not feel. They looked at each other seriously, their eyes conveying the unspoken fear.

Hours later, after all the patients were settled down for the night, Josie, Rebecca, and Jane sat around a small kitchen table. "Why didn't you say anything, Jane?" the outlaw asked with a tone that expressed her disapproval.

"By the time I realized you were here, you'd already been exposed to it. T'wernt nothing I could've done 'bout it." Calamity settled back and rolled herself a cigarette. "You see what I'm up against. Half those men would've been dead if you hadn't stayed to help. And that little girl of yours was a big comfort to 'em as well. She's a real huckleberry above a persimmon." Rebecca smiled at the compliment from the sharpshooter. "Course don't know why a purdy thing like yerself would be hanging out with someone who's all horns and rattles."

"Hey," Josie protested. She looked over to Rebecca and gave her a small smile. "She has a...calming effect on people. It's a rare quality." Turning back to her old friend, her smile faded. "You should have told me, Jane."

"There's nothing we can do about it now, Josie," Rebecca said as she rose from the table. "I'm going to go check on Michael," she held up a hand to block the outlaw's protest. "Josie, he's all alone and he needs me. I'll be fine."

Josie rose to her feet and stood in the doorway, effectively blocking the blonde's exit. "I don't want you up there with those sick people."

"It's too late," Rebecca said. "If I was gonna get it, I would have. Please, he's all alone."

Please Sprite, don't look at me like that, Josie thought to herself as soft green eyes pleaded with her. Lowering her head, she reluctantly nodded and took a step back. "Don't stay long."

Calamity waited until Rebecca was gone before pulling a jug of whiskey out from under the sink. "Tarantula juice?" she asked, holding the jug up.

"No. Damn it to tarnation, Jane, you should have told me."

"Josie, I'm sorry." Jane took a long pull on the jug. "She's a beautiful girl. I'm sure she'll be fine."

Josie crossed the room in an instant, pressing Calamity up against the counter. "She'd better be." The thought of Rebecca coming down with smallpox was too frightening for her to contemplate. "I'm going to check on the horses," she said abruptly, turning and leaving the room before her anger took control.

When Josie went upstairs two hours later to fetch Rebecca for bed, she was surprised to see how many people there were in the large room. With all the dead that had been brought down, she had believed only a few remained. Looking about, she counted at least a dozen people remaining. Pulling her bandanna up over her nose and mouth, she entered.

Rebecca was kneeling next to Michael's bed holding his hand within hers. Josie stood back and leaned against a post, close enough to hear but not close enough to be noticed.

"...and the rabbit slipped into the hole and escaped from the hungry wolf," she finished her story and ran a wet cloth across his burning forehead. "How was that?"

"Thank you, Rebecca," he said as he reached up and touched her cheek with his fingertips. "You're a very beautiful creature. I'm sorry."

"Shh, you need to rest now." She moved a lock of his dark hair away from his eyes. "Everything will be fine, just have faith."

"No..." he gasped. "I know, Rebecca. I know what's wrong with me."

"Then you also know that you need to rest. You can survive this, you know." She maintained her low, soft tones as she tried to lull him back into sleep. He brought his free hand up and grabbed her wrist.

"Don't leave me, Rebecca. Please...stay and tell me another story."

"Michael, I can't. I promised Josie..."

"Please." He closed his eyes and swallowed. "Just one more."

No, Josie's mind screamed. *Come downstairs. Get away from all these people.* To her dismay, Rebecca began reciting another tale. She thought about stepping forward and making the young woman come with her but seeing the peaceful look on Michael's face and hearing the gentle tones of Rebecca's voice, Josie knew the decision wasn't hers to make.

Closing the door behind her, Josie leaned her forehead against the jamb. A small voice in the back of her mind asked if she could handle losing Rebecca. Pushing the depressing thought out of her head, she purposefully headed down the stairs to their sleeping area. Knowing that thoughts of a peaceful sleep were hopeless, she turned and went to check on the patients.

As the days went on, Rebecca never left Michael's side. The high fever gave way to delusional ranting and the night chills left him a helpless shell of a once vibrant young man. She stayed there telling stories or quietly holding his hand. Red pox marks now covered his entire body, signaling just how close the end really was.

"Rebecca, I...I can't see...everything's black," he cried, his voice hoarse and low. The strength he used to move patients was gone, taken by the vicious disease. As the tears streamed down the sides of his face; she brushed them away with her fingers.

"It's all right, Michael. Just rest now. It's going to be all right." Her voice cracked as she choked on the truth she could no longer ignore.

"I know, Rebecca." He reached up with a shaky hand to touch her face. "So beautiful." His hand fell back limply. Eyes closing for the final time, he rasped, "I'm so sorry, Rebecca...so sorry."

Through blinding tears, Rebecca ran downstairs and into Josie's arms. The young woman sobbed hysterically against the outlaw's chest. "Why?" she cried over and over, her tears soaking the cotton shirt. Unsure of what to do, Josie stroked the blonde hair in a comforting motion.

"Shh, it's gonna be all right, Sprite." She looked helplessly at Jane. The sharpshooter nodded and went into the kitchen, returning minutes later with a cup of tea.

"It'll calm her down," she said as she handed the mug to Josie. It took some convincing to get the upset girl to drink the strong liquid. Within minutes Rebecca started yawning and was amiable to being directed to the corner where their bedrolls were.

"What was in that?" Josie asked later, after they had gotten Rebecca to sleep and removed Michael's body. They were in the kitchen, the door to the parlor closed to keep their voices from carrying and waking anyone.

"'Nuff laudanum to make her sleep through the night, is all," Jane said as she scratched herself. "What's a purdy young thing like that hanging 'round with you fer, anyway?"

"What are you doing playing nursemaid to a bunch of miners?" Josie returned, ignoring the question.

"Someone has to," she quipped. "'Sides, you knew I was always purdy good at caring for people." Calamity leaned back and put her booted foot upon the table. Scratching her head, she tried to use her fingers to put her wayward hair under control. Success was limited to keeping the greasy strands from falling into her eyes. "What I don't git is why you ain't robbin' 'n lootin' no more. "

"She depends on me," Josie said, nodding toward Rebecca.

"There's no going back, ya know. Once you git a price on yer head, it'll always be there. 'Tain't nothin' gonna change that." Calamity took a long pull on her flask. "Them bounty hunters don't care none that you changed, they just care 'bout the money they been promised." Josie was just about to tell Jane that she had joined the ranks of the bounty hunters herself when their conversation was interrupted by a low moan that was unmistakably Rebecca's. Josie leapt from her seat and shouldered her way through the door, not stopping until she was kneeling next to the bedrolls. The sweaty, flushed complexion that met her struck fear into the outlaw's heart. "No," she whispered, pushing the sweat soaked hair off Rebecca's forehead. The unmistakable heat of fever rose to meet her fingers.

The next three days were a blur to Josie. Every moment was spent at Rebecca's bedside, placing cool cloths across her sweat-soaked body in a feeble attempt to break the raging fever.

"We…we have to get the chickens into the coop before the coyotes get them," Rebecca mumbled. Josie removed the cloth from the young woman's forehead and dipped it in the bowl of now tepid water. It was the second time in an hour that Rebecca's fever had completely dried out the cloth.

"I already took care of the chickens, Rebecca. You just rest now," she said as she placed the cloth back on the young woman's forehead. The incoherent ramblings had started that morning and only served to heighten Josie's sense of dread. She knew the fever was just as likely to kill her friend as the infection from the blistering lumps now beginning to appear on Rebecca's extremities.

"Josie, you can't do nothin' fer her, ya know. Either it kills her or it don't; ain't nothin' you can do 'bout it," Jane said as she placed another bucket of water next to her.

"We'll see about that," the outlaw said as she soaked several cloths in the fresh water, only slightly cooler than the previous bucket. Jane shook her head and walked away, never seeing the look on Josie's face as she reapplied the wet cloths.

"Hang in there, Sprite," she whispered. "You just hang in there."

Rebecca's temperature rose steadily during the night until it reached a dangerous level. Her lips moved, but all that came out were unintelligible mumbles. The reddish lumps were spreading from her arms and legs to the rest of her body. Many of the wounded were moved out of the boarding house as soon as they were able, leaving only a dozen people for Jane to nurse. Josie left Rebecca's side only to use the outhouse. She even slept on the floor next to the stricken girl's bed, refusing to leave her alone any longer than necessary.

Dawn was just breaking over the horizon when Josie rose to look out the window. The rest of the boarding house was still asleep, but concern for her friend kept her up all night. Rebecca's temperature had not risen for hours, but it had not diminished either. The wet cloths she had placed on her friend's body made no difference, except to make the outlaw feel like she was doing something useful. Leaning her forehead against the cool glass, Josie closed her eyes and tried to think of a way to get her friend's temperature down. When the idea finally came, the desperate woman stormed into Jane's room, not caring that the sharpshooter was sound asleep.

"Jane! Jane, wake up!" Josie's quick reflexes allowed her to catch the fist that came flying toward her face.

"What in Sam Hill do you think yer doin'?" the groggy woman cursed as she sat up and rubbed the sleep out of her eyes.

"I need two strong mules for the buckboard."

"Wagon? Mules? Now just hold on a minute, what are you talkin' about?"

"Ice. We need ice to bring Rebecca's fever down. The ice-wagon can't come into town because of the quarantine so I have to go get it." She grabbed Jane's arm and pulled her from the bed. Calamity jerked her arm free.

"I know yer worried 'bout her and that's all that's keeping you from eatin' lead. When this is over, one way or 'nother, we're gonna talk 'bout wakin' Martha Jane Canary up from a sound sleep," she muttered and reached for her britches. "Sides, how're you gonna get past the army? 'Tain't no way yer gonna get through their roadblocks with a wagon."

"I'll just have to find a way," Josie said firmly.

It was easier said than done, Josie realized when she finally got a look at the sentries placed a safe distance from the town. She knew they had orders to kill anyone who tried to leave before the quarantine was lifted. While she could slip in and out without being detected, she had to admit Jane was right; there was no way she could get a wagon through. *I'll just have to think of another way,* she thought before disappearing into a nearby thicket.

Once past the sentries, it was no problem to follow the trail uphill to the icehouse. The sun slowly moved across the sky during the six hours it took her to walk up the steep mountainside. Sweat rolled down her face despite the gradual drop in temperature and her legs screamed for a break, but Josie refused to slow her pace. She was close now, she was certain. *Come on,* she told herself. *Just a bit further.*

The wooden buildings were a welcome sight. Being careful not to be noticed, Josie slipped into a storage shed, removing a large set of ice tongs and two saddle blankets. She folded one into thirds and tucked part of it under her collar, letting the rest lay against her back. After folding the other blanket into thirds and then rolling it up, she headed for the icehouse. If the sentries were not in place, it would have been a simple matter to load the buckboard with blocks of ice. But such luck was not with her today. Worried about how much ice would melt on the way down the mountain, Josie grabbed the biggest block she felt she could heft onto her back. After covering it with the second blanket, she jabbed the ice tongs into it. Bending down and turning around, she leaned the block of ice against the blanket on her back and pushed up with her legs. It took a moment to get her balance, which she could do only by bending over slightly. Making certain she was not spotted, Josie left the icehouse and started the long trek back down the mountain.

Josie had been right in assuming the cool air and the blankets would help maintain the life of the ice block, but she had erred in thinking one blanket was enough protection for her back from the cold. At least twice an hour she had to stop to rest her aching arms, and also to let her back warm up again. Several times she contemplated breaking the block down to a smaller size. The vision of her best friend, her only true friend, burning up with an uncontrollable fever filled her with a sense of guilt over her selfishness. Rebecca would need every piece of ice she could get in order to hopefully break her fever. With a grunt, Josie hefted the block onto her back again and continued her slow walk.

Halfway down, her burning legs, aching back, and screaming arms demanded a longer rest period than a few minutes. Darkness had fallen, making the dirt road hard to see. Knowing if she pushed herself too hard she would never make it, Josie set the block down and leaned up against a tree. Looking at nothing in particular, the blue eyes came to rest upon the moonbeam bouncing off a willow tree. Leaning her head back and closing her eyes, Josie tried to remember what the old medicine woman had told her about willow trees. She looked again at the tree. It was a white willow, the bark of which when ground into a tea was a natural fever reducer. Forcing herself to her feet, the outlaw walked over to the tree. Pulling a knife out of her boot, Josie gouged out several long strips of bark and placed them in various pockets. With renewed hope, she jerked the block onto her back and set out again.

The sound of a boot kicking repeatedly at the door woke Jane from her sound sleep. Cursing loudly, she cocked her Colt and opened the door. "Put her in the tub," Josie said, pushing her way past Calamity and letting the heavy block fall to the ground. Her fingers remained curled up from being held in such a tight grip for so long. With painful slowness, she forced them to straighten. She did not even try to hide the look of anguish on her face when she straightened up and tried to move her fingers. The first thing she did when she finally felt the feeling return was to reach into her pocket and pull out a piece of the bark. "I need to grind this down and make a tea out of it. It'll help bring her fever down." She pulled more pieces out of her pockets, and the sharpshooter reached out and took them from her.

"I'll take care of this. You go sit down before you fall down," Jane said as she guided Josie to a nearby chair.

"The tub…"

"Don't you go worrying none 'bout the tub," Calamity said, pushing on the exhausted woman's shoulder to keep her seated. "It's gonna take me a few minutes to git her into the tub and git the ice in there. You sit there for now." Josie nodded reluctantly. Her legs felt like oak trees, the strength sapped by the grueling walk.

"Just let me know when she's in," Josie said. "I'll take care of her then." Pushing her body far beyond its limits coupled with the lack of sleep made it impossible for the gunslinger to keep her eyes open.

Josie woke less than an hour later, the ache in her back cutting through her sleep. It took a moment for her completely exhausted senses to re-member what was happening. With slow movements and a deep groan, she trudged off to check on Rebecca.

"Yup. This should bring that fever down in no time," the sharpshooter said as she added a few more pieces of ice into the water. "Just got her in there. Took a while to get the water and then haul that blasted block in here. Had ta drag it. Tarnation woman, that block would break a mule's back. You daffy?"

"We needed as much ice as we could get," Josie said as she knelt down next to the tub. Rebecca was propped into a half sitting position, her che-mise plastered to her wet skin. "Hey…" the gunslinger said softly while dropping pieces of ice into the water. Rebecca's eyelids fluttered, but never opened. She seemed to be too weak to perform even that simple task. "All right now, you just relax, Sprite. I've got you." Once there was enough ice in the water to cool it down, she lowered Rebecca's head back until just her nose and mouth were above water. She placed towels under the young woman's head to keep it at that level while she moved the water about with her hand, forcing it to circulate around Rebecca's overheated body. Jane handed Josie the tall mug of tea made from the ground-up bark.

Josie nodded and took the mug. She dipped part of a clean cloth into the tea before bringing the fabric to Rebecca's lips. Parting them with her fingers, Josie squeezed the cloth, allowing a few drops at a time to fall into the young woman's mouth. As hoped, her body unconsciously swallowed. Ignoring the ache in her back and fingers, Josie continued to drip the tea into Rebecca's mouth until it was all gone.

As the minutes ticked by, Josie sat in quiet vigil, removing water and adding ice when necessary and constantly keeping the water flowing around in a clockwise motion. Her fingers resembled prunes from the lengthy immersion. The lack of sleep was catching up with Josie as she fought to stay awake. The repetitive motion of churning the water did not help; nor did her refusal to look at anything other than Rebecca's face, desperately hoping the flush would diminish.

Jane checked in on them an hour later to find the outlaw sleeping on the floor next to the tub. She noted that at some point extra towels had been placed in the tub to support and brace the young woman's head. It was as though Josie knew she would fall asleep and still tried to take care of Rebecca. Jane checked the water temperature, then placed her hand on the young woman's forehead. Turning her hand over, she checked both of the blonde woman's cheeks before checking her forehead again. "Cooler," she said softly as she broke into a rare smile. "You did it, Josie," she said to the sleeping woman on the floor. "You broke her fever. The ice worked." She reached into the tub and lifted the small woman out. "I don't know how you did it, child, but if you only knew how much that woman went through for you. You just made a person who's killed more people 'n me go through hell 'n back to save you."

Josie woke to find herself lying next to Rebecca in Jane's large bed. She quickly looked around for her gun, disoriented. "Relax, Josie," Jane's voice called out from the darkened shadows of dusk. The oil lamp was burning low on the table next to the bed, but it cast enough light for the sharpshooter to see Josie reach over to check on Rebecca. "She's fine...at least the fever broke anyway." Jane watched as the outlaw ran the backs of her fingers over the young woman's cheeks. "She woke up earlier fer a few minutes. Saw you there and fell back asleep." Jane quieted down when she realized the gunslinger was paying no attention to her.

"You did it, didn't you?" Josie whispered as she gave Rebecca a soft kiss on the forehead. "You fought it and you beat it." Josie pulled her into her aching arms and held her close. "It's going to be fine now; everything will be all right, Sprite."

Jane quietly extinguished the lamp and closed the door behind her, leaving the sleeping women to their dreams.

Morning found Rebecca awake and alert and itching like crazy. The fever had given way to the second phase of smallpox; the burning, painful blisters that spread from the extremities to the rest of the body. Their extreme itchiness often made victims scratch themselves to the point of bleeding, increasing their chances for severe infections, which just as often killed the victims as the fever. By the time Josie entered with breakfast and tea, the young woman had scratched her left forearm raw and was starting on the right one. "What are you doing?" she growled as she set the tray down and grabbed Rebecca's wrists to stop her. "Rebecca, you know better than that," Josie looked at the red, irritated skin. Some spots were starting to bleed from the intense clawing. She sighed, knowing how difficult this stage in healing would be. "Look, I know it itches, but you have to keep from scratching. It'll only get worse." With that admonition she released Rebecca's wrists.

"I know..." she said in a small voice. "But it itches so much." Her green eyes held Josie with a look of pain and discomfort. Rebecca started to rub the underside of her left wrist against her knee, covertly trying to scratch without being caught.

"No!" Josie said, reaching out and grabbing the young woman's wrists again. Inside, Josie's heart was overflowing with compassion for her young friend's pain and irritation, but she knew the chance of scarring and infection would be significantly decreased if she could keep the blisters from being scratched open.

"They itch and they hurt," Rebecca cried as she tried to pull her arms away from the much stronger woman. "Josie, please, I can't take it..." Her words broke into sobs as she tried again to wrench her wrists out of the outlaw's grasp. The desperation to scratch showing in her eyes equaled the determination not to let her in Josie's.

"I know it's hard, but you have to fight it," she said in a gentle voice.

"I can't," Rebecca cried as the tears streamed down her face. Not knowing what else to do, Josie pulled the young woman into her arms and held her. Within seconds, she felt the young woman's arms moving against her back and quickly realized what she was up to. She again grabbed the young woman's wrists.

"Jane!" she called out and waited for the sharpshooter to enter the room. "I need two wide strips of cloth, try and find the softest material you can." She watched as Rebecca's eyes grew wide at the realization of what was about to happen.

"Josie...no...please." The stream of tears increased along with her struggle to free herself. "You can't do this; you just can't."

The gunslinger's heart lurched at the impassioned plea, filling her with guilt for causing the hysterical tears. Jane returned with two wide strips of cloth from an old sheet. Together they held the struggling Rebecca down and tied her wrists securely to the bed frame. A tantrum ensued as the young woman flailed her legs wildly in a feeble attempt to escape her confinement. One bare foot connected with the side of Calamity's face, a nail causing a slight scratch on her cheek. Josie held her breath and tensed, well aware of the sharpshooter's quick temper. To her surprise and relief, Jane merely wiped the small trickle of blood from her face and stepped out of range of the kicking legs. "Scrappy thing, ain't she?" she quipped, cutting through the momentary tension.

"That she is," Josie replied, careful to avoid the green eyes that were blazing with anger and frustration.

"Let...me...GO!" She continued her kicking, which did nothing more than fuel her frustration. "You can't do this to me, Josie." She pounded the bed with her feet. "You're nothing but an overgrown bully," she said kicking again. She saw Jane heading for the door. "Please, you can't leave me like this. Don't let her do this to me." The door closed, leaving the outlaw with her charge.

"You're just going to wear yourself out with all that kicking," Josie said calmly, yet still keeping her distance from the flailing legs.

"I don't care! You let me out of this...." Rebecca jerked her wrists against the restraints. "Josie, you know this isn't fair. I wouldn't make you suffer like this." She knew her words were hurting her friend, her best friend. But at the moment, all thoughts of kindness and compassion were gone, replaced with the burning desire to ease the painful prickling feeling in her arms and legs. "Please. Remember when you were shot and we were at Belle's ranch? I took care of you. I didn't..." She tugged hard against the cloths holding her wrists. "I didn't tie you down like an animal." The muscles in Josie's jaw tightened as she fought to remind herself that Rebecca was only lashing out because of the pain.

"I'm going to find something to help with the itching. Until then you'll have to stay tied up."

"Josie, please..." She stopped kicking and turned her green eyes to lock with the gunslinger's. Rebecca moved her right foot and used a toenail to scratch an itch on the back of her left leg. The movement did not go unnoticed by Josie, who turned and left the room for a moment, only to return with two more strips of cloth.

"I'm sorry, Rebecca. You give me no choice," she said as she approached.

"NO! No, you can't, please," Rebecca begged, frantically kicking to keep out of Josie's grasp. Her left foot was caught briefly before she managed to connect with her right and force the gunslinger to let go and back up out of range. But with her hands restrained, the struggle was soon lost as Josie pinned her down and tied the knots that would prevent her from scratching. With all her thrashing about, Rebecca never saw the misting in her best friend's eyes. "Damn you to tarnation, Josie Hunter!" she screamed.

"I have to do it," the gunslinger replied as she stood up and reached for the sheet.

"No you don't!" Tears of frustration poured out of her eyes. "You can't leave me like this."

Josie covered her with the sheet and leaned in close, allowing her to see the scratches caused by her vicious kicks. "I promise I'll find a way to make this better, Sprite."

"Please let me go," Rebecca whispered pleadingly. She felt a calloused thumb on her cheek brushing away her tears.

"I wish I could."

Josie stared at her reflection in the mirror. The large purpling spot on her jaw was still tender to the touch even hours after Rebecca's heel had connected with it. Using a clean cloth, she carefully tended to the scratches that dotted her face and arms from her young friend's frantic attempt to keep her legs free. "You're losing your touch, old girl," she muttered. She always prided herself on her alertness and her ability to stay out of harm's way. With Rebecca, she never saw the blow coming, a rare thing indeed for the experienced gunslinger. With a quiet sigh, she set the cloth down on the edge of the sink and left the boarding house, needing a few minutes alone to sort out her thoughts.

Once outside, Josie sought the shelter of a small grove of trees on the edge of town. Her still recovering muscles groaned at her thought of climbing up into the branches and she relented, deciding instead to sit on the ground and lean her back up against the trunk of a tall deadwood tree. She closed her eyes, letting her mind go through the litany of ways to ease Rebecca's suffering. The most common treatment for the blisters was a paste made of sulfa drugs. Of course the apothecary's store had long ago run out of such drugs. Soap root would help, but her searches of the creek banks turned up no sign of the plant. *Damn quarantine*, she thought to herself. There was not enough time for her to slip out of town, go to Rapid City for the medicine, and still make it back to Deadwood in time to save Rebecca. Josie brought her strong fingers up to firmly rub her temples in a vain attempt to ward off the impending headache. *There just has to be a way. There has to be something...* Her keen hearing picked up the sound of a wagon approaching in the distance. Of course, with the amount of noise the wagon was making, anyone would have heard it. Josie listened carefully, picking out the various sounds. It was obviously a wooden wagon, based on the sound of metal clanging against metal and wood. That sound was most likely pots and pans banging against the sides. The hoof beats indicated at least two large horses carrying a heavy load. Whatever it was, it was worth investigating, she decided as she rose to her feet and took off in the direction of the sound. It took her only a few minutes to reach the trail that ran past the town, now guarded by soldiers from the nearby fort.

"This town is under quarantine. No one in or out. Turn around and head back to Rapid City," the soldier said as he approached the wagon, his attention on the portly man at the reins. Josie watched quietly from her vantage point behind a nearby bush.

"Ooh, a captive audience, how delightful," the driver said, his voice slightly higher than one would expect from a man with his girth. His face sported a short beard, the same dark color that his hair once was, now graying with age. "Look, I can help whatever is wrong with them. I have medicines and elixirs and..."

"I said no one enters, by order of Governor Mellette," the soldier said, bringing his rifle up against his body to make sure the man understood the meaning.

"Oh...I see what you're saying. No one enters." He forced a laugh to cover his intensely growing fear. "Well then, I guess I'll just be off."

A sound in the bushes caused both men to turn around. What they saw was Josie somersaulting through the air at them. Before the soldier could raise his rifle into firing position, her boots landed squarely against his chest. A quick blow to his temple from the butt of her gun was all it took to send him into blackness. She turned her attention back to the man on the wagon, who looked like he was either going to cry or faint with his fear.

"Now, I don't have much here, miss...ah...I mean...."

"Shut up," she snarled as she headed to the side of the wagon. This was obviously a patent medicine man, she thought to herself. It was a traveling show wagon, with doors on the side and back, with a fold-up stage for performing. Most likely he had a dancer or juggler inside the wagon who would come out and perform in towns to draw the crowds before he made his appearance, hawking elixirs that were little more than alcohol and syrup. Removing one Colt from her holster, she aimed at the door. "Come on out," she said in her most intimidating voice. Without turning around, Josie pulled her other Colt out and shot the hand of the soldier, forcing him to drop the rifle that was trained on her. A young man and woman exited the wagon. The man looked to be in his early twenties, thin and gangly with extremely thinning blond hair. His face bore more acne scars than Josie had ever seen before. The young woman, on the other hand, was quite the pleasant sight to look at. Her flaming red hair was tied up in a swirling bun on her head, her worn dress hugging her bosom forcing it up to tantalize and distract. Josie was certain that this woman was little more than a traveling strumpet doubling as an assistant to the flim-flam man.

"P-please allow me to introduce myself," the bearded man said nervously as he stepped down from the wagon. "My name is Salvatore, but most people call me Sal. Do you perhaps have an ailment that requires my attention?" he asked in a hopeful tone.

"Sulfa drugs, all you have."

Sal laughed nervously and wrung his hands together. "I ah...I mean sulfa drugs are extremely costly, if you know what I mean...urumph!" He found himself being held by the throat, his body off the ground and pressed against the side of the wooden wagon with enough force to rattle the warped door.

"Where?" She growled menacingly. She extended her arm and stepped back a bit, worried that the extremely terrified man would lose control of his bladder. Her biceps screamed at the strain, but her concern for Rebecca overrode the pain.

"I-inside," he cried, quickly scrambling out of reach when Josie released her grip. Once inside the rickety wagon, it took only a few minutes for her to look through the different elixirs and creams. She found four crates of soap root and two jars of salve made from sulfa drugs along with several bottles of laudanum. The majority of the remaining bottles contained mixtures that were mostly syrup and alcohol - good for making someone forget what ails them, but not much else. It was obvious that he had recently restocked his supplies. The gunslinger smiled at her good fortune. *There's enough medicine here to care for everyone at the boardinghouse.*

"But you can't just take all my medicine...." Sal protested as Josie climbed up and took the reins. He scrambled up next to her, terrified of her but just as terrified of One-Eyed Henry back in Rapid City, the man who loaned him the money to pay for the supplies. Death from this madwoman would be a comfort compared to what Henry would do to him if he did not show up in three days with the money plus substantial interest.

"If you and your friends haven't been exposed to smallpox before it would be a good idea to stay here."

"Smallpox? Did you say smallpox? Well, why didn't you say so? Just wait a second." He climbed down and spoke quickly to his assistants before pulling a small tent and other camping supplies off their various positions on the wagon and placing them on the ground. "My town suffered through the pox back in the fifties," Sal said as he climbed back into the seat. "Why do you think I wear a beard in the middle of July?" He pointed to several small pitted scars that were mostly hidden by his facial hair. "Here, Buttercup and Raven are a bit skittish with unfamiliar people," he said, taking the reins from the gunslinger. With a cluck of his tongue, they were off toward town. "They're just kids," he said once they were on the road into town, referring to his two companions.

"They'll be fine out here for a few days. Billy's a bit of a Jonathan, what with his family coming from Delaware and all, but he knows enough to keep them alive for a few days." He noted the faraway look in Josie's eyes and asked with genuine concern in his voice, "Someone you love got the pox?" He hoped he would not end up with a bullet for his question.

"There are a dozen people suffering from it right now. Most of the others have died," she said, her blue eyes never leaving the road before them, her senses working to pick up any sign of trouble. The key to saving Rebecca was in this wagon and she was going to defend it with her life if necessary. Sal figured out the unspoken answer and gave the rein a flick, sending the horses into a trot.

The now unusual sound of a wagon pulling up outside brought Calamity Jane to the door. Her heart leapt with joy at the sign of the patent medicine man's wagon. "We've got soap root and some sulfa paste," Josie said as she swung her long legs and jumped down from the seat. Sal used the handles and carefully stepped down. Together, the three of them brought all the usable medicine inside. Sal left to tend to his horses.

Using mortars and pestles, the women ground the soap root into a fine powder. Although not as effective as the sulfa paste, the tuber would be enough to ease the painful itching and help to draw out some of the blisters. Jane went to tend the others while Josie took up residence next to Rebecca.

"Howdy," she said groggily. Jane had given the young woman several doses of laudanum in an attempt, quite simply, to make her too drunk and doped to fight the restraints.

"Howdy yourself," Josie answered softly as she examined the rash, which now had moved up her arms and legs to cover most of Rebecca's body. The youthful face was mottled with several small red marks. "I have some medicine to help you."

Rebecca knew better than to ask Josie to untie her again. The pasty mix of soap root and sulfa drugs was cool against her overheated skin. She closed her eyes and relaxed under the older woman's gentle treatment. Josie worked slowly, making sure to carefully cover every inch of Rebecca's body with the healing salve. "Josie, aren't you afraid of catching it?"

Josie paused for a moment, remembering a time long ago. Her blue eyes took on a faraway look. "There was an outbreak of smallpox on the reservation. The disease was new to the Cherokee; they had no natural defense to it." Like alcohol, she thought ruefully. "Smallpox wiped out most of the people in my tribe. I was around it the whole time and never got sick. I guess I'm just immune to it." A momentary flash of pain crossed her face as she remembered all the sick and dying, and her helplessness to do anything about it.

"Josie..." the little blonde said, trying to bring her friend back to the present. "I'm sorry about earlier...." Her gaze fell on the purple bruise on the gunslinger's cheek.

"Don't worry about it, Rebecca," she smiled, trying to lighten the mood. "Just don't get the idea that you'll ever get away with it again." Josie held up a mock fist in jest. Both shared the rare playful mood for a few more moments while she finished applying the salve.

Sal returned a short time later, his arms burdened down with a crate full of items he felt would be helpful to the suffering people. Without hesitation, he followed Jane's directions and started to help. He chatted amiably with people, holding some hands and generally lifting the mood with his infectious smile and chatter.

"Who is that?" Rebecca asked. "He looks like a used wagon salesman."

"Actually, he's one of those traveling medicine men. He was kind enough to supply us with all this medicine," she allowed a tone of gratitude to filter into her voice. "I found him on the trail."

"How did you convince him to come into a town with smallpox?" she asked. Thinking better of it she added, "Never mind. I'm sure I don't want to know."

Josie chuckled. "No, you probably don't. Why don't you try to rest for a while?" She adjusted the pillow and turned down the lamp next to the bed.

"Josie, you need to rest too."

"I will, Rebecca. I just need to check on the others first. I'll be back in a little bit."

Having Rebecca tied to the four corners of the bed made it impossible for Josie to sleep next to her. She contemplated undoing the straps for the night, but realized that the general movements of sleep could rub the salve off the young woman's skin. With a sigh, Josie pulled the comforter off the end of the bed and laid it out on the floor.

Although Josie used most of the sulfa paste to blend with the soap root, she kept a small amount aside, using the concentrated form on Rebecca's face, determined to do her best to prevent her pretty, young friend from being scarred severely from the pox. Her efforts paid off handsomely as the days wore on. The itching stopped and Rebecca was finally untied, much to everyone's relief. Despite her normally gentle nature, the words and phrases Rebecca came up with were enough to make a harlot blush. Although Josie abhorred physical discipline, she was sorely tempted to throw her young friend over her knee several times for her sharp retorts and biting words. There was no doubt that Rebecca could match words with the best of them. The blisters scabbed over, but were showing little, if any, signs of scarring.

Before Sal arrived with the medicine, less than one out of ten had survived the pox. Ten of the twelve remaining victims survived and, thanks to the sulfa and soap root, most came out of it with only a few mild scars. The only sign of scarring on Rebecca's face was a small spot below her jawbone, unnoticeable unless pointed out. Within two weeks, the quarantine was lifted and the boardinghouse was returned to its normal use.

Rebecca and Josie escorted Sal to the stables. "I have to go see if Billy and Mary are still waiting for me," he forced a small laugh. "They've probably gone back to Rapid City."

"They're waiting for you in Rapid City, Sal," Josie said as she stepped forward. "Go to the Horses Mouth Inn. It's been paid for and so has your debt to One-Eyed Henry."

"B-but how did you...?"

"Sal, I've learned that Josie works in mysterious ways," Rebecca said as she put her arm around his shoulder. "It's better most of the time not to ask; just accept it." Josie smiled at her friend's insight into her character.

"Well then, I thank you most kindly, Josie." He knew better than to comment on her reputation as a murdering thief and train robber. Despite all the weapons and her usual menacing stare, Sal just could not see her in that light anymore. He had watched her the past few days as Josie had stayed by her friend's bedside, keeping her company and constantly tending to her. Being a light sleeper, he had been awakened one night by the crystal voice of the gunslinger talking to the sleeping blonde. For an endless length of time, Josie spoke of hopes, dreams, and wishes that she dared not reveal in the light of day. He understood now that there was a special bond between the two women. Sal had assumed it was the young woman who needed Josie, when in fact it was just the opposite.

25: Sinners?

When Rebecca had recovered her strength sufficiently to travel, the pair set out for Wyoming Territory in search of an outlaw who was reported to have been last seen in Cheyenne. The man was known to have murdered a woman and her child because they got in his way as he was fleeing from a bank robbery. The cold-blooded murder of such innocents put him high on Josie's list of fugitives to find, and she was itching to get on the road as soon as Rebecca was able.

The long hot days of summer were shortening with the coming of fall, but the weather was still unusually hot and dry. The two women drew to a stop on a hill over-looking a good-sized town spread out on the plain below them. It was close enough to Cheyenne to use as a starting point for tracking down the killer, but hopefully far enough away that he would not get wind of her nosing around. Deciding it would be better to enter the town separately, Rebecca changed into her new dress and headed off on foot, entering the town in time to coincide with the arrival of the overland stagecoach. Josie found an abandoned corral that looked as though it was once used by the pony express before the trains came through, and left the wagon and Flossy there with an ample supply of water and access to grass. Josie rode in on horseback a short while later, noting the sign over the entrance to the main street proclaiming the town to be Rosewood.

She took Phoenix to the stable and secured her lodgings before heading for the boardinghouse. An older woman whose brown hair was liberally salted with gray met her at the door. Rebecca was seated in the parlor with a glass of lemonade; Josie could see her over the woman's shoulder. "I am Miss Emily and this is my place." She looked at the tall gunslinger, brown eyes meeting blue. "I run a clean, respectable place here, uh...miss. I don't want any trouble," she said as her gaze fell on the guns on Josie's hips. Rebecca walked over and placed her hand on the old woman's forearm.

"She's the friend I told you about. I assure you there will be no trouble. We're tired and really just want a place to sleep and eat." She took the pouch containing the money from Josie's belt and counted out six dollars for the lodging. Emily's eyes moved from the gunslinger to the pile of money in her hand, greed outweighing concern.

"I don't provide meals other than morning coffee...one cup each," she said firmly. "Git your grub over at the Red Diamond. At least you'll fit in there," her last comment was directed at the woman in black. Down the street to the west of the boardinghouse was the saloon, a two-story structure with a porch and balcony. Several scantily clad women fanned themselves and watched the street from their vantage on the balcony. Red curtains adorned the windows and several men were entering the saloon downstairs through the swinging doors. The hairs on the back of Josie's neck prickled with a warning that something was amiss. As Emily led them upstairs to their room, the gunslinger's eyes kept darting around, trying to pinpoint the source causing her senses to be on alert.

Rebecca flopped back on the straw-filled mattress and let out a sigh. Josie's back was to her so the young woman was unable to see the smile that crossed her face before she resumed her normal stoic look. Their room was in the front, giving them an unobstructed view of the street below. No matter which direction she looked all Josie saw was the normal activities of a small town. People walking and riding about, storekeepers helping people load their purchases into their wagons, ladies with parasols walking arm-in-arm with well-dressed men. There was nothing out of the ordinary. Her brow furrowed as she tried to figure out the answer to the puzzle. "Guess we'll go get something to eat."

"Eat? Sounds good." Rebecca smiled as she rose from the bed and headed for the door, reaching the handle before the gunslinger.

"Never saw you move so fast, Rebecca," Josie teased. The young woman's green eyes twinkled.

"Food has that effect on me," she replied. "Come on, you could use a good meal, too."

As Josie expected, the Red Diamond was the local hangout for all the lower forms of life in town. Several round tables were filled with men playing poker while the women she had seen on the balcony earlier were either lining the bar and stairs, or were trying to talk the men into giving up some of their money in the name of carnal pleasure. Josie allowed the corners of her lips to rise slightly. *This is more like it*, she thought.

Rebecca looked around the brightly-lit room, but most of her attention was on the common ladies of the evening who milled about. She also noted the looks from some of the men as they passed through the door. Most saw the tall gunslinger first and their faces registered the immediate fear. Those that managed to see past the woman in black and spotted her wore looks of undisguised lust. She felt like a sheep surrounded by a pack of hungry wolves and moved deliberately close to Josie, silently indicating that she had protection.

"Whiskey," Josie said brusquely as she sat down on a stool at the bar, indicating with her eyes that her companion should sit next to her. The barkeep quickly produced a shot glass and the bottle. He looked to Rebecca for her order.

"Sarsaparilla," she said quietly, not wanting the others in the place to hear. The barkeep snorted and went to look for the bottle of soda he was certain was around somewhere, all the while thinking that the tall woman and short blonde made an odd couple

Josie drained her shot of liquor and refilled her glass. A burly man who reeked of unwashed skin and clothes that had not seen soap in far too long came up behind them. Both women smelled him before he made his presence known by slapping his grimy hand on Rebecca's shoulder. "And just how much would ye be costin' me, little one?" His rancid breath made her forget about food.

"Just a broken arm," Josie snarled as she moved with lightning speed off her seat and grabbed his hand, twisting it off her companion's shoulder and up behind his back. "Apologize," she hissed in his ear, pressing his arm upward sharply, driving home her point. "I said apologize to the lady."

"S-sorry," he grumbled, his eyes tight from the pain shooting through his shoulder. "Now please...let me go."

Josie took a long look around the saloon, making eye contact with all who were paying attention with a silent warning. Releasing her grip, she stepped back, waiting to see if the man was stupid enough to fight her. Fortunately for him, the idea of slipping back into an alcoholic haze was more enticing then going up against the taller and better-armed woman. He muttered something unintelligible and moved on back to his table. Josie resumed her seat next to Rebecca, whose eyes never left the gunslinger. "Thank you," she said. Josie nodded and downed another drink.

Josie ordered two dinners and looked around for the table she wanted. With Rebecca and the bottle in tow, she walked through the crowd and glared at four men until they decided to take their card game somewhere else. She took the seat against the wall, affording her a clear view of the whole room but not the stairs, which ran up the wall behind her. Rebecca reached for the chair opposite her, but the gunslinger indicated with her hand to take the chair next to her.

"Did you want to talk about something?" she asked once settled.

"No."

"Then why did you make me sit over here instead of over there?"

"You were blocking my view of the door," Josie said simply, pouring whiskey into her glass. "I told you there's a reason for everything I do, Sprite." Josie downed two more drinks before dinner finally arrived. She sniffed at the unfamiliar dish. "Um..."

Rebecca looked up from her plate with the same quizzical expression. "Do you..."

"Not a clue," Josie replied, taking a tentative poke at the meat with her fork. "It's a stew...I think."

"Maybe it's better if we don't know," the young woman said, picking around the meat to stab a cube of potato. Josie agreed.

Rebecca was halfway through the greasy stew when she noticed the gunslinger staring intently at a man sitting by himself in the far corner. His hat was pulled down over his eyes, obscuring most of his face. She reached over and lightly placed her fingertips on Josie's forearm to get her attention. "You know him?" she whispered. The bounty hunter's eyes never left her quarry.

"He's wanted. I saw him in the group of wanted posters I looked at before."

"Wanted for what?"

"Rape and murder. That's Lefty Brown." Her eyes narrowed slightly. A commotion in the street drew everyone's attention to the door. "Stay here," Josie said firmly as she rose from her chair, her hands never far from her pistols.

Outside the crowd had begun to gather, listening earnestly to the preacher standing atop a barrel. "Well, if it ain't ol' Reverend Righteous himself," one of the men behind Josie snorted.

A man dressed in a black coat stood upon a soapbox in the middle of the main street. "Citizens of Rosewood, hear me. These sinners must be stopped. They bring nothing but disease and degradation to our fair town." His deep voice boomed over the crowd, drawing yells of approval. John Righteous, as he was called, stroked his short, black beard as he thought of his next statement. "These harlots...these whores bring disease to our men, engaging in the vilest of acts," he said, the venom clear in his voice. Several of the women in question looked down from the balcony. The crowd outside the saloon grew as people poured out of every building to join the fray. Righteous smiled. All was going according to plan. "These harlots must be stopped before they ruin all of us, so sayeth the lord," he shouted the last words.

"So sayeth the lord!" the crowd responded. Josie now knew what made her so concerned earlier. She moved away from the door, not caring who she shoved out of her way, to reach Rebecca.

"Go out the back door and get back to the boarding house."

"Josie...."

"Now!" she growled, grabbing Rebecca firmly by the upper arm and hauling her out of her seat. "Rebecca, please just do what I say and ask questions later."

The young woman nodded, but the fear still remained on her face. Josie led her over to the black oak door and slid the bolt. "Go, I'll get there when I can. Pack up our stuff, just in case." She waited until Rebecca was out the door, then bolted up the stairs, taking them two at a time.

Josie used her brute strength to bust down the first door she reached and entered the room. It held only a small table, lamp, and bed. The window was open, leading to the balcony. She pulled the curtains down to get them out of her way, opened the window, and leaned out. "Over here!" she called, catching the attention of the now frightened harlots. The crowd was whipped up to a frenzied level, totally entranced by the reverend and his poisonous words. From her position at the window, Josie heard the calls for lynching from the mob.

"No, my friends, hanging them will not end the scourge!" Reverend Righteous shouted, quieting the crowd down. "No, more will come to replace them. We need to cleanse this bastion of evil. From the ashes shall grow a new place free from sin."

Josie's eyes widened as she understood the reverend's intentions. "Move!" she yelled, breaking the whore's attention from the crowd. "Let's go; this place is going to burn!" she barked. One by one, she helped the women through the window. Most headed down the stairs and out the back door, but some ran to their rooms and grabbed whatever personal belongings they could carry in their arms before escaping.

"Is that it?" Josie asked. Already she could see the torches being lit.

"I think so," the frightened woman said. Not having time to waste, Josie pushed her toward the open door. "Go." She looked out one last time to make certain all the women were out before racing down the back stairs herself. In all, seven women were waiting for Josie by the time she made it out the back door. The first torch sailed through the front window, smashing it to pieces.

The seven woman looked at Josie expectantly, waiting for her to tell them what to do next. In her concern to get them out of the building, she never gave much thought about what to do with them afterward. Running her fingers through her raven hair, she took a moment to think.

"Do any of you have horses?" The shaking of heads caused her hopes for a quick escape to sink.

One woman stepped forward, her flaming red hair billowing in the warm breeze.

"I've got two horses and a wagon at the corral. Be big enough to get us out of town," she said.

"Good, we'll get it after dark," Josie replied. She looked around. Apparently the mob was too focused on their task to notice they were missing. "Let's go," she said, hoping in her mind that Rebecca's powers of persuasion would work.

"Absolutely not, I won't hear of it," Emily said firmly as she shook her head. "It's bad enough that I let this...this..." she tried to find just the right word to describe the tall woman in black without insulting her, "...person be here, but there is no way on God's green earth that I'm going to allow my home to be used as a hideout for those sinners."

"Look at them," Rebecca said, trying to get the old woman to at least cast a glance at the whores. "Do you think they wanted to be doing this? Do you think they want to sell their bodies for money to drunken men?" She avoided looking at the whores herself, afraid they would take her words the wrong way. "Don't you think their lives would have been different if they had been given a chance?"

"They're sinners!" Emily shot back.

"And you're not? You've never committed a sin? What about the men who pay for their services? Aren't they sinners, too? Yet you let them stay here. Why are they any different?" Rebecca watched as the hard lines on the woman's face softened a bit at the logic of her words. She pressed on, knowing that the advantage was hers. "Most of these women never had the chance you had. What would you do to feed yourself if you didn't have this boarding house?" She paused for effect. "Give them this one chance; let them stay until tonight. Then I promise we'll get them out of here."

Before Emily could answer, another loud commotion ensued outside. The angry mob, in their haste to burn down the saloon, forgot that there were buildings on either side of it. Both the assayer's and the telegraph offices were now on fire. The bucket brigade had been started, with young boys running back and forth from the rain barrels with pails and buckets, handing them over to the grown men that were desperately trying to save that side of the street. Josie looked out the window, her eyes carefully scanning the street. She turned around and addressed the group of women. "Now is the perfect time to get out of here."

Even though she was certain she had not been spotted rescuing the women, Josie nevertheless felt it safest for Rebecca if they left town as well before the mob realized what had happened. The only obstacle for them was Phoenix, who was stabled at the opposite end of town from the corral where Stacey's wagon and horses were kept. With as much stealth as was possible for seven brightly colored ladies in billowing dresses, they slipped around the back of the buildings and made their way up to the corral. Josie led the group with Rebecca never more than an arm's length away from her. One gun was drawn in the unlikely event that they were seen.

No one noticed the wagon pull out of the corral and leave town, nor did they notice the tall woman in black climbing from rooftop to rooftop as she made her way down the street to the stable. It took no time at all for Josie to saddle her steed and make her escape unnoticed. She rode Phoenix hard, forcing her into a full-out gallop as soon as they cleared the burning town. The fire had spread, rapidly traveling along the rooftops until the entire side of the street was burning. The banker was screaming frantically at the sheriff, who was busy trying to calm down the assayer, who was screaming about chemicals. The town was almost out of her sight when the explosions started. Josie guided Phoenix in a wide arc around the outskirts until she was finally heading in the same direction as the wagon. There was no doubt in the gunslinger's mind that the men of the town would be far too busy trying to save it to bother with forming a posse. She slowed the horse down to a less punishing gait and followed the twin rows of tracks laid down by the wagon. The hoof-prints indicated that Stacey had slowed her horses down, so there was no need for the gunslinger to push her beloved mare. Within two miles, she caught up to the women. Rebecca was sitting in the back of the open wagon, chatting animatedly with several of the younger ladies of ill repute. Moving Phoenix in front of the wagon, Josie led them off the trail for several miles before finding what she considered to be a safe place to stop. A small stream nearby would provide water and the gunslinger was certain she could round up some kind of meat for them to eat.

26: The Ladies of the Evening

The horses were groomed and fed with the remainder of the oats in Phoenix's saddlebag while Rebecca and the other women washed up at the brook. Only Stacey and Josie remained behind. The prostitute tied her red hair up into a bun and pinned it into place to keep it off her neck in the heat of the late day sun. Josie leaned back against the wagon wheel, her black hat pulled down far enough to block Stacey's view of her ice blue eyes. For the longest time, not one word had passed between them as the gunslinger methodically cleaned her weapons while the prostitute watched. It was Josie who finally broke the silence. "Something you find interesting about me?" she asked, her eyes never leaving her task.

"Actually there is."

"Yeah?" she asked with no sound of interest in her voice.

"Why would someone like you help someone like us?" the redhead asked, her tone indicating her fear as well as her feelings about the woman with all the guns that she assumed to be a common murderer.

Josie looked up, her blue eyes locking with the green across from her. "You mean a thieving, murdering pile of dung like me?" she said in mock distaste. The green eyes dropped immediately, guilty that her feelings were so obvious. Josie looked back down at her gun, spinning the barrel before snapping it shut and looking down the sight. She returned it to her holster and removed the other one before continuing. "I don't like to see women punished by the very men that put them in that position." In a lower voice she asked, "How many of the men in that crowd were regular customers?"

"More than I'd care to admit," Stacey replied. Her gaze drifted off to the clouds as her mind traveled back to a simpler time. "After my husband died, I didn't...."

"You don't owe me an explanation," Josie interrupted as she rose in one fluid motion. "I'd better go check on the others." She pulled the gun out of her left holster and held it out, butt first, toward the whore. "You know how?"

"Yes," the redhead replied, rising to her feet and taking the offered weapon. The gunslinger nodded and walked off in search of the rest of the group.

Two women were sunning themselves on the flat of a large rock. Their clothes were scattered nearby. Even in the distance, Josie was able to pick out the telltale crisscross marks of repeated whippings on the back of one of the women. Her black hair was not long enough to cover the red welts of a recent beating. Unable to look any longer, the gunslinger turned her attention to finding Rebecca. It took only a moment to spot the familiar blonde hair bobbing around, laughing and splashing with two of the younger women. The others were milling about in the water, enjoying the freedom of being naked without being pawed at. Josie called out, getting their attention. The women started getting out of the water, all naked save for Rebecca, who retained her thin cotton slip. The gunslinger smiled slightly at the young woman's modesty as she watched her gather her clothes and move behind the large rock to change. The others simply stood in the open and helped each other get dressed. Josie leaned back against a nearby tree and waited. She kept one eye on the rock that Rebecca was behind and the other on the naked bodies prancing about in front of her.

Josie discovered that Elaine, the woman with the whip marks, was an excellent shot and the two of them set out to catch enough meat for dinner. In less than two hours, they had caught more than enough jackrabbits to feed the group. Neither spoke a single word during the hunt, but both learned much about the other. Elaine remained focused on her task, refusing to allow herself to be distracted by the distant sounds of the coyotes, or fooled by the wind rustling the leaves of the brush. Josie understood this woman's determination to succeed in securing dinner for her friends. Elaine was clearly the one they turned to for guidance and protection.

They were walking back toward the camp, each carrying three skinned and cleaned rabbits. The evening sun had set, the orange now only a slit on the horizon, the sky a dark gray, providing just enough light to see the camp clearly in the distance. "I could have caught enough for us by myself," Elaine said, her hazel eyes staring forward. "I didn't ask you to help."

"Didn't matter; I had to catch food for us anyway," Josie shrugged, not bothering to look at her.

"That Rebecca is quite the child."

"Meaning?" The gunslinger felt herself tense up, unsure what the whore meant.

"Just that she is naive. She knows nothing of the world around her, yet she rides with you, a woman with a price on her head." Elaine held her hands up in a defensive position when the gunslinger stopped suddenly and turned to face her. "Don't take much to figure out you're wanted for something. Innocent people don't run around with that many guns." Josie started walking again and the prostitute fell into step. The bounty hunter's eyes stared straight ahead. "What I can't figure out is why you let that girl ride around with you," Elaine said. "All you're going to do is get her an early trip to the pearly gates."

"Would you rather she became a whore like you?" the gunslinger snapped.

Elaine stopped and faced Josie. Her fingers dug into the carcasses as she fought to control her anger. "I guess that'd be a far sight better than being a murderer."

"Perhaps," Josie replied, her voice betraying none of her feelings. "But be either long enough and it makes no difference." She turned and started walking again, not waiting for a response.

The sun was low in the sky when they returned to camp. Josie deposited the dead animals near the fire and pulled Rebecca aside. "I have to go get the wagon."

"Now?" she asked, looking at the sky. "Josie, it's almost dark. Can't we go get it in the morning?"

"No. Stay here with them. I'll leave you the shotgun for protection."

"How long will you be gone?" she asked. The gunslinger caught the tinge of fear in her young friend's voice.

"I should be back by midnight." At her surprised look, Josie added, "I have to take the long way around the town coming back with the wagon."

"Josie?" Rebecca's green eyes locked with those of the gunslinger. "Promise you'll be careful?" she asked, concerned. The bounty hunter looked at her for a moment before answering.

"I promise, Rebecca. You try to stay out of trouble."

"Me?" she asked, feigning innocence. Josie arched an eyebrow before grinning with her friend. The mirth ended a moment later when the gunslinger whistled for Phoenix. She mounted the steed and with one backward glance, she took off to retrieve their belongings. Rebecca stood there and watched until Josie was no longer in sight before turning around and joining the rest of the women.

The aroma of roasting jackrabbit filled the air as the women circled around the fire and settled in for the evening. Victoria, the brown-headed woman who was the last one rescued from the saloon, reached under the seat of the wagon and pulled out several bottles of whiskey and rum.

"Victoria!" Stacey exclaimed as she rose and took one of the bottles out of the younger woman's hands. "When did you hide these in there?"

"I been hidin' 'em there for a few months now. I take one every week or so. Nobody seemed to notice." Victoria looked over at Rebecca and added, "I got a few bottles of sarsaparilla too, if ya want."

Rebecca hopped up and moved over to the opposite side of the fire, joining Victoria next to the wagon. They were born only months apart, and the proximity in age helped to make them fast friends. Within minutes, bottles were passed around along with pieces of cooked meat, skewered on sticks. Elaine and Stacey dumped part of a bottle of sarsaparilla out and replaced it with rum before passing it to Rebecca. The young woman gratefully accepted the bottle and drank deeply. The sarsaparilla tasted a bit odd to her, but determined to be polite, Rebecca took another sip and smiled.

As the evening wore on, Rebecca found that she liked the taste of the soda more and more. Victoria giggled slightly when she turned her head to see Stacey pouring out over half of the remaining bottle of sarsaparilla and refilling it with the rum. One look at her new friend's green eyes in the firelight told her just how drunk she was.

"Give it a try, Rebecca," Victoria urged, nudging the blonde woman with the half-empty bottle of rum. While they all had a turn with the bottle, the majority of the missing liquor was used to spike Rebecca's drinks.

"All right bust jussta lill slip," she replied, unaware that her speech was slurred. All Rebecca knew was that she was feeling good and everything seemed funny to her. The others realized this as well and began to pepper her with jokes that no respectable woman would dare repeat, sending the young woman into fits of giggles. The soft laughter reached Josie's ears as she returned to camp with Flossy and the wagon. She looked up and saw Rebecca surrounded by the women she had rescued, all laughing and giggling. Although she could not see her friend, Josie did see the almost empty bottle being passed around. She had no doubt that Rebecca was drunk. The gunslinger took a deep breath before walking over to them.

"Where ya going?" Stacey asked the slightly swaying Victoria, who had a firm grip on Rebecca's shoulder to keep herself from falling.

"I gotta pee," she said, her eyes closing for a moment as she fought to keep her balance.

"Ooh, me too," Rebecca said as she got to her feet a little too quickly and lost her balance. She unceremoniously flopped back down to the ground, taking Victoria with her, a feat that she found incredibly funny. The crowd of drunken prostitutes around her parted as the imposing gunslinger made her way through. Rebecca looked up, her head feeling twice as heavy as normal, to a not-so-happy face glaring down at her. "Uh...hi Josie," she said before breaking out into another giggle fit. Nervous looks were exchanged between the other women as they realized just who it was who had rescued them from the saloon, but their sense of fear was eased when they saw her squat in front of the drunken blonde and scoop her up gently into her arms.

"You're drunk," Josie said as she carried her friend off to a private area in the nearby brush.

"I am?" Rebecca asked in all seriousness. She looked around and realized for the first time that she was being carried. "Oh...guess I am," she said softly before breaking into giggles again. Her sides hurt from the constant laughter. Josie smiled softly.

"Yes you are. Here we go. I'm going to stand you up now; don't fall," she said as she set Rebecca's feet down on the ground. The drunken woman wavered for a moment before gripping the gunslinger's upper arm for support. The laughter ceased as a new feeling washed over her.

"Josie, I don't feel good."

The gunslinger watched the sudden change and recognized it for what it was. Without wasting time, she got Rebecca down on her knees and held her hair out of her face as the contents of her stomach churned out onto the ground. Josie was aware of the small crowd forming behind her. "How much did you give her?" she demanded.

"Enough," Elaine said.

"Too much," Stacey corrected with a touch of regret, noting the continued nausea that gripped the blonde woman. Josie shook her head in annoyance at their reckless actions as she continued to care for Rebecca. She leaned in closer and softened the tone of her voice. "You feel better, Sprite?"

Rebecca nodded, but a second later lurched forward for another round.

"Uh huh, that's right, let it out," Josie said softly, one hand rubbing the young woman's back while the other continued to hold the blonde hair out of the way. The other women discreetly left Josie to care for her friend.

Rebecca woke in the middle of the night to find a cool cloth on her forehead and a concerned Josie sitting next to her. "How ya feeling?"

"Awful."

"You should. From what I gather, you drank quite a bit tonight." She sighed at the thought of the hangover that would visit her young friend in the morning. The green eyes closed once more and Josie allowed herself to relax and lay down on her blanket, keeping herself a mere arm's length away from Rebecca.

Elaine watched the scene from her side of the fire. Although she could not hear the words exchanged, she knew how long the tall woman had been awake, watching over her friend. She remembered the conversation she had with the reclusive gunslinger earlier in the day. She never would have suspected the woman in black to be so understanding and compassionate toward someone who was simply drunk. Elaine fully expected Josie to have yelled at them or worse for getting her friend in such a condition. Yet she said not a word to them when she returned to the camp. All she did was help Rebecca into her blankets and sit next to her. No one dared to disturb them. There was not one of them who had not heard tales of Josie the train robber. They said she killed at will, sometimes just for target practice. Elaine looked over at the couple again. She had no doubts that Rebecca would be up during the night, nor did she doubt that the gunslinger would be right there to lend assistance if needed.

27: It's Only Natural

Rebecca covered her eyes with her forearm as the bright morning sun beat down on her. Her head was pounding so hard she was sure everyone could hear it. Her stomach ached, her throat was sore, and she was certain she would never rid her mouth of the foul taste. She felt the soft leather of the canteen press against her elbow.

"Here," Josie said softly, although to the young woman it sounded much louder. Rebecca rolled onto her side, away from the offending sun and toward the woman who had cared for her the previous night. She propped herself up on one elbow and took the offered water. With her eyes still shut tightly, Rebecca rinsed her mouth out, then took several long draughts before handing the canteen back to the tall woman in black.

"I feel awful," she moaned as she rolled onto her back, one hand reaching down to cover her aching belly.

"You should," Josie said. "You were blind drunk." Her tone was not condescending, but it was not especially pleasant, either.

"Sorry," Rebecca mumbled as she slowly opened her eyes. The gunslinger held out her hand and brusquely helped the young woman to her feet.

"Don't be sorry, Rebecca. Just improve."

The young woman let out an exasperated sigh. "Fine," she said as she turned and headed for the brush. Josie's blue eyes flashed a hint of anger as she followed with deliberate steps. The instant they were out of earshot of the rest of the group, the gunslinger reached out and grabbed Rebecca by the upper arm, jerking her around to face her.

"You listen to me, Rebecca. I'm not upset that you got drunk. It happens." From the look on the young blonde's face she realized the strength with which she held her and eased up the pressure.

"Then what?"

"There's a time and a place for it. In the open with the possibility of a posse after us isn't it. What would you have done if something happened? By the skies above, girl, you can't even defend yourself," Josie said. She released her hold and ran her fingers through her raven hair, waiting for a retort from the young woman. Rebecca lowered her eyes for a moment as if lost in thought, then raised her head to face the gunslinger. Unsure what to say, the blonde nodded and stepped behind the brush. Josie turned and walked back to camp, but her ears still heard the ragged breathing that usually preceded sobbing.

Rebecca returned a short time later, her eyes a bit puffier than usual. Without looking at the gunslinger, she headed for the coffeepot and poured a mug for both of them. She walked over to Josie and held out the cup as if holding a peace offering. The gunslinger took it and nodded her thanks before indicating that the young woman should sit down next to her. Stacey and Elaine approached.

"Josie, we wanted to thank you for rescuing us and to apologize for getting Rebecca so drunk last night," Stacey said, her tone conveying her remorse. Elaine nodded. The gunslinger waved off the apology.

"We'll escort you to Fort Laramie. If we follow the river, we'll be there in less than a week," Josie said as she stood up and headed to her own wagon. Rebecca tossed the remainder of their coffee into the dying fire and quickly followed. Within a half-hour, the two wagons started their trek westward along the Platte. Elaine and Victoria rode with Rebecca while Stacey and the others rode in the larger wagon. Josie rode further ahead on Phoenix, her eyes constantly searching the area for any sign of trouble. Elaine held Flossy's reins while Rebecca and Victoria rode in the back, using the short sides of the wagon as a backrest.

"...so I moved to Rosewood," Victoria said, finishing her tale. She took the offered canteen from Rebecca and took a deep swallow. "So how about you? How'd ya end up like this? Away from yer family and all."

"I ran away," she replied, her gaze fixed on a knot in the wood on the other side of the wagon. There was a long pause before the blonde woman spoke again. "How did you...?"

"Become a whore?" Victoria offered. Rebecca smiled, a bit embarrassed that she was even asking the question, and nodded. The brown-headed woman took another sip of water and leaned her head back against the top of the wooden side of the wagon. "Well, I told ya that me daddy died. I had to feed myself someway."

"What will you do now?"

She shrugged as if to say there really was not much choice. "Prob'ly find me another whorehouse to work in."

"But you have another chance!" Rebecca exclaimed. "You can do something else."

"The only thing I'm good at is spreadin' my legs for men, Rebecca. I got no other skills." Victoria looked at her new friend and went on, "Yer the lucky one. Ya got that big one," she nodded toward Josie atop the bay mare, "to watch out fer ya. You'll be all right."

Rebecca did not know what to say. She knew she was lucky to be able to read and write and that she would be dead by now without Josie. But she was still afraid the gunslinger would grow tired of her being around and just leave her someplace. Shaking her head as if to clear the negative thoughts, she decided it was time to change the subject. An impish grin came to her face as she turned and whispered to Victoria, not wanting Elaine to overhear. Of course the older prostitute was not paying a bit of attention to the two young women in the back of the wagon anyway. "What's it like?"

"What?" Victoria replied. Rebecca turned a light shade of pink.

"You know..." she looked down at her boots, totally embarrassed to ask, "...sex."

The laughter that boomed from Victoria caused Elaine to turn around to see what was going on. From the wagon following, Stacey shook her head as if to say "I don't know." Elaine smiled and shook her head before turning around and redirecting her attention to where she was going. Up in the distance, Josie kept Phoenix at a steady pace, never allowing herself to get too far ahead of the wagons.

Rebecca knew without anyone telling her that her ears were bright red from embarrassment. "Shh," she hissed, poking the prostitute in the ribs. Victoria snorted and fought to bring herself under control again.

"Heh heh, sorry, Rebecca," she said. "It's just that I ain't used to people not knowin' about it."

"I know what it is, Victoria," she hissed. "I just don't know what it's...like." Her cheeks became flushed again as her friend let loose another round of laughter.

"I knew you was pure-like."

"Will you stop?" Rebecca asked through gritted teeth as she looked around to make sure the others had not heard. If Elaine heard, she made no indication of it and Stacey's wagon was too far away, the noise of the wagons moving along making it impossible for her to hear what was making the young blonde so red.

"Well..." Victoria said after she calmed down and took a swig of water, "...it depends."

"Depends on what?"

"Depends on who ya do it with. Most men don't care about ya, so it's mostly borin'. If ya want it done right, ya gotta count on rosy palm and her five friends," Victoria said, holding her hand out as if inspecting her fingernails.

"Who are they?"

Rebecca's innocent question sent her friend into a bout of laughter and mirth so bad that tears were streaming down Victoria's cheeks before she could stop. Elaine turned to look at them. Victoria was holding her sides from laughing so hard and the poor blonde was scowling. "What is so damn funny?" she said, annoyed. "All I did was ask who Rosy Palm and her friends were." With the wagons stopped, all the women heard what was said and Rebecca found herself surrounded by hysterical women.

"Ask Josie," Stacey called to the wagon in front. "I'm sure she knows exactly who they are."

Josie looked back at the stopped wagons. There was no obvious sign of danger and no one exited either wagon so it could not have been a relief stop. She moved Phoenix closer and heard the peals of laughter. *Great,* she thought as she rolled her eyes. The gunslinger let the horse nibble on the sparse grass for a few moments while she waited for the wagons to start moving again. Just as she started to head for them, Elaine snapped the reins and Flossy started moving again, most of the women having regained their composure. Rebecca quickly changed the subject to something she knew about while Stacey took pity on her and held her wagon back a bit, putting some distance between the blonde and the women who were still playfully ribbing her about asking the tall gunslinger who Rosy and her friends were.

When they stopped for a break, Josie took the opportunity to scout ahead, resting Phoenix further along the trail while waiting for them to catch up. Rebecca entertained the women with a story while they ate and soon everyone forgot about the question the blonde woman had for the gunslinger. The routine repeated itself at every break with Josie remaining far away until they finally stopped for the night. The sun was a bright orange in the lower western sky when the wagons were unpacked, and camp was set up while Josie and two other women went to the river to catch some fish. The gunslinger used her knives, throwing them with deadly accuracy as she pinned one fish after another to the sandy streambed before scooping them up and tossing them on the bank for the others to clean.

One of the girls found some wild scallions growing on the edge of the river and quickly harvested them for the evening meal.

Rebecca decided to wait to ask Josie her question until after dinner. The gunslinger always seemed more relaxed after a good meal. Night had fallen and only the warm glow of the fire gave them any light. Josie tossed another log on the fire and settled back against the wagon wheel, mug of coffee in hand. Rebecca poured herself some and sat down next to her. "Josie, can I ask you a question?"

"You just did," she replied as she brought the cup to her mouth.

"Do you know who Rosy Palm and her five friends are?"

Coffee sprayed from Josie's mouth, dribbling down her chin to soak her neck and shirt with the hot liquid as she looked at Rebecca in astonishment at the question. Howls of laughter were heard around the camp as the other women realized what had happened. The gunslinger leveled a stern gaze at them that, although diminished by the lack of light, still managed to quiet down the group. She grabbed Rebecca by the wrist and pulled her to her feet, forcing her to follow her until they were out of earshot.

Once Josie was certain they would not be overheard, she stopped and released her grip on her friend's wrist. She kept her back to Rebecca. "What did they say to you?"

"Well...I asked Victoria...um...about sex." She was beginning to seriously regret having asked the woman about the subject. "And she said that only those people knew how to do it right." There was a long pause before Rebecca spoke again. "Josie, do you know who they are?" She watched as the gunslinger scratched her head while obviously trying to find the right words to explain. She turned around and grabbed the blonde woman's wrist, turning the hand around.

"You see this?" she asked, describing a wide circle with her finger in the middle of Rebecca's hand. "This is rosy palm, and these..." Josie pointed to her fingers and let her voice trail off as a look of almost comprehension came into the younger woman's eyes.

"Oh," Rebecca said quietly, still not quite understanding. She wiggled her fingers and thought about what Victoria had said. It finally came to her just what they were suggesting Rosy's "friends" do, and Rebecca's eyes grew wide. "Oh!" she exclaimed.

"Rebecca, it's a natural thing. Everyone does it," she said, although she found herself unable to meet the eyes of her friend. "We just don't talk about it," she added.

"Well...um...I see...well all right, thanks for explaining that." She turned and started to walk briskly back to camp. It took only a few strides of the gunslinger's longer, more powerful legs to catch up to her.

"Rebecca," she said softly, turning her around to face her. "You don't have to be embarrassed about this."

"W-we didn't talk about things like...like that."

Josie put her hands on the younger woman's shoulders and gently squeezed. "Rebecca, listen to me. Nothing that feels that good can be bad." She let go and took a step back, her face betraying no emotions. "We need to get back to camp," she said firmly, ending the discussion.

The gunslinger was settled quite nicely into her blankets when Rebecca scooted up next to her and whispered in her ear. "Do you?"

"Do I what?" the half-awake woman mumbled before realizing what she meant. "Oh, sometimes," she said matter-of-factly. "Go to sleep, Rebecca."

"Sorry, good night."

"'Night."

"Sorry."

"Rebecca...." The gunslinger whispered in a low warning tone. The blonde quietly moved away and the only sound to be heard was the crackling of the banked fire and the soft snickers of the eavesdroppers to the conversation.

28: Making Friends

All the next morning Rebecca had a six-foot shadow. Once the gun-slinger realized that all the laughter the previous day was at her friend's expense, she refused to leave her alone with the more worldly women. Despite her lack of education, Victoria understood the tall woman's actions and the reason why. Josie tossed the metal coffee mug into the back of their wagon and reached for Phoenix's saddle. "Let's try not to wake up the dead with all the noise today," she said firmly. The gunslinger made eye contact with each one of them, silently conveying a different message, one that was easily understood…no picking on her young friend.

The next three days passed quickly. The small caravan continued its trek westward until the river took a turn north. The breaks were less frequent as the women adjusted to the long ride and required fewer stops to rest. Rebecca and Victoria continued to ride in the back of the first wagon, although the conversation never went anywhere near the subject that embarrassed the blonde so much. Only Josie noticed the recent horse tracks. She shortened the distance between her and the wagons. Their route took them through a small canyon full of blind turns and twists, all of which served to heighten the gunslinger's anxiety. Removing her remaining gun from its holster, she now wished she had not given the other firearm to Stacey and the shotgun to Elaine to protect the wagons.

The short hairs on the back of Josie's neck prickled, but it was too late. Three riders appeared in the path ahead, all fully armed and aiming straight at them. Her blue eyes narrowed when she realized that the leader was none other than Lefty Brown, the man she wanted to capture back in Rosewood. She pulled Phoenix to a stop, her mind calculating whether she could get all three of them before they managed to get a shot off. A commotion behind her caused the gunslinger to turn in the saddle. Two more men appeared from behind them, their shotguns pointed at the women in the rear wagon. Lefty laughed, showing a mouth of crooked yellow teeth. "Well, well... lookie what we found, boys." His brown eyes locked on the gun in Josie's hand. He moved his horse forward and disarmed the tall woman who offered no resistance. From the clothing he assumed her to be the leader of the group and thus the most dangerous. With a vicious laugh, he landed the butt of his gun against her temple, sending the gunslinger pitching forward into blackness.

The small adobe structure served as the gang's hideout. There was no roof to block the sun and draperies hung on ropes strung about served to separate the area into two rooms. The nine women were against one wall, pieces of rope keeping their hands behind their backs. The unconscious Josie was in the corner, her temple purple from the force of the blow. Lefty turned the bowie knife he had taken from the gunslinger's boot over and over in his hand, admiring the quality for a moment before fixing his attention on something else he admired. "Hey Johnny, you picked one out yet?" he called to the short, squat man kneeling in front of the women.

"Oh hell, Lefty, you know they're all the same at the bottom," he replied, reaching out with a grimy paw to squeeze the redhead's breast. Stacey closed her eyes, knowing there was no way to avoid the inevitable as Johnny pulled her roughly to her feet. As they headed to the other side of the curtain, she put her mind into a working mode, pretending that this was just another paying customer instead of a man intent on raping her. One by one, the other men stepped forward and chose their pleasures. The women went without protest, knowing from experience that it was of no use. As Elaine was being led away, she swore they would all pay if any of her girls got hurt.

Victoria and Rebecca were sitting next to each other, the remaining two women several feet away. The gunslinger still had not stirred, heightening Rebecca's fear as Lefty moved forward and squatted in front of the two young women. It took all of her control not to cry or whimper when he reached forward and slowly ran the point of the blade across her right breast, not deep enough to cut, but firm enough to make his intentions clear. Victoria found her voice. "Sassy, did you get rid of that itch yet?"

It took only a second for Rebecca to understand what her friend was doing. "Uh...no. Doc says I need a cream or something," she replied, squirming slightly as if trying to ease the imaginary discomfort between her legs. The blade retreated as Lefty backed away from her. He did not know if the bitches were lying or not but he had no intention of finding out. The little blonde was not worth it.

"Looks like yer it, sweet thing," he said as he turned his attentions to Victoria.

Josie listened to the exchange with her eyes still closed to feign unconsciousness as her fingers worked to slip under her belt, finding the small slit that hid the secret compartment. With dexterity born out of practice, she released the small knife from its hiding place and sliced through the ropes soundlessly. The ropes fell loosely to the ground behind her as she gripped the tip of the blade between her right thumb and forefinger. The blue eyes opened and focused as she brought her arm around. With a flick of the wrist, she sent the small blade through the air with blinding speed and force, imbedding it deep into Lefty's neck, severing his jugular as well as his windpipe. In an instant she was upon him, taking the bowie knife from his hand and imbedding it deep into his chest. She took just a second to look at Rebecca before removing the weapon from his lifeless body. Josie cut the bonds that held the young women and retrieved her revolvers. Without a sound, she slipped between the curtains. Four shots rang out, the proximity hurting Rebecca's ears.

Elaine looked down at the man lying dead at her feet. Looking around, she saw Josie helping Stacey roll the dead man off her while the other two women ran from the room. The gunslinger did not see the man slowly rising to his feet, blood covering the front of his filthy shirt. He brought his gun up, his dying energy spent trying to aim. Elaine reached down and grabbed the gun from the holster of the dead man at her feet and fired. Josie's head snapped around to see and her blue eyes locked with the hazel eyes of the prostitute. Both nodded slightly in silent appreciation of the other.

The women assembled in the larger room. Victoria took the knife from Lefty's throat and used it to free the other two women. Rebecca never moved from her position except to draw her knees up and bury her head in her arms as her body shook. Josie knelt down next to her, uncertain of what to say. The young woman sensed her presence and flung herself against the gunslinger with enough force to knock the older woman back on her rear. The events and emotions caught up with Rebecca as she wrapped her arms around Josie's neck and sobbed. Some of her tears were for herself, for how close she had come to being raped, but some were for her new friends, who actually were. Prostitutes or not, they were still women taken against their will and Rebecca could not stop herself from crying.

Josie was clearly uncomfortable with the outpouring of emotions, but she made no effort to extricate herself from her friend, instead placing a stiff arm against Rebecca's back and squeezing slightly. She waited a couple of minutes for the young woman's breathing to calm down before she moved her arm and stiffened her back, silently indicating the end of the embrace. Rebecca sniffled and sat back, wiping her eyes with the sleeves of her shirt. Josie looked over at Elaine, silently pleading for help. The black-headed woman understood and whispered something in Victoria's ear. The young woman went over, sitting cross-legged next to Rebecca and putting her hand on her shoulder. Elaine followed and stood behind them, facing the gunslinger.

"Can you help me get the bodies on the wagon?"

"I guess we'd better," Josie said and rose a little too enthusiastically, grateful for the excuse to get away. Victoria spoke quietly with Rebecca, keeping the young woman distracted as the dead bodies were dragged out.

The dead men were piled into the back of the whore's wagon while the women sat either in the back of the lead wagon, or rode the men's horses. They used a piece of canvas found at the hideout to cover the bodies to keep the sun from rotting them any quicker than necessary, and to keep the buzzards away. The gunslinger pushed the group hard, wanting to get to town as soon as possible. It was close to nightfall when they saw the first signs of Fort Laramie. A collective sigh of relief was heard when Josie pulled the group to a stop a mile outside of town. She pulled Phoenix alongside the lead wagon. "We need to bring the bodies to the marshal. Elaine, you come with me. You others stay here." She leveled her gaze at Rebecca to make certain she was understood. Seeing her nod in assent, Josie looked over the rest of the group. "You might as well set up camp; I don't think we'll be back before morning."

Josie stopped the wagon in front of the jail and handed the reins to Elaine before getting out. She entered the building and returned a few minutes later with a stack of wanted posters and the marshal. He held a lantern up near the faces of the dead men. "Well, looks like Lefty, all right," he said, double-checking his information on the wanted poster. "Them others look familiar too. Lemme see." He took the pile of posters from Josie and shuffled through them, pulling out the ones that seemed to be possibilities. Within an hour, they had identified three of the men as being wanted, with the total sum running just over two hundred dollars. The gunslinger was a bit disappointed in the bounty, but said nothing as she followed the marshal and the wagon to the undertaker's place on the edge of town. Once their business was done, Josie made arrangements with the marshal to meet her at the bank in the morning while Elaine took the horses and wagon to the stable.

Josie had just enough money to get a small room in the flophouse after paying for the stable and a few drinks in the saloon. The room was lit with one small lantern, casting a dim, orange glow throughout the room. "What are you going to do now?" Elaine asked as she sat on the edge of the bed. The gunslinger reached down and untied the leather straps that held her holsters to her thighs.

"We'll get the money in the morning and replenish the supplies. It'll take a couple days to get to Cheyenne, and I have a friend there who can help." She removed her gun belts and set them on the floor next to the bed before sitting down and pulling off her boots.

"Josie..." Elaine began, not looking at the tall woman seated next to her. "I wanted to thank you...for everything." She turned to study the gunslinger's profile. As the bounty hunter tucked her boots under the bed, Elaine rose and removed her dress to stand before Josie, clad only in the thinnest and most revealing of slips. "I really want to thank you," she said seductively, moving closer and straddling the gunslinger's hips.

"You don't have..." Josie began.

"Shh," Elaine said, silencing the protest with her lips. "I want to." Her hands reached for the buttons of Josie's shirt.

Back at camp, the women finished off the last of their liquor supply while Rebecca entertained them with one of her endless cache of stories. She occasionally pretended to take a sip as the bottle was passed back and forth, but in fact carefully avoided allowing the liquid to run into her mouth. The events of the day faded away as several women began to tell raunchy stories and jokes. While the conversation was slightly embarrassing to Rebecca, it was not as bad as when they first started, and she had became comfortable enough to laugh with them at some of the jokes. They all settled in early, mostly because of the booze. Rebecca laid her blanket down next to the wagon wheel, apart from the others. She had a second blanket that usually cushioned her from the hard earth, but realizing the others did not have true blankets had offered it up for use. Coupled with both of Josie's and the saddle blankets, there were just enough to go around.

Rolling up Josie's duster and using it for a pillow, Rebecca settled down onto the firm earth. Time drifted as her thoughts swirled aimlessly before settling on one thought. Rebecca opened one eye and looked about. The others were in various stages of sleeping and paid no attention to her. She nervously brought her hand under the blanket and unbuttoned most of her shirt. Slowly her hand crept beneath the cotton material, her fingertips fluttering across her nipple to make the coral skin harden and contract to a point. Her fingers splayed out as she rubbed her palm across the tip before squeezing the whole mound firmly. *Oh yes, this feels so good.* Her other hand crept under the cover, giving both breasts equal attention. In her mind, she saw the knight ravishing the princess, still in his suit of armor, his face hidden. Her thumb and forefingers captured her hard nipples, rolling and pinching them as she arched into her own touch. Her breathing quickened as she continued to pleasure her breasts and the heat increased between her legs.

Slowly lowering her right hand down, she unbuttoned her britches, her left hand never easing up on its assault of her nipple. She reached beneath her under drawers and let her fingers comb through her soft, blonde curls. She let out a soft sigh as her fingertips touched the wet ringlets. The tight britches denied her access to her most private area. Opening her eyes, she looked over at the women before bringing her other hand down to help push the clothes off her hips and down until she could spread her knees apart. *I can't believe I'm doing this,* she thought but the rational part of her mind gave way to the overpowering need. Lifting one knee up to brace her leg against the wagon, Rebecca's hand made its way between her thighs. She was surprised to find how wet and slick her thighs were until she touched her swollen outer folds and felt the flood coat her fingers. *Oh my.* She pressed against herself, the palm rubbing back and forth against her aching sex. Her middle finger slipped between the folds and pressed near her opening. Rebecca began a slow exploration of herself, her fingertips tracing every fold, discovering what felt nice and what did not. She focused on the image of the knight and princess as her middle and index fingers found themselves on either side of her most sensitive spot, and she squeezed rhythmically. *Mmm...oh yes.* Her breath started coming in short gasps and her hips moved of their own volition. She instinctively moved her fingers, pressing against the small hood of skin above the hard nub. Her blood pounded in her ears as she planted her feet and lifted her hips off the ground, her fingers never losing their position or pace as they swirled about. She gritted her teeth as a wave of indescribable pleasure gushed through her body. Letting out a small cry, Rebecca fell limply back to the now damp ground and shuddered as her body pulsed with aftershocks.

Two of the women had been wakened by the sound, but seeing nothing amiss, rolled over and went back to sleep. Rebecca lay there, wide-awake, reveling in the new sensation. It was a long time before she found the strength to reach down and fix her clothing, and even that movement caused a small shudder to pass through her. She finally got into a sleeping position, a lazy smile never leaving her face. *Josie was right,* she thought. *Nothing that feels this good could possibly be bad.*

29:   The Gift

Josie left the bank with her small pile of bills. She met Elaine at the trading post and spent most of the money getting the vast amount of supplies they would need to keep nine women going for the length of the journey. The gunslinger insisted on staying away from the smaller towns along the way, as the large group of women would most surely be noticed. On impulse, Josie went to the Express office to wire money and a telegram on to Cheyenne.

"Ready?" Elaine asked when the gunslinger returned from the Express office. Climbing up on the wagon, Josie nodded and took the reins, sending the horses into motion. She spotted the doctor's office and pulled back on the reins.

"Stay here, I'll be right back," Josie hopped down and entered the small building, returning a few minutes later with a large, heavy, dusty book. She tossed it up on the seat and climbed in, pushing it over until it was between her and Elaine. "Rebecca likes to read," was her reply to the curious look she received from the black-headed harlot. As they rode back to the camp, Elaine noticed that the gunslinger used her new bandanna to wipe away the years of built-up dust on the large book. By the time they reached the others, no one would have known the book had resided on a bottom shelf in a back closet of the doctor's office for the past ten years.

They pulled up and were quickly surrounded by the women, excitedly asking about the bounty or looking at the fresh load of supplies. Rebecca spotted the small jar of pickles. She was working on the latch that held the Mason jar closed when Victoria came over to see what she was up to. They each took a pickle and munched happily. Josie came up behind Rebecca and tapped her on the shoulder. "Come with me."

They walked over to their wagon. "I bought you something," Josie said a bit nervously as she leaned over the edge of the buckboard and hefted out the medical text.

"Oh... oh my." Rebecca took the book from the gunslinger. Even though she knew it was heavy, she was not quite prepared for the weight and Josie had to make a lightning-fast move to keep it from dropping on the young woman's toes. Rebecca opened the book, supporting the spine on the edge of the wagon, and flipped through the pages reverently, her fingers running over the lines of text and drawings.

"It's a beginner's medical text," Josie said, stating the obvious to the overjoyed blonde. Rebecca set the book back in the wagon and gave the gunslinger a huge hug.

"Thank you so much," she gushed as she continued to squeeze against Josie. The appreciation was so genuine and the affection so honest that the normally stoic bounty hunter smiled and gave Rebecca's shoulders a gentle squeeze.

When she pulled back, Josie frowned as she saw the tears spilling out from Rebecca's eyes. She fought the urge to wipe them from the blonde's cheeks. *I won't get attached to you, Rebecca*, she thought, but could not stop herself from asking, "What's wrong?"

"It's just that... well no one ever gave me something so... so wonderful before," she said as she wiped the tears from her face. "I don't know what to say." She looked up at the gunslinger with a smile that could warm the coldest of hearts. Josie smiled, but clearly looked uncomfortable. Rebecca realized this and gave the gunslinger a gentle squeeze on the forearm. "Thank you, Josie."

"Sure. Glad you liked it. I'd better go help get the gear unloaded."

"Uh, yeah, right. Good idea," Rebecca said, the smile never leaving her face. As soon as the gunslinger left, she pulled the book out and sat on the ground. She did not move until dinnertime except to turn the page. Had someone paid close attention to Josie, they would have noticed her smile every time she looked over at the voracious reader.

Dinner of salt pork and beans was eaten in shifts, as they had only the few plates they had taken from the men whose final stupid plan had involved an attempted rape of Rebecca. Only a few utensils were purchased since the money was best used on meats and supplies. The funds that Josie spent on Rebecca's book kept her from getting a keg of ale she had been looking forward to, but she had no regrets. Rebecca was still sitting against the wagon with the book in her lap. She was eating and reading at the same time, trying to absorb as much as possible before the sun set for the evening. Victoria tried to talk to her a couple of times, but the blonde smiled apologetically and pointed at the book. Only when the light became so dim that it hurt her eyes to read did Rebecca set the book back gingerly in the wagon and join the others. Josie sat apart from the rest, leaning against a tree cleaning her guns. She frowned at the multitude of fingerprints that littered her Winchester. *What'd they do, all take turns touching it?* she wondered as she ran the oily cloth up and down the barrel.

For the next several days, the routine stayed the same. Up at dawn, ride until noon, rest for a while, ride until almost sunset, and then camp for the night. The bumpy ride made it impossible for Rebecca to read so she spent most of her time in the back of the wagon with Victoria. The supplies were split between the two wagons since the women were now riding the horses taken from the dead men. Josie drove her wagon with Phoenix tethered behind, while Stacey's wagon brought up the rear with the extra horses nestled safely between them. While the gunslinger appreciated the respite from the blonde's usual chatter, she found herself listening every so often to the two young women talking behind her, smiling when she heard Rebecca tell something funny. Even though the blonde became close to the women - Victoria in particular - Josie kept her distance from the group whenever possible. Every so often she would exchange a knowing glance with Elaine, but never did she approach her. Both understood the reasons why. Repeat performances create complications.

The late summer sun gave way to an unseasonably cold night. The fire gave off some heat, but there was no way for all nine women to sleep around it. Several of the women coupled off to share body heat and blankets; only Stacey remained alone, taking up the fourth side of the fire. Rebecca set hers and Josie's blankets down next to the wagon in a heap. "Josie, aren't we sleeping by the fire?" she asked as she watched the gunslinger remove the items from the ground and set them neatly back in the wagon.

"No, there's not enough room. And it'll be warmer up here in the back of the wagon than on the ground." She pulled the sheepskin from the seat and laid it out in the back, covering it with one of her blankets. Rebecca walked to the other side of the wagon and helped to straighten out the covers as they made their makeshift bed. Without thinking, she pulled Josie's rolled up duster out of the pile of belongings and set it at the head of the blankets. The gunslinger arched an eyebrow and looked at her for an explanation.

"Oh, this? Well, I uh... kinda borrowed it," Rebecca said sheepishly. Josie reached out and moved the duster from the blonde's side of the wagon to her side.

"If it's going to be used as a pillow, at least I should be the one to use it."

There was enough room between them for a third person to have fit comfortably, yet Josie still felt the young woman shiver. She mentally berated herself for not making space for Rebecca at the fire, not counting on the temperature dropping quite so much. She moved closer and pressed her body up against the young woman's back. "I didn't think it would be this cold," she said apologetically.

"I didn't say anything," Rebecca said softly, yet her body instinctively moved closer to Josie's, craving the body heat.

"I know. Lift your head," she said, placing part of the rolled up duster under Rebecca's head. Their bodies shifted and moved as they adjusted to each other. Josie was not totally certain she could sleep so close to another person. Even during the night with Elaine, she slept on her side of the bed, making certain there was space between them. She laid awake for a few moments as one thought continued to race through her mind. "Why?"

"Hmm?" the half-awake blonde responded.

"Why, Rebecca?" She propped herself up on one elbow and looked down at her. "Why didn't you tell me you were so cold?"

Rebecca rolled onto her back and looked up, the gunslinger's blue eyes demanding the truth. "I... I didn't want you to think I couldn't handle one night in the cold," she said in a small voice, unsure of what Josie's reaction would be. The gunslinger understood the implication behind the words.

"Roll over." She settled back down and wrapped one long arm around the blonde woman's waist. "Don't do that again. And I don't think that," she added softly. She felt Rebecca relax against her, soon falling into a deep sleep. The gunslinger laid awake a while longer, watching the steady rise and fall of the young woman's chest and wondering just what it was about the little sprite that made her care so much about her. Years of running and depending on no one but herself had built a wall of armor around her heart that no one could penetrate. Josie cared for no one and no one cared for her. That was just how it was and she always felt comfortable with that fact. Then came Rebecca; in a mere three months she had managed to make the gunslinger care for her, enough to give up her own personal pleasures for the sake of a smile. "My friend," she whispered to the sleeping form in front of her. Josie allowed herself to relax and be lulled to sleep by the blonde's gentle snoring.

30: Called Out

Several miles from Cheyenne the group came upon a covered wagon all but blocking the trail and preventing them from passing. A large blonde woman with deep green eyes sat patiently on the seat. A small scar-faced man sat next to her, holding the reins. On the ground next to the wagon a cat lay curled up. He was white except for dark gray feet, face, and ears. Nervous looks were exchanged between the women as Josie pulled the wagon to a stop. "Stay here," she said firmly to Rebecca as she hopped out and walked over to the covered wagon.

The young woman watched the gunslinger, noting the way Josie's hands never strayed far from her talking irons as she approached the strangers. Even in situations that did not appear to hold any danger Josie felt the need to be on her guard. The blonde in the covered wagon climbed down, aided by the gunslinger's strong arms.

"It's so good to see you," she said as she wrapped her arms around the woman in black.

"It's good to see you too, Sandy," Josie replied, taking a step back from the embrace. She looked up at the small man. "Earl," she said with a nod, receiving the same in response.

"Your wire said you needed help," Sandy said as she walked with Josie back to the caravan.

"I don't; these women do," the gunslinger replied, waving with her arm to indicate the others. Sandy looked from one woman to the next, mentally assessing them. Elaine dismounted and walked over to her. The others took that as their cue to dismount. Many of them were rubbing their aching thighs and rears from the long ride. Rebecca climbed down and stood just behind Josie, close enough to hear the conversations without being in the way.

After brief introductions, they settled down to business. "I have room for five women, but if necessary, I can probably find positions for the others at one of the other houses," Sandy said. Her eyes locked on the small blonde standing behind the gunslinger. "I don't know about this one, Josie. She looks a little too innocent. Reminds men of their daughters. A serving girl, perhaps."

Rebecca's eyes flashed indignantly, but she held her tongue. Josie smirked at her friend before turning to face Sandy. "She's with me."

"Didn't think you went for the young ones, Josie," Sandy quipped, drawing a confused look from Rebecca and a warning glare from the gunslinger.

"Can we get going?" Josie asked, but it was more of a statement.

"Yes, of course." Sandy turned her attention to the prostitutes. "I don't want to be seen bringing all of you into town. You'll have to hide in the back of my wagon."

One by one the women were put in the safety of the covered wagon. Only Josie, Rebecca, Stacey, and Elaine remained behind to deal with the horses and wagons. Sandy scooped up the purring feline and climbed back up into the seat on her wagon. The short man snapped the reins and set the horses into motion, turning in a wide arc to head back into town. Josie waited a few minutes before indicating that everyone should mount up.

"What's going on?" Rebecca asked once they were settled back on the sheepskin-covered seat. Josie slapped the reins on her flanks to get Flossy going before answering.

"Sandy operates the largest whorehouse in Cheyenne. She'll take care of them, give them jobs."

"But why hide them in the back of the wagon?"

"Can you imagine what would happen if people see a half dozen whores suddenly show up in town? Sandy will slip them in through a back entrance. In time no one will realize they weren't there before." Although it seemed perfectly clear to her, Josie did not seem to mind explaining everything to her young friend. "We'll enter separately and get a room at the boarding house."

Seeing that Rebecca was satisfied with her explanation, Josie concentrated on guiding Flossy to the livery stable with Elaine following on her horse, leading one of the rider-less mares. Stacey brought up the rear as usual, the remaining horses tethered to the back of her wagon. A heated discussion occurred at the livery between the gunslinger and the stable owner over the price. Rebecca was certain that Josie was at the point of handling the situation with her irons when she stepped in, smiling pleasantly.

"Sir, you see these fine pieces of horseflesh?" she indicated the small string of horses. "What are they worth to you?" He rubbed the stubble on his chin as his mind worked feverishly to come up with a price.

"Best I can do is one hundred dollars for the whole lot, including the wagons."

"What!" Josie said loudly, pushing Rebecca gently out of the way so she could tower over the man.

"Uh... er... I mean..."

"You mean that two hundred for the horses alone is a fair price. That also includes stabling the others and storing the wagons." Her deep blue eyes dared him to argue.

"Uh... yeah," he said, defeated.

"I could have gotten a better price for the horses, you know," Rebecca said as they walked to the saloon. Stacey and Elaine walked behind them, exchanging amused glances as the young woman made the statement for the third time in as many minutes. As before, Josie chose to simply ignore the comment. Rebecca let out an exasperated huff and scowled. "If you would have just been patient."

"I didn't feel like waiting an hour for the two of you to haggle," Josie replied matter-of-factly as they reached the saloon. The scowl was replaced with a look of hurt, reaching straight into the gunslinger's heart and filling her with guilt. She looked back at the others. "You two go on ahead. Sandy will be waiting for you. We'll be along."

Stacey and Elaine nodded, understanding the two women's need to have a moment of privacy. Josie pulled Rebecca away from the swinging doors and out of sight of the other women. "Rebecca, I'm sorry I didn't want to wait. I have no doubt that you could have talked him up on the price. Next time I'll be more patient." She managed to get the words out without choking on them. Apologizing was something that the gunslinger just did not do, but looking at the hurt in Rebecca's eyes and knowing she was the cause was more than she could bear. She would have said anything to see a smile on that sweet, young face.

"Come on, you can make it up to me with dinner in that nice restaurant I saw as we entered town," Rebecca said, forcing a smile to her face to show the gunslinger she was not upset at her anymore. The comment Josie made about the next time filled the young woman's heart with hope. It was the first time the bounty hunter had spoken to her as though they would be together in the future.

"Deal," Josie said, showing a smile full of teeth. "I need a drink. Let's go."

The saloon was typical of a large city. The long bar covered the left wall while the right wall contained a small stage and piano. Straight ahead was the white staircase that led to the pleasures upstairs. Scattered about were several round tables, mostly empty as the men were still working in the mines or fields. A large chandelier hung auspiciously in the center of the room, the intricate design clearly out of place in the dusty tavern. The light from the multitude of candles reflected through the teardrop-shaped pieces of lead glass, casting a soft glow on the room. Josie looked around and noted that the women were all upstairs. The parched feeling in her throat helped her make her decision. "We're going to have a drink first, then we'll go check on everyone," she said, knowing that Rebecca would want to see how Victoria was doing.

"Sure," Rebecca agreed. Her mouth was as hot and dry as the gunslinger's. They moseyed up to the bar and sat down on adjacent stools. As the bartender approached, Rebecca felt Josie press a dollar bill into her hand under the edge of the bar. The gunslinger kept her eyes on the bartender and acted as if nothing had happened.

"Whiskey," Josie said firmly. "And an ale."

"Sarsaparilla," Rebecca added. The gunslinger watched out of the corner of her eye as the young woman paid for the drinks with the bill she had been given. Although Josie's face showed no signs as to her thoughts, inside she was smiling at the look of pride on Rebecca's face.

They were on their second round of drinks when a large boar of a man entered, flanked by two smaller but equally evil-looking men. Josie watched them through the mirror behind the bar as they looked around the saloon. The bartender nonchalantly pulled on a rope that extended through the ceiling to a bell upstairs. The men took up residence two stools down from the bounty hunter. Within minutes, Sandy came down the stairs with Bobo bounding down after her. She fixed the largest of the newcomers with a glare and hissed at him.

"Felix! I told you to stay out of here," she said as she approached the corner of the bar, making sure she was out of arm's reach.

"Now, Miss Sandy, you know what happened was an accident," he said as if it were true, sending the men with him into laughter. "I was just havin' a bit o' fun."

"Your bit of fun cost me one of my best girls," she snarled. "Now you get out of here. None of the girls want anything to do with you."

Felix moved off his stool slowly, the look on his face menacing as he took a step closer to the madam. "She said for you to leave," Josie said firmly, her attention seeming to never leave the glass in front of her. Felix stopped his advance and turned to look at the woman in black.

"You got somethin' to say, woman?" he said, the last word spoken more as an insult. "Try usin' yer talking irons."

"You calling me out?" she replied as she downed the last of her ale. Rebecca's eyes grew wide as she followed the route of the conversation.

"Josie..." she hissed, pulling on the gunslinger's forearm to get her attention. "What are you doing?" Josie slid off the stool gracefully, her imposing frame towering over the smaller woman.

"Go with Sandy...now," she said in a tone that brooked no arguments. Josie walked to the door, deliberately keeping her gaze away from the young woman's face. Sandy walked past the men and put her arm around Rebecca's shoulders.

"Come on, child. This is no place for you right now," she said as the men followed the gunslinger outside, joking and slapping Felix on the back in anticipation of his victory.

"No!" Rebecca yelped, wrenching herself from the older woman's grasp. Sandy quickly recovered and wrapped both arms around the smaller woman's waist, pinning her arms. Jon, the bartender, frantically pulled on the rope, getting the attention of the women upstairs. Elaine was the first to arrive, skipping half the steps in her haste.

"Child, please, Josie doesn't want you out there," Sandy said, trying to get the squirming woman to understand. Elaine assessed the situation quickly and went to the doorway. In the middle of the street, Josie and Felix stood paces apart, paying no attention to the rapidly growing crowd of spectators. An enterprising man with a short, black goatee was taking bets on the outcome, favoring the man with the bandoleers over the tall woman. Rebecca worked her way free by relaxing her leg muscles, sinking out of the madam's grasp. Elaine grabbed her at the doorway.

"Rebecca, don't you understand? Whatever happened, she can't back down now," Elaine said and then watched as a flicker of understanding appeared in the green eyes. She lowered her tone. "If you go out there, you'll only distract her. You don't want that, do you?"

"No," Rebecca said softly. It was obvious that the young woman was terrified for the gunslinger and very near the point of tears.

"You don't need to watch this," Elaine offered. Rebecca sniffled and cleared her throat, straightening her back and raising her chin.

"Yes, I do," she said firmly. Elaine nodded and stepped to the side to make room for her to see out the doorway. Victoria came up behind them and put her hand on Rebecca's shoulder, squeezing softly.

Josie's fingers twitched, flexing and relaxing in anticipation. She watched his movements carefully. He seemed relaxed and assured, as if no one could draw faster than him, let alone a woman. He reached for his gun, his fingers closing around the familiar piece of steel. He only got as far as pulling it out of his holster when his chest took the impact of Josie's bullet. It was over in the blink of an eye. The gunslinger stood there, smoking gun drawn, looking at the mortally wounded man slumping forward. His face registered his profound surprise as he pitched forward, dead before he hit the ground. For a moment no one moved except for the man with the goatee, who decided that sticking around was not such a good idea. Josie holstered her weapon as Felix's friends dragged his body off the street. The marshal waited for her at the doors to the saloon.

"Nice shooting," he commented as she passed. Her face was an unreadable mask.

"I did what I had to do. He called me out." She pushed her way through the doors and was quickly hugged by an emotional Rebecca. Josie stiffened and pulled back, giving the young woman a quick squeeze on her upper arms. In a tone that only Rebecca could hear, she said. "I'm all right, Sprite."

The barkeep set the bottle of whiskey and a fresh glass of ale on the counter in front of Josie. Sandy moved over and spoke quietly with the marshal. Rebecca felt the last of her reserves waning and raced out of the saloon, Victoria at her heels. Josie looked at the retreating form, debating about whether to follow her or not.

"Let her go," Elaine said from just behind the gunslinger. Josie turned to look at her. "She was pretty upset. Hasn't she seen you kill before?" she asked as she led the bounty hunter back to the bar. Josie downed the shot of whiskey and drained half of her glass of ale before answering.

"Not like that. She's never seen me called out before." Josie stared into the amber liquid, suddenly feeling very empty. Elaine recognized the look; she had seen it on the faces of countless men over the years.

"Josie..." she said softly, running a fingernail up the length of the powerful forearm. For a brief moment the thought of drowning herself in the throes of carnal pleasure appealed to the gunslinger, but only for a brief moment. She stood up.

"I'd better go find Rebecca," she said, politely refusing the offer. Elaine gave a little smile of understanding.

"I'll be here if you need me, Josie. You're welcome...anytime," the last word said in an unmistakable tone of invitation. Elaine turned and went up the stairs, giving a most flirtatious smile to the barkeep as she passed. It never hurt to get in good with the bartender. It always made for the best chance of getting the better clients.

Rebecca sat on the ground with her back pressed up against the back of the building. The alleyway was empty except for her and Victoria. "Why did she do it?" she said between tears. "Doesn't she realize how easily she could have been killed?"

"Dunno," Victoria replied. "Suppose she must. Bet she had done it before."

"Then why? Why take such a chance?" Rebecca said as she picked up a small stone and flung it as hard as she could against the building on the other side of the alleyway.

"She's not like you, Rebecca. She a killer, that's fer sure. In her blood, I think. She said he called her out. A killer can't not go then. Looks bad," Victoria said, hoping that her words would help, but noticing that the expression of anger and fear did not leave her friend's face. "If she didn't, he'd have killed her right there in the saloon."

"There has to be another way," Rebecca said adamantly. "She shouldn't keep putting herself in danger like that. She was out there, right in the open. If she wanted to, she could have talked her way out of it."

"She ain't you, Rebecca. She talks with her guns, not her mouth. If you don't accept it, you'd best git away from her afore ya git yer heart broke."

Rebecca watched as Victoria stood and headed back to the saloon. She remained there for a few minutes more, letting the waves of emotions run their course. Josie watched silently from the edge of the alleyway, not moving until she saw the young woman wipe the tears from her face and stand up. The gunslinger crossed the remaining distance between them. There was a long silence as blue eyes met green, Rebecca's unguarded face betraying all of her emotions. Finally she broke the silence.

"I know why you did it, Josie, but I don't have to like it," she said firmly.

"No, I suppose you don't," the gunslinger agreed. "But you also can't get in my way or we could both be killed."

"Josie, am I your friend?" she asked softly, her eyes begging for a response. Josie took a step forward and put her hands on the young woman's shoulders.

"Being my friend will only put you in danger, Rebecca, but yes... you are my friend," the gunslinger said firmly, admitting it to both of them. For a moment, she allowed herself to feel the tenderness of the moment, the feeling of knowing that she was not alone anymore, that they were no longer two people traveling together, but now something more, something much deeper. Friends. The word echoing through her head brought a rare smile to her face. "Come on, friend. Let's mosey over to the restaurant and get something for dinner."

The mention of food paled in significance to "friend," but Rebecca readily agreed to the offer of a warm meal, happy just to be with Josie. As they passed the theater, the young woman's eyes lit up at the sign announcing a performance later that evening. Then she saw the admission price of four bits per person and the smile left her face. The gunslinger noted both and smiled to herself, knowing exactly where they would be going after dinner.

31: An Evening Together

At Rebecca's insistence, they stopped at the boarding house to relieve the gunslinger of some of her weapons. Josie had started to protest, but the young woman explained that it was bad enough that her clothes would make people nervous. A pair of deadly revolvers might make the other patrons too scared to eat. While the bounty hunter reluctantly acknowledged this fact, she still made a point of carrying her knives in their various locations. There was no way she was going to be completely unarmed.

Josie received a curious and mostly disgusted look from the waitress, but stubbornly waited to be seated. She was not surprised when the short, round woman led them to a table in the far corner, near the kitchen and most likely the least enjoyable spot in the place. As they made their way, Josie kept her hand resting lightly on the small of Rebecca's back, guiding her through the maze of chairs and potted cactus that littered the area. A stout man at a nearby table rose and held the chair out for Rebecca as they arrived. Josie was pleased by the respectable gesture, as unusual as it was in that part of the country, but nonetheless kept her eye on him for any sign of trouble. He smiled and returned to his wife and son at his table.

"Thank you, sir," Rebecca said sweetly as he pushed in her chair. He moved over to get Josie's chair but the gunslinger waved him off and pulled it out herself. They waited ten minutes for the waitress to pass by and drop off the menus. Rebecca thought that Josie was fuming inside as the minutes passed, and then she was certain of it from the slight tenseness in the gunslinger's jaw and the almost imperceptible narrowing of her eyes. Yet Josie said nothing, merely studying the patterns on the utensils or glancing about the room. Rebecca had tried to make small talk, but the bounty hunter's attention kept shifting to the other patrons and the young woman gave up.

"Sorry, what was that?"

"I said the beef looks good," Rebecca replied, hoping to draw Josie's attention back to her and away from the rest of the room. The gunslinger gave a quick lopsided grin and looked at the menu for the first time.

"I have a hankering for the elk. Where is that woman anyway?" Josie said, looking around the room. As if she could feel the blue eyes boring into her back, the waitress turned around from chatting with a patron and saw that the two women were ready. The glare she received from the tall one in black guaranteed that she would return immediately with their drinks.

While waiting for their dinner to arrive, Rebecca chatted about the new things she had learned from the medical book Josie had purchased. Josie smiled and paid attention, noting that the young woman did not mention any diseases or give any detailed descriptions that might have affected the enjoyment of dinner. "You know, Josie, it says that some of the best medicines are known only to the Indians."

"That's true," the gunslinger replied, letting a bit of pride show through. "The Medicine Elders - you call them medicine men - know far more about herbs and roots than the white man does."

"I'll bet I could learn a lot from one of them," Rebecca mused softly. The words did not escape Josie's ears as an idea formed in her mind. Perhaps she could take her to the Cherokees, to her people, and let her learn the medicines of old. The gunslinger was well aware of the need for good healers.

"I'm sure you could, Rebecca. Would you like that? To meet a real Medicine Elder and learn from him?" In her mind, the gunslinger was calculating just how far they were from the Cherokees, less than three weeks by wagon over the Cimarron Crossing. It was more dangerous than the Cheyenne Trail, but was also more direct. The trail would take them at least another week to ten days, adding considerably to the cost of their supplies.

"Oh, Josie, I'd love to. I could learn so much more than the book can teach me," she said enthusiastically. The waitress arrived with the platter containing their dinners. Both women were silent while the not-so-nice-smelling woman plopped their plates down in front of them.

"Anything else?" she asked, moving quickly away without waiting for an answer. Rebecca reached out and placed her hand on top of the gunslinger's fist.

"Josie..."

"I'm fine. Just don't care for the likes of her," she replied as she relaxed her hand and pulled it out from under the blonde's grasp. She sampled a piece of the elk before speaking. "I can take you there."

"Take me where?" she replied around a mouth full of food.

"To meet a Medicine Elder. To learn healing." She stabbed another piece of meat with her fork. "I can take you to the Cherokees," she said as she popped the morsel in her mouth and began to chew.

Rebecca's fork stopped halfway to her mouth as she looked across the table dumbfounded. Josie smirked and took another bite of food. "Of course if you don't want to go..." she said idly, twirling her fork in the air.

"Yes! Yes, I want to go," the blonde said enthusiastically as soon as her voice returned. "Oh, Josie, that would be so wonderful!"

"Now hear me out," the gunslinger replied, setting her fork down and leaning in to give her most serious expression. "It won't be easy. We'll be going through dangerous territory."

"I don't mind," Rebecca interrupted. Josie gave a quick frown.

"The first thing you have to remember is not to interrupt me. Next is to pay attention; don't make me tell you something twice." She waited until Rebecca nodded solemnly. The gunslinger leaned back in her chair and stared at her half-eaten dinner. "Of course, that's only if you're going to keep riding with me. Any time we find a town that you think you'd be happy in...."

She did not get to finish her thought as Rebecca bolted from her chair and gave the seated woman a hug. Josie stiffened noticeably but still managed to put a smile on her face for the blonde's sake. "Rebecca, not in public," she hissed quietly but gently. The young woman gave one last squeeze before returning to her seat, smiling with a glow that melted just a little bit more of the ice surrounding the bounty hunter's heart.

The pair strolled down the street, the warm meal and dessert still settling in their bellies. Despite the waitress's surliness, they still managed to get two large pieces of pie for dessert, of which Rebecca ate hers and half of the gunslinger's. Josie deliberately shortened her normally long gait so the shorter woman would not have to walk fast to keep up. Truth be told, the bounty hunter was actually enjoying the evening. The night air was the perfect temperature; the lights from the buildings along with the half moon cast enough light to see easily. There was a gaiety about the night as families and couples headed for the theater, all chattering away happily. Men stopped to shake hands with each other while the wives exchanged pleasantries and, judging from the conspiratorial giggles in some cases, the latest gossip. As they reached their destination, Josie noted that the stout, balding man who had held Rebecca's chair at the restaurant was standing outside the entrance to the theater with what she could only assume was his wife and son. The father touched his fingers to the brim of his bowler and nodded as the women passed. Rebecca smiled and wished him a good evening, although her attention was drawn more to his son, a dapper young man who was most likely only a year or two older than she.

Rebecca went up and down the aisle, pointing out possible seats for them but the gunslinger shook her head at each one. None of the available adjoining seats were in the aisle. Josie spotted what she decided to be the perfect location, not caring that it was already occupied, and headed for it. Her long strides took her there quickly and, by the time Rebecca caught up, the young men who had been sitting in the desired seats were already heading up the aisle, suddenly deciding that the view would be much better somewhere else.

"What did you say to them?" Rebecca asked as she took the inside seat. Josie flopped back casually into hers, a knowing smirk on her face. She crossed her long legs, placing her booted foot up on her knee with the toes pressed against the seat in front of them.

"I suggested that they be gentlemen-like and offer their seats to a couple of women," the gunslinger said with feigned innocence.

"Uh huh, that's why they hightailed it to the back, huh?" the young women replied with a grin. "I can just imagine what you said to intimidate them." She leaned over and spoke in hushed tones, as if she was not stating the obvious. "You are intimidating, you know."

"Can't be too bad; haven't been able to get rid of you yet," Josie quipped without thinking. Rebecca lost her smile and straightened up, fixing her gaze on the stage.

"Do you want to, Josie?" she asked fearfully, not daring to look at the gunslinger.

Her mind raced; the skills and techniques she had used over the years to avoid any kind of commitment or responsibility snapped into place as the answer came to her. "How can I get rid of you, Sprite? Even if I tried, you'd probably just follow me anyway," she said as she gave the young woman a playful shove on the shoulder. Rebecca reacted well, grinning at the tease and settling back in her chair, but inside she noted that Josie deliberately avoided answering the question. She thought about pursuing the matter, but decided against the possibility of putting a damper on the otherwise enjoyable evening. Josie was glad that Rebecca turned her interest to the men scurrying about the stage getting it ready for the performance, rather than to continuing the conversation.

A polite cough drew their attention to the aisle. The man with the bowler and his family stood patiently and waited for the gunslinger to sit up and pull her long legs in so they could pass. As the young man did so, his leg brushed up against Rebecca's knee. He apologized immediately, taking the seat next to her as he did so.

"I'm so sorry, Miss," he said, his accent clearly that of a Yankee. "Oh, how rude of me." He wiped his hand on his britches before reaching out to grasp Rebecca's hand and placing his lips briefly on the back of her hand. "Lance," he said by way of introduction, and looked at her inquiringly.

"Rebecca," she replied. He kissed the back of her hand once more before releasing it.

"I'm most pleased to make your acquaintance, Miss Rebecca."

Despite his dapper appearance and impeccable manners, he still managed to earn a warning glare from the gunslinger. She learned long ago to trust no one, especially those who appear to be the trustworthiest. It was nothing compared to his mother's look as she reached down and grabbed him by the earlobe. "Lance, I'm sure the young lady didn't come to the theater to listen to you all night, talking that sweet molasses talk of yours. Now you move over and leave her and her mother alone."

It was all Rebecca could do not to burst into a fit of laughter. Lance was unceremoniously led by his ear to a seat further down while the gunslinger glared at his mother's back. The young woman leaned over and whispered in the still fuming Josie's ear. "I guess we do make an odd pair of cards, huh?"

"I do not look old enough to be your mother," Josie hissed back, fully insulted. Rebecca chuckled silently and gently tapped the gunslinger's leg reassuringly.

"I know, Josie," she said, trying to sound convincing, but her smile remained. The lights were extinguished moments later, leaving only the stage visible to the audience. A man stepped on stage to the roar of clapping. Rebecca leaned over, her smirk now absolutely mischievous.

"Are you going to read me a bedtime story, Mother?"

Without taking her eyes off the stage, Josie leaned over until her lips were just a hair from the young woman's ear. "Keep it up and you'll be sleeping with Flossy, darling daughter," she teased back.

The play was a slapstick comedy about bumbling robbers trying to hold up a stagecoach. Josie rolled her eyes when she saw the two robbers prance out on stage riding stick horses and wearing lace scarves over their mouths. "It's supposed to be funny, Josie," Rebecca whispered at the frowning gunslinger.

"Uh huh," she said sarcastically as they watched the two robbers run into each other and fall down. The rest of the audience laughed uproariously. The gunslinger slumped in her seat, doing her best not to look too bored. Rebecca was smiling and apparently enjoying the antics on stage. The stagecoach prop was brought on stage, complete with the "helpless damsel in distress" riding inside. The robbers circled the wagon on their stick horses, yelling at the woman to toss her valuables out. Josie straightened up in her seat slightly. "That's not how you rob a stage."

"Oh, that's right. You're the expert," Rebecca teased, drawing a smile from the gunslinger as she realized how silly she was being. "That's better. Now sit back and enjoy the show."

"Shh!" Lance's mother hissed at the chatty young woman, despite the fact that most of the theater was laughing at the activities on stage. The damsel in distress was now out of the stagecoach and running around after the robbers, who had given up their stick horses, beating them repeatedly with her bag. At this Josie gave a chuckle and relaxed visibly. Within minutes the bounty hunter was laughing along with Rebecca, both thoroughly enjoying the show.

When the show finished everyone got up at once to leave. Unfortunately, the people in the doorway seemed intent on talking to each other and not on getting outside. Grumbling and complaints were heard from the men and women waiting to leave. Josie leaned over and whispered in Rebecca's ear. "Stay right behind me." She put on her most intimidating face and tapped the shoulder of the man in front of her. "Move, now."

"Miss, 'tain't no way you gonna get out. That's Charlie up there jabbering. He don't never shut up," the man said.

"You want to get out of here?" Josie said loudly, her voice carrying above the din to reach the ears of the frustrated patrons. Several shook their heads in the affirmative or yelled "yes" back at her. "Let me through. I'll make them move."

"You? A woman?" a large and rather dangerous-looking man sneered. Several of his buddies started to laugh until they watched her grab his meaty arm and twist it up behind his back, sending him up on his tiptoes.

"Still think I can't make them move?" she asked rhetorically as she released his arm. The patrons moved back to let her through, with Rebecca following closely behind. The crowd realized that the tall woman would, in fact, get Mouthy Charlie out of the way and started to close up the space behind her, all trying to be the first ones out in case a good fight got going. Rebecca reached out and hooked her fingers around the top of the gunslinger's belt. Josie turned her head slightly, making sure it was her friend that was attached to her before continuing to make her way through the crowd.

"So how's Bertha?"

"She's doin' fine, yep. Her little doggie be due to birth them pups near about anytime now...," Charlie said as he felt a very firm tapping on his shoulder. "Go 'round. There's room," he said without looking around. The tap changed to a firm poke. "Tarnation, what in blue blazes...." He turned and faced the bluest eyes he had ever seen just as the firm hand that was poking him now took hold of a fair amount of his hair.

"Didn't your mother ever tell you it was rude to block other people's way?" she asked as she bodily escorted him out of the doorway and into a nearby trough. She was rewarded with a chorus of cheers from the crowd as people finally made their way out of the theater.

Rebecca caught up with Josie just as she felt a soft touch on her shoulder. The young woman turned to find the dapper young man standing there nervously twisting his hat in his hands. "I uh... just wanted to say that it was nice meeting you, Rebecca."

"It was nice meeting you too, Lance," she replied shyly, feeling her cheeks warming.

"Lance! Get over here and stop pestering that young girl," his mother called. He quickly grabbed Rebecca's hand and kissed the back of it.

"'Bye," he said grinning foolishly and returned to his mother's side before she decided to yell again. Rebecca sensed the gunslinger standing just behind her.

"He's nice," she said a little dreamily. Lance turned around and waved, smiling even more when she returned the gesture.

"You ready?" Josie said a bit more harshly than she meant to. Her blue eyes stayed on the young man as the family walked further down the street. The gunslinger could not put her finger on it, but something about him annoyed her. He was almost out of sight when Rebecca turned to look at her.

"I'm sorry, did you say something?"

"It's getting late," Josie replied, slightly annoyed at being ignored.

"Oh, sorry, Josie. I just...." She gazed at the darkened street where moments ago Lance had waved at her. The dreamy look settled on her face again. "He's nice," she said softly, apparently unable to describe him any other way.

"Uh huh, let's go." This time the gunslinger started walking, her long strides forcing Rebecca to jog to catch up. Only then did she slow down to a more reasonable gait.

"Josie?" The tentative tone made the gunslinger stop and turn to look at her. Rebecca looked down at her boots. "Um... are you mad at me for something?" she asked softly. The wave of guilt passed over the bounty hunter as she realized that she was taking her feelings for the boy out on the blonde. Instantly her features softened and she put her hand on Rebecca's shoulder gently.

"No, I guess I'm still mad at that codger who was blocking the door," she moved closer and put her arm lazily around the smaller woman's shoulders. "Look up there, Rebecca," she said pointing at the stars that twinkled brightly in the clear night. "It's like you can almost reach out and touch them."

"Yes," the young woman replied softly. "They're so pretty; the way they sparkle, it's just like little diamonds in the sky." She started humming the children's melody to herself and was completely surprised when Josie joined in. Rebecca smiled and put her arm around the taller woman's waist, giving her a squeeze. The gunslinger returned the gesture of affection before pulling away.

"Come on, Sprite. Let's get back," she said, giving Rebecca a friendly smile as they started walking again.

The cool night breeze fluttered in through the window as both women got ready for bed. The moon cast enough light for them to see the bed and barely make out each other, so there had been no need to use the lantern. Josie sat down next to her on the bed and pulled off her boots, quickly putting them as far away from the bed as possible. Rebecca untied the thin bow at the neck of her dress and stood, wiggling her arms out of it while turning her back to the gunslinger. She reached down and pushed the dress past her hips, letting it slide down to the floor. Josie placed her guns in a convenient location near the bed, making a mental note to clean them in the morning. She stripped down to her drawers and pulled the covers back on the bed. Rebecca straightened out the sleeves on her flannel nightgown and crawled into bed, scooting up against the wall to make room for her friend.

Josie loosely wrapped an arm around Rebecca's waist. "Is this all right? There's not much room on the bed..." she said, knowing full well that there was plenty of room on the straw-filled mattress. Somehow it just felt right to hold the little blonde in her arms. Rebecca reached down and patted the strong hand resting on her belly.

"It's fine," she replied, smiling in the darkness. She felt so safe and protected in Josie's arms, as if just being in her presence was enough to make all her worries disappear. She sighed contentedly and nuzzled her head deeper into the pillow.

"Good," the gunslinger whispered, moving just a fraction of an inch closer. She was so close that they ended up sharing the same pillow. A thin smile crossed Josie's lips as she drifted off to a sleep undisturbed by nightmares.

The knight fought valiantly, slaying one dragon after another in the quest to rescue the princess. At last the hero was victorious and knelt before the fair maiden. Try as she might, the sleeping woman could not make out the knight's face when the helmet was removed. All she could see was a dark head bending down to kiss the princess. Slowly the lips moved closer until only one thin beam of light passed between them. The light became less and less until total darkness ended her dream.

32: Just Desserts

Typical of most mornings in the saloon, the women were all gathered around the tables, enjoying breakfast and each other's company before the patrons arrived. Rebecca sat with Victoria at a small table near the stairs, drinking coffee and listening to the brown-headed woman talk about her new room and the differences between this whorehouse and the one she left behind in Rosewood. Josie sat with Sandy, quietly drinking coffee and catching up with her old friend. A tall, thin man walked in, his walking stick tapping on the floor in cadence to his steps. The room suddenly quieted and Sandy exchanged a worried look with Josie before rising to meet him halfway.

"Miss Sandy," he said none too politely as he surveyed the room, taking in the sight of the new women. He stroked his handlebar mustache thoughtfully.

"Look, Sam, I've done already paid you for this week." She tried to sound forceful, but her genuine fear prevailed. Sam smiled wickedly.

"Ah, but you didn't pay me enough. Why, I see you have some new ones. I do believe that makes the price higher, don't you?" He reached forward and pulled a small roll of bills out from between the madam's ample breasts. The sound of a chair scraping against the floor was heard as Josie rose to her feet quickly, her right hand hovering just over her shooting irons. Sam shoved the whore out of his way and stood directly in front of the woman in black. "You don't look like the type to be spreading your

legs, so you best just get back to your own business," he spoke threaten-
ingly, yet his eyes remained fixed on Josie's weapons. The gunslinger
desperately wanted to introduce her fist to his teeth but the madam stepped
between them.

"Look, there's no need for this kind of talk," Sandy said, trying to
diffuse the situation. "You got what you came for, so git out and leave us
alone."

Sam looked around, paying close attention to the women's faces, noting which ones were scared of him and which were not. "Nice merchan-
dise, Miss Sandy. Perhaps I might just have me a sample or two, hmm?"
he said lecherously, his mind filling with thoughts of one of the women
lying helpless beneath him. A thin sneer formed on his lips. "I'll be back,"
he said before turning and leaving, the tapping of his walking stick echoing
off into the distance. Josie waited until the sound was completely gone
before sitting back down. Sandy joined her and sat quietly for a moment,
letting the tension ease a bit before speaking. The other women resumed
their conversations, although several still cast nervous glances at the doorway. Sandy motioned for the bartender and within seconds a full bottle of
whiskey and two glasses were placed on her table. She filled them both
before speaking.

"He's Sam Hutchins. Owns the bank, the brewery, just about anything
in town that has a profit to it," she said solemnly, wishing that the cactus
juice could take away her feeling of dread.

"What's his business with you?" Josie asked as she looked around the
room again, making brief eye contact with Rebecca and smiling before
turning her attention back to the blonde madam.

"He holds the note to the saloon."

"So he thinks that he owns everything..." Josie lowered her voice in
disgust, "...and everyone in it."

"That'd be about right," Sandy replied, reaching down to pick up Bobo.
"We pay the mortgage but he still demands more, a part of the profit each
week."

"Is he dangerous?"

"No, just greedier than a prospector. Thinks he's entitled to whatever
he wants."

Josie finished her drink and looked at her friend. "Do you want my
help?" The blonde madam immediately stiffened and shook her head.

"No, Josie. There's no need. I can handle him," she said firmly. She
would live to regret those words.

It was late afternoon when the men came pouring in from their day of
labor. Everyone was known by name and greeted with hearty handshakes
and smiles when they entered. Josie had long ago traded her cactus juice

for ale, drinking slowly to keep her senses alert. There had been no sign of Hutchins since he left five hours ago, but the gunslinger still felt uneasy and insisted on staying. Rebecca passed the time chatting with Victoria until the customers started coming in. Josie decided that her young friend did not need to see her friends working and took her back to the boarding house. In the hour after they left, the saloon became so busy that no one noticed Sam Hutchins enter and go up the stairs.

He hid in a small vestibule and watched a door open and two people exit. The man tipped his hat and headed down the stairs. Victoria leaned over the railing and caught the attention of Sandy, indicating with her gestures that she was taking a break. The blonde madam nodded and went back to her duties. The young woman returned to her room. Locking the door behind her, she sat down in front of her small dresser and began to brush her hair, not paying attention to the image in the mirror until it was too late. Sam lunged forward, wrapping one arm around her throat and pulling her from the chair. With all the sounds of lust and passion coming from the rooms, no one heard the small yelp before she was gagged.

Sandy knocked on the door. "Victoria?" When there was no answer she knocked again. "Victoria, unlock the door."

"What's going on?" Elaine asked as she came out of her room. Her last customer of the night had left a short time ago and she was getting ready for bed when she heard the blonde woman's poundings on the door across the hall.

"Victoria must have fallen asleep or something. The door's locked and no one's seen her for a few hours," she said as she reached in her pocket for the set of skeleton keys she kept there. Elaine became concerned and pounded hard on the door, shaking it on the hinges and drawing the other women from their rooms. They were asking each other if they knew what was going on as they all crowded around Victoria's door. Sandy turned the key and opened the door. Elaine rushed over to the bed, pulling the battered woman into her arms and removing the gag from her mouth. The curtain flapped against the frame of the open window.

"I'll get the doc," Stacey said, heading for the stairs. Sandy ran out of the room and caught the redhead at the landing.

"Doc Brooks met Saint Peter last week. Cheating at cards, I think. He never cared none for doctoring us anyway," the blonde woman said. Elaine came out of the room and shut the door behind her. Everyone quieted down and looked at her, waiting for news.

"She says it's the man with the curly mustache."

"Sam!" Sandy said in disgust. She turned to the redhead. "Get Josie."

Josie reached over and took the large book out from under the blonde's nose and closed it. She had been watching Rebecca reading the same paragraph for the better part of an hour. "I think it's time to visit the sandman, Sprite. Let's go," she put her hand around the smaller woman's upper arm and helped her stand up. Rebecca stretched and groaned as her body moved for the first time in hours.

"Yeah, I think... you're right," she said yawning. She had been reading about the skeletal structure of the human body and found it too fascinating to put down, even when her eyes had trouble staying focused. She looked at the inviting pillow and aimed for it with her tired body only to be stopped by the gunslinger's strong arms.

"Hold your horses there. You're not going to sleep in your boots. My shins wouldn't survive the way you toss about," Josie said as she turned Rebecca around and sat her down on the edge of the bed. She debated about helping the young woman when the sound of rapidly approaching footsteps made the decision for her. The gunslinger moved to the side of the door and readied one of her Colts, holding it up in position to press against the head of the intruder. She unlocked the door and turned the handle slowly.

Stacey reached out to pound on the door when it suddenly flew open and she was roughly pulled inside and found herself looking down the barrel of Josie's gun. A split second later the gun was withdrawn and back in its holster. "What's wrong?" the gunslinger barked while ushering her back out the door. The look on the redhead's face told her without a doubt that something had happened at the saloon.

"Victoria's hurt. That damn banker came back and..."

"Rebecca, grab the saddlebag!" Josie interrupted. The young woman did as ordered and within seconds they were heading down the stairs, Rebecca now very wide-awake.

Rebecca almost cried out when she saw the battered face of her friend. Victoria's right eye was swollen shut, and a crimson line of blood trailed from her nose. Her disheveled brown hair only added to the appearance of being run over by a wagon train. The blonde was relieved and a bit confused to see Victoria still clothed. She looked at Elaine expectantly. The black-headed woman shook her head, causing Rebecca to let out a sigh of relief. Josie was about to reach for the saddlebag when the young blonde moved to the edge of the bed and set it down beside her, opening the flap and rummaging through it looking for the strips of cloth they used for bandages. Without saying a word, the gunslinger motioned for everyone else to move away from the bed. Sandy followed that up with gestures for the women to leave the room. Only Josie, Sandy, and Stacey remained behind to watch the young woman care for her friend.

Her hands trembled slightly from nervousness as she wet the strip of cloth. As delicately as she could, Rebecca gently wiped the blood that had run from Victoria's nose down to her chin. "You're gonna be just fine," she said softly. The brown-headed woman nodded and let a dry, cracked sound come from her lips. "Shh... don't try to talk," her soothing tone and gentle touch calmed the battered woman. Rebecca reached over and poured some water from the pitcher into a tin cup. Using her left arm to support Victoria's head, she lifted her up and placed the cup to her lips. It was then that Rebecca noticed the split lip, previously hidden by the bloody nose. "Stitches," she said quietly. Rebecca swallowed nervously as she realized that all the hours of sewing practice were about to be tested for the first time on a person. She forced her hands not to tremble as she reached into the side pouch and pulled out the needle and thread kept for that purpose. She narrowed her concentration, blocking out the other women in the room and focusing on the task at hand. Belle's voice echoed in her head, reminding her to make small, neat stitches. She took Victoria's hand and pressed it against the cloth on her lip. "Hold this."

With ease born of practice, Rebecca threaded the needle, making a small knot in the end of the thread. She placed her hand reassuringly on the prostitute's shoulder. "Everything will be fine, Victoria, but your lip is cut pretty bad." She held up the needle and thread so the battered woman could see them. The young woman waited until her friend nodded in understanding. "This may hurt," Rebecca said apologetically as she pulled the cloth away and studied the uneven gash. In her mind's eye, she saw exactly where each stitch had to go to properly seal up the wound. Still, the idea of actually putting the needle and thread through a person's skin caused her stomach to churn. She closed her eyes for a moment and waited for the queasy feeling to pass. After a moment she opened them, the cloud of doubt and hesitation now gone. Victoria lay very still as she watched her friend bring the needle slowly to her lip. Although she trusted Rebecca, she still flinched and turned her head when she felt the pressure of the point against her skin. The young woman stopped and pulled back a bit, placing the cloth back over the bleeding wound. The direct approach was not going to work. "Victoria, do you know the story about Jim Bowie and the Alamo?" she asked, leaning over and dabbing at the wound with the cloth in one hand while bringing the needle closer. The brown-headed woman shook her head slightly. "Well, lucky for you I do." Rebecca spoke in a tone that made the upcoming story sound interesting. She began her tale, continuing to press down with the cloth as if cleaning the area. She had

Victoria's complete attention on her story when she finally pushed the point of the needle through the broken skin.

The battered woman did not realize what she had done until she saw Rebecca's hand come up, drawing the thread tight. The touch was so gentle, the tones filling her ears so soft that she had no choice but to fall under the spell her friend was weaving. Victoria felt very little discomfort as the needle was passed through again and the thread drawn tight with small, gentle tugs. Rebecca smiled at her. "There, that wasn't so bad, now was it?" she said, continuing to press against the cut with the bloody cloth, maintaining activity in the area. "Now, where was I? Oh yes, he met up with Daniel Boone..."

Josie watched with rapt fascination as Rebecca continued to stitch up the wound. When she had first closed her eyes, the gunslinger had taken a step forward, prepared to take over. But when the green eyes opened with a flash of confidence, Josie decided to stay where she was and watch what happened. She did not move when Victoria flinched, and was quite impressed by the way Rebecca handled it. The gunslinger realized that her friend had a special talent, not just for healing with her hands, but for soothing with her voice. Josie noted that Victoria no longer had the fearful look in her eyes, but was calmly looking at her friend as she finished suturing the wound. Rebecca continued to tell her story while she looked for more signs of injury. Gone was the look of hesitation and nervousness, replaced by a newfound confidence in her abilities. The bounty hunter understood that a great change had happened to her friend. Rebecca was no longer the frightened young caterpillar she had rescued such a short time ago. The woman she looked at now was undergoing the transformation, and Josie knew that it was only a matter of time before a beautiful butterfly emerged to cast her gentle glow over all she touched.

Rebecca listened carefully as Victoria whispered to her the places that hurt. Even that little bit of talking hurt her. The inside of her mouth was cut up from his fist punching her cheek against her teeth time and time again, not to mention the puffy and split lip. There was little more that Rebecca could do for her friend. Most of the remaining injuries were bruises, her face, neck, and upper arms taking the brunt of it. Victoria touched her fingertips to her swollen lip, wincing at the pain. "Guess he done got me good... ow."

"Yeah...he did," Rebecca said softly, her green eyes misting up.

"Shh... twer..." She motioned for the water and took a sip, mindful of her lip, before continuing. "...'twern't the first time I got beat." Victoria looked away from her friend, unable to face the look of innocence, the innocence she lost so long ago. "Prob'ly won't be the last." Her voice was tinged with the anger she felt welling up inside her. Rebecca placed a gentle hand on her forearm.

"Victoria, it doesn't have to be that way. You can leave this all behind you. Make a new start. We'll help you, if you let us. Everyone deserves a second chance." She spoke in her most convincing tone of voice, yet the brown-headed woman maintained the defeated look on her face.

"Whores don't usually git second chances."

"No?" Rebecca reached over, opened the pouch, and pulled out the small bible she had found when she first started following Josie around. She opened it to the New Testament and flipped through until she found the page for which she was looking. She took a sip of water and began to read: "Now the scribes and the Pharisees brought a woman caught at adultery, and, after standing her in their midst, they said to him 'Teacher, this woman has been caught in the act of committing adultery. In the Law of Moses it is prescribed for us to stone such sort of women. What, really, do you say?'" She looked up from the book to catch Victoria's eyes with her own. "And do you know what he said? He said 'Let he who is without sin be the first to cast a stone at her.' Victoria, no one threw a stone because no one is above sin. We all make mistakes, and we all deserve a second chance."

Josie motioned for the others to follow her out of the room, confident that her young friend had things well in hand and, in fact, was probably doing a better job than she would have been able to do. For just a moment she caught the green eyes with her own. The depth of compassion and caring that Josie saw there was too much for her. Suddenly uncomfortable, the gunslinger simply followed the others out, closing the door behind her. She had no doubt that this would be a very long night for both of them. "Sandy, put coffee on," she called out to the blonde woman at the bottom of the stairs.

A short time later, the three women were sitting about one of the small round tables. Not wanting to draw attention to the saloon at such a late hour, they chose to light only one small lamp, setting it on a nearby table. Josie picked up her cup of coffee and leaned back in her chair, resting her booted foot on the table in a most unladylike manner. "Why does he do that?"

Sandy looked down at the half empty cup of coffee. "It's how he gets it done. Can't do it no other way," she let a small smirk cross her face. "You know how he needs that there stick o' his to walk with? Well..." she leaned forward as she shared the secret. "Damn fool was twirling his gun around and shot himself. Ain't got hardly nothing left now." They all had a good laugh at his expense before she continued. "But he still feels, I guess. 'Tain't the first time this happened. Beat three girls so bad they can't work no more, and another... well, she ain't right in the head no more. He up and punched her stupid."

"So what do we do now?" Stacey asked.

"Nothin' we can do," Sandy replied. "I do what I can to keep him away from the girls, but sometimes he still gets through. You know the law ain't gonna touch him just on our say so. We're good enough to go round the mountain with but not good enough to believe over that no-good excuse for a man," she said bitterly. "I just hope somebody puts him in a wooden overcoat soon."

"Perhaps sooner than you think," Josie said softly, putting her finger on her lips. Soon they also heard the unmistakable sound of Sam's walking stick tapping the ground as he approached. Stacey reached over and pulled the gun from Josie's left holster. The gunslinger had no time to react as the creak of rusty hinges announced his arrival. She quickly pulled her right gun out and readied it for action. The redhead would have hell to pay later, the gunslinger thought.

"Ladies, why are you sitting in the dark? Surely you won't attract customers that way," he said smugly as he moved over to the bar and lit another lamp, turning the wick up to cast a dark orange light. Sandy rose, followed quickly by Stacey, and walked across the floor to meet him halfway. Josie remained in her seat with her gun aimed directly at him from under the table. She knew without looking exactly where her weapon was pointing. With his attention directed at the approaching woman, it was easy for her to reach over and turn the wick down on the lamp near her, leaving it still burning, but too low to cast light on her.

"Get out of here!" Sandy hissed. The redhead stood behind her, the revolver sandwiched between their bodies. "You may not have nothin' else, but you sure got balls coming back here after what you done."

"Done?" he said, feigning innocence. "I haven't been here since earlier today. I was in my office all evening." Hutchins stroked the curl of his mustache. "Of course no one saw me," he said with a sly grin.

"You bastard!" Sandy lunged at him, her anger at all the women hurt at his hands flooding through her. Her sudden movement put her between the banker and Josie, blocking any shot she may have had. The gunslinger leapt to her feet, ready to join the fray and protect her friends.

Everything happened in the blink of an eye. Sam swung his cane, striking Sandy just below the left temple. As the woman fell, he raised his arm for another blow. Both Josie and Stacey leveled their weapons. It was the redhead who fired first, striking him in the center of his forehead. The force kicked his head back, causing the gunslinger's bullet to fly harmlessly into the wood behind the bar. His eyes rolled up into his head as a thin stream of blood poured down the front of his face, and he pitched backward. His lifeless body landed across the blonde madam's legs. Stacey's hand started shaking violently with the realization of what happened. Josie reached her quickly and wrenched the gun out of her hands, putting it back in its holster. She pulled out a chair and forced the redhead to sit down before she fell down.

The gunshot brought all the women out of their rooms. Rebecca flew down the stairs, her focus solely on Josie and not on the possible danger. The gunslinger rolled Hutchins off Sandy and helped her to her feet just as the young woman reached the bottom of the stairs. The other women looked down from the upstairs railing. Josie's eyes narrowed as she stormed over and grabbed the young woman by the upper arm, pulling her over to a far corner before releasing her. Unmindful of the gunslinger's anger, Rebecca wrapped her arms around the taller woman and hugged her tightly. "When I heard..." she inhaled sharply and shook her head against Josie's chest, unable to voice her fears.

The bounty hunter looked down at her, understanding the mixture of emotions running through Rebecca. The anger she had with her for running headlong into an unknown danger dissipated as she tentatively wrapped her arms around the young woman's shoulders, resting her chin on the top of the blonde head. "We'll talk later," she said gently. Rebecca nodded, knowing she had made a mistake and that most likely the gunslinger was angry with her about it. A soft smile came to her lips. Although angry, Josie still allowed her this comforting embrace. She gave one more squeeze before stepping back.

The women looked expectantly at Josie. If anyone knew how to hide a killing, it was the tall gunslinger. She walked over to Sandy. "Want him found?" she said seriously, her mind already working on where to deposit the body for the buzzards to pick clean.

"I think that's best. If he don't show back up, they'll be looking for him," the blonde madam replied, much to the gunslinger's dismay. It would have been much easier to make him disappear.

"And if anyone saw him here..." Josie left the thought unfinished as she looked around the room. Her eyes gazed upon the large chandelier full of dangling diamond shaped pieces of lead glass. She turned to Rebecca. "I want you to take Stacey upstairs, all right? Tell everyone to meet us in Victoria's room."

"What are you...?"

"Rebecca, go," Josie asked more than said.

"Uh... yeah," she said, understanding the unspoken message in the blue eyes. The gunslinger did not want her to see what she was going to do. "I'll wait for you upstairs." She turned and went to get Stacey, leaving the gunslinger to her task.

Josie waited until everyone was out of sight except for Sandy, who was keeping an eye out for any signs of life on the street. Apparently no one heard the gunshots, as there were no signs of activity. The blonde could only hope that no one would be wakened by the next sound to come from the saloon. Josie walked to the corner and looked at the rope. One end was tied to a rung in the wall. The other ran up through a pulley to the top of the chandelier. She smiled. This was the part she loved, the execution of a brilliant plan. Pulling off the impossible. That was what made her such a good train robber, what kept her alive. The ability to think quickly on her feet was a skill she hoped would never fail her or Rebecca. After a quick glance upstairs, Josie focused her attention on the knot holding the rope to the anchor on the wall.

The women from Rosewood were gathered in Victoria's room, the others waiting in the hall outside the doorway due to the lack of space. Rebecca sat on the bed next to the upright Victoria, quietly explaining what she knew. Elaine and the others were comforting Stacey, who was in a complete state of shock over taking a human life. The sound of the large chandelier crashing to the floor caused all of them to jump. Bobo, who had been sleeping quietly under the dresser, tore off like a shot across the room and dived under the bed. Josie came bounding up the stairs, her long legs avoiding every other step. Everyone poured out into the hallway to hear what happened. Josie waited until she saw Rebecca come out of the room, the battered Victoria in tow. "Get the saddlebag," she said, and watched as the blonde disappeared back into the room to return with their gear. The gunslinger turned her attention to the whores, all looking at her for an explanation.

"Sandy has gone for the sheriff," the gunslinger raised her voice slightly to make sure everyone heard her. "Act confused. You have no idea why he was here or what he was doing. You don't know anything and hadn't seen him since early afternoon." Her words were met with a chorus of nods. "All you heard was a loud crash downstairs. That's all." Her tone warned them that the previous sound of a gun was not to be mentioned. Josie reached for Rebecca's arm. "We need to go... now."

Josie did not say a word as they walked back to the boarding house and her body language made it clear that Rebecca was not to speak either. They took the route through the alleyways, carefully avoiding the main street and the possibility of being seen. Once inside the privacy of their room, the gunslinger sat down on the edge of the bed and motioned for Rebecca to sit next to her. In the darkness, all they could see of each other were dim silhouettes. Josie sat quietly, waiting for the inevitable questions.

"Why did you do that? Drop the chandelier on him, I mean. Won't they see the bullet hole?" she asked, not entirely sure she wanted to hear the answer.

"With all the cuts, looking for a small hole like that would be like looking for a needle in a haystack," Josie said assuredly, although she secretly worried that someone might have heard the gunshot. It would only take one person commenting on a previous sound before the crashing glass to cause a closer look to be taken at the dead body.

"What did Sandy tell the sheriff?"

"That Hutchins insisted on lighting the chandelier and when she went to lower it, the rope slipped out of her hands. A tragic accident."

"Do you think the sheriff will believe her?" Rebecca asked.

Josie pondered the question for a brief moment. "If Sandy put her mind to it, she could convince an assayer to buy fools gold. She's a fast thinker, that one. Nope, unless he sees something wrong, the sheriff will buy her story."

"Good," the young woman said as she let out a sigh of relief. An awkward silence fell between them.

"Rebecca..." she said, trying to break the deafening silence. "You did a good job taking care of Victoria." Josie turned and pulled one leg up on the bed so she could face the young woman. "From what I saw, her lip will heal up just fine."

"I tried to concentrate on what Belle taught me about stitching," she said modestly, but in the darkness of the night, she was beaming ear to ear from the compliment.

"No, you did more than that. You comforted her while you tended to her. That's a special talent, Rebecca. Not everyone can do both." Josie took a deep breath and paused for a moment. The blonde swallowed, understanding that the topic was about to change and knowing what was coming. "When you heard the gunshot, your first instinct should have been to get to safety, not to run headlong into danger." As she spoke, Josie was careful not to let her fear for Rebecca's safety express itself as anger in her voice. "Next time, act; don't react," she said as she reached out and placed a hand on the young woman's shoulder.

"Josie... I didn't mean to scare you." The sudden tension in the hand on her shoulder told Rebecca that she had accurately guessed the gunslinger's feelings. She patted her hand gently. "I worry about you, you know. I care."

"You still have to be careful, not take chances," Josie said firmly, not thinking about the words until after they had left her mouth.

"Said the desert to the grain of sand," she shot back. "I worry about you because you give me reason to worry, Josie. One of these days someone is going to call you out and..." Rebecca stopped when she realized her mistake. The gunslinger's shoulders slumped and she let her hand fall to rest on the young woman's knee.

"You're still upset about yesterday." It was a statement, but also a question. Rebecca nodded.

"Hey," she said, smiling in the darkness and putting her hand on top of the gunslinger's. "I'll make a deal with you. I won't take unnecessary chances if you won't."

"It's a deal," Josie said as she tried to stifle a yawn. "Now let's get some sleep." She rose and quickly stripped down to her drawers. Rebecca took longer to get down to her slip. They curled up together as they had the previous night, the gunslinger's arm wrapped protectively around the young woman's waist, their bodies so close that only one pillow was needed. A couple of minor adjustments and both settled into a comfortable position. Lying in the warm embrace, the outside world melted away for Rebecca. The vision of her friend beaten, the stress of putting the needle through skin, all the actions of the day slipped from her mind. There was no dead man, no danger, only the safety that came from the strong arms wrapped around her. Just as Rebecca crossed the line to sleep, the rich voice behind her ear whispered "Good night, Sprite," as the strong arm around her belly squeezed gently.

Sleep did not come so easily to the gunslinger. Her mind raced with thoughts of the possible activities going on up the street. She lay there until she heard the steady breathing that indicated her companion was asleep. Being careful not to disturb Rebecca, Josie slipped out of bed and went to the window to cast an eye up the street.

33:   Lance in the Pants

Rebecca woke to see the tall gunslinger staring out the window, mug in hand. "'Morning," she said with a yawn.

"'Morning," Josie replied, her gaze never leaving the bustle of activity at the saloon. She recognized the long, flat wagon of an undertaker sitting outside. Rebecca trudged over to the small table and picked up the tin mug.

"Josie, where's my coffee?" she asked as she looked at the empty cup. She received a sheepish grin as the gunslinger held out the mug she was holding. The young woman took the half-empty cup and frowned. She downed it in a few swallows and set it on the table. "You know, Josie, if I got up before you and drank your coffee, you'd have my head on a stick."

"Yeah, but you'll never wake up before I do," the gunslinger said confidently, turning her attention from the activities outside and looking at the young woman. Josie looked back out the window, but not before seeing the blonde stick her tongue out at her. She watched as the canvas-wrapped body was placed in the back of the wagon, and the sheriff exchanged words with the undertaker. The undertaker shook hands with him and both men went on their way. Sandy left the saloon, heading up the street toward the boarding house. "We've got company, Rebecca."

The young woman was dressed and ready by the time Sandy knocked on the door to their room. "How'd it go?" Josie asked, as the blonde madam entered the room.

"Just like you said it would. Old man Henry is taking him to the dirt pile now," she said. The gunslinger gave a grim smile of satisfaction. With no doctor in town, it was up to the undertaker to decide if an autopsy was called for, and apparently the old man was not interested in trying to keep the body until one could be called from another town.

"Good," Josie said as she flopped down on the bed, guns, boots and all. It had been a long night, and the news that it was over finally gave her a chance to relax. She closed her eyes, hoping that today would be a lazy day and she could catch up on her sleep.

"How's Stacey?" Rebecca asked as she motioned for Sandy to sit at the table with her. The young woman had no doubt that Josie had stayed up the remaining hours until dawn. She deliberately kept her voice low, hoping that the gunslinger would get some much-needed rest. Sandy understood and kept her voice at the same low level.

"She's doing better. Elaine managed to keep her quiet and hidden when the sheriff was around. Poor thing's pretty shook up, though."

As they spoke quietly about the previous night's events, Rebecca glanced over at the bed frequently, checking on her friend. It was not long before Josie was in a deep and apparently peaceful sleep. "Sandy..." she whispered, pointing at the sleeping gunslinger.

"Come on, Rebecca. I'll buy you breakfast," the madam whispered back.

As quietly as possible, they left. The sound of the door closing woke Josie, but after a second of deliberation, she decided that they would be fine and rolled over and went back to sleep.

Sandy took Rebecca to the small restaurant. The same waitress was there, but this time she was much more pleasant and gave them a table near the pot-bellied stove. The young woman was quite happy at that, since the coffeepot was kept warming there. She quickly helped herself to a cup while waiting.

"I guess they let anyone in here," a woman said to her husband as they passed their table. Sandy gave her a withering glare. The pompous woman let go of her husband's arm and turned to face them with her hands on her hips. "I heard that Sam Hutchins died there last night. No doubt fitting punishment for visiting a whore." She turned her attention to Rebecca. "And what's this, a new one? How old are you, child? Seventeen? Eighteen? You should be home, learnin' cookin' 'n sewin' 'n worrying about finding yourself a husband." She paused for a moment to study the face before her. "You're pretty enough; shouldn't have no problem finding yourself a man."

"Now you look here, you high and mighty bitch!" Sandy said, rising to her feet. Rebecca rose as well, hoping to avoid a conflict in the middle of the restaurant.

"Ladies!" she said, putting her hands up to silence them. "Please." She looked at the indignant woman and her cowed husband. "Ma'am, we just want to get something to eat. You were leaving, weren't you?"

"It's bad enough you have that brothel of sin and booze. You should keep yourselves there and not come out to sully a fine, respectable place like this." She looked at Rebecca and went on, "I won't stand by and watch a new one like this come in and corrupt our fine men." Her face twisted with self-righteous anger and hate as her body tensed, ready to strike.

"Sweetheart?" Everyone turned to see the brown-headed young man approach.

Rebecca breathed a sigh of relief as she recognized Lance. The woman relaxed her body, clearly confused. Lance stepped close and kissed the blonde on the cheek. "So you did decide to have breakfast with your aunt. I wish you would have told me, darling. I was worried."

Rebecca looked at him blankly for a moment before she caught on. "Uh...yeah." She forced a smile to her face, not that it was too hard seeing as how he just swept in and rescued her from trouble. "I should have told you." She turned to her companion and continued, "Aunt Sandy, this is Lance." Sandy quickly put a happy smile on her face and she held her arms out.

"Lance, darling, so nice to finally meet you. Rebecca has told me so much about you." They embraced as though truly glad to see each other.

Thoroughly embarrassed, the woman said gruffly to her husband, "Come on, Harold," as she headed for the exit. Rebecca barely suppressed a giggle as she watched them leave. She smiled and held her hand out, pointing at an empty chair.

"Thank you so much. Please join us."

Lance smiled at his good fortune and quickly helped both women with their chairs before taking his own seat. Rebecca smiled at him and he smiled back, neither one of them speaking. Sandy watched the interaction and smiled to herself. Ah, young love. So pure and sweet in its innocence. Rebecca briefly explained to her that they had met before as she continued to smile at Lance.

The waitress brought their food and set it down gently on the table in front of them, frowning slightly when she saw the young man. "You have to eat something to stay here," she said firmly.

"Oh, dear me," Sandy said rising once again to her feet. "I have to get back. Lance, would you be a dear and escort Rebecca back to the saloon after she finishes? You're welcome to mine," she said as she pushed the plate in front of him. She opened her purse to pull out money, but the young man held up his hand.

"Please, let me. It would be my sincere pleasure." He turned back to Rebecca. "Would you like some more coffee?" He was already moving out of his chair and reaching for the potholder hanging on a hook next to the stove. Sandy looked at her, silently asking if she would be all right. Rebecca smiled and nodded slightly. Lance leaned over and filled her cup, smiling at her the entire time and almost spilling the coffee. Sandy smiled and gracefully left them alone.

"So, Rebecca... are you new to Cheyenne?" he asked as he buttered her bread for her.

"Thank you," she said accepting the bread from him with a smile, "We're just passing through, actually." She took a small bite of her bread and returned the coffee mug to her lips, looking over it at the handsome young man. Rebecca was acutely aware that the toes of their boots were touching. "And you?"

"We moved here about six months ago, from Tucson. We have a small cattle ranch a few miles out of town," he said, completely mesmerized by the green eyes looking at him from beneath soft lashes. "You are very beautiful," he murmured, smiling when her cheeks flushed pink and she looked down at her plate.

He reached out and took her hand in his own. "I mean it, Rebecca. You truly are a work of art, worthy of being in one of those museums in New York City."

"Stop," she said, embarrassed. "You don't know me, Lance." She gently pulled her hand back to her lap, noting that it was the first time a man had touched her so gently.

"I'd like the opportunity to get to know you better, Rebecca," he said sincerely. "And I hope the feeling is mutual."

Rebecca's heart picked up its pace slightly. This well-mannered, handsome, charming gentleman was trying to court her. She put her hands on the table and found them instantly encased within his warm and gentle ones.

The sun was high in the sky when Josie woke. She looked around for a moment before remembering that Rebecca had gone to eat with Sandy. She got out of bed and stretched before reaching down and scratching the area under her breasts while yawning, looking every bit like a bear coming out of hibernation. She looked out the window. Horses, wagons, and people all filled the street as they went about their business. Her eyes narrowed when she saw the familiar blonde head walking arm-in-arm with a man. She looked closer and realized that it was the boy from the theater. Her jaw clenched unconsciously when she saw him put his arm around Rebecca's waist. It took less than four strides of her long legs to reach the door.

Sandy stared at the clock nervously. Josie would kill her if she knew she had let Rebecca out of her sight, the madam was sure of it. Her quiet friend did not speak of why she was traveling with the young woman, but Sandy knew from watching the gunslinger that Rebecca was special to her. They had not gone 'round the mountain yet, Sandy was certain of that, especially after talking with Elaine. She knew the blonde was no relation of the half-Cherokee, but she could not think of any other reason for them to be traveling together. If not for love or money, then why? And what of Rebecca's reason for being with Josie? Sandy found it most interesting that the gunslinger made no mention of any recent robberies and, in fact, the madam realized that she had not heard anything about the raven-headed woman since the news article quite a while back about the robbery in the midwest, which reported the death of the outlaw. Perhaps the young blonde had something to do with that. Certainly Josie seemed more at ease around people since the last time she had seen her, and the way she had held Rebecca after the shooting was most surprising to the madam. She had no idea Josie could be so gentle and caring.

The madam breathed a sigh of relief when she saw Rebecca and Lance enter the saloon, only to see Josie come in just seconds behind them. She took a quick note of their position and headed straight for Sandy. "I thought you were going to keep an eye on her," she said in a disapproving tone, then stepped back a bit when she realized just how much like a mother hen she sounded. The madam decided that a change in subject was the best course of action.

"Josie, how about you and me go in the back room and play some pool?" she suggested. She moved closer and lowered her voice. "I'll even throw in a jug of cactus juice I've got hidden back there." She followed the gunslinger's line of sight back to the couple sitting opposite each other at a small table in the back.

"Come on, Josie, let those kids have some fun. It looks like he's quite taken with her."

"Yeah... well, he'd better not get too taken with her. He won't be a happy person if he does." Her tone was serious enough to make the madam gulp nervously. She had seen Josie in action and knew just how swiftly she could cut a man down. Sandy looked at the couple again. They were just quietly talking, each with a sarsaparilla in front of them. She hoped for Lance's sake that he was as much of a gentleman as he seemed.

Josie realized that she was feeling more anger toward the young man than she should have. He had done nothing out of the ordinary and Rebecca seemed happy enough. *Get a grip, Josie*, she chided herself. *If she wants to spend time with him, well that's just fine with me. We don't have to spend all of our time together.* With that in mind, the gunslinger turned and headed to the back room, followed closely by Sandy.

Rebecca turned her head slightly to watch them go into the back room.

Lance's back was to the door and thus he did not see the glare given him by the gunslinger. Rebecca wondered briefly why Josie did not come over to talk to her, but was drawn back to Lance by a polite cough. "Oh, I'm sorry. What?"

"I asked if you would do me the honor of accompanying me tonight? My father is having a barbecue to celebrate his forty-fifth birthday. Nothing fancy, just a bunch of the ranch hands and some friends of the family," he said quickly, his nervousness showing through. He flashed her a hopeful smile. "You can even bring your mother along if you want to," he said, receiving a guffaw from Rebecca.

"Lance, she isn't my mother. She's just a friend."

"Oh," he said, embarrassed.

"It's all right," she said, still grinning. "We get a lot of funny looks." She decided not to tell him that most of the looks showed fear of the tall, intimidating gunslinger.

"Well, if you want, you can bring her along, I guess. I'm sure my mother will keep her company," he offered, willing to do anything to get the beautiful blonde to accept his offer.

"No. I don't think your mother and Josie would have much in common to talk about," she smirked as she thought about the possible conversations between the two women. Lance's mother trying to talk about the recent harvest and the gunslinger talking about why Colt Peacemakers are the best shooting irons around. She gave a small giggle at the thought. Lance smiled, although he did not get the joke.

"So will you? Go with me, I mean?"

"Um..." She flashed him a shy smile, "...yes, I'd like that," she said. He relaxed visibly and let out a deep breath as he ran his hand through his hair.

"That's great! Um...I'll pick you up at six... uh, I don't know where you live," he said apologetically.

"I'm staying at the boarding house."

"Fine. I'll pick you up there at six."

"That'd be nice," she replied, wondering why her heart was racing again. Then she realized this was the first time she was going on an actual date.

"Well, I'd better get back to the ranch before Pop has a fit," he said as he stood up, taking her hand into his and kissing it. "I'll see you tonight, fair lady."

"Oh…." She rose to her feet and nervously pulled her hand back. "Tonight, then," she said as she watched him leave. When he was no longer in sight, she turned to go find Josie and instead she saw Victoria leaning against the upstairs rail. With a wave and a smile, she went to go visit with her for a little while.

Josie checked and double-checked the angle and position of the balls before taking her shot. With a crack, the cue ball struck the nine ball, just off from where she had intended it to, sending the white ball into the side pocket. "I thought you were good at pool, Josie," Sandy said as she refilled the gunslinger's glass again.

"I would be if the cues weren't warped," she complained, turning the stick in her hands to study it. "And if you would stop trying to get me drunk," she added half-jokingly as she pulled the cue ball out of the pocket and handed it to the blonde madam. Sandy smirked and handed Josie the full glass.

"I have to do something to have an even chance, don't I?" she said as she took aim, sending the nine ball into the corner pocket easily. "After a while, you get used to the curves of the cues. Don't even notice anymore." She set the cue against the wall and sat down on the couch. "I do believe it's your turn to rack them."

It was after three when Rebecca came down and knocked on the door. She poked her head inside and looked at Josie. "Can I talk to you?"

"Come on in, Rebecca," Sandy said as she tossed her stick on the table. "I've got to get ready for tonight anyway."

"Josie," she began hesitantly after the madam left. "Lance has asked me to his ranch for a party tonight."

"Have fun," she replied with no sign of emotion.

"Well…." Rebecca turned, but not before Josie saw the look of hurt on her face. "I guess I'd better get back and get ready."

"Rebecca, wait," she said as she walked over and closed the door. "Sit down." They each took a seat on the couch, Josie mentally chastising herself for not realizing how much the young woman was looking for her approval and encouragement. "I'm sorry. I didn't mean to sound like I didn't care. I do care."

"You think I'm just a child, Josie. I'm not." She was upset enough to let her hurt and anger through. "I wasn't asking your permission, Josie. I was trying to share something important to me with you."

"Rebecca, I don't think you're a child."

"Really, Josie? What was that look when you saw Lance and me together? You didn't look happy."

"I..." she scrambled to explain what she felt when she saw them together. "I was just surprised to see you with someone other than Sandy, that's all. Call it my protective nature." She forced a toothy smile, hoping to lighten the mood. Rebecca relented, unwilling to remain angry with her best friend.

"All right, but I really do need to get going." She looked down at her dress, trying to smooth out the wrinkles, then down at her boots. Josie caught the look on her face and frowned in understanding. A quick mental count told her she did not have enough money to get Rebecca both a nice pair of shoes and a new dress. There was a flicker in her blue eyes as she thought of a solution to the problem.

"Rebecca, go on to the house and get washed up. I'll be there in a little while," Josie said handing her the money to pay for the bath. When their hands touched to exchange the bill, Josie gripped it for a moment. "In the bottom of the saddlebag on my side is a small bottle of Katec toilet water. It's strong, so don't drown yourself with it." The smile she received was worth far more than the two bits the perfume cost. After Rebecca left, the gunslinger smiled and headed upstairs.

The bathtub was located in a back room downstairs. The lock was nothing more than a piece of wood nailed to the door that turned to block it from being pulled open. Looking at it as she turned it into position, Rebecca decided that even she could pull the door open, the nail hole worn enough to allow the wood to swivel easily. One good tug and it was certain to fall to the floor. She silently wished that she had known so she could have had Josie stand outside the door. Too late now, she mused as she removed her clothes, setting them in a small pile on the floor, save the dress, which she draped on a nail sticking out of the wall for just such a purpose. She placed her clean under drawers and slip on the small shelf and carefully stepped into the claw-foot tub.

She had been soaking for some time when she heard the firm but non-threatening knock on the door. "Rebecca?"

"Hang on, Josie," she said, climbing from the tub and wrapping a towel around her. She turned the lock and opened the door enough to poke her head out.

"Let me in." The look on the gunslinger's face reminded Rebecca of her sister's face when she was giving someone a present. She stepped back and let Josie in, closing and securing the door behind her. She was holding a light green and white lace dress as well as a pair of white, button down boots. "I thought you might like to wear this to the party," she said as she set the boots down and hung the dress up, tossing Rebecca's old one on the floor with the rest of the dirty clothes. "I couldn't afford both, but Sandy found the dress in one of the closets. I think it'll fit you just right," she said, not bothering to mention that it took her the better part of an hour to find and purchase the boots. She was not expecting quite the reaction she got. Rebecca's eyes filled up and she gave Josie the best imitation of a bear hug she could, before softening it and laying her head on the older woman's chest.

"Thank you, Josie," she murmured, her hand splaying out and rubbing up and down the gunslinger's back slowly. The movement of her upper arm caused her towel to fall open exposing her whole back as it hung loosely, trapped between their bodies. Josie was returning the embrace when she felt the smooth skin beneath her fingers instead of the towel. Rebecca made no effort to move when she felt the strong arms wrap around her bare skin and squeeze gently. After a moment, a feeling of awkwardness set in for the gunslinger and she reached down and gathered the ends of the towel, securing it back around her friend's body.

"I guess I'd better let you get ready." She turned and reached for the door handle. "Is this their idea of a lock?"

"Yeah," Rebecca replied, still staring in awe at the new dress and boots.

"I'll be outside when you're done," Josie said authoritatively. She took a quick look to make sure the blonde was still covered before she opened the door and stepped out. Another boarder was in the adjoining parlor and glanced in her direction. One quick glare from her and his attention went back into the week old newspaper in his hand.

Rebecca looked in the small mirror, trying to see as much of herself as she could. As Josie had predicted, the dress fit perfectly. *Although it's a bit snug in the chest*, she thought, as she looked down to see exactly how much cleavage was showing through the white lace that started barely above her nipples. To her relief, the lace was intricate enough to cover everything, although it still clearly defined her pushed up bosom, making her appear larger than she was used to, and causing her to feel a bit self-conscious. She looked down at the delicate boots and smiled again. They were completely impractical for traveling and were clearly an indulgence on Josie's part. The boots had to have taken up most of the money not set aside for supplies. Rebecca ran her fingertips across the pearly buttons. "Oh Josie..." she whispered as a teary smile came to her face. She picked up the boots in one hand and her dirty clothes and traveling boots in the other, pressing the garments against her body to keep them from falling, and opened the door.

Josie immediately moved from her position leaning against the wall to help Rebecca with her clothes. "Give me those. You don't want that clean dress to smell like your dirty clothes, do you? Come on." As they went upstairs, Josie's boots struck the wood in sharp contrast to the young woman's bare feet. Once inside the room, the gunslinger put the boots in the corner and the clothes in the growing pile of laundry in another corner. Rebecca sat down on the bed and pulled her leg up over her knee to put on her boot. She slipped the leather and cloth over her foot, frowning when she realized that the buttons were on the outside. "Why do they do that?" she grumbled as she tried to reach around and fasten the buttons. Josie chuckled and knelt down in front of her.

"Let me," she said as she pulled Rebecca's ankle off her knee. "They button on the outside because they expect all 'ladies' to have someone helping them get dressed." Her nimble fingers worked quickly, securing all the small buttons up the calf.

"Well, it seems a little silly, doesn't it?" Rebecca replied, surprised at the gentle manner in which Josie put her foot into her boot. She held the calf with one hand and gently slipped the shoe part of the boot onto the young woman's foot, then rested the foot back on the ground before methodically buttoning it.

"That's why I don't wear them. Just like corsets," Josie replied as she stood up. "All right, let's get a look at you."

Rebecca stood and self-consciously turned around in place. She stopped and watched the gunslinger's gaze go up and down her body slowly, as if memorizing her. "Josie? How do I look?"

"Beautiful," she replied, suddenly realizing that her mouth was quite dry. She swallowed and looked into the blonde's eyes, unnerved by how deep the green seemed to be in them, almost an emerald color. *You are no child, Rebecca,* she thought to herself as her eyes drank in the vision before her. *No child at all.* "You'll be the prettiest one there," she said with a teasing glint in her eyes. "Now just try not to get sauce all over the front of your dress. I know how you eat." She followed her words up with hand gestures depicting a most unladylike manner of eating.

"Oh, you..." Rebecca huffed playfully. "This from the woman who makes noises with her armpits."

"Hey, I told you I have many skills."

"Oh yeah, and that's one that'll be sure to land you a husband." She did not understand the knowing smirk that came to the gunslinger's lips. Rebecca was about to comment on the look when the church bell chimed off in the distance, drawing her attention to the time.

"Oh no, he's going to be here any second," she gasped as she raced around in search of the brush. "Oh Josie, my hair is a mess and..."

"Relax, Rebecca. Here." She pulled the brush out from the saddlebag and walked over to the window. "Stand here and watch for him. I'll take care of your hair."

As promised, Josie gently brushed Rebecca's hair while the blonde watched the street below. The green eyes were half-closed in enjoyment of the unexpected luxury of having someone else do her hair. Long fingers aided the brush through the soft blonde hair. The strokes were far gentler than she had ever done for herself and Rebecca made a mental note to ask her to do it again sometime, perhaps in exchange for a backrub. Josie always did like backrubs. The young woman smiled at the thought. She enjoyed giving massages to the gunslinger, to run her fingers over the strong muscles, to hear the soft murmur of relaxation that came from her mouth. She wished Josie would ask for one more often, not just when she was in pain.

The sound of a wagon approaching drew her focus away from the spot on the wall to which it had strayed during the brushing, and back down to the street below. "He's here," she whispered nervously, pulling the gunslinger from her musings as well.

"Oh," Josie replied, setting the brush down on the table. She put her hands on Rebecca's shoulders and turned the smaller woman to face her. "Listen to me. Have fun, enjoy yourself, but be careful." She did not even realize that her voice was in "mother" mode. "I know you're a grown woman and what you do is your business, but remember that you don't have to do anything that you don't want to do."

"Yes, mother," Rebecca said with a smile as she tried to cover up her nervousness. It did not work.

"You'll be fine; stop worrying," Josie said reassuringly. "You'd better go before he thinks you've stood him up."

"Oh... bye," she said as she headed out the door, only to turn around and give her friend a quick hug. "I'll be back early... I promise." Then in a rustle of skirts, she was gone.

Josie stood at the window, watching as Lance put a soapbox on the ground for Rebecca to use as a step to get into the wagon. Despite her upbringing, Rebecca acted every bit the proper lady, holding her hand out to be assisted up the step, sitting with her hands crossed over each other in her lap. The only thing missing was a hat. *Damn, forgot about the hat,* Josie thought to herself. *How could I forget that? Oh, Rebecca, I hope no one mentions it.* She watched the wagon until it was no longer in sight before turning away from the window. Josie lay down on the bed with her fingers interlaced behind her head, staring at nothing. What had happened at the saloon? Why did she get so angry whenever she saw them together? She blew stray strands of hair out of her eyes as she let out an exasperated sigh. She should be happy that Rebecca had found a nice, young man to give her attention. From what the gunslinger could gather about the young woman's past, something not spoken of any more than her own, she was not used to receiving such positive attention. Josie rubbed her eyes. Sitting here staring at the ceiling was not going to help her understand. She rose to her feet and set out for the saloon.

The wagon moved slowly out of town, the pale gray of evening settling around them like a dark blanket. "You look very beautiful," Lance said as he admired the vision sitting next to him.

"Thank you," Rebecca replied softly, finding herself unexpectedly shy. "Lance, you don't sound like you come from these parts. Where are you from originally?"

"Well, our family is from back east, near Albany. We moved out here about two years ago. Pop was a banker; came out here to settle down and raise cattle," he looked out at the setting sun. "Don't think he expected it to be so hard, though." He smiled and took her hands in his hand, the reins tangling between them. "But I guess it's worth it to see such a pretty girl as yourself. But how'd you know we weren't from around here?"

"Your accent," she replied. "You have one, even if you don't realize it. Like coffee. You pronounce it caw-fee."

"I do not have an accent," he said indignantly. "Only people from the south and from New England have accents."

"You do. Listen... coffee... walk... you say them," she said. He repeated the words. "See? Caw-fee and wok. You have an accent," she said triumphantly. Lance nodded in defeat.

"I didn't know. You're very intelligent as well as beautiful, Rebecca." He pulled her hand up for a kiss. She smiled, thinking how nice the attention was, then discreetly pulled her hand away, thinking that a refined lady would do the same. Lance smiled and untangled the reins, shifting in his seat and leaning forward to watch the road in the dimming light. For several minutes there was no sound save the steady rhythm of the horse's hooves against the ground and the creak of the wagon. "Rebecca, if she's not your mother, then why do you travel with her?" He sat up in his seat and looked at her. "You have to admit she's not like most women."

Rebecca grinned. "No, she's not. But that's part of what makes her so special. She is different. Maybe she doesn't fit into the mold of a perfect lady, but generally, I think proper ladies are boring. Josie's fun; you never know what to expect next from her. It's exciting." She did not realize how big her smile was when she spoke of her friend, but he noticed.

"She looks like the kind that likes trouble. Seems to me you'd be better off settling down somewhere."

"Oh, I'll settle down eventually. I just haven't seen enough of the world to decide what I want to be yet."

"Want to be? What do you mean, want to be? Don't you want to be a wife and mother like all women?"

"Well, of course I do, Lance," she said huffily, not at all happy about having to defend herself. "It's just that I want more than that. Lance, I want to learn about medicine, how to help the sick and injured. I want to do more than cook and clean and raise babies." She quieted down as they passed through the gates to the ranch.

"Seems to me that's all any woman would want," he said, keeping his eyes straight ahead as his perfect vision was shattered.

"You didn't remind me about a hat," Josie growled to Sandy as she entered the saloon and bellied up to the bar. "What if someone says something to her?"

"Josie..." Sandy motioned behind the gunslinger's back at the barkeep to bring the bottle along with the glass he was holding. "I didn't think about the hat. She'll be fine. Rebecca certainly is pretty enough to go without a hat." She poured a glass of whiskey and pushed it in front of the raven-headed woman.

"Did you find the boots you were looking for?"

"Yes." The blue eyes lit up with rare excitement. "They fit her perfectly. You should see them, Sandy, nice white leather with shimmering white buttons like pearls. She looked so nice in them, and in the dress too. You had her size right." Josie stopped when she realized just how much she had said and how she had said it. She quickly drained her glass and refilled it.

"I wish I had remembered the damned hat," she mumbled into the glass.

"Next time you'll remember the hat, Josie. In the meantime, the girl is out having fun, why don't you? There're fresh cigars in my desk and the pool table is free," she suggested, trying hard to keep the smirk off her face. The tall gunslinger was acting like a typical mother worrying about her child's first date. *That girl's got something on you, Josie: I can feel it,* the madam thought. *You've changed, and I'd swear on a stack of bibles held by Jesus himself that it's all because of that girl.*

"Fine... beats sitting around here looking at all these codgers," Josie grumbled, breaking Sandy out of her reverie. The gunslinger grabbed the nearly full bottle and they headed for the back room.

"Rebecca, this is my mother and father, Mister and Missus Jon Van Doren." Lance turned to face his parents. "Mother, Father, this is Rebecca."

Mister Van Doren kissed the back of Rebecca's hand, and Missus Van Doren smiled and said, "Nice to meet you, Rebecca...?"

"Cameron, Rebecca Cameron. Pleasure to meet you as well," she replied, leaning down to accept the offered kiss on the cheek.

"Ah, well now Rebecca, we've met before, haven't we?" Lance's father asked. Like his son, he never forgot a pretty face.

"Yes, at the theater," she replied, instantly regretting it when she saw the look on the older woman's face, that of a cat about to pounce on an unsuspecting mouse.

"Ah yes, the theater. Lovely establishment, wouldn't you say? Not nearly as grand as say, the Palace, but still rather nice for such a rustic area." She turned to see if there was anyone around who was more important she could talk with, and finding none, she returned her attention to the young woman. "What were we talking about? Oh yes, the theater. You were there with your mother, weren't you?" Lance opened his mouth to correct her, but shut it when he felt the gentle poke in his side.

"The actors were very funny, didn't you think?" Rebecca asked, trying desperately to change the subject.

"The actors? Oh, I suppose so." She dismissed the topic with a wave of her hand as if it was not even worth discussing, and then went on. "But tell me, dear, why does your mother wear your father's clothes? And in public?" she said in a disapproving tone. Rebecca's mind raced quickly as she tried to come up with an acceptable explanation.

"Oh, well, you see... that's for my benefit. You see, if people see her like that with me, well, they just assume that she's a man and they don't bother me. Mother's just trying to protect my virtue." She smiled, trying to look as innocent and ladylike as possible.

"Ah, I knew there had to be some explanation." Her curiosity satisfied she turned to her husband. "Come along now, Jon. We have others to attend to." Missus Van Doren gave Rebecca a smile that looked as if it were made of paste, and hooking her arm through her husband's, she propelled him off in the direction of a small crowd of people who had just arrived.

"Sorry about that," Lance said once his parents were out of earshot. "Mother can be a bit... nosy at times."

"It's all right," Rebecca replied. The smell of fresh ribs cooking assailed her nose. "Mmm, smells wonderful," she said sincerely.

"Oh, you haven't lived until you taste Pedro's cooking. His ribs melt in your mouth," he chuckled. "Of course, you'd better make sure you have a tall glass of water next to you. It's a bit spicy."

"I can handle spicy, Lance. One time, my father came home from the trading post with a small little pepper and gosh was it hot."

"Well, I guess you can handle Pedro's sauce then. Come on, let's see if we can get some before the ranch hands take it all."

"You think she's having a nice time?" Josie asked absentmindedly for the fifth time in the past hour.

"Josie, she's fine. She'll be back anytime now, I'm sure of it. Just relax," Sandy said with a sigh, pulling two thin cigars out of a humidor on the desk. "Now I think I've seen his family around here before. Don't get out much, ya know. They look like real nice people. I'm sure she's just fine," she said as she handed the cue ball to the gunslinger. "I do believe it's your shot."

"Yeah," Josie replied noncommittally. To herself she wondered, *Are you safe, Sprite? Are you all right? Please be careful.*

"Did you enjoy yourself, Rebecca?" he asked as they walked near the stable.

"Yes I did, thank you. The food was wonderful, and the company was nice too," she said shyly, turning her head away slightly.

"Yes it was," he said, his voice slightly deeper than before. They were standing just outside the stable. Lance moved, positioning her between him and the wall of the building. "Rebecca..." he said as he moved closer, causing her to back up against the whitewashed wood. "You are very pretty." He had noticed the way she smiled earlier that night whenever he said that and he tried to use it to his advantage now. "Your lips, they were made for kissing." He ran his thumb across her lower lip, causing her heart to pick up its beat slightly. Rebecca looked at him uncertainly, not knowing what to do or say, afraid she was about to be kissed and afraid that she was not.

"Oh?" was all she could think of to say. Lance smiled.

"Yeah." He bent down and pressed his lips to hers, pushing her harder against the wall. His arms came out to rest against the wood on either side of her head. "Rebecca..." he whispered as he came up for air before planting another firm kiss against her mouth. She felt his tongue slip past his lips, demanding entry.

"No," she said as she pressed her hands against his chest, trying to back him away from her. Lance did not back up, but he made no effort to continue.

"Rebecca... all girls kiss," he said as if stating the obvious.

"I did kiss you... but I don't want to do... that," she said, wishing that Josie was there at that moment. "Lance, a real gentleman wouldn't try to push a lady further than she wanted to go."

He ran his fingers through his brown hair as he tried to maintain control. This small, blonde woman was so tempting. He longed to taste her mouth, to take her to his bed. She would be a good mother, he thought as he looked at the womanly flare of her hips. His mother always said to look at their hips; the larger they were, the better for bearing children. Rebecca's hips were not that wide, but certainly looked nice enough to keep the flames going for quite some time. Lance smiled at her and placed his hand beside her head again, leaning in ever so slightly. "I'm not trying to push you, sweet Rebecca. I am, after all, nothing if not a gentleman." He made no effort to change his position just as she made no effort to remove her hands from his chest, lest he move forward to kiss her again. "But you need to understand that when a man kisses you, you have to let him kiss you the way he wants to. Have you ever been kissed like that before?"

"N-no. Lance, I think I'd better get back now." She tried to duck under his arms but he was too fast for her. He quickly wrapped his arms around her and held her close.

"Rebecca... I'm not trying to rape you; I just want a kiss." He brought his mouth to hers again, this time with more authority. He forced her mouth open with his tongue, yelping and letting go of her when he felt the bite of her teeth on his lower lip. "Ow... you bitch," he spat, his hand going to his tender lip.

"I said no," she said nervously, visions of the women of Rosewood and the things that Lefty's men did to them filling her mind, making panic rise in her throat.

"Well... I guess you did, didn't you?" he said in a defeated tone. "If that's how you want to be..." Rebecca understood the implication. He was not interested in her anymore. He looked over at the crowd of ranch hands milling about. "Hey, Matt!" he called. One of the men separated himself from the crowd and began walking their way. "Matt will take you home," he said, effectively dismissing her as he walked to meet with the ranch hand. He said a few words to the man, gesturing in her direction and, without a backward glance, he rejoined the celebration up at the main house. Matt looked apologetic as he escorted her to the wagons and helped her into the one the ranch hands used for hauling hay about the fields.

"Sorry, ma'am. This here's the only one that Mister Van Doren lets us use. Seat's pretty clean, though," he pulled out his handkerchief and wiped the wooden seat before she sat down anyway. "I'll have you home in no time." He sat down and snapped the reins, sending the horse into motion. Rebecca remained quiet on the way back, wishing only to be back with

Josie, to have her tell her that she had done nothing wrong, and that everything would be all right, but mostly just to be with her.

Josie paced back and forth from the window to the door of the back room. Sandy looked at the clock nervously. It was after ten and there was no sign of Rebecca. A half dozen whores sat around playing cards. The menacing look of the gunslinger had driven away most of the evening's business since she had come out of the back room shortly after eight and began her relentless pacing. "Josie, please come sit down... you're making me dizzy."

"How much longer can she possibly be? She said she'd be back early," the gunslinger growled. The creak of a wagon in the distance drew her back to the window. "She's back," Josie said with relief evident in her voice, and she headed for the door.

"Good night," Sandy said to the retreating form.

Josie made it back to the boarding house a minute or two before Rebecca. She had the lamp turned up and was sitting in the chair, waiting for the young woman to come upstairs and tell her about her evening. She listened to the rhythm of the young woman's steps in the hall. They stopped at the door, but Rebecca did not enter immediately. Seconds passed as Josie waited. A grave fear set in as the gunslinger leapt from her chair and opened the door. Instantly Rebecca was in her arms, sobbing shamelessly. Josie's body softened immediately as she enveloped the young woman in her arms and closed the door. She led them to the bed and sat down, keeping her arms around Rebecca. Anger, fear, concern, and a twinge of guilt for not being there all filled the gunslinger as she waited for the tears and ragged breathing to cease and her friend to be able to speak again.

It was several minutes before Rebecca calmed down enough to speak. Josie had spent the time holding her, doing her best to keep her anger in check and promising herself that Lance would suffer if he hurt her friend in any way. Slowly the tears and haggard breathing eased to a point where Josie felt comfortable letting go. "What happened?" the gunslinger asked tentatively, not fully certain she wanted to know the answer. Her eyes inspected Rebecca, noting no tears in the dress, nor bruising anywhere, except perhaps her lips. The young woman took a shaky breath before speaking, her eyes fixed upon a spot on the floor.

"He kissed me," she said softly. "I wanted him to, but..." her voice trailed off. Josie placed her fingers on the young woman's chin and forced her to meet her gaze.

"But what, Rebecca? What did he do?" She fought to keep her anger in check and not let it show in her voice. "Tell me," she said softly.

"He tried..." she paused but did not turn away. Josie swore she could see the young woman gathering the strength to speak. "He tried to kiss me more than I wanted... and when I said no, he... he got mad and had one of the men drive me home."

"He wasn't man enough to escort you home?" This time Josie made no effort to hide her anger, only the intensity of it.

"But he had Matt bring me... he's a nice fellow." She saw no change in the gunslinger's expression. "Josie, he didn't try anything. Matt was a perfect gentleman."

"Shame Lance wasn't," she growled, rising and going to the window. It was taking great effort to stay in the room and not go knock some sense into the young man, or just knock him around. A very unpleasant thought came to her. "Rebecca... is there anything else? I mean did he...try to touch you?" It was an effort to get out the words.

"No," was the soft reply. Josie visibly relaxed and returned to the bed. Without thought, she put her arm around Rebecca's shoulders and pulled her in for another hug.

"It's all right now, Sprite. You're safe here," she whispered into the younger woman's ear. "I wish it had gone better."

"I had a nice time otherwise," Rebecca offered, trying to lighten the mood. "They have a cook, Pedro. He makes the best barbecue ribs... they were so good."

"How many racks did you eat, my little eating machine?" the gunslinger teased good-naturedly, also trying to eradicate the somber mood. The young woman smiled and wiped her eyes.

"I only had a few pieces. Had to act like a lady, after all. Oh, they had a small band there, too...." She went on for several minutes describing the rest of the party, deliberately leaving out her conversation with Lance's mother. She let out a long yawn in the middle of describing the ranch itself.

"I think it's time for bed," Josie said as she rose to her feet.

Rebecca nodded and reached down to unbutton her boots. Without a word, the gunslinger dropped to the floor and made quick work of the buttons.

"Thanks." She picked one of the boots up and stared at it thoughtfully. "You know, Josie, someday I'm going to give you something. Something that only I can give you. Something irreplaceable." She gingerly ran her fingers over the leather of the boot. "Something that makes you feel as special as I do tonight. You didn't have to get me these beautiful boots, you didn't have to find me the dress." Before Josie could react, Rebecca put her arms around her and gave her a loving embrace. "Someday..."

Josie looked down at the blonde head resting under her chin. She thought back over the past few months, trying to pinpoint exactly when the young woman in her arms had slipped past her defenses and become such an important part of her life, not just an unexpected burden. She tightened her grip slightly, smiling to herself when she felt it returned. "Come on, Sprite. You've had a long day. Let's get you to bed."

Long after Rebecca had fallen asleep, Josie lay awake trying to quell the anger that burned inside her. Despite the young woman's protests that he did nothing other than try to kiss her more than she wanted to, the gunslinger still felt an almost uncontrollable rage towards Lance. How dare he try to force his way on Rebecca. Only when she looked at the angelic face sleeping beside her did Josie feel any sense of calm. Moving gently so as not to disturb her, the gunslinger curled her body around Rebecca's and soon joined her in sleep.

After breakfast, they went to the saloon to return the dress and to visit with their friends. Sandy adamantly refused to accept the garment, citing that it had been collecting dust in the closet for months after its original owner left. She gave Rebecca a small carpetbag to keep the dress in while they traveled. Josie sat at a table with three other women, intent on playing a few hands of poker while the young blonde went upstairs to visit with Stacey and Victoria, both of whom had remained in their rooms.

"Full house," Elaine said triumphantly as she lay her cards down and reached for the pot. Despite having a flush in her hand, Josie tossed her cards down. Something else had captured her interest.

"I'll be back," she said firmly as she rose from her chair and stormed out the door. Elaine and the others looked at each other for just a brief moment before the black-headed woman went in search of Sandy. She had no idea who or what the tall woman had seen, but whatever it was, the gunslinger was most definitely angry when she left.

Lance stepped down from the wooden walk in front of the mercantile, totally oblivious to his surroundings. The next thing he knew, he was being thrown hard against the side of the building, an extremely angry woman in black glaring at him, her hands clenching the front of his shirt. There was a fire in the ice blue eyes, a fire that was reserved for him and he knew it. Never in his young life had he felt so much fear as he did at that very moment. "I-I-I..." he stammered helplessly.

"You are a very lucky man, you know that?" Josie growled, pushing him against the wall again for emphasis. "I don't like men who try to take advantage of young women, especially... my... friend." She accentuated the last three words with little shoves into his chest, each shove slamming him hard against the wood.

"I-I... all I did was kiss her," he cried, his eyes darting around in a vain attempt to find someone to help him. "I swear I didn't try anything else, I swear!"

"If you had tried something else..." Josie moved close, her face scant inches away from his, "...the only 'lance' you would have left is the one in your signature." She looked down at his crotch, then back up at his face, and arched an eyebrow. "Got it?"

He swallowed nervously as beads of perspiration rolled off his brow. Josie pulled him forward slightly and shoved him against the wall again, slightly harder than before. She knew he would end up with little more than a few bruises on his shoulder blades and perhaps a ruined pair of britches, but in her eyes, that was a small price to pay for making Rebecca's first date an unpleasant experience. "Rebecca is a very forgiving person, but I'm not. Be thankful that you get to walk away with all your body parts intact." She gave him one more shove and then let go of his shirt. "Hurt her again and I swear you won't live to regret it."

Lance slumped down on the ground next to the wall, grateful to be alive. Josie gave him one more menacing stare before turning to head back to the saloon. She stopped short when she saw Rebecca standing at the mouth of the alleyway staring at her. Neither paid any attention as the scared young man quickly took his leave, smartly heading in the opposite direction. Josie approached her, trying to keep her face as expressionless as possible despite the gnawing fear that the young woman would think her little more than an animal for attacking him. By the time the gunslinger was within touching distance of Rebecca, she was certain that the young woman would walk away from her, never to return.

"How much did you see?" Josie asked, managing to avoid eye contact, certain of the disappointment she would find there. She was startled to feel a gentle touch on her forearm as Rebecca reached out to her.

"Enough," she said softly. "Did you hurt him?"

"Not nearly as much as I wanted to," the gunslinger admitted. "I held back."

"Why? Hey..." she put her fingers on Josie's cheek, "...look at me... that's better. Why did you hold back? Because of me?" she asked gently. The blue eyes flickered for the briefest of moments, giving Rebecca her answer. The unspoken admission was enough to make Josie visibly uncomfortable. The young woman pulled her hand back and smiled warmly, as she understood the unspoken fear. She also understood that her tall companion was not ready to voice that fear or have it voiced for her. This was not a case of the gunslinger protecting someone from harm. Rebecca realized that it went much deeper than that. What happened in the alleyway was revenge, pure and simple. Josie wanted to punish Lance for hurting her. As much as the thought of physical violence bothered her, Rebecca nevertheless felt a warm, comfortable feeling at the knowledge that the gunslinger cared enough about her to do such a thing. She captured the blue eyes with her own. "I'm glad you didn't beat the stuffing out of him, even if he did deserve it."

The words eased the tightness that Josie was feeling in her chest, as she understood that Rebecca was not upset with her. "I wanted to, you know. I wanted to push his little head right through the wall." Her muscled forearms tensed as she remembered the feeling of slamming him against the wooden side of the building.

"I know you did, Josie. But don't you see? You didn't. You didn't hurt him; well, not badly anyway, and you didn't lose control," she said reassuringly, frowning when she noticed that the gunslinger's jaw was still clenched as tightly as her fists. "Josie, you're not the monster people think you are, or even you think you are. What you did today wasn't done out of anger or hatred, it was done out of care and concern for another human being." She touched the gunslinger's arm again and maintained the contact, wrapping her small fingers around the powerful wrist. "For me," Rebecca said softly, almost in awe that her sadness could affect Josie so.

The gunslinger cleared her throat and politely pulled her arm back, the emotions becoming too much for her once again. "I don't think you have to worry about old lance in the pants again."

"Josie!" Rebecca said, shocked at her friend's comment. "I don't believe you said that. How awful." A huge grin broke out on her face as she thought about the comment some more. The grin turned into a smile, which in turn became a giggle. She swatted her tall friend's arm playfully. "You are bad."

"Stick around me and you'll learn just how bad I can be," Josie said wickedly. "Come on, I'll buy you a drink. If you're a good girl, I'll even teach you how to play pool."

"Really?" Rebecca said excitedly. "You would, really? Teach me, I mean."

Josie smiled at the childish look of excitement in her friend's face. "Rebecca, I'll teach you how to play pool and anything else you want. I warn you though, I'm a hard taskmaster; worse than Belle."

"If you're my teacher, I don't think I'll mind. I'm a fast learner, you'll see," she said enthusiastically. "I won't let you down."

"I'm sure you won't," Josie agreed as they entered the saloon.

34: Endings and Beginnings

"They want to leave?" Josie asked as she took her shot, sinking the four ball cleanly in the corner pocket.

"Yup. Both of them. I can understand Stacey, what with the shooting and all," Sandy replied as she watched the seven ball fall into the side pocket. "And Victoria, well, I think your Rebecca had something to do with that. She said she wasn't doing no more whoring."

"What is she going to do?" She passed the cue back to the blonde madam and ignored the "your Rebecca" remark. "From what I understand, she doesn't have any skills."

"I don't know, Josie. She's still young. Maybe she can find herself a man and have a family." She bent over and took aim. "Of course she can't do that around here; someone might pass through town and recognize her from Rosewood." Sandy pulled her arm back and let loose, sending two balls into the pocket. Unfortunately, one of them was the cue ball. Josie held her hand out for the stick, her face an unreadable mask.

"Think she'd make it if she wasn't around here?"

"I don't know. Even without an education, she's a smart girl. I imagine if she gets somewhere where she can make a new start she'll be all right," the madam said. "Don't know her too well, though. You'd be better off asking Elaine or even Rebecca."

"Hmm." Josie let the conversation drop as she took her shot, letting out a low growl, as the eight ball bounced off the green felt bumper. She set the cue stick down on the pool table. "Sandy, I have to go somewhere. Keep an eye on Rebecca."

"Well, that should be no problem. She's probably with Victoria anyway. Where are you going?" Sandy asked.

"Express office."

Despite Rebecca's best efforts at dinner to get the gunslinger to tell her why she had to go to the Express office, Josie adamantly refused. It was half past eight and they were settled in for the night in their room, the bounty hunter cleaning and polishing her guns and the young woman studying her medical text. The blonde head poked up from behind the large book. "Did you send a telegram somewhere?"

"Rebecca..." she warned gently.

"I'm sorry, Josie. If you'd just tell me what you were up to then I wouldn't bother you about it," she coaxed, anxious to quench her curiosity. The gunslinger merely smirked and continued to rub the cloth over the steel.

"Nope," she said smugly, watching Rebecca get more and more frustrated.

"Josie... come on, tell me."

"Nope."

"Please? I'll give you a backrub."

"Nope," she said, even though the offer was tempting. Not being on the road, there had really been no physical activity to strain her back. The scuffle with Lance was nothing. Josie missed those moments when she could relax and let her friend rub the tension out of her. But she was not going to give in on this one, no matter what Rebecca tried.

"Josie... you know I'm just going to keep asking until you tell me, so you might as well just tell me now and get it over with," she grinned mischievously.

"Nope."

"Please?"

"No."

"Come on, please?" Each time she asked only served to make her more aggravated, much to the gunslinger's amusement. She could just imagine what Rebecca was like on Christmas.

"I'm going downstairs to take a bath," Josie said, rising. The young woman was about to beg again when the words registered. Rebecca lifted her arm slightly and lowered it quickly. The hot afternoon had done nothing to help her aroma.

"Um, Josie?" she asked with all seriousness, the change in tone drawing the gunslinger's attention to her and away from the door handle that her fingers were about to close on. "If you don't mind, I'll watch the door for you if you watch the door for me? I'd um... feel safer with you there," she said, fairly certain that Josie would agree, especially after the way the gunslinger reacted to seeing the flimsy lock yesterday. What Rebecca did not expect was the momentary look of affection on her face. Josie picked up the second towel and held it out to her.

"Come on," she said with a gentle smile, understanding what the offer truly was. *Never fear, Rebecca. I'll always protect you,* she thought as she watched the young blonde grab her nightgown from the edge of the bed.

"Josie, I know you sent a telegram. Come on, where'd you send it?" she asked through the closed door. The raven-headed woman lifted her leg straight up in the air.

"Give up, Rebecca... and stop yelling through the door," she called. "If you want to talk to me then come in here." She washed and lowered her leg back into the warm water. Josie watched the latch slowly lift and the door open. She had not bothered to twist the useless piece of wood when she entered, knowing full well that even without her weapons, she could handle anything that happened. The claw-foot tub was not really deep enough for the tall woman, causing the water to lap gently against the underside of her breasts. Rebecca entered, trying not to look at the naked woman, and she crossed the room to sit on the floor with her back against the porcelain and steel fixture. Josie laughed lightly. "You don't have to sit on the floor, Rebecca. There's a perfectly good stool over there, just scootch it over."

"Uh... no, I can't. I'm fine here, really," she said, her embarrassment showing. Josie smiled softly, although the little blonde could not see it.

"You've seen me naked before, Rebecca." She did her best to keep her tone gentle and understanding, not wanting to do anything to further embarrass her young friend.

"Well, yeah, but only for a few seconds while you're changing. We've never talked with you... like that." She kept her eyes focused on a knot in the door panel.

"I sleep topless against you every night," Josie tried again.

"I know... and I know I'm being silly," Rebecca said, turning her head toward the gunslinger, but not far enough to see anything. A long, wet arm slipped out of the tub and lightly patted the blonde head.

"It's all right, Rebecca. If you're more comfortable there, that's fine. I'll tell you what, why don't you tell me a story," Josie said, hoping to make her more comfortable. It really was annoying to have to turn around every time the young woman got dressed or undressed.

"Which one do you want to hear?"

"I don't know... tell me something I haven't heard before," the gunslinger replied as she lathered up the cloth until it was covered with a bubbly white foam. She twisted her arm up behind her and tried to wash her back, grunting as she stretched her fingertips to try and reach that one area that was always impossible to get to.

"What are you doing?" Rebecca asked, getting to her knees as she twisted to see Josie.

"Trying to wash my back, what does it look like I'm doing?" she replied testily.

"Well, if you'd ask for help," the young woman replied as she rose to her feet and walked over to the corner. She picked up the stool and set it down at the head of the tub. "Lean forward please," Rebecca said as she took the soapy cloth from the long fingers and started to wash her friend's broad shoulder. Josie reached back and gathered the long black tresses in her hand, pulling them to one side and out of the way so the young woman could continue her task.

Rebecca hummed a tune as she continued to run the washcloth over the gunslinger's back, gently rubbing the well-defined muscles as she passed over them. Josie closed her eyes and let her head fall forward, her hair spilling forward, the black tips sinking into the soapy water. "How's that feel?"

"Mmm, good," the gunslinger murmured, lulled into relaxation by the gentle hands sliding over her skin, aided by the soap. Rebecca dipped the washcloth back into the water before raising it and squeezing the water out over Josie's shoulder. She repeated the procedure until she was certain that every last trace of soap was off. Only then did she drape the cloth over the edge of the tub and sit back on the stool. She was disappointed slightly that it was over. Rebecca did not know what it was, but there was just something so enjoyable about giving the stronger woman a massage. To feel those muscles loosen under her touch, to see the small smile that formed on Josie's face, to know there was something that she could do, no matter how small, that made the older woman feel comfortable and relaxed. Twice that she was sure of Rebecca had made the gunslinger fall asleep. She wished that Josie would ask for backrubs more often.

The raven-headed woman took the now cool cloth from the side of the tub. "Thanks, Rebecca," Josie said as she quickly finished up, the water now cooled down to an uncomfortable level. "Could you hand me the towel please?"

"Oh... um, yeah." Rebecca stood up and retrieved Josie's towel from the shelf. She held it out and waited for the gunslinger to rise and exit the tub.

"Thanks," Josie said as she took the towel and began drying off.

"Oh, I forgot!" Rebecca exclaimed. "I put water on to heat. It's probably all boiled away by now." She could not keep the disappointment from showing on her face. She had been looking forward to soaking away all the sweat and dust. "I'd better go see."

Josie watched the door close behind the young woman. She rolled her shoulders, enjoying the lack of tension within them. She picked up the clean pair of drawers and stepped into them, pulling them up just as she heard a soft knock on the door. "Josie? Can you get the door? My hands are full." The gunslinger pushed her arms through the sleeves of her shirt, letting it hang loosely on her body as she headed toward the door.

The stronger woman opened the door and took the two heavy pails from Rebecca, careful not to pinch the blonde's fingers during the exchange. Within seconds, both pails were emptied into the tub, causing wisps of steam to rise. "Guess you didn't boil it away," she said as she set the empty containers on the floor.

"No," Rebecca said in a relieved tone. "I guess the stove wasn't that hot." She stood there for a moment and then asked hesitantly, "Josie... aren't you going to leave?"

"Sure, I'll wait outside," she said, buttoning up her shirt as she headed for the door. The gunslinger had thought the young woman wanted her to stay and wash her back. *Sprite, you really need to get over this modesty,* Josie thought to herself as she closed the door behind her and flopped down on the nearby stool. She leaned her head against the wall and closed her eyes, planning on taking a short catnap while Rebecca soaked.

Josie heard in one instant the splash of water, the startled cry, and the thud. She leapt to her feet and flung open the door in time to see Rebecca lying on the floor, one foot still on the side of the tub. "Are you all right?" the gunslinger asked as she knelt down next to her and helped the young woman get her leg down and sit up. "Did you get hurt?" she asked. Rebecca shook her head, waving her hand to say that she was fine.

"Just my pride, I guess." A slight tinge of embarrassment colored her cheeks. She drew her knees up and rested her arms on them, her back against the tub. "I'm fine, Josie." She looked at the door expectantly.

"Rebecca..." she said sternly, "If you think I'm going to take a chance of you falling again, you're sadly mistaken. You're lucky you didn't crack your head on the side of the tub." The gunslinger felt her heartbeat slowly return to normal. She had slipped once in a tub and been knocked out; only her long frame kept her from slipping under the water and drowning. Josie stood up and held out her hand.

"I'm fine. Go on. I'll be all right now," Rebecca said, not moving from her position against the tub. The gunslinger noted that the young woman's position did nothing to hide her personal areas from view. She knew that Rebecca had to be a bit shook up from the fall, but it still did not make sense that she made no attempt to cover herself yet still insisted on being left alone.

"Stand up and let me help you into the tub," she said firmly, regretting her tone the instant she saw the sad look in the green eyes. For a long moment, neither moved from her respective position. Rebecca reached out tentatively and took Josie's hand, allowing the taller woman to help her to her feet. She faced the gunslinger, green eyes locking with blue as she lifted one leg up and into the slippery tub. She felt the strong hand grip hers tighter as she lifted the other leg and stepped in. Rebecca twisted and sat down in the tub careful not to move so fast as to make the water splash out. She leaned her back against the slight slant of the end and looked up at Josie. "I'm in now," she said, stating the obvious.

"I see that," the gunslinger said as she moved to the head of the tub and sat down on the stool. "Since I'm here I might as well wash your back, seeing as how you washed mine."

"Josie?" came the small voice, "I-I don't want you to, all right?"

Instantly the raven-headed woman moved to the side of the tub and knelt down until she was eye level with the now visibly upset woman. Josie folded her arms and leaned against the cool porcelain, her face showing her concern. "What's got you so scared, Sprite? What are you afraid of me finding out?" she asked gently, silently willing her friend to confide in her, to trust her with whatever was wrong. A thought occurred to her. "Rebecca, are you afraid of me?"

"No!" She sat up and caught the blue eyes with her own. "It's not you, Josie, honest," the blonde lowered her head, staring at her hands underwater. It took only seconds for Rebecca to lose the battle to control her emotions. Her heart told her to take the chance and a small voice in her mind screamed at her not to tell. The green eyes closed yet the tears still came unbidden, leaking out to leave wet trails down her cheeks.

Rebecca found herself instantly enfolded in strong, flannel-covered arms. Her tears gave way to outright sobs and she wrapped her arms around Josie's neck, squeezing tightly. The gunslinger held her, unmindful of the hard tub pressing against her ribs. Nothing mattered except trying to get her friend calmed down. Josie pulled her closer, the shift causing her to look over the blonde's shoulder and there she saw what had gotten her so upset.

There was no need for words; the faded scars told the tale all too clearly. Josie swallowed and took a deep breath to quell her rising anger and outrage at the sight. She felt the small woman stiffen in her arms and she held tight. "No, it's all right, Sprite. It's all right. I know." She repeated the words over and over like a mantra into the young woman's ear, rocking her gently in the process. Josie was dimly aware of a growing pain in her ribs from the tub, but chose to ignore it. Her friend was more important at the moment.

In the darkness of the older woman's comforting shoulder, Rebecca cried. She cried for the pain of a young girl who only wanted to be loved. She cried for the loss of happiness and joy within herself at the hands of those who were supposed to protect and care for her. She cried until no more tears were left; only the feeling of a great weight removed from her remained. Rebecca took several deep haggard breaths before pulling back from Josie's embrace. They sat there silently, both needing time to compose themselves. The bounty hunter's hand went to her own ribs, touching lightly and wincing at the pain. She did not realize how hard she had been pressing against the tub. "You all right?" Rebecca asked softly, her voice a bit raspy.

"I'm fine. What about you?" Josie asked as she moved back to the stool, her back protesting from being kept in that position for so long.

The young woman nodded slightly, both knowing that it was not the complete truth. "This water's getting cold."

"Well then let's get you washed up quickly, shall we?" Josie replied, grabbing the soapy washcloth. With the gentleness of a washerwoman cleaning the floor, she scrubbed the smaller woman's shoulder.

"Hey!"

"Sorry," she replied, leaning forward and giving Rebecca a lopsided grin. "I guess I'm not used to washing other people. I'll go easier."

Josie wrapped the cloth around two of her fingers and gently rubbed the young woman's other shoulder, using small circular motions. Her lips set in a tight line when her hand passed over the most prominent streak of white against Rebecca's skin. *I guess you're not such an innocent after all, are you, Sprite?* she thought. *You should have been protected from him, from his rage. How could anyone raise his hand to someone as gentle and caring as you?* "Never again," she said, realizing that she had spoken aloud.

"What?" Rebecca asked as she turned in the tub to face her. Josie handed her the washcloth and forced a smile.

"I said I'm done. Finish up," the gunslinger lied. She waited until the young woman was done and helped her out of the tub before leaving her to dry off and get dressed.

Leaning against the wall outside the washroom, Josie's mind raced while she waited for Rebecca to finish. She tried to think of all the reasons why having the young woman stay with her was no good. It was too dangerous. She could get hurt. A dozen reasons later, Josie rubbed her face with her hands vigorously and sighed. The decision was made.

Once in their room, Josie turned the lamp down and joined Rebecca in bed. As had quickly become the habit, the gunslinger wrapped her arm around the smaller woman's waist and curled up against her back. Both lay there, wide-awake and deep in thought. "Can't sleep?" the blonde inquired. Josie propped herself up on one elbow and looked down at Rebecca, who rolled onto her back to look at her companion.

"Do you..." the gunslinger began. "Do you want to stay with me? Traveling from place to place with no roots and no home? Is that what you want?"

"Josie... I had a home and a family and I was miserable." She lowered her eyes. "I want to stay with you, if you'll let me." Rebecca wanted to plead, to beg, to offer anything just to continue being with her friend, her protector. But she held back, still not daring to hope that Josie wanted the same thing.

"You know it's dangerous... you can get hurt, or worse."

"I could get hurt or worse anywhere."

"Don't you want to settle down? Raise a family?"

Rebecca raised herself up on one elbow, her face inches away from the gunslinger's. "Josie, I'm not ready to settle down yet. There's too much to see, too much to do. I know it won't be easy, but I'm willing to try. Neither one of us has to be alone again." She lowered her head, her voice quavering as she continued. "I don't want to go back, Josie. If you don't want me to stay with you then leave me here, but I won't go back to Chancetown... I-I can't."

"No. I won't let them hurt you again, Rebecca. Never again." Josie said firmly, her own outrage and anger at her friend's pain showing through. "I can't promise that it'll always be easy."

"Are you saying that I can stay with you?" she asked hopefully.

"Yes," was all the gunslinger could get out before she was knocked onto her back by the smaller woman's fierce hug. Rebecca held on tight, her emotions a mixture of relief and joy. Josie smiled in the darkness, feeling her own sense of joy at the young woman's reaction. She wrapped her own arms around Rebecca. "Yes, Sprite, you can stay with me. I won't make you leave, I swear."

Long after the young woman had fallen asleep in her arms, Josie lay awake, her own emotions still churning about. Her head and heart warred with each other over her decision, her mind telling her that someone as gentle and caring as Rebecca could only get hurt being around her, and her heart quietly saying that she had no other choice. She looked down at the sleeping blonde, noting the soft smile that graced her lips and the gentle, even breathing of a most peaceful rest. "Neither one of us will be alone again. I'll die to protect you," Josie whispered before placing a soft kiss on the young woman's forehead and settling down to let sleep claim her.

Rebecca woke to find herself alone, a cool cup of coffee waiting for her on the table. She stretched and yawned, wondering where the gunslinger went at such an early hour. "Damn," she swore when she realized. She peeled off her nightgown, not bothering to notice where it landed, and quickly dressed.

Josie exited the express office, telegram and draft note in hand.

"You gonna tell me now?" She turned to see Rebecca sitting on the small bench next to the doorway. The young woman hopped up and stood beside the gunslinger, trying her hardest to steal a peek at the note.

"Nope," Josie said as she folded up the papers and tucked them into her vest pocket. Out of the corner of her eye, she caught the frustrated and furious look on her young friend's face and smirked.

"Josie..." She followed the gunslinger up the street, walking quickly to keep up with the taller woman's longer stride. "Josie... you know you can trust me with anything... Josie are you listening to me? What is it? Friends share things, you know.... Come on, Josie...." All she heard was a deep, throaty chuckle from the woman in black.

Sandy watched the tall woman enter with a bemused expression on her face, followed closely by Rebecca, who was pestering her about something. "Why won't you tell me? Come on, Josie, I'm no good at surprises."

"Rebecca, go get Stacey and Victoria and have them meet us in the back room," Josie said just as Sandy reached them. "I swear I'll tell you what's in the note then."

"Oh, all right," the young woman replied, a bit disappointed. "You wait, Josie," she said as she reached the stairs. "Someday I'm gonna have a secret and you just see if you can get it out of me," she said smugly, although deep down inside she knew she would probably have a hard time keeping anything from Josie if she really wanted to know.

Sandy and the gunslinger entered the back room and waited for the others to arrive. Josie leaned against the pool table, one leg bent and resting on the green felt. The madam frowned but said nothing, choosing instead to take a seat on the couch. Stacey, Victoria, and Rebecca entered, the two prostitutes choosing to stand at the end of the billiard table while the young blonde stood next to Josie. The tall woman looked at the two women at the end of the table. "I understand you both want to leave, to go somewhere and make a fresh start." Both women nodded in agreement. A rare public smile formed on Josie's face as she pulled the notes out of her pocket and unfolded them. She passed the telegram to Stacey. "There are jobs waiting for both of you as well as a place to stay," the gunslinger said. The redhead read the note aloud for Victoria.

J
MOST PLEASED TO HEAR FROM YOU STOP
ARRANGEMENTS MADE STOP
REPORT TO MRS STANTON 128 W 140TH STOP
DRAFT ATTACHED STOP
SBA STOP

She set the telegram down and looked at Josie. "I don't..."

"You both need work and somewhere to live. Missus Stanton needs two maids," the gunslinger explained. To Victoria's surprised look, she replied. "Missus Stanton is a friend of the family. I've known her since before I was Rebecca's age."

"But I don't know nothing about being a maid," the young brown-headed woman protested. Josie held up her hand to forestall any more argument.

"Elizabeth is a good woman, very well-educated, and part of the suffrage movement. She'll take care of you and help you find something you're suitable for. Most likely she'd even teach you how to read and write if you wanted."

Victoria looked squarely at Rebecca. "Is this the second chance you were talking about?"

"Yes." She moved closer and took Victoria's hands in her own. "I don't know this Missus Stanton but I do know Josie. If she says it's the right thing, then I believe her. Victoria, think of it: New York City. A place to live and an honorable job," Rebecca cast quick glances at the others. "No offense."

"None taken, child. We know you didn't mean nothing by it," Sandy said. Stacey stared down at the note again.

"I know that working for someone who treats women as people and not objects is a far cry better than this," the redhead said to Victoria. She turned her attention to Josie. "She said there was a draft attached?"

The gunslinger smiled a self-satisfied smile and nodded. "Plenty for both of you to take a stage to Saint Louis and then a train the rest of the way," she said, handing Stacey the draft note. "The stage will be here in just over four hours. You have enough time to get to the bank and the mercantile to get the things you need for traveling. There's enough money for that, too."

"Josie?" They were lying in bed, darkness long since fallen.

"What?"

"Do you think Victoria will be all right? I mean, what if she gets there and that woman doesn't like her?"

"You worry too much, Rebecca. Go to sleep." She tightened her hold around the younger woman's waist. "She'll be fine. Elizabeth will make sure of it. It's not the first time she's taken people in and helped them."

"You said she and the one who you sent the telegram to are friends of yours?" Rebecca had trouble believing that anyone who had the money and position to hire maids at will would be a friend to a known outlaw.

"Well, she and Susan are friends of my mother's mostly. I know them through her," Josie explained. "They used to hold meetings with other suffragists at my mother's home. Victoria will be fine. Besides, Stacey's with her. Can we go to sleep now?"

"Yeah. What time are we leaving tomorrow?" She heard the exasperated and rather tired sigh behind her.

"Rebecca, once we're up and ready to go, then we'll leave."

"All right."

It was silent for several moments before Josie spoke. "You can buy all the supplies from now on."

"W-what?" Rebecca turned in the older woman's arms, her left arm trapped between their bellies. "You mean it?"

"Of course. You get better prices than I do. I never would have been able to get all the supplies for the price that you did. You're good at that haggling stuff. Now roll over and go to sleep," Josie said, pushing gently on the young woman's side in an attempt to get her to move.

Rebecca rolled over happily and grinned in the darkness.

"I do get better prices, don't I?" she said smugly. "Hmm, wonder what else I do better than you."

"Talk... and talk and talk," the gunslinger teased. She felt the light swat on her forearm and chuckled before becoming serious. "You have your own skills and talents, Rebecca. You just have to discover them." She snuggled deeper into her pillow. "Now go to sleep."

"Before you shoot me?" the teasing blonde inquired. Both bodies shook together as they remembered the old threat and realized how funny it seemed to them now. It was not long before sleep claimed both the gunslinger and the young woman curled up in her powerful arms.

Late morning found them at the stable, readying the horses and wagon for departure. Despite Josie's best attempts, the good-byes from Rebecca to all the other women dragged on far longer than planned. It seemed that the young woman had a speech prepared for each one of them, the ones from Rosewood as well as the women from Cheyenne, whom Rebecca knew very little about. All were treated to parting wishes of the best for them and several offered and received hugs from the bubbling young woman. Of course the most they received from the gunslinger was a polite nod and a mumbled "You're welcome" to the women from Rosewood's repeated thanks. Josie and Elaine exchanged a knowing nod and Sandy received a handshake, but no one else dared get that close to the well-armed woman. Once all their good-byes were said, Rebecca told Josie she had an errand to run before she would be ready to go, so Josie went on ahead to get their gear stowed in the wagon and the horses ready.

"Ready?" Josie asked as she climbed up into the sheepskin-covered seat and took the reins from Rebecca.

"Yeah," she said as she put her hat on and adjusted the brim to keep the sun out of her eyes. "Josie, how long do you think it'll take to get there?"

"Shouldn't be more than a week, but it's not going to be an easy ride," the gunslinger said as she double-checked the position of the Winchester leaning against the seat between them. "The Cimarron Cutoff is a dry and dangerous route, but it cuts at least five days off our journey." She turned in her seat and looked at Rebecca, wondering not for the first time if she should just take the much longer yet safer route.

"Is that why you bought the extra barrel for water?" the young woman asked, reaching back and laying her hand against the large, heavy wooden container. Josie nodded, not mentioning that it was also why she bought extra boxes of shells for the Winchester as well as for the Colts. The Cimarron Cutoff was known as a route where ambushes were common from both bandits and renegade Indians. Josie took one more look at the contents of the wagon to make certain she had not forgotten anything before they left town. Not that she would ever forget something she considered necessary for traveling, but there was also Rebecca to consider. Thus there was a small box of rock candy hidden underneath Josie's saddlebag, as well as a dime novel entitled *Tom Sawyer* that she had seen the young woman pick up and look at while they were at the mercantile. There were also two more blankets in preparation of the upcoming cold nights. With a flick of her wrist, Josie set Flossy in motion, and the wagon made its way slowly out of town with Phoenix tethered behind.

35: Cimarron Crossing

Despite the late start, they still made good time before dusk began to settle and Josie decided to stop for the night. She turned the wagon off the trail, stopping it only when she was certain she was far enough away that a fire would not attract attention from the rutted road. They unhitched the horses and tended to their needs before going about setting up the camp. Josie went in search of dry brush and wood for the fire while Rebecca unpacked the gear they would need for the night.

After sleeping next to Josie for the past few nights, it seemed strange to her to set their blankets on opposite sides of the fire. However, it did not seem right to set them side-by-side either. Rebecca solved her dilemma by setting her blankets ninety degrees from Josie's around the fire. She was careful to place her pillow on the end closest to the gunslinger, knowing full well what her feet were like after a long, hot day packed in her boots. Thinking about her companion's own ability to smell like she traipsed through a swamp whenever she removed her black boots, Rebecca set Josie's pillow in a similar manner. The end result was that their heads would be less than four feet apart during the night, close enough to be near without being on top of each other. Once the sleeping arrangements were settled, Rebecca began to position the ring of stones that would circle the fire before setting out the coffee and cooking pots, their flat metal plates for eating, and their utensils.

The young woman was rummaging through the supplies, trying to figure out where Josie had packed their tin mugs when she felt the sensation of being watched. Rebecca's heart raced and her breathing increased, and her mouth suddenly felt very dry. She knew the gunslinger would most likely be within earshot, but found herself unable to utter a sound. Her eyes fell on the Winchester lying propped against the seat of the wagon. Acting as though she were still looking for the elusive mugs, Rebecca climbed up in the back of the wagon and slowly moved forward until she was within arm's reach of the rifle. "What are you looking for?"

Rebecca jumped visibly at the sound of Josie's voice behind her. "Oh, land sakes, Josie, you scared the daylights out of me," she said as she turned to face the grinning gunslinger. "I thought there was a bandit sneaking up on us." She placed her hand over her still rapidly beating heart. Her fear turned to anger as she watched the older woman smile even wider and hold her hand out to help Rebecca off the wagon. "Why did you do that to me?" she said in annoyance as she stepped down.

"I wasn't trying to scare you, Rebecca, I was trying to find out what you were up to." The smile disappeared and Josie became serious. "You did good, though. You didn't panic or scream. That's an improvement."

"I would have shot you if you hadn't spoken up," the young woman said with an angry tone in her voice.

"Uh huh," she replied, not believing a word of it.

"Well, I would have waited to see who it was first, but then..." she pointed her finger at the gunslinger and made the motion of a hammer falling.

"You would have waited to see who it was and even then tried to talk the person into surrendering," Josie said confidently. Rebecca smiled in acknowledgment.

"Yeah... come on. Let's find the mugs so we can get the dinner fixings going," she said, turning back to the wagon to look for the missing items again. "Josie, where did you hide the cups?"

The tall woman reached over Rebecca's shoulder and picked up the one canvas sack she had not checked yet. "Josie, why did you put them in there? That's where the towels are. I don't want to taste towel fuzz in my coffee."

"Would you rather have had them bounce around the wagon and make more noise than a dozen washboards? We don't need to be announcing our presence from miles away," the gunslinger replied. Rebecca looked at the wagon again, noting for the first time that there was a piece of leather nailed on one side of the washboard, the other end going over the wood and metal object and hooking on a nail on the opposite side.

"You think of everything, don't you?" the young woman said in awe of her friend's foresight.

"Not everything... I haven't figured out a way to cook the jackrabbit I caught while looking for firewood without some matches to start the fire." She arched her eyebrow and looked at her young companion, and received a sheepish grin in reply as Rebecca turned and retrieved a match from their supply.

The evening passed fairly quietly with the gunslinger cleaning her weapons and Rebecca repairing yet another tear Josie managed to make in her shirt. Staring at the thin and worn material in her hands, the young woman contemplated tossing the black shirt in the fire "accidentally," but instead sighed and continued her precise stitching.

Sleep was another matter altogether. Twice Josie woke the younger woman up with her thrashing about when demons visited her dreams. Rebecca sat scant inches away from the gunslinger's head, softly speaking to her. "Shh, it's all right now... it's all right..." She continued to gently try to coax Josie back to a peaceful rest, her own heart feeling the pain the sleeping woman was suffering through. She crawled to Josie's side and brought her head to her breast. With feather light touches she stroked her hair as she sang one song after another until the gunslinger was still, her breathing even. Morning would find the outlaw sleeping with her face pillowed on Rebecca's soft breast. She did not know when the young woman came to join her, but the feeling of contentment she felt upon waking to find her so close made her want to kiss her until she wakened. With a sigh she realized that Rebecca had never given her any reason to believe she would welcome her advances, so reluctantly she untangled her limbs from the sleeping woman and rose to start the day.

The sun shone brightly down on the small campsite. Josie took a sip of the coffee and winced. She really wished Rebecca was an early riser or at least had set the coffee up the night before. No matter how hard she tried, Josie was unable to make the beverage taste right. She looked over at the sleeping form, buried deep beneath the blankets the gunslinger had covered her with upon waking to find her friend uncovered. Josie could only surmise that she had once again woken Rebecca up with her nightmares. Feeling a bit guilty, she decided to let the young woman sleep instead of waking her.

Rebecca woke to the smell of bacon burning in the frying pan. She wrinkled her nose and poked her head out from under the blankets, squinting from the bright sunshine. "Are you trying to cook?" she asked groggily, her eyes focusing on the gunslinger as she frantically tried to move the smoking meat from the pan onto the metal plate.

"Trying," Josie muttered, looking down at the blackened strips. "Glad to see you're awake."

"Why?" she said as she sat up and stretched.

"Because I'm hungry," she replied smiling. "I, uh, tried to make coffee too," she said holding out the tin mug to Rebecca, who took one sniff and shook her head.

"Let me take care of nature and I'll get breakfast ready," she said, rising to her feet.

"And coffee, don't forget about that," Josie said to the retreating blonde.

"And coffee," Rebecca yelled back, grinning. She heard the splash of the gunslinger's attempt at the morning drink being dumped on the ground. Josie's many skills obviously did not include anything domestic, the young woman joked to herself.

The next two days continued in much the same fashion, except that the gunslinger did not try to cook anything. Rebecca had, at Josie's suggestion, set up the coffee pot the night before so all the tall woman would have to do was add water and heat it up when she woke. It worked out well, allowing Josie to enjoy some private time in the morning and affording Rebecca a couple of much needed extra hours of sleep. The beds stayed in the same position and the nightmares continued. Despite the young woman's protests that she was not always awakened by Josie's cries during the night, the gunslinger did not believe her, especially when the telltale dark circles began to appear under the green eyes.

On the third day, they were taken by surprise by a sudden storm. Within seconds, what began as a light spattering of drops developed into an all-out, teeming downpour. Josie pulled the wagon to a stop and both women tried frantically to cover their belongings with a large piece of canvas, but the sudden gusts of wind threatened to take the cloth away from them before they could get it tied down. There was no time to look for Josie's riding duster or Rebecca's cloak before they were both soaked to the skin. "Lay down on top of the canvas to hold it down," the gunslinger yelled, trying to be heard over the driving rain. "I'm going to try to find us some shelter. Hold on!" Flossy seemed as eager as the outlaw to find a place out of the deluge and she responded by breaking into a trot when Josie slapped the reins on her backside.

Josie could barely see the trail in front of her, and if not for Rebecca they would have passed by the little sod cabin in a stand of trees. Rebecca did not think she could make herself heard, so she simply tapped Josie on her thigh and pointed toward the cabin. Josie veered off the trail and pulled the wagon sharply to a stop under the trees. She leaped from the seat and nearly lost her footing in the rivulets of water that coursed through the trees. The thick canopy of leaves did offer some shelter for the horses from the worst of the rain, so she figured to leave them there while she and Rebecca made a dash for the soddy. Clutching the side of the wagon to keep her feet, Josie held out her free hand to Rebecca to help her from the wagon. "Come on," she yelled over the pounding rain, "We can come back later for what we need after the rain lets up!" Rebecca scrambled over the side, and reached back to make sure that the canvas was securely tied over their belongings. Josie grabbed her hand and pulled her away. "Don't worry about that now. Let's get out of this downpour."

They took off for the cabin at a run and when they reached the door, Rebecca insisted they knock in case someone was still in residence there. It appeared from the outside to be deserted, but she did not want to assume that and burst in and frighten some poor settler. Josie humored her and gave a perfunctory knock and immediately opened the door. She rushed through, dragging Rebecca behind her, and slammed the door.

As Josie thought, the soddy had been deserted for some time, and rain fell steadily through several holes in the thatched roof. The corner closest to the stone fireplace was relatively dry, and they threw themselves down on the floor there, grateful to be out of the rain.

They caught their breath from the dash to the cabin and sat closely together on the floor, allowing their eyes to grow accustomed to the dimness so they could see if there was anything of use to them. It was a one-room cabin constructed solely of sod bricks. The stone fireplace was the only thing in sight not made of dirt. No furniture had been left by the builders of the cabin or, if it had, it had long ago been carried away or put to use by other needy travelers. There was no wood with which to start a fire and no sign of a blanket that they could use to warm themselves.

They sat in silence for what seemed like a very long time but which in reality was no more than a few minutes, listening to the rain beat against the walls and roof of their little shelter. At last, with a little sigh, Josie climbed to her feet and took a few steps in the direction of the door.

"Where are you going? Josie, it's pouring buckets out there," Rebecca exclaimed as she moved to follow the gunslinger.

Both women were freezing cold and wanted nothing more than to dry off and warm up, but there was still work to be done, and they both knew it. Josie removed her gun belts and set them on a dry spot of the dirt floor. All they were doing at the moment was adding to the weight of her soaked britches.

"We need blankets and dry clothes and some wood for a fire. Stay here; I'll be back as soon as I can." She frowned when she saw Rebecca stand up defiantly and place her hat on her head.

"That's right, I'm as soaked as you are and if you're going to go out there, I'm going to go out there." She crossed her arms in front of her chest and looked up at Josie. Rebecca's green eyes burned with determination under the rain-soaked brim of her hat. The gunslinger knew that it was not worth it to try and argue. They were both soaked through and having the extra set of hands would only help to get them warm and dry quicker.

"All right," Josie agreed. "I'll see about getting some wood for a fire, and you get the blankets and clothes out of the wagon." Rebecca nodded, and the two of them started for the door. They stood for a moment in the open doorway looking out at the still teeming rain. They turned and looked at each other briefly and then stepped outside.

They had a woefully small supply of kindling in the wagon, but it was way in front and would require removing all of the canvas to get to it, something Josie did not want to do. She made a mental note to move the wood to the rear of the buckboard once weather permitted and struck off into the stand of trees to look for fallen branches that might be somewhat protected from the rain.

Rebecca fumbled with the knots in the rope that held the canvas down. They were swollen from the water, and she was ready to cry from frustration when finally the knot on one corner came loose and she was able to peel back the canvas. She grabbed the carpetbags containing hers and Josie's spare clothes, and shoved as many blankets as she could reach into each bag before she turned and ran for the soddy. She returned to the wagon several times for additional supplies that they would need. The wind had picked up considerably while she was making her trips, and it drove the rain right through her clothes and into her skin like thousands of needles. By the time she returned from her last trip, she was chilled to the bone and too numb to do anything but sink down into a heap on the floor.

The gunslinger returned with an armful of wood covered by her vest, which was the only thing she could think of to keep at least some of the rain off the timber. Setting the pile down beside the hearth, Josie knelt to prepare the fire. Noticing Rebecca sitting in the corner, she wondered why the blonde had not changed into the dry clothes that had been brought in. "Rebecca, get out of those wet clothes," she said. "I'll have the fire going in a few minutes." She started piling the smaller pieces of wood in the fireplace, but stopped moving the sticks around when she heard no movement from her friend. "Sprite?" Josie came closer and saw she was in the midst of an all-over shiver. "Blazes," the gunslinger muttered and drew even closer to the young woman. "Come on, let's get you out of these wet things."

"H-how'd it get so cold so fast?" Rebecca said through chattering teeth as her numb fingers tried to undo her shirt.

"Northers. That wind comes down from the north and the temperature just drops through the floorboards," the gunslinger replied while removing

Rebecca's hat and toweling the blonde hair dry. "Little early for them, but I guess there isn't much we can do about it." She dried Rebecca's hair as much as she could before using the damp towel on her own hair, trying to save the remaining towel for their bodies.

Josie helped her peel the shirt off her soaked skin and handed her the dry towel. The gunslinger shivered uncontrollably for a moment, drawing her concern to herself for the first time. She quickly wiggled out of her own clothes, the boots being the hardest to remove and requiring help from Rebecca. Josie laid one of the blankets out on the ground and sat down on it. She ignored the goosebumps that covered her flesh as she helped the young woman remove her clothes. Josie pulled her close and wrapped the remaining blanket around them, trying to generate body heat. "Once I get you warmed up a bit, I'll get the fire going," the gunslinger said softly as she ran her hands rapidly up and down Rebecca's forearms.

"G-guess we'll keep the dusters under the s-seat from now on, huh?" She felt the strong arms wrapped around her tighten, drawing her closer to the warm body behind her.

"I reckon. Not to mention the tent. You know I put the sack of oats on top of it?" Josie said in an 'I can't believe I did that' tone of voice. "I think before we head out tomorrow we'll re-pack the wagon." She smiled to herself when she felt Rebecca's body stop shivering and start to warm up.

"All right," Josie said after a few minutes, pulling herself out from under the blanket and tucking it in around Rebecca. "I'll get the fire going. Once it's warm enough, we'll worry about eating." She waited until the young woman nodded before moving to the clothes pile and donning her long underwear and a warm pair of stockings. Within minutes the fire was beginning to burn nicely. Josie added more logs than she normally would have, more concerned at the moment with warmth than with someone else spotting the smoke from the little chimney. She highly doubted that even the most desperate rogue would be out in the downpour if he could help it. The gunslinger took a moment to warm her hands up in front of the fire before grabbing Rebecca's clothes and moving over to the woman who still sat wrapped up in the blanket. As quickly as she could, Rebecca dressed and scooted as close as she could get to the edge of the fireplace. Josie picked up the damp blankets and laid them out near the fire, hoping they might dry a little before they had to try and sleep with them.

Dinner was nothing more than coffee and warmed up slices of dried beef, too thick to be jerky but too thin to be satisfying. Now dried, neither woman was interested in running out to the wagon for the rest of their staples. By unspoken agreement, both women were too chilled to talk or do anything else but stare at the fire and try to keep warm. The rain had let up only slightly by the time they were ready to go to sleep. They placed

two blankets on the ground, using them as a cushion from the cool dampness of the earth. Josie placed one still wet pistol between Rebecca and the
fire, making sure she could reach it easily from her sleeping position and
promising to clean it in the morning. There was no doubt that they would
sleep close together with the damp cold permeating the area. She lay down
and made room between her and the fire for Rebecca. The young woman
curled up and pressed her back against the taller woman, snuggling closer
when she felt the warm heat against her. "Ooh, you're warm."

"And you're cold. Come here," Josie said, pulling her even closer. It
was too early for bed and neither of the women were sleepy, but with virtually all of their things still out in the wagon, there was nothing for them to
do. They sat in companionable silence for a while, and Rebecca began to
softly hum. It made Josie think of an angelic voice she sometimes heard in
her dreams, and she had to smile. Josie's chin was resting on Rebecca's
shoulder, and she whispered into her ear, "Sing me a song, Sprite."

Rebecca jumped when she felt Josie's warm breath on her ear. She
shivered, even though she was no longer cold, and felt warmth suffuse the
area between her legs. Josie noticed the shiver, and believing that Rebecca
was still cold, she wrapped her arms tightly around the smaller woman and
asked, "Is that better?"

"What?" Rebecca croaked, and the raspy sound of her voice surprised
both of them. She cleared her throat and said, "Yes. Yes, it's better now,
thanks."

Josie relaxed her grip around Rebecca's ribcage just a bit thinking that
perhaps she had restricted her breathing, which would explain the breath-
lessness in her voice. If she did not know better, she might almost think
Rebecca had been sexually aroused, from the tone of her voice. She chided
herself for projecting her own wishful thinking onto her innocent friend,
and with a sigh, she said again, "How about that song?"

"Oh, I can't carry a tune in a bucket," Rebecca protested. "Why don't
I tell you a story instead? Have I ever...."

"You've told me every story you know at least twice," Josie interrupted.
"Besides, I could hear your voice just now as you were humming, and it
sounded like you were carrying a tune just fine."

"Not to hear my mother tell it. She plays the organ in the church and
sings for all the church socials. I learned the words to all the songs from
listening to her practice, but every time I tried to sing along, she would tell
me to run along and play." Her voice was wistful as she spoke of her mother,
and Josie could tell that even though her father treated her badly, she still
missed her mother. Josie gave her friend what she hoped was a motherly
pat on her shoulder and Rebecca turned and smiled at her and went on.
"My mother now, she has the voice of an angel. I could sit for hours and

listen to her play and sing. She should never have married; she could have done something with her life, something...."

"She did," Josie said softly, "she created a beautiful and talented daughter, who's going to sing for me now."

"All right. But remember, you asked for it." Rebecca sat up so she could breathe freely and wrapped a blanket around her shoulders. Josie snuggled down in her own blanket and gazed into Rebecca's face. "What would you like to hear?" she asked.

"Anything but hymns. I never had much use for the white man's religion or their songs."

"How about the songs of Stephen Foster? He's written some great ones."

"Never heard of him. But if you like them, I'm sure I will too."

Rebecca took a swig of water from a canteen and began to sing. Josie was enraptured by the beautiful voice and amazed that anyone could know so many songs. Some of them seemed familiar to her - "Oh! Susanna," "Old Folks at Home," "Beautiful Dreamer," "My Old Kentucky Home," "Nelly Bly" - she could swear she had heard before. Josie was starting to doze off but when Rebecca started to sing "Jeanie with the Light Brown Hair," her eyes opened wide and she sat up, staring open-mouthed at the young blonde. Rebecca immediately stopped singing, and Josie grasped her by her arms and said frantically, "No, please don't stop!"

Rebecca started over again, "*I dream of Jeanie with the light brown hair, borne like a vapor on the summer air. I see her tripping where the bright streams play, gay as the daisies along her way....*" Rebecca could see tears glistening in Josie's eyes as she sang. Her heart ached for the pain she could see in those beautiful eyes. She wished she could take her in her arms and protect her from that pain as Josie had protected her since the day they met. She sang the last line of the song: "*I dream of Jeanie with the light brown hair, floating like vapor on the soft summer air.*" In the silence following the song, she could hear Josie softly sobbing, no longer trying to keep the tears from flowing.

Rebecca crawled to where Josie sat on the floor and wrapped her arms around her, drawing her head down to her chest. Instinctively Josie tried to pull back, but Rebecca would not let her go. "Josie, please don't pull away from me," she pleaded. "Let someone else be strong for once in your life. Do you trust me?" Josie could not speak, so she simply nodded. "Then tell me. Let me share it with you." Josie nodded again, but still did not trust herself to speak, so she held up her hand to indicate that Rebecca should wait. Rebecca stroked her hair, and felt her warm tears soaking into the cloth of her nightgown. After a few minutes the tears began to abate. Josie lifted her head from Rebecca's chest.

"Hand me the canteen please," she asked, and Rebecca complied. She took a long draught and then a deep breath. "This is..." she began and then stopped and started over. "I've never told this to anyone before. It didn't... there was no one who ever cared enough to want to know."

"Oh, I care Josie." She thought, *I wish I could tell you how much I care.* But she was not even sure what that meant, and so she said nothing more.

"My father wrote for the Cherokee Phoenix, which was a newspaper published in both Cherokee and English, and he always said what was on his mind. The Cherokee were forced off their land time after time by the government. When valuable gold deposits were found on tribal land, the land was seized and the Cherokee forced to move on. No matter how God-forsaken the land they were allowed to settle on, the whites would find something there of value and push them farther. And even when there was no gold on the land, the railroads wanted to expand, and so they appealed to the government and were granted the right to build the railroads across Cherokee land. They slaughtered the buffalo as they went, leaving the Cherokee and other tribes to starve. My father was a man of peace, but he was also a Cherokee. He told the truth about what the railroads were doing. The tribe sent him to Washington to protest to the government and try to influence them to divert the railroads to other lands. He was not able to make any headway with the bureaucrats in Washington, but he did meet my mother there. Over the objections of her family, they were married, and she moved west with him. I was born a year later." She paused to take another sip from the canteen and then continued.

"I was fifteen when my father was killed; gunned down in front of me by one of the railroad's hired thugs. I saw the man clearly and described him to the local authorities, but because I was a child and there were no other witnesses, they made no effort to catch him. I knew that if my father had been white, my word would have been enough to convict the man." Her eyes glittered with hate as she recalled hers and her mothers repeated attempts to see justice done in the killing of her father. She looked at Rebecca's face, so full of sympathy for the innocent child that she was. She resumed her tale.

"My mother was devastated by the death of my father. She moved back east to her family, who were living in New York at that time, and took me with her. My grandmother wanted to dress me in fancy clothes and send me to finishing schools and debutante balls." Josie could tell by the look on Rebecca's face that she was having a hard time picturing her tall form in a fancy gown. "I hated it there," she said bitterly. "I felt like an animal in a cage. I stayed as long as I could for mother's sake, but when I was sixteen I returned to the Cherokees. And, in the little trading post town that bordered on the reservation I met Genie."

"Excuse me." Josie felt a tap on her shoulder and turned to a petite young woman with sparkling green eyes and light brown hair that hung down in ringlets. She was smiling up at her and dimples indented both of her cheeks. Pale freckles were scattered over her nose and cheeks. She reminded Josie of a leprechaun. Her smile was contagious.

"Yes?" she replied.

"I wonder if you could reach that washboard down from that shelf up there?" the girl asked, pointing to a shelf a good foot out of her reach.

"Sure," Josie answered. She walked to the shelf and stood on tiptoe to grasp the washboard. She presented it to the girl with a smile and a bow. "At your service."

"Thanks," the young girl said brightly, and once again Josie found herself unable to resist smiling. "That's the hardest part about working here. Seems like nobody ever wants anything from a shelf I can reach." The girl ducked behind the counter where she was in the middle of putting together some supplies for a woman Josie recognized as the schoolteacher from town.

"Afternoon, Miz Bohler," Josie said, nodding to the teacher. The older woman turned to her, and for a few moments the look on her face was blank as she tried to place this tall, young woman. Then it came to her, and she grinned broadly.

"Josie Hunter! Land sakes, you've certainly grown since I last saw you. I thought you had moved back east?"

"I did. I... came back. Mother's still in New York." The teacher took Josie's hand in both of hers and patted it in a comforting way.

"I was just sick to hear about your father," the woman said sincerely. "He was a good and kind man. I... well, if I can do anything for you, you let me know." She turned her attention back to the counter where her purchases were all bundled and ready to go.

"I will, Miz Bohler," Josie said, trying hard to keep the quaver from her voice that usually preceded tears. She busied herself searching for saddle soap, which was the reason for her trip into the trading post. The teacher waved and smiled at Josie as she left the store. Josie waved back and then approached the counter, where Genie was busily rolling the string she had not needed to wrap her previous customer's packages. She tucked the ball of string back under the counter and turned her attention to her only remaining customer. Josie laid the saddle soap on the counter. "Good thing I was here," she said smiling at the impish brunette, "This was on a high shelf."

Genie laughed and the sound was musical to Josie's ears. The girl - for Josie could scarcely think of her as a woman since she had to be about her own age - made her forget her anger and sorrow over her father's death. Made her forget how miserable she was in New York. Made her forget everything, in fact, except the soft tinkling sound of her laughter. "It's a very good thing you were here," Genie agreed. "If I only sell the things I can reach, Mr. Eberhard will sure be unhappy when he comes back."

That was what was missing, Josie realized. It had not occurred to her until that moment that Mr. Eberhard owned the store, and that it should be his face across the counter instead of the leprechaun. "Where is Mr. Eberhard?" she asked, although she was happier than she could possibly say that he was not there, if it meant having the girl wait on her.

"Broke his leg," Genie said seriously. "Pretty bad, too. He'll be laid up for a while. He's a friend of my Pa's, and Pa offered to have me mind the store for him. I'm Genie Sanders." She extended her hand and Josie grasped it with her own. Genie's grip was firm but her hand was soft. Josie was sure her hand felt like cactus by comparison, and after a moment she withdrew it self-consciously.

"I'm Josie Hunter," she said in reply.

"Well, Josie Hunter, I think you earned yourself a handful of this penny candy for your help," Genie said as she removed the lid from a bin of lemon drops. Josie reached in and took a piece and popped it in her mouth. The candy was so sour it caused her to squinch up her face and half close her eyes, which made Genie laugh again. Josie would have been willing to stand there all day eating one candy after another just to hear that laugh.

"Take some more," Genie said when her laughter was under control. Josie could not tell her that she really did not care much for the taste. She simply put her hand in the bin and grabbed a handful of the hard candies to please Genie.

And that was the beginning of what was to be the most intense friendship either of the girls had ever known. Josie volunteered to make trips to the mercantile for any of her friends who needed anything. As a result, she was making the trip to town three or four times a week, and each time she would spend more and more time in the company of the little imp. She helped her stock the shelves and was always there when something needed to be fetched from a high shelf. During the frequent gaps between customers they talked about anything and everything and nothing. Josie told Genie about her father's death, and it was one of the few times she saw a look on Genie's face that did not make her feel like smiling. Even before Josie was finished recounting the horror of the night her father was shot,

Genie was beside her with her arm around her shoulder. The kindness and gentleness of the girl somehow made Josie cry, and Genie pulled her head down to her chest and hugged her and soothed her as they both sobbed. Genie was as angry as Josie at the injustice that had been done. They spoke of what they would like to do to the killer, a lot of which involved putting things in various parts of the anatomy that neither of them knew first hand, but it sounded unpleasant and therefore what he deserved.

"I wish I knew how to handle a gun, and I'd call him out," Josie said with bitterness in her voice. Her father had been a firm believer in "Live by the gun, die by the gun," and he refused to have weapons in the house.

"We could learn," Genie said enthusiastically. "My Pa has more guns than anybody, and he wouldn't miss one if we took it out to practice shooting."

Josie smiled but shook her head. "Oh, I was just dreaming," she said softly. "We'd need to know more than just shooting. You have to be able to draw and do it faster than the other guy. I wouldn't want to be the next Hunter killed by the railroad."

"We can draw on each other... without bullets, of course," Genie said, convinced that it was possible to learn to be a fast draw without firing a shot. She started pacing around, intent on planning their lessons. "So, we'll need holsters as well as guns, and a bunch of ammunition. I'm sure Mr. Eberhard wouldn't mind me taking a few boxes of shells instead of money. And we can go out to Pa's wood lot; it's far enough away from the ranch that nobody will hear the shots, and there's a nice clearing there where we can set up targets. In a couple of days Mr. Eberhard will be back and we'll have plenty of time..."

And so their plans were made. Josie made the trip to the clearing in the woods every day at the same time, and Genie would usually be waiting for her. True to her word, she was able to get two guns and holsters out of the house without anyone knowing they were gone, and at the end of their practice they cleaned them and stuffed the guns and supplies in a hollow log. Josie had a natural aptitude for shooting. Her hand was steady and her eye was unerring, and she seldom missed her target. As time went on, she was able to put several bullets so close together in her target that it almost appeared as if there was only one hole, until you looked closely. She also found that she could draw with a speed that she was certain would rival almost any man. Genie would still be pulling her gun from her holster when Josie had her gun out and aimed at her. Of course, it was a whole different kettle of fish to draw a fully loaded gun with the intent to kill someone, and despite her bravado, Josie was not sure she would be able to do it if the time came. As fate would have it, she had the opportu-

nity to find out much sooner than she imagined, as Genie told her one afternoon about the horse thieves and her plan for her and Josie to catch them. What she did not tell Josie was that her father had long ago forbidden her from seeing that, as he called her, "No account half- breed." She hoped that, by showing him Josie was willing to risk her life protecting his horses, he would relent and allow them to see each other openly. Instead, Genie was killed, and the outlaw Josie Hunter was born.

Rebecca was unable to stop the tears from flowing down her cheeks as the stoic gunslinger recounted the tale of meeting and then losing her precious friend.

Josie picked up the canteen and took a long drink of water. She felt once again the pain of losing Genie as keenly as if it had happened yesterday. Her mouth was dry, and she trembled from the emotions she had kept bottled up for so many years.

"It sounds like she was very... special," Rebecca said softly. She felt a twinge of jealousy that another woman was able to carve a niche in Josie's heart so large that she felt the loss this strongly across all the years. Rebecca chastised herself for thinking that way; Genie had been robbed of her life and it was small of her to begrudge the girl the happy times she had with Josie. Rebecca took Josie's hand in hers and held it softly while running her thumb across the back of her knuckles. The gunslinger did not flinch or try to pull away as she normally did, and Rebecca hoped that meant Josie was feeling as close to her as she was to Josie.

"She was more than special. She was...." Her voice trailed off. How could she tell Rebecca what Genie had meant to her? Rebecca was only a year or two older than Genie was when she died and almost as innocent.

Before she could think of a way of putting it that the girl would understand, Rebecca summed it up for her in seven words. "You must have loved her very much."

Josie closed her eyes, and tears leaked out from behind the lids as she said, "More than... I could tell her. She never knew...." Josie swallowed to choke back the sobs that caused her chest to ache from holding them in.

Josie and Rebecca had separated while Josie was talking. Seeing the look on Josie's face, Rebecca opened up her arms and simply said, "Come here." Once again the tall woman buried her face in the soft bosom of the little blonde, who soothed her with her soft voice and hands. "Shh, baby, it's all right."

"No, it's not all right," the gunslinger said, her voice husky with emotion. "She died because of me, and nothing can ever make that all right!"

"That's not true. She died because of someone else's greed."

"She wouldn't have even been in that barn if not for me! Don't you see it was my need to take revenge on the man who killed my father that made her learn to use a gun? She thought that being right made us invincible, and I should have told her otherwise. I might as well have pulled the trigger myself...."

"Oh, Josie, that's wrong. You can't blame yourself for other people's misfortunes. If she had never even met you she still might have gone to that barn with a gun, because that's the kind of person she was. Just because something you do starts something in motion doesn't make you responsible for everything that happens as a result of that act."

"Believe what you want to," Josie said in a resigned voice. She sat up and looked into Rebecca's eyes. "In here," she said putting her fist over her heart, "I feel responsible for her death and I always will."

"But...."

"I can't talk about her any more," Josie cut her off sharply.

"I'm sorry. I'm sorry. I wasn't trying to argue with you," Rebecca said quickly. "I only wanted to understand. And to help," she finished softly.

Josie could not miss the hurt tone in Rebecca's voice, and she wanted to reach out to the young woman, but her years of keeping people at arm's length reasserted itself and instead she simply sat with her arms clasped around her knees.

Rebecca knew better than to pursue the subject any further, but she still was itching to know how Josie went from being on the run as an alleged murderer and horse thief to being the "Terror of the Railway," which was the title of the first dime novel that featured the woman outlaw. Careful to avoid any mention of Genie she asked, "What happened after you jumped out of the barn?"

"I became what they thought I was, a horse thief. I had to get as far away from there as I could, and I didn't have a horse of my own. I took a horse that belonged to one of Sanders ranch hands and headed for the woods. I didn't slow down even when I took a bullet in the arm. I knew some places where I had played as a child near the reservation, and I figured they wouldn't find me there. I holed up there all the next day, but I was afraid I would lose my arm from the gunshot wound, and I came out to see if I could get some medical attention. I was weak from loss of blood and lack of food. I guess I must have fainted, because I found myself lying on the ground, and the horse had run away. I thought I was heading toward the reservation, but my sense of direction was out of kilter, and I was actually heading back toward the Sanders Ranch."

The sun was almost gone for the day when the ranch hand spotted the wounded half-breed lying in the dirt. A half-hour later and he would not have seen her and she would probably have bled to death where she lay. The horse she had taken returned to the ranch riderless with a good deal of blood on the reins and saddle, and all he had to do was follow the tracks back the way the horse had come until he found the woman. He smiled as he looked down at her still form, already devising ways of spending the reward he was sure to get from Sanders for bringing in the one who shot his daughter.

He turned her over onto her back and poured some water from his canteen over her face to revive her. He cursed himself for coming out on foot to search for her, since it did not appear as though she were going to be able to get back under her own steam. He did not relish the idea of having to carry her all the way to the ranch, since she was taller than he was himself. When the water hit her she opened her eyes, but in the dusky gloom she did not spot him for several seconds, and by that time he had a gun trained on her.

"I wouldn't reach for none a them guns if I was you," he cautioned her. "I expect you'd be worth about as much dead as you was alive, so it don't make much difference to me. Dead's probably easier." Josie nodded her understanding and forced herself to relax back onto the ground. She would wait for an opportunity. The cowpoke grabbed hold of her good arm and yanked her to her feet. She was lightheaded and thought she might pass out again.

"Please let me have a drink of your water," she croaked. "I promise not to try anything."

"Why not," he said, but when she reached for the canteen with her uninjured arm, the man pulled it away. "Oh, no, I'll just hold onto it myself." Her thirst was so great she would have agreed to drink the water out of an old shoe served by the devil himself, so she simply nodded and allowed him to pour water down her throat. The water went a long way toward reviving her. She was careful not to let him see that she was strong enough to walk on her own and instead allowed him to halfway support her. She needed to conserve as much of her strength as possible if she hoped to succeed when she made her bid for freedom.

The two of them stumbled toward the ranch like a pair of drunken sailors. Josie made a grab for his gun when she saw the lights of the ranch come into view, figuring that she had a better chance against one man than the whole crew. But her reflexes were slow and his were not; he yanked the gun out of her reach, and immediately brought it back in a vicious arc that connected with her temple. She blacked out for a moment but his arm around her waist prevented her from falling. He half dragged her the rest of the way to the ranch and then dumped her in the dirt in front of the door of the main house. Unwilling to leave his prize alone, he yelled for Genie's father to come out of the house. A few moments later Sanders appeared at the door with a shotgun in his hand.

"I got the half-breed, Mr. Sanders," the ranch hand said proudly. Sanders eyes glittered with something akin to madness as he stared at the creature who he believed had shot his daughter. He stepped down from the porch and walked in a circle around Josie as she lay where she had been tossed like a broken toy. She allowed Genie's father to prod her with his toe and continued to feign unconsciousness.

"Get her up on a horse, boys," he said to the cowpokes who gathered around to watch the excitement. "The wheels of justice turn way too slow out here, so we're gonna string up this murdering Indian ourselves."

While two of the men went to fetch horses, two others pulled her to her feet. Sanders stood in front of her and grasped her chin in his hand, forcing her head up. He stared straight into her eyes, his own filled with loathing and disgust. "You got anything to say for yourself before we carry out your sentence?"

As twisted with hate as he was, Josie knew there was little point in protesting her innocence, but still she had to try. "I... loved her, Mr. Sanders. I didn't shoot her; I would never do anything to hurt her."

"That's not the way I hear it," he spat into her face. Two men on horseback rode up to the little group leading three saddled horses. "Tie her hands," Sanders ordered, and one of the cowhands threw a length of rope to one of the men holding her up. He drew her hands behind her back, which caused her wounded arm to begin bleeding again, and wound the rope around her wrists. When that was done, they lifted her none too gently into the saddle and, mounting their own horses, they waited for Sanders to lead them. "We'll take her to the Indian reservation," Sanders said. "I'd just as soon the sheriff didn't connect this hanging to me." He swung into the saddle and grasped the reins of Josie's horse and they made their way toward the reservation.

It was full dark by the time they reached a spot that suited Sanders. He wished they had waited until the next morning to do this so that he would be able to see the agony on her face, but having come all the way out there he was not going to leave without completing his mission. He tied the end of a rope to one sturdy branch of a huge oak tree and tossed the end with the noose over another branch. He led the horse under the branches of the tree and roughly pulled the noose over her head.

"You might think about praying to whatever God it is you heathens believe in," he said with a voice full of venom. He turned his horse back the way they had come and gave a tug on the reins of Josie's horse. The animal was confused when her rider did not seem to be accompanying her and she stopped for a moment, but he pulled sharply on the reins again *and she bolted out from under the helpless woman. "Let's go, boys," Sanders said to his men. He was anxious to get home before full dark set in and figured it would take the half-breed some time to die, time he did not have to waste.*

Josie could feel her field of vision begin to narrow as her body reacted to being deprived of air. As spots danced before her eyes, she clawed frantically at the secret pocket in her belt until she freed her knife, and she sawed at the rope that bound her wrists. It was awkward and painful, and for a few moments she feared she would lose consciousness before she was able to free her hands, but at last the rope fell away. The precious seconds required to loosen the bonds on her hands brought her even closer to losing consciousness. She had to fight her natural instinct to thrash and kick, as she knew it would only serve to tighten the loop on her neck. Her lungs screamed for air and her eyes widened in fear as she brought the knife up to her neck with her uninjured arm until the point of the knife was pushing against the rope under her chin. If she slipped she knew she would finish off the job Sanders had started, but she could not ignore her rising panic, and she sawed frantically at the rope with no regard to what damage she might inflict with the knife. Darkness enveloped her completely, and she went limp, dropping the knife from her lifeless fingers. Seconds later, the rope, which had been sawed almost completely through, unraveled and released its hold on her and she tumbled to the ground.

The impact caused her to draw in a huge breath, and she lay there for several minutes gasping for air, almost unable to believe she was alive. Her throat was raw from the friction of the rope and bleeding from the cuts she had inflicted on herself, but she smiled with satisfaction for having survived. She almost laughed when she realized that the rancher had strung her up virtually on top of an underground spring and within easy walking distance of the village. She stumbled to the fountain of water that welled up out of the ground and gulped the cool liquid. She splashed water on her face and neck and it helped to cool the heat of the rope burns. The pain in her arm reminded her that there was still a bullet in there that needed removing, and quickly, before infection set in. She knew she could rely on the discretion of the Medicine Elders on the reservation to keep her survival a secret. Once she was able to travel, she would put some distance between herself and Genie's father, knowing he would not hesitate to finish what he had started. Her heart heavy with the weight of the loss of her dearest friend, she made her way toward the reservation and safety.

Rebecca listened in silence as Josie recounted the events of the night that had so drastically altered the course of a young woman's life. When Josie fell silent, Rebecca found herself shaking with anger and outrage at the injustice that had been done to her friend. Seeing the way the outlaw huddled against the wall of the soddy with her face drawn in pain, compassion overrode the anger Rebecca felt, and she found herself crawling to where Josie sat and putting her arms around her shoulders. Josie made no effort to move away, and in fact she lowered her head to Rebecca's breast and relaxed. Not a word was exchanged, but Rebecca knew that something had changed between them that night. She sensed that Josie had let down the barriers that always kept Rebecca at arm's length, and instead of shutting her out, Josie's protective walls enclosed her. As she did when the gunslinger was caught in one of her nightmares, Rebecca stroked Josie's ebony mane and she began to sing. Within minutes she could tell by the rhythmic breathing that Josie had fallen asleep. She gently lowered her to the floor and then lay down beside her, burying her face in the crook of the taller woman's neck. She released a soft sigh of contentment and quickly fell asleep.

36: A New Friend

The bottom of the wagon was covered with caked-on mud, as were both women from the splattering of the wheels. The strong rains left puddles of indeterminate depth in their path, forcing both travelers to sit as close to the center of the seat as possible in order to avoid the constant splashes. One particularly large one caught the young blonde in the face, causing her to sputter and curse while Josie chuckled at her predicament. She chuckled, that is, until an equally strong splash caught the gunslinger even worse than the one that had soaked Rebecca. Josie used her bandanna to wipe off the muddy water while the young woman guffawed.

A cracking sound, almost like a rifle shot, rang out and the wagon lurched and came to a shuddering stop. Josie's brow furrowed as she handed the reins to Rebecca and vaulted over the side of the wagon. "What's wrong?" Rebecca called to the gunslinger who crouched next to the wheels. "Not another bad wheel?"

"No, not the wheel," Josie said dejectedly. "The axle."

"What?" She climbed down immediately and squatted down next to the gunslinger. The tall woman pointed to the edge where the axle met the wagon. The wood was clearly fractured to the point where one more solid jostling would cause its demise. "What are we going to do?"

Josie stood up and looked around, trying to keep her frustration from erupting in a litany of expletives guaranteed to color her younger friend's ears. "Good question, Rebecca. We're too far away from anywhere to get a cartwright or smith to help. I don't think that axle will last more than five miles." She gripped the edge of the buckboard so tightly that her knuckles whitened, an action not unnoticed by Rebecca.

"It's all right, Josie. We'll figure something out." She reached over and placed her smaller hand on top of the gunslinger's. "Look, you said we're too far away to go back, right? So let's just keep going forward. We know there's nothing behind us." Rebecca felt the grip beneath her hand ease. "Who knows what will show up within the next five miles."

"What or who," the gunslinger corrected, pulling out one of her colts and checking it. She untied Phoenix from the back of the wagon and began to saddle her up. "You lead Flossy, but be gentle about it. She's used to being driven, not led."

As an added precaution, they redistributed the weight so that the majority was above the rear wheel opposite the stress point. While it made the load seem heavier to Flossy, it still was within her limits and she slowly moved forward. Josie rode Phoenix, keeping near the damaged axle yet still keeping Rebecca and the road within her vision. Although her face betrayed no emotion, inside she was fuming at her inability to repair the wagon. Even just a few nails and strips of metal, both items that they did not have, would help her brace it until they reached Boise City. It was a slow trek, with Josie stopping them now and again to guide the wagon around some of the deeper bumps in the road. Rebecca went slowly. She watched the trail carefully for the deceiving puddles that could spell disaster for the buckboard. The combined care from both women resulted in the axle lasting more than twice the distance the gunslinger had predicted. Josie heard the creaking, jumped off Phoenix, and had a barrel wedged under the wagon before the axle groaned and snapped like a handful of pencils. The corner dropped only a couple of inches before landing on the flat top of the barrel. The instant she heard the gunslinger dismount, Rebecca stopped Flossy and watched in amazement as her friend moved with a fluidity and grace that was both strong and supple at the same time. She knew that Josie was a strong woman, stronger than any she had ever met, but to see her lift a barrel half-filled with water with little more than a grunt was enough to leave the young woman speechless. Never had she seen even one of the men in Chancetown lift something so heavy so easily.

"Rebecca?" The gunslinger looked at her and immediately recognized the expression of awe. She had seen it before from various men when she had bested them in arm wrestling or boxing.

"Huh? Oh, what?" she said, snapping out of her trance.

"Nothing. We're going to have to leave the wagon here. Unhitch Flossy and pack her up as much as possible." She watched as Rebecca nodded and went about her task. Josie smiled to herself as she started to

load up Phoenix's saddlebags. *Think I'm a huckleberry above a persimmon, do ya, Sprite?* she thought. *Don't put me on a pedestal; I'm no hero.*
Within minutes, everything of importance that they could strap to the two horses was in place and they set out on foot, Josie in the lead. Mud sucked at their feet and both women were mud-splattered and bedraggled looking when, less than a mile later, they came upon a small ranch set far from the trail, yet still noticeable to someone with vision as keen as the gunslinger's. Removing the saddlebags from Phoenix and tossing them on the ground, Josie motioned for Rebecca to come close. "I'm going up to check it out. You stay here with Flossy and the gear. No matter what, don't move until I come and get you, understand?" She waited for the young woman to agree before mounting Phoenix and riding off toward the ranch.

The house was in such disrepair that Josie wondered if anyone lived there at all until she heard the familiar sound of a rifle bolt being readied behind the door. She carefully crouched down and cocked the hammer on her colt. "I don't want any trouble."

"Then what in Sam Hill do you want?" a voice hoarse from too many years of smoking called from behind the door.

"My wagon broke down. If you have a flat piece of metal and a couple of nails, I'll gladly pay you for them and be on my way." She kept her voice non-threatening, not wanting to scare the old codger.

"Where's your husband?" the old man asked while moving from window to window looking for signs of an ambush.

"Don't have one. Look, I'm not gonna hurt you. If I can just go into your barn, I'm sure I can find what I need and be gone." She put her gun back in its holster, confident that the old man was not a danger.

"Wagon broke?" he asked, his voice right behind the door. She carefully lowered her left gun belt to the ground, not wanting to appear too armed but also not wanting to appear defenseless either.

"Yes. Back a ways." She stood up from her crouched position, keeping her hand near her sidearm just in case. One brown eye looked out from the Indian door, a small hinged opening at eye level within the paneling of the main door.

"And you say you're alone?" The Indian door opened wider, revealing an old man not much taller than Rebecca. Glasses with thick, black metal frames rested upon his nose, his white hair receded at the temples.

"I said I didn't have a husband." she responded, not wanting to give too much information away. The Indian door closed and the latch on the front door lifted slightly. Josie remained still as the old man pushed the muzzle of his sixteen shot rifle through the small opening before following it onto the porch. In the daylight, the gunslinger got her first clear look at the old man. Easily in his sixties, his drawn face still reflected the handsome man of his youth. He returned the gaze, studying the strange woman standing before him, noting the muscles that showed so clearly beneath the worn, black shirt and the menacing looking gun strapped to her thigh. After a moment, he spoke.

"How bad is it?" he said, lowering his rifle slightly.

"Axle," she replied. "I can brace it with a piece of metal and some nails, at least enough to get to Boise City."

"Doubt it," he said, taking a cigarette out of his shirt pocket along with a match. He struck the match against the porch rail and lit the cigarette, taking a long drag before exhaling. "Nothing like fine tobacco. Road between here and Cheyenne is flat compared to from here to Boise City. Nope, what you need is a new axle." He walked over and sat down on his porch swing, the weapon resting non-threateningly next to him. Josie hooked her thumbs through her leather belt, deliberately keeping her right hand away from her Colt, and sat down on the porch step. He looked off at nothing, flicking the ashes of his cigarette onto the wooden porch. "Yup, a new axle, that'd be all that'll get you there." With a flick of his fingers, the remains of the cigarette flew in an arc off the porch and onto the ground, joining a dozen other butts scattered nearby. "I have one."

"How much?" she asked, hoping to end the visit and get on her way. He smiled at her, revealing a full set of false teeth and chuckled.

"Money don't do me no good, little girl." He looked around the overgrown field, then up at the roof of the porch, inspecting the many holes that allowed sunlight to pour through. "Nope, what I need is an honest day's work, if you and whoever you got hiding somewhere got the mind to do it."

"What do you want done?" she asked, certain that she was not going to like the terms.

"I need a new roof. Been leaking for close to a year now. You fix that, you can have the axle." He sat back and waited for her answer.

Josie glanced up at the porch, noting that a simple patch job would not do any good. The wood was far too rotted.

"It would take a couple days to replace the roof," she replied, indicating in her tone that the price was too high. He laughed deep in his chest, causing a short coughing fit before he regained his composure.

"Take you more than a couple days, missy. I'm meaning the whole roof," he said, pointing to the house. Josie's blue eyes narrowed.

"That's an outrageous amount of work just for an axle," she protested.

"Suit yourself," he replied. "Don't matter none to me. I'm not the one with a broken wagon."

They sat there for several long moments, he smoking another cigarette and she fighting the urge to just intimidate him into a more reasonable trade. A vision of him trying to climb up on the roof and repair it himself flashed through her mind. "I'll fix your roof in trade for the axle, but you have to provide me and my companion with a place to stay until I'm finished."

"I don't put up with none of that fornicating in my home," he said, tossing the cigarette over the porch rail to join the others. "I have one extra room. You can stay there; he can sleep in the barn."

"It's not a he; it's a she," Josie replied. "A young woman. Good cook too." The old man smiled at that information.

"Well then...." He looked up at the setting sun. "It's too late to do anything today. Go get your friend and you can start in the morning," he said as he rose and walked to the door. "If your friend has a mind to, there's vittles in the kitchen. Tell her I don't mind none if she feels like cooking something for dinner." He said it matter-of-factly, but the look in his eyes told another story. She wondered how long it had been since he had someone else cook a meal for him.

Josie remained seated on the porch for a few minutes after the door closed, thinking about the old man and the deal to which she had agreed. Redoing a roof was a tall order and far too high a price for a simple axle, but she also knew there was no other way he was going to get his roof fixed. She stood and stretched, knowing full well it would be the last time for quite a while that her muscles would not feel sore. Picking up her discarded gun belt, she turned and headed for Phoenix.

"Any luck?" Rebecca asked once the gunslinger was within earshot. Josie dismounted and dropped the reins, letting Phoenix munch on the overgrown grass.

"There's an old man that lives there. He has an axle, but I have to do a job for him before he'll let us have it," she explained while picking up her discarded saddlebags. "We'll be staying here for a few days."

"A few days? What kind of job is it?" Rebecca asked apprehensively.

"He needs a new roof," she replied. "And perhaps some company. Looks like he's been alone for some time."

"A roof is an awful lot of work, Josie."

"I don't have a choice. We need that axle, unless you want to walk the rest of the way," she said as she secured the gear to Phoenix.

"Walk the rest of the way? Oh, no thanks. But I'm not getting up on a roof."

"Don't worry, Rebecca. I'll be the carpenter. You get to be the washerwoman. Place looks like it hasn't seen a woman's touch in years," she said, grinning when she saw the younger woman roll her eyes.

They were within arm's reach of the porch when the door opened and the old man stepped out. Rebecca smiled warmly and headed toward him.

Josie, always distrustful of strangers, stayed back and lowered her hands until they were within easy reach of her guns.

"Hello, my name is Rebecca," she said.

"Charles... Charles Bragg." He took the offered hand and kissed it, as befitting a young lady. "Welcome to my home," he said as he pushed open the door and held his hand out, inviting her to enter first. In the blink of an eye, Josie was on the porch and within easy reach of both of them, not wanting to let her young friend out of her sight, despite the lack of any feeling of danger. Rebecca entered and stood just inside the doorway, trying to take everything in with one polite glance. Stale smoke and air assaulted her nose, as well as layers upon layers of dust. Josie had not been kidding when she said she did not think the place had seen a woman's touch in years. The front door opened into what was obviously once a parlor, now nothing more than a dusty living area. It was apparent from the pillow and blanket on the couch that Charles spent most, if not all, of his time there. Empty whiskey jugs and tin cans were scattered about the floor, as were dozens of cigarette butts. A metal plate on the end table overflowed with the burnt-out matches used to light the rolled tobacco. To the right was the kitchen, a place where Charles obviously spent very little time, if any at all. Everything, except the well pump, was covered in the same thick layer of dust as the parlor. Cobwebs littered every corner and crevice possible. Had he not been standing next to her, Rebecca would have sworn that no one had occupied the house in years. "Oh, let me get you a chair, Miss," Charles said apologetically, moving past her to dust the seat of a wooden chair with an equally dusty rag. "I don't usually get company, 'cept my brother Horace, and he don't mind the place the way it is."

The fresh wave of dust tickled Rebecca's nose, causing her to sneeze uncontrollably. "Would you... achoo... excuse me p-p-p'achoo... please?" She made a hasty retreat out to the fresh air. She leaned forward against the rail of the porch and breathed deeply.

"Pretty bad, huh?" the gunslinger said from behind her, fully expecting the young woman to jump and completely surprised when she did not. "Rebecca?"

"There's more dirt there than in boot hill," the younger woman said, pulling her handkerchief out of her pocket.

"Rebecca, how did you know I was behind you?" Josie asked, leaning against the rail next to the blonde.

"Oh, I recognized your footsteps. Charles isn't wearing boots, but you are," she said simply. She blinked twice and looked at the gunslinger. "Hey, that's pretty good, huh? I figured out who it was without looking." Her voice was so full of pride at the feat that Josie had no choice but to smile. Rebecca enjoyed the feeling for a moment before she became serious again. "How can someone live like that? He must be lonely."

"I think he is, but we're only here as long as it takes for me to fix the roof." Josie thought about adding 'Don't get attached,' but knew better. Nothing she said would make a difference in that department. "Do you think you can work the stove? From what I saw from the doorway, looks like it hasn't seen a fire in years."

"If the flue is clear, I shouldn't have any problem," the young woman replied. "We'd better check that."

Charles took the horses to the barn while the women went into the kitchen and checked the stovepipe for obstructions. Josie pulled her soot-covered arm from the pipe. "Feels clear," she said, wiping her hand against her shirt.

"Josie, do you know how hard it is to get soot out of a shirt?" Rebecca chastised as she handed the gunslinger a damp rag.

"But it's a black shirt," she said innocently. "That's why I wear them. Hides everything." She wiped her hands as best she could and handed the rag back to the young woman.

"Keep it up and you can do your own laundry, Miss 'I don't do laundry.'"

"But Rebecca..." she rubbed some of the soot off her shirtsleeve with her forefinger, "that's what I have you for," she said sweetly, touching the tip of the young woman's nose with her soot-covered finger. She held the blackened digit up for Rebecca to see while taking a step back and smiling wickedly.

"You didn't...." The young woman touched her nose and inspected her fingers. "You did." Her green eyes narrowed. "I'll get you for that one, just you wait." She picked up the damp rag without thinking and tried to wipe the soot off her nose. Josie took one look at the smeared black mess on Rebecca's face and laughed lightly while removing her bandanna.

"I'm sure you think you will, Rebecca," she said as she wrapped the scarf around her finger and spit on it. "Come here."

"Are you joshing?" the young woman protested, stepping back against the edge of the sink.

"Rebecca, everyone knows that spit removes everything," Josie said, reaching forward with one hand to hold the young woman's head still while she wiped the soot off. "There, all better."

"Land sakes, Josie, I'm not a little kid," she scowled. "It's your fault anyway. I'm still going to get you back for that, you know," she said, wagging a finger at the taller woman.

"Uh huh," the gunslinger smirked. "We'll see about that, Sprite."

Rebecca smiled at the pet name and looked around the dusty kitchen. "Uh, do you want to ask him where he keeps his food?"

Josie took a long look around. "Not a chance." She put her hat on just as Charles entered. He nodded and sat down on the couch. Opening the tin on the end table, he pulled out a cigarette and match. "I'm going to see if I can round up a rabbit or two," Josie said. She knelt down and pulled the bowie knife from her left boot and slipped it into the younger woman's right one before standing back up. "Just in case," she whispered. Rebecca nodded, knowing full well in her heart that everything would be fine.

"So, Charles," Rebecca said while trying to get a fire going in the long-cold stove. "How long have you lived here?"

"I reckon been close to twenty years now; moved out here back in 'fifty-seven. Horace, now he's only been out here for about five years, since his wife died and all. Runs trade from Boise City to Cheyenne once a month. Always stops here both ways for a spell and to drop off fixins for me."

"So that's how you get your food and tobacco?" she asked, taking a seat on the bench opposite his, forgetting all about getting the stove working.

"Yup. Every month he brings me two tins of tobacco and a score of Van Camps," he said as he lit another cigarette.

"All you eat is beans from a can?" she said incredulously. "You don't get any meat or bread?"

"Sometimes Horace'll bring in some salt pork, but ain't too often." He reached over and patted her hand. "Now don't you go worrying about me. I've been living this way ever since Ruth passed on and I've been just fine. You and your friend there have better...." He looked around, noticing for the first time that the tall, dark-headed woman was nowhere in sight. "Where'd your friend go?"

"She went to get something other than beans to eat. Oh, that reminds me...." She got up and went back to the stove. "Charles? If you didn't use the stove or a pot to heat your beans up with, what did you use?"

He grinned, stood up, and walked over to the fireplace. "I have to use this to keep the place warm now that the Northers are coming. I just put the can here." He pointed to the large, black pot hanging from a hinged arm. "And swing it out over the fire. Few minutes it's done." He busied himself with picking up the multitude of cans that littered the floor near the fireplace while Rebecca silently prayed that Josie was successful in her hunting.

Josie returned with two small rabbits. The look on her face when she handed the skinned carcasses over made it clear that she was just as disappointed as her friend. "Don't you worry about me, I've got my Van Camps;

you two go on ahead," he said. Josie walked up behind Rebecca, so close that only they could hear each other.

"Stew?"

"Stew," the young woman replied. Josie gave a gentle squeeze on her shoulder. She knew that Rebecca was tired of stew and had been looking forward to some fried meat for a change.

"Charles, save the beans for another night. Rebecca's making rabbit stew and there'll be plenty for everyone." The look in his aged eyes reminded the gunslinger of the look she received when she gave Rebecca the medical book.

"Well, if you're sure," he said, the can of beans that was in his hand already put back with the rest of the pile. "If you need flour, I'm sure Ruth had some around here..." He went into the kitchen and started to open drawers that had not seen the light of day in ages. Josie quickly went over and put her hand out to block him from the rest of the drawers.

"No, don't worry about it. We have plenty of flour, don't we Rebecca?" The thought of adding anything to the meal that came from the dust-covered drawers had no appeal to the gunslinger.

"Plenty," the young woman agreed emphatically, making a mental note to empty the drawers first thing tomorrow.

It was almost dusk by the time dinner was finished. Josie went to check on the horses, the best excuse she could come up with for not staying put and being sociable, while Rebecca washed up the dishes and made a pot of coffee.

"Well, guess it's time," Charles said as he rose from his chair and headed for the front door.

"Time for what?" the young woman asked, following him.

"Time to lower the flag of course."

They stood in the front yard next to the tall wooden pole. With great reverence, he slowly lowered the flag. "Your flag's wrong," Rebecca commented. He stopped lowering it and looked at her. "I mean, there's only thirty-six stars on it. There're thirty-eight states now."

"Missy, when I served this country in the Great War of the states, there were only thirty-four. By the time the army let me go, there were thirty-six. This is the flag they gave me when I was discharged and this is the flag I'll fly," he said adamantly. "Bad enough we keep adding states without having to worry about how many darn stars are on the flag. At the rate Hayes is talking, we'll have a hundred of 'em before the century's out." He finished lowering the flag and folded it up for the night.

Josie managed to hide out in the barn until it was almost bedtime. Only then did she return to the others. Charles added some logs to the fire, readying it for the long night. "The bedroom is over there. Don't know what you'll find, haven't been in that room in ages. Used to be my daughter Lillian's room before she up and moved to Illinois," he said as he opened a tin and pulled out a cigarette. "Now I snore a little bit, so you just don't pay me no attention."

Both women made quick trips to the outhouse before turning in. Rebecca did not like the look of either the mattress or the blankets that had long covered it. She stripped it and replaced the linens with their own blankets and pillows, setting Josie's on the outside of the bed, as she knew the ever-cautious gunslinger would want. Rebecca changed into her long nightgown and climbed into bed, moving as close to the wall as possible to make room on the narrow mattress for Josie. The gunslinger stripped down to her long johns and slipped between the covers, her arm automatically going around the younger woman's waist. Rebecca settled back against her and both fell asleep within minutes.

"Rebecca... Rebecca, it's time to wake up," Josie tried gently, knowing that it probably would not work. She was tempted to let her young friend sleep, especially knowing that it was the first good night's sleep Rebecca had gotten since they left Cheyenne. Looking at the sleeping face, the gunslinger noticed the dark circles that had ringed her eyes were gone. Josie had been relieved to wake up and find that she had gone the entire night without a nightmare. Sometimes she was not sure which was worse, the nightmares or knowing that she kept waking up her friend. Rebecca stirred and buried her head deeper into her pillow. "Oh no you don't. I want coffee," the gunslinger muttered. She shook the young woman on the shoulder. "Come on, Rebecca."

"Hrrmmphf."

"Is that your way of saying good morning?"

"Hrmmpf... go away."

"Rebecca..." she said sternly.

"All right, all right," the tired voice said. A half-awake Rebecca crawled out of bed, eyes practically closed, and headed for the spot near the wall where their boots were sitting. One green eye focused on the two pairs, one black, and the other deep brown. She slipped her feet into the black ones.

"What are you doing?"

"Easier," she mumbled before opening the bedroom door and heading to the outhouse, the oversized boots clumping against the floor.

An hour later, all three were up, dressed, and sitting around the table drinking coffee. "I reckon I'd better get started. Where are your tools?" Josie asked.

"Everything's in the work shed. At least it should be. Haven't been out there in a while," Charles responded.

"No matter, I'm sure I'll find what I need." She stood up and downed the last of her coffee. "I want to change that axle first and bring our wagon up."

Charles leapt from his seat, his brown eyes wide. "No! You can't have the axle until the roof is fixed. We have a deal." The look on his face was near panic. Rebecca reached over and put her hand on the gunslinger's thigh. When she had the gunslinger's attention, she shook her head slightly, imploring the taller woman to let it go.

"Fine. I'll fix the roof, but I have to go back and get the rest of our supplies. Can I use your wagon?" She was met with a hearty laugh.

"Child, my wagon hasn't moved in eleven years."

"Terrific," she growled. "Guess I'll be up on the roof if you need me."

"Josie, be careful up there, all right?" Rebecca said. The gunslinger, still aggravated over the whole turn of events, merely nodded and put her hat on. The young woman watched her leave, then looked around the room. The bright morning light made all the dust and grime seem ten times worse than it had the day before. She decided that another cup of coffee was in order before she started her new chore, that being to make the neglected house look livable.

Once inside the work barn, Josie found the pile of lumber in the corner as well as a bucket of nails and a worn-out hammer. "Uh huh, one swing and the head is gonna go flying," she said out loud. She tossed the useless tool back down on the workbench and looked around the barn. In the far corner sat a wagon missing all its wheels. She went over and inspected the front axle, pleased to see that despite its neglected appearance it was still in good shape. She picked up the rusty crowbar and hooked it though her belt before hefting the wooden ladder onto her shoulder and leaving the barn.

She sat on the top of the pitched roof, one leg straddling each side, and began the slow process of pulling out the cedar shingles. Josie inspected each one carefully, tossing the rotted ones to the left and the good ones to the right for reuse. The morning sun beat down on her mercilessly, forcing her to wrap her bandanna around her forehead to keep the sweat out of her eyes. The day had just started yet her arms were already beginning to protest from her straining to remove old rusted nails.

Rebecca wrapped her bandanna around her head to keep her hair back. She used the corn broom to sweep out the cobwebs from the corners. Two hours later, all the dishes were piled on the table awaiting washing and the counters were wiped down. She stopped and wiped her brow with the back of her hand. Charles was nowhere in sight. Above her head she heard the sounds of Josie still working hard on the roof. As much as she wanted to stop and rest, there was no way she was going to until Josie did. With renewed determination, Rebecca threw herself back into her task, this time with a song on her lips.

The soft, melodic voice filtered up to Josie's ears from the open door below. She recognized the haunting strains of "I Dream of Jeanie" and felt a familiar tightness around her heart she supposed that song would always evoke in her. She paused in her work to listen to the words, even though she knew they would likely bring tears to her eyes, but she was surprised to hear that Rebecca had changed the lyrics to 'I dream of Josie with the coal-black hair…' Josie could scarcely believe what she was hearing. At first she thought that perhaps the young woman was trying to avoid the emotional scene that occurred the first time she sang that song for her. But the more she listened, the more likely it seemed that Rebecca was not even aware that her voice would be audible to Josie, and she was singing for herself.

She was struck by the honesty in the girl's voice; every word seemed to pour straight from her heart. She found herself wondering what truly had inspired Rebecca to change the lyrics. It was more than she could hope for that the younger woman might be falling for her. She had not truly realized until that moment how very much she loved Rebecca; her feelings had changed so subtly. She could no longer fool herself into believing that she simply wanted to protect the innocent girl until she could find a place to safely deposit her. She wanted Rebecca in her life. More than just wanted. She needed the stabilizing influence that Rebecca brought to her. Since she had made the choice to live outside the law so many years ago, this was the first time she found a reason to try to atone for the wrong she had done.

Tears brimmed in her eyes as she listened to the heart-felt words. She wanted to climb down from the roof and take Rebecca in her arms and make love with her until they both collapsed. Fearing that would scare the innocent young girl away, she decided instead to court her. If Rebecca seemed responsive to her overtures, she would take the next steps. In her adult life, she had never allowed herself to be really touched by another human being, since she had lost every person she loved in her life. Her motto had been if you don't let them touch you, they can't hurt you, and she had been successful at keeping people at arm's length. She could not maintain that distance with Rebecca. Slowly the pretty blonde had chipped away at her defenses until Josie no longer wanted her to keep her distance.

Josie was disappointed when the song ended, so wrapped up was she in the sound of Rebecca's voice. When she started a new song, Josie found herself joining in, albeit so softly that the younger woman could not hear her. The time and the work flew by until the sun was high in the sky. Josie's shirt was stuck to her back and both her bandanna and the brim of her hat were soaked from her efforts. She tossed the crowbar over the side of the roof and climbed down the ladder, all the muscles in her upper body protesting the abuse to which she had subjected them.

She had just put her foot on the ground when she saw Charles emerge from behind a clump of cottonwood trees, his glasses in his hands. Josie's keen vision noted the redness surrounding his soft brown eyes. She looked over at the trees, knowing without question that his wife's grave lay beyond them. The gunslinger waited until he was inside before she collected the pile of rotted cedar and set it with the rest of kindling on the side of the house. As she put the wood down, she noticed a patch of wild flowers and decided to pick a bunch for Rebecca. She gathered what she considered to be a lovely assortment of flowers and, dusting the grime from the roof off her clothes, she headed in for lunch.

Charles was seated at the table while Rebecca stirred the contents of the pot on the stove. Josie tossed her hat on the peg near the door and walked to where Rebecca stood, the flowers hidden behind her back. When she had Rebecca's attention, she whipped the flowers around and handed them to her with a flourish. "The only thing in this room prettier than these flowers is you," she said softly so Charles would not hear. Rebecca's mouth dropped open slightly and she stared first at the flowers and then at Josie, not sure what to make of such a display of affection. Rebecca's cheeks flushed to think of Josie out picking flowers for her, and she grinned shyly at the gunslinger, not knowing what to say. When Rebecca made no move to put the flowers in water, Josie said, "Better put them in a vase or they'll wilt like me." She sat down on the bench opposite the old man, her hands wrapping gratefully around the mug of water Rebecca had poured for her right before she came in.

"Uh... right. Charles, do you have a vase?"

"Should be one in that cupboard to your left," he replied with a sad smile. "Ruth loved those flowers," he said as Rebecca rummaged among the contents of the cupboard, finally finding what she sought. The vase was full of dirt, and she pumped some water into the sink and began to wash it. "Spring and summer and right into the fall, I picked her flowers every day as long as they were blooming. The house always smelled like a garden. I haven't... picked any flowers since she died."

Rebecca put the vase full of flowers in the center of the table, and the whole room seemed brighter and more cheerful. She patted Charles' hand and said, "After lunch we can pick some flowers for Ruth."

"She'd like that," the old man said with a smile. Rebecca returned to the stove where she ladled stew into bowls. She set the steaming stew in front of Charles and Josie, and noticed as she did that Josie's cheeks were more ruddy looking than usual, and the skin at the base of her throat was flushed red. She touched her face, and was surprised at the heat coming off the gunslinger.

"You're burning up," she said with a note of alarm in her voice. "Give me your bandanna," she said firmly. Josie was too hot to argue. The young woman took it to the pump and rinsed it with fresh water. She wrung it out slightly and unraveled it before giving it back.

"Thanks," the gunslinger replied, slowly wiping her face with the cool cloth. Rebecca smiled and went back to the stove to get her own bowl of stew, and then she sat down on the bench next to her friend.

"Thank you," Charles said to Rebecca as he dug into his stew. Around a mouthful he asked Josie, "How's the roof coming?"

"Slowly. There's a lot of shingles that have to come down before I can even reach the boards. Just hope it doesn't rain again," the gunslinger responded.

"Yup, got that wood oh... about two years ago, I guess. Horace brought it on one of his trips. Just ain't been able to get to it," he said with a shrug. "He'll be coming again in a couple of weeks. Be mighty surprised to find that roof done."

"Bet he will. Probably figured it'd never get done," Josie replied. She drained her mug of water, but before she could rise to get another, the cup was out of her hand and Rebecca was standing at the pump. Rather than filling the mug with the first water from the pump, she raised and lowered the arm several times, resulting in a much cooler cup of water for the over-heated gunslinger. Josie thanked her and drank half of it with one long series of swallows.

After lunch, Josie ran the cool water from the pump over her head, soaking her hair and bandanna before picking up her hat and going back out to face the afternoon sun. With each groan from her aching muscles, the gunslinger silently reminded herself to get Rebecca to rub her down later.

Rebecca swept the main room while Charles settled himself on the couch and watched. "You don't have to do that," he said.

"It's all right, I don't mind," she replied, stopping for a moment to rub her itching nose.

"That's a good woman. You'll make some young man a fine wife." He opened the tin and pulled out the last rolled cigarette. "Now my Ruth, she was a fine woman. Kept the place spotless, she did. Never complained, no matter how bad it got." His brown eyes focused on the tin daguerreotype resting on the mantle. The picture showed a young man sitting next to a beautiful dark-headed woman holding an equally dark-headed child on her lap. Rebecca looked and noticed for the first time that it was the only thing in the room that was not covered with dust. "When the war broke out, we had to choose sides. Now we didn't care none about them coloreds or nothing, but I didn't want to see the country split neither. Sent Ruth and Lillian up to Boston with my kin and I ended up with the Union." He motioned for her to take a seat in the chair opposite the couch. "When they say it was brother against brother, they weren't joshing none. For us, it was cousin against cousin."

"You fought your own cousin?"

Charles took a long drag on his cigarette before answering. "That I did. Of course I was just a lowly sergeant and he was a general. General Braxton Bragg, full of piss and vinegar, he was. Darn fool so arrogant he called his cannons Matthew, Mark, Luke, and John. Thought he had God on his side. For a while it seemed like he did. I served under General George Thomas in Chickamauga. We joined up with General Rosecrans, poorest excuse for a general I ever saw, and fought Braxton and his men. 'Twernt that many more of them than us, but those cannons sure made the difference. Nothing but smoke and blood everywhere. We could have taken him, 'cepting that no-good Rosecrans up and retreated. Old Pap Thomas, well he ordered us to stay put and keep fighting. Worst battle I ever saw and I believe one of the worst of the whole war. Well, Braxton got his wish and took Chickamauga from us, but we got him back for it." He paused to take a drink from his mug, and then continued. "He got too sure of himself, tried to take Chattanooga as well. Stationed his troops up on Lookout Mountain; guess he figured he was safe there until reinforcements arrived. Well, Old Pap didn't care to wait. We went up that mountain and surprised him. Whoeee! You should have seen them rebels run. One of the biggest battles of the war if you ask me. We followed them right down the mountain, chased them clear out of Tennessee." His eyes took a faraway look as he relived old memories. "Was a damn stupid war if you ask me. Too many men dying for nothing."

"It wasn't for nothing, Charles. You fought to keep the country together, to end slavery."

"Pshaw, don't matter none now. Braxton's dead, Old Pap Thomas is dead, suppose I'll go soon too. Seventeen years I served the United States, what have I got to show for it? A run down shack in the middle of nowhere, dinner from a tin can, having to have a woman fix my roof." His voice was tinged with frustration and anger. Above them the steady sound of Josie pulling shingles echoed through. Charles looked at the picture on the mantle. "Oh, Ruth, why'd you leave me?"

Rebecca was at his side immediately, offering her shoulder for his tears. Time passed as she cradled him in her arms, the youth comforting the elder. Through his tears, he told her of the day he woke up to find his beloved lying next to him in eternal sleep. How he buried her beyond the cottonwoods. How his life changed from being happy and full to being empty and sad, and how he only wished now for a quick end to the loneliness. Rebecca cried with him, her sensitive nature not allowing otherwise. They passed the afternoon together, Charles sharing with her his life, reliving through his words all the good times he shared with his beloved Ruth, how they used to pass the evenings on the porch swing, looking at the stars and just being happy with each other's company. He told her of their journey across the country after his discharge from the Union army and how they lived in Boise City while he built their home. He spoke of Lillian and the many adventures that made up her childhood. By the time they heard Josie climb off the roof, Rebecca knew the sweet man's entire, colorful life and felt enriched for it.

Josie set the crowbar down on the workbench in the barn along with the pile of good shingles. She was about to leave when she noticed the pile of firewood in the corner along with an ax. She stepped outside and looked again at the stack of cut wood. There was enough to last at least a week, but not much more. She rolled her shoulders, noting the stiffness, and decided that the wood could wait for another day.

In an attempt to stretch their remaining food, Rebecca made a simple fare for dinner, mixing together the remainder of their bacon with some cans of Charles' beans and adding some molasses. As worn out and tired as Josie was, she still held the plate out for seconds, as did Charles. Rebecca kept an eye on the gunslinger, concerned that she might have pushed herself too hard. Her suspicions were confirmed when Josie asked for a third cup of water and winced noticeably when she reached up to take it from her.

After dinner, Charles sat down with a fresh tin of tobacco and his rolling papers to make more cigarettes. To his surprise, Josie sat in the chair opposite him and Rebecca sat on the floor next to him and all three passed the evening converting the tin of tobacco into a tin of freshly rolled cigarettes. At first, every one Rebecca made either fell apart or did not look anything like a cigarette. Noting her friend's frustration, Josie slipped out of the chair and sat down next to her. "Like this," she said, slowly showing her the proper way to roll. The gunslinger was a patient teacher, demonstrating time and time again until Rebecca got the hang of it. Only then did Josie get back up in the chair, sighing audibly when she leaned back into the overstuffed cushion.

Rebecca entertained them with stories throughout the evening, pausing only to answer the multitude of questions posed to her by Charles, who had never heard the story of the battle of Saratoga. Although Josie had heard the story before from Rebecca, she still sat there, drawn in by the young woman's vivid descriptions and animated voice. Even when all the tobacco was rolled they continued to sit there, refusing to move until the story was complete.

Josie sat down on the edge of the bed and pulled her leg up to remove her boot. She did not even realize she had groaned until Rebecca knelt down in front of her. "Let me help," she said taking the boot in her hands and pulling. She repeated the process with the other boot before standing up. "Your back hurts, doesn't it?" Although spoken as a question, the young woman made it sound more like a statement. Josie nodded.

"Guess I overdid it today," she admitted. Rebecca walked over to their saddlebags and rummaged around until she found the liniment. Josie smiled at the silent offer and quickly stripped down to her under drawers while Rebecca changed into her nightgown. "You don't have to do this, you know," the gunslinger said as she lay down in the middle of the bed.

"I know, but I want to," Rebecca said as she climbed up onto the bed. She hiked her nightgown up to her thighs and straddled Josie's hips. "This all right?"

"Hang on a second." The gunslinger arched her back and lowered herself slowly, allowing her breasts to find a more comfortable position. "That's better."

Rebecca very carefully poured a small amount of the liniment onto Josie's back and began to work it in gently. She ran her fingertips lightly over the muscled planes of her friend's back, adding more of the pungent liquid as necessary until her hands slid smoothly over the skin. She brought both hands to Josie's left shoulder and rubbed gently, eliciting a moan from the older woman. "I'm sorry, did I hurt you?"

"Mmm, yeah, but don't stop. It feels good," the gunslinger mumbled. Rebecca smiled and continued her task. She focused her attention on each muscle, taking the time to thoroughly relax one before moving on to another. She moved from one shoulder to the other and repeated the process, noting from the moans and sharp intakes of air from Josie which muscles hurt more than others. She moved her body forward until she was on the small of the gunslinger's back, using her knees to help support most of her weight. The new position allowed her to use her thumbs to gently massage Josie's neck, every movement causing soft groans from the older woman. "Am I doing all right?"

"Wonderful," the gunslinger murmured with a thin smile on her lips. At the first touch, her eyes closed involuntarily and remained that way. "You give wonderful backrubs."

Rebecca smiled. "It's a good thing, too, considering the way you push yourself," She moved back onto Josie's hips and began to work her hands down the length of the gunslinger's back, alternating between a gentle caress with her palm to firm pressure with the heel of her hand. Every movement caused the dark-headed woman to moan and sigh as the aches and pains of the day slowly disappeared. One by one the muscles relaxed under Rebecca's gentle touch. She ran her thumbs along the lines of Josie's ribs, stopping when she found a small round indentation she had never felt before. Of course she'd never done such a thorough massage before, either. "What happened?" she said, her finger pressing on the indentation.

"Hmm?" Josie picked her head up, disappointed that Rebecca had stopped until she realized what she was referring to. "Oh, nothing, happened a long time ago." She put her head back down and waited for the young woman to continue her glorious massage. When she did not, Josie picked her head up again and twisted slightly, trying to look at the blonde woman in the dark. Gentle but firm hands pushed her back down.

"What happened, Josie?"

"Shot. Mmm... oh, right there... yessss." She closed her eyes again. "Nothing important. I got away and it wasn't that deep."

"How many times have you been shot?" Rebecca asked as she continued the massage. Josie thought about it for a few moments before answering.

"Four times... yeouch! Easy there."

"Sorry." She eased up the pressure on the sensitive muscle. "This one, the time I was with you, and the night Genie died. What else?"

"It's not important, Rebecca... There... no, to the left a little... yeah."

"Tell me," she gently prodded.

"It's stupid. It was a long time ago, when I was younger."

"Well of course you were younger. What happened? I'll stop rubbing your back if you don't tell me."

"Fine." Josie let out an exasperated breath as she prepared herself for the inevitable. *Why don't I win arguments with you, Sprite?* "I was fourteen and got hold of a gun that belonged to the hired man who worked for us."

"You shot yourself?"

"In the foot." Immediately Rebecca rolled off her and pivoted to look at the gunslinger's feet. Sure enough, on the right foot near the big toe was a small bullet hole scar. She gently touched it with her fingertips.

"That must've hurt something awful." Without thinking, Rebecca began to massage the ball of Josie's foot with her thumbs. She was rewarded with a deep groan. She rubbed again and received another lethargic groan. She sat cross-legged at the end of the bed. "Roll over."

Josie complied and was treated to the utter bliss of having both of her normally aching feet massaged with the same tenderness that her back and shoulders received. No one had ever rubbed her feet before and she could not believe how nice it felt. With infinite care and gentleness, Rebecca pressed her thumbs into the callused skin while her fingers glided over the smooth tops of Josie's feet. Her hands traveled upward, past the ankles until she reached the well-defined calf muscles. She leaned over and retrieved the bottle of liniment. Josie realized what she was going to do and happily rolled back over without being asked. "Mmm... this is better than sex," she murmured. The fingers pressing into the backs of her legs suddenly stopped.

"It is?" Rebecca asked. Josie chuckled and shook her head.

"No, but it sure feels that way right now."

"Oh," she said with a sigh of relief. She resumed her painstaking massage, working up until she reached Josie's knees. She looked at her friend's thighs, covered by her drawers. "Um... do you want..." She left the question unfinished.

"No, that's all right, Rebecca. Your arms are probably getting tired by now anyway," Josie replied, sensing her friend's discomfort. "Besides, I've got 'it' right now."

"Oh, all right," she replied, knowing that the gunslinger was lying. They had been together long enough for her to know when it was Josie's time of the month, although it seemed like their times were getting closer to each other. "So tell me how you managed to shoot yourself in the foot, oh great and mighty gunfighter," she said as she moved up and straddled Josie's hips again, running her hands over her lower back.

"Mmm... harder... it was nothing, just an accident... oh... ah, yup, right there."

"Tell me," Rebecca said, deliberately easing up the pressure on Josie's muscles, teasing her by gliding her fingertips over them.

"If I tell you, will you continue?" She felt the slightest increase in the fingers on her skin. "I was playing with it, doing target practice. I had it down at my side, hammer cocked and my mother came out and caught me." Josie could feel her cheeks turning pink. "She screamed so loud that it startled me and I pulled the trigger." She felt the body on her rear tremble with unreleased laughter. "She was so mad that she grounded me for a month. Wasn't even my fault; she's the one who yelled."

Rebecca lost control and laughed hysterically, rolling off the gunslinger and onto the bed. Only Josie's quick reflexes kept her from falling off the side. It took a few minutes for the young woman to get herself under control. "I keep seeing this little girl all dressed in black, and her mother coming out and chastising her," Rebecca chuckled. "Oh Josie, I just bet you were a handful when you were younger," she added as she rolled back onto the gunslinger and began her massage anew.

"Hmm... I was." She closed her eyes and fell back into enjoying the younger woman's ministrations, so gentle, so caring. Josie was certain that no one had ever treated her this way before, so... so... she could not come up with a word to describe the tenderness that Rebecca put into each touch. Small hands left her back and she groaned in protest until she felt them on her upper arms, wet with a fresh application of liniment. She spread her arms out, giving the younger woman total access. With the same patience and thoroughness that Rebecca used on her back, feet, and legs, both her arms were massaged from shoulder to fingertips. While there was something scary about being so completely relaxed with another person, Josie still felt safe and protected, as if no harm could come to her as long as the gentle woman continued to touch her. She felt a sense of loss and regret when Rebecca slid off her, although the blonde kept one hand on the small of her back.

"How was that?" she asked softly.

"Wonderful," Josie replied, rolling onto her side to look at her friend. Both women were propped up on their elbows facing each other. "You do that very nicely, thank you." She rolled her free shoulder and smiled. "You have no idea how good that feels."

"I'm glad you liked it," Rebecca said, smiling. She hopped off the bed and pulled the blanket down as far as she could with the gunslinger still on the bed.

"Hey, what about your backrub?" Josie asked, rising to her knees. "I can't let you give me the best rubdown I've ever had and not return the favor." She laced her fingers together and cracked her knuckles in preparation.

Rebecca sat down on the edge of the bed, put her hands in her lap, and looked down. "I don't think I want... I can't...." Her voice was so low that only someone with Josie's keen hearing could have heard. She knew immediately what was wrong.

"Rebecca..." She moved closer and put her hand on the younger woman's shoulder, noting the tension. Josie cupped her chin, forcing the green eyes to look at her in the dim light of the moon coming through the window. "Do you trust me?"

"Yes, of course I do," she said with conviction. "You know that."

"Then trust me not to hurt you, Rebecca. You can't tell me that all that sweeping and dusting didn't give you sore muscles too." She released her hold on the younger woman's chin. "You trusted me to wash your back; trust me to do this."

They sat there quietly for a minute while Rebecca made her decision. Without a word, she stood up and peeled off her nightgown. Josie stood and pulled the blankets back the rest of the way and waited for her to lie down before placing one knee on either side of Rebecca's waist and reaching for the liniment. Remembering how gently the younger woman had given her a massage, Josie imitated the motions, lightly running her fingers over Rebecca's back until it was covered with a thin layer of liniment.

Josie worked slowly, letting her get used to the feeling of hands traveling over her back. "How are you doing?"

"All right," Rebecca said, her senses still alert to every movement. The taller woman continued to gently run her hands all over her back and shoulders, feeling the almost imperceptible relaxing of the muscles underneath. Josie made no attempt to deepen the pressure, seemingly content to just let her hands glide over the smooth skin. "How about now?"

"Mmmmmhmm," was the mumbled reply. The gunslinger smiled and began to let her fingers seek out the bunched up and sore muscles. She marveled at the way Rebecca's body responded to her touch. Muscles that were tight and clenched relaxed completely under her manipulations. Her ears were rewarded with the softest of sighs as her hands continued to roam. She listened to Rebecca's breathing deepen and become even followed by the softest of snores.

Josie leaned back, making sure to keep her weight off the sleeping woman, and yawned. She was about to move off when she noticed a thin white scar illuminated by the pale moonlight. She let her finger lightly run the length of it before putting her hands on either side of Rebecca and bending down. She placed a gentle kiss, much like a mother would kiss a child's injury to make it feel better. "Goodnight, Sprite," she whispered before pulling the blankets up and lying down next to her friend. When she went to wrap her arm around Rebecca's waist, Josie felt the sensation of her breasts pressing up against bare skin. The last time she had been like this with Rebecca, it was pouring down buckets and did not feel anywhere near as pleasant as it did at that moment. Josie snuggled closer, buried her face into the soft golden hair, and fell to sleep in seconds. Her last waking thought was of how nice it felt to hold someone. *No, not just someone*, she corrected herself. *To hold Rebecca.*

37: Whittling Away the Time

Josie woke to find one arm and one leg draped casually over her, and Rebecca's head resting on her shoulder. She did not want to disturb the comfortably sleeping woman, but her bladder was protesting too much. As gently as she could, the gunslinger slipped out from under her and got out of bed. The early morning chill raised gooseflesh on her skin and the rough and tumble gunslinger really wished they had a chamber pot as she reached for her long johns. After making certain that Rebecca was covered with the blankets, she picked up her boots and one gun belt and quietly left the room.

Josie was already up on the roof pulling away shingles when Charles left the house, rifle in hand, and headed through the clump of cottonwoods. Rebecca came out a few minutes later with a cup of coffee in her hand. She stood on the ground and looked up at the woman in black, already sweating from the heat of the morning sun. "Hi," she called up.

"Hi yourself."

"Brought you some coffee. Sorry I forgot to set the pot up for you last night." She walked over to the ladder and waited for Josie to come down. "Thanks for letting me sleep," she said when she handed the mug over to the gunslinger.

"It's all right. Did Charles say where he was going?"

"No," Rebecca replied. "I'm sure he'll be fine, though. He was in a good mood when he left."

Josie downed the rest of the coffee and handed the cup back to her. "I need you to take Flossy and go get the rest of our things from the wagon before someone happens upon it. Should only take you three or four trips if you load the horse up right." Since the wagon was less than a mile from the house, and thus within earshot, Josie did not make her take a gun along. The gunslinger did, however, still insist on Rebecca taking one of the bowie knives, just in case.

It was late afternoon when Rebecca finished getting the rest of their things. She had just finished brushing down Flossy and putting her back in her stall when a shot rang out from beyond the trees. She ran out of the barn in time to see Josie race down the ladder and pull her gun from the holster. "Get inside and don't come out I until tell you to," Josie yelled as she ran into the cottonwoods and disappeared from sight. Rebecca stood frozen to the spot, unable to move. Several minutes later another shot rang out. There was no sign of either Charles or Josie. Rebecca headed for the woods, forgetting all about her friend's instructions in her worry. She almost reached the trees when the gunslinger appeared.

"I thought I told you to go inside and wait," she said, concerned about the look on the young woman's face. "What's wrong?"

"I was worried," Rebecca replied. "Where's Charles?"

"He's back with the deer. Fresh meat for dinner tonight. Hope you know how to cook venison."

"That's what those shots were? Heck, Josie, I thought someone was attacking you two." The gunslinger caught the tone of worry in the young woman's voice and immediately felt bad for scaring her so. Without saying a word, she held her arms out slightly and invited Rebecca in for a brief hug.

"I was trying to keep you safe, not scare you," she said to the top of the blonde head.

"Well, I was," she admitted. "Don't do that to me again." She pulled back from the hug and smiled. "So, venison for dinner, huh? I'll cook it, but you're gonna have to skin it."

"Deal," the gunslinger replied. "Just came back to get some rope. It's a small buck, but he sure is heavy. Gonna have to drag him."

"You just make sure that you wash up before coming in to eat," Rebecca said, wagging her finger. "And I mean it, with soap and everything."

"Yes, Mother," the gunslinger said mockingly, receiving a playful backhand to the belly.

"Keep it up and you can go sleep with Phoenix."

"At least Phoenix doesn't snore," Josie teased back.

"You're right, she doesn't; but then again, Phoenix doesn't give backrubs."

Josie held up her hands in defeat. "I'll wash, I'll wash. I'm not giving up those backrubs for anything." She watched as the broadest grin came over the young woman's face and realized with a slight smile that she would be lucky if she ever won an argument with Rebecca again.

After a filling meal of venison steaks, Josie took the rest of the meat to the smokehouse while Rebecca cleaned up after dinner and Charles worked on getting a fire going in the fireplace. Once again in possession of her medical text, the young woman sat down in the chair, turned the wick up on the lamp, and resumed her reading.

"That's a mighty big book you got there," Charles commented. "What's it for?"

"Oh, it's about medicine and healing. Josie got it for me," she added proudly.

"Wanna be a doctor, do ya?" he said as he lit a cigarette.

"Oh no, I could never be a doctor, too much schooling. I would like to help people though."

"My Lillian wanted to be a nurse once. Girl's too darn smart for schooling, though. Ever seen one like that? Too smart to be taught, that's what she was. Ruth tried. She bought her books and even took her to the library at Harvard a lot when they were living with my kin in Boston. For almost four years she took her there every week. Lillian spent hours there, just reading everything. When I came home, I couldn't believe how much she knew. Like a sponge, that one was." His eyes took on a lost glaze, remembering a happy time so long ago. Rebecca reached out and squeezed his hand, receiving a smile in return. "Well," he sniffed, "I guess that's enough talk about things long past." He reached out with his free hand and patted hers. "We should do something fun."

"Like what?" she said, putting her book down gently on the floor.

"Now I know I have some cards around here somewhere," he said as he stood up. He walked into the kitchen and opened and closed several drawers before he found what he was looking for. "I knew I had some." He returned to the parlor holding a worn deck of playing cards in his hand. "What would you like to play?"

"Oh, I'm afraid I don't know how to play cards," she said apologetically. Charles smiled a warm, grandfatherly smile and began to shuffle the deck.

"Well then, now is a good time to learn. What would you like to learn? Ruth used to play cards all the time. You see that piece of wood over there?" He pointed to a thin board, two feet by three feet, leaning against the wall. "She'd put that across her lap right in that chair and play solitaire for hours. I couldn't tell you how many decks of cards she went through. Horace used to bring a new deck each time he'd visit." He stopped shuffling and waited for her answer. She thought about what kind of card game would be good to learn.

"Can you teach me how to play poker? I know Josie knows how to play that game." She thought it might be nice to play a game with her friend. "Oh, but I don't have any money to play with."

Charles chuckled. "Not to worry, we'll use what Horace and I use when we play." He got up, went back out into the kitchen, and removed two small sacks from the drawer. "It'll be easier to play at the table," he suggested, setting the sacks on the table. Rebecca joined him and took the offered bag.

"Beans?"

"Yup, Horace and I never play for money." He dealt out the cards, smiling when he saw the look of total concentration on the young face. Oh yes, this was going to be much more fun than playing with his brother, who insisted on playing cutthroat poker. "Do you like wild cards, honey?"

"What are wild cards?" she asked innocently.

"Wonderful," he said with a smile.

Once all the meat was cut up and hung around the inside of the smokehouse, Josie went to the barn to get some kindling. She picked up the ax and ran her thumb along the end, checking it for sharpness. Not at all pleased with it, she went over the workbench to get the whetstone. Sitting next to the stone was a knife with a short blade and a long handle, perfect for whittling. Setting the ax down, Josie walked back over to the woodpile and picked up a piece of split wood. She sat down on a stool and turned the wood over in her hands, studying the grain and inspecting it for knots. She treated six more pieces to the same scrutiny before selecting one and setting it on the workbench next to the knife. She pulled the handmade wheelbarrow over to the pile of wood and loaded it for the smokehouse.

"So when is Horace coming?" Rebecca asked, laying two cards face down on the table. Charles handed her two new ones before taking three for himself.

"Hmm, should be in about ten days or so. He'll stay overnight, then move on. I'll see him about a week after that on his return trip." He pushed two dry beans into the pile on the center of the table.

"Do you think Josie will be done with the roof by then?" She met his two beans and raised him two.

"I don't think so, Rebecca. There's a lot of work to be done up there. I know she's a strong woman, but even a strapping young man wouldn't be able to get it done in ten days." He matched her two beans. "What'cha got?"

"Three nines. Well, I guess that means we'll be here for my birthday. It's in eleven days," she said, setting her cards down to show him.

"Your birthday? How old will you be? Three tens." He took the pot, leaving one bean behind for the ante.

"Twenty," she answered while he dealt another hand.

"Well then, we'll have to have a little celebration for you," he said as he discarded one card.

"Oh please, don't think about it. All it means is that I'm another year older. It's no great shakes. Three cards please."

After making sure the fire was going nicely, Josie left the smokehouse and returned to the barn. She picked up the piece of wood and the whittling knife and headed for the porch swing. The late afternoon sun cast its orange light upon the sky while the dark-headed woman put the blade to the wood. Thin, curly slivers began to multiply on the porch floor. Josie continued to shave off pieces of the wood, not giving any thought as to what she was making. The foot long quartered log found its edges rounded under her blade. Far away a coyote cried out to the approaching moon. She tucked one leg up underneath her and used her other foot to set the swing into a gentle rocking motion. By the time darkness made it impossible for her to go on, the entire floor and seat around her was covered with the slivers of wood. She stood up, set the wood and knife on the swing, and brushed the slivers off her britches before going in.

She found Rebecca and Charles seated at the table, the younger with a huge pile of beans in front of her and cards in her hand. "Charles, what are you teaching her?"

"Full house, right?" Rebecca said as she laid her hand down and smiled.

"That's exactly what it is, child. You win again," he said, passing the deck to her. Josie walked over and looked at the cards on the table.

"She doesn't have a full house, she's got two fives, two sixes, and a two."

"Twos are wild," Rebecca said, pulling the cards together and shuffling. She did it slowly, worried about sending them all over the table and floor again like she did when she first tried to follow the kindly old man's instructions.

"Wild cards are for old ladies and children," the gunslinger muttered under her breath.

"You wanna play, Josie?" she said, looking expectantly at the older woman. "You can have some of my beans." Her eyes took on the expression of a puppy dog and her lips formed a slight pout. The bounty hunter pulled the chair from the parlor to the end of the table, tucking her feet under herself to make up some of the difference in height from the chair to the table. Rebecca pushed a pile of beans over to her and started to deal the cards.

"Threes are wild."

"Wonderful," Josie said, trying hard not to groan at how silly it was to play like that. She picked her cards up one at a time. Three, ten, three, nine, queen. A straight with no effort. She counted out ten beans and pushed them forward only to be stopped by a smaller hand.

"The most you can bet is three beans."

"You're kidding."

"Nope. Three's the limit. Want any cards?"

"No. I'm fine," she said sourly as she slouched back in her seat. Charles took two and Rebecca took three, her face lighting up as she put the new cards into her hand.

"Nice poker face," the gunslinger drawled. "If you have a good hand, try not to show any expression. Otherwise everyone will fold and you won't win any money."

"Oh, all right," she said, trying to make her face as expressionless as possible. Charles folded. "Your bet, Josie."

"Two." She pushed two beans into the pot and the younger woman matched it. "Straight to the king," she said with a smirk. Rebecca broke into a broad grin.

"Flush." She laid down a hand full of hearts.

"Beginner's luck," Josie growled. "Deal."

"That's one thing she has," Charles said with a wry smile. "At the rate she's going, I'll be broke within an hour," he said, waving his hand toward his dwindling supply of dry beans.

"Don't worry, Charles, I'll be happy to loan you some, just like Josie."

"Loan me? You mean I owe you these beans?"

"Of course," Rebecca said with a mischievous smile. "So you'd better hurry up and win a hand so you can start paying me back."

"Oh, I'll pay you back all right," Josie playfully threatened as she picked up the new hand of cards. Charles chuckled and tossed his bean in the pot.

The winnings passed back and forth amongst the three of them for hours. Rebecca won more than the others, but continued to feed her pile of beans across and down the table to keep the others in the game, not wanting it to end. When Josie saw her fighting to stay awake, the gunslinger tossed her cards down on the table. "I think it's time for the sandman." She rose to her feet and put the chair back where it belonged. Rebecca collected all the cards into one neat pile and left them on the table along with the beans.

"Yeah... I am pretty tired," she said. "Goodnight, Charles."

"Goodnight, Rebecca."

Within minutes they were under the covers, the gunslinger in her long johns and Rebecca in her nightgown. "Thanks for playing tonight," the young woman said softly.

"I'm glad you enjoyed it. Just don't go getting any ideas in your head about walking into a saloon and sitting down at a table," Josie warned gently. "They don't play with wild cards."

"Oh I won't, I promise. I'll leave that kind of stuff up to you," she said as she snuggled deeper into the older woman's embrace. Both well fed and comfortable, it was only a matter of moments before they were sound asleep.

38: Preparations

The routine they had established varied little as the days went by. Each morning it was harder for Josie to pull herself away from the sleeping form next to her. Instead of separating herself from Rebecca, she found her arms snaking around her to draw her even closer. And even in her sleep, Rebecca returned the embrace, wrapping her own arm around Josie's middle and draping her leg over Josie's thigh. Josie had never felt such contentment. She would wait until she heard Charles puttering around in the house and finally, with a soft kiss to Rebecca's lips, she would drag herself out of bed.

Before Josie climbed up on the roof, both she and Charles trooped to the flower garden to pick a handful of flowers. With a wave, Charles would then make his way to the cottonwoods to visit with his wife, and Josie would put the fresh flowers in the vase for Rebecca.

On the fifth morning before he walked away, Charles called out to Josie who stopped and turned around. "Been meaning to ask you, you know Rebecca's birthday is coming up in a few days…" he began, but stopped when the look on her face made it clear she had not known.

"No, she didn't tell me," she said. She was hurt that Rebecca had told Charles about her birthday, but did not share it with her. She squared her shoulders and tried to act like it did not matter. "What day is it?"

"The twenty-first. I want to do something special for her, but I don't know her well enough to know what she'd like. Maybe you could give me some ideas?"

Josie thought about it for a few moments and then said, "Well, she loves to read. A book would be nice. Or some fabric and embroidery thread," she added, remembering how much Rebecca had enjoyed embroidery once she finally caught on.

Charles' face lit up; he had the perfect gift for her. "Thanks, Josie. Oh, and not a word to Rebecca, all right?"

"Count on it," she said as she watched him walk off with a lightness in his step she had not seen before. She only wished she had an idea of what she could give Rebecca. And then it came to her. The piece of wood she had been half-heartedly whittling on for several days had gradually resolved itself into a fairly decent looking totem. If she could finish it in time she was certain Rebecca would like it, fascinated as she was with all things Cherokee. It would mean she would have to stop work on the roof earlier in the day so she would have more daylight hours to work on it. Rebecca had been occupied with her own tasks and did not seem to notice what the gunslinger was up to, so she figured she could accomplish it without her being any the wiser. Josie hummed as she went about her work on the roof and thought of things she could do to make Rebecca's birthday a very special day.

Horace arrived two days before Rebecca's birthday. From her vantage point on the roof Josie could see the dust of his wagon even before the wagon itself was visible. She was fairly certain it must be Charles' brother coming down the road, but to be on the safe side she climbed down from the roof and strapped on a gun. When he pulled into the door yard with a jangling of harness and was met by a tall woman dressed in black with her hand lightly resting on the handle of her gun, he pulled up short with a look of confusion on his face that changed to fear. "Has something happened to my brother?" he asked, his voice tinged with hysteria. Josie removed her hand from her gun and held both hands in front of her as a sign of peace.

"No, he's fine," she said quickly to relieve his anxiety. "He's out in the grove yonder," she said gesturing toward the cottonwoods, and Horace nodded in understanding. He often found his brother out there when he came to visit. "My friend and I have been helping him around the place in exchange for an axle for our wagon."

Horace visibly relaxed when he realized his brother was in no danger. He looked around then and it was obvious that a lot of work had been done to the place since the last time he was there. The roof was almost completely replaced, the yard was neatly trimmed, and the rubbish that had accumulated over the years was gone. Even the flowerbeds, which had been overrun with weeds when last he noticed, were neat looking and color-ful. It did not look like the same place at all, but instead looked as it had when Ruth was alive. He shook his head, incredulous. "I wouldn't a recog-nized the place," he said, smiling and stepping forward with his hand out-stretched. "I'm Horace, Charles' younger brother," he said as he pumped her hand vigorously.

"Josie…." She nearly blurted out her last name, but realized that Horace was more a man of the world than his brother and might be inclined to turn her in for the reward if he knew who she was.

"Purely pleased to make your acquaintance," he said brightly. "You have surely done wonders here. My brother is lucky to have found you."

"Oh, I only did the roof. Charles and my friend Rebecca have been working on the rest of the place. And speaking of Rebecca, I have a favor to ask of you…" she added conspiratorially.

When Rebecca walked through the door that evening with a bucket of wild blackberries she had picked down by the creek, Josie and Charles abruptly fell silent. It seemed that every time she came upon them un-awares these days they were in the middle of a heated discussion that ended the moment she appeared. Since she had never in her life had anything special done for her birthday, it did not occur to her that they were planning something pleasant. Rather she feared that Josie might be softening her up with flowers and kindness every day because she was conspiring with Charles to leave her there when she departed. Certainly Josie was not act-ing like she wanted to leave her and, in fact, the opposite seemed to be true. And Josie had promised never to leave her behind as long as she wanted to stay with her, so Rebecca was truly confused about what was going on.

The one thing she was not confused about was the way she felt every time Josie brushed her finger over her lips, or whispered into her ear, or twined her fingers together with her own. Josie's smile made her weak in the knees, and when she spooned her body around Rebecca's in bed at night, Rebecca could feel the wetness bloom between her legs. She had never realized that it was possible for two women to love each other as a man and a woman did, but when Josie told her about Genie, it was obvious from the pain in her voice that Josie had been in love with Genie. Dare she hope that Josie's actions were those of a woman in love? It seemed so, but Rebecca's lack of experience made her uncertain. She promised herself that she would pluck up her courage and ask the beautiful outlaw outright. But she did not. Josie excused herself right after supper and went out to the barn to *work on something*. Rebecca cleaned up the kitchen as fast as she could and was putting a shawl around her shoulders to go out and speak to Josie when Charles practically pounced on her.

"Where you off to?" He asked innocently enough, but it appeared to Rebecca that he was more than simply curious.

"Thought I'd go see if I could help Josie with whatever she's working on," she replied. She continued toward the door, and Charles bounded in front of her and hooked his arm through hers.

"Aw, I kinda hoped you might want to play some card games with me. Josie's about finished with that roof and you folks'll be movin' on. There's still lots of games I need to teach you before you go."

He sounded almost desperate to the girl, and she realized that when they did leave – and she was determined Josie would not leave her behind – Charles would be even lonelier than he was before they came, having become used to the presence of other people. With a sigh she took off her shawl and draped it back on the peg by the door and, smiling at the old man, she took a seat at the table. "All right, Charles, what can I beat you out of today?" she said with a grin. She would talk to Josie later.

"Gin," Rebecca said triumphantly, lying her cards out on the table with a flourish. Charles groaned and threw his cards down on the table and scowled playfully at his young protégé.

"Upon my soul girl, if I hadn't dealt those cards myself, I'd have to wonder if you weren't pulling a fast one on old Charlie."

"Beginner's luck. Again," she said with a laugh as she gathered up the cards. When she had finished putting the cards together, she stood up and stretched. They had been playing for at least an hour or more, and the hard wooden chairs were less than comfortable. She stifled a yawn. "Excuse me. I'm about done in," she said apologetically. "Think I'll just go see if…."

"You can't quit without letting me have a chance to get even," Charles said quickly. "How about best three out of five? You already have two to my one, so it shouldn't take long." He started shuffling the cards and dealt out the hands without waiting for a response from the little blonde. She shook her head as if to say there was no winning an argument with this stubborn old man, gave another stretch and started to sit down. At that moment the door opened and Josie stepped through, surprised to see Rebecca still up. The young woman normally went to bed shortly after finishing her chores in the kitchen. There was a silent conversation between Josie's eyes and Charles', and the gunslinger realized that he had been keeping the little blonde from going out to see what Josie was up to. She mouthed "thank you" at him as she walked into the kitchen to pour herself a glass of water.

"Your little friend whupped my tail at gin all night," Charles grumbled lightly as he gathered up the cards. Turning to Rebecca he smiled and said,

"Think you got the right idea, Punkin'. I'm plumb wore out myself. Suppose we have us a grudge match tomorrow, what do you say?"

"Sounds good to me," Rebecca agreed quickly, glad he had abandoned the notion of playing another game. "I'm just going to make a little trip to the uh…" She nodded in the general direction of the back of the house where the outhouse was located, then continued, "…and then I'm going to bed. How about you, Josie?"

Josie laughed. "I think I'll let you go to the 'uh' by yourself, and I'll be along to bed directly." Rebecca gave her a big smile as she threw her shawl around her shoulders once again and, picking up a lantern, she headed out into the night. Taking advantage of her absence, Josie filled Charles in on the errand she had sent Horace on for the next day, which relieved his mind. His brother was seldom late, and he had been concerned when Horace had not shown up that day as he said he would.

Her hands were red-brown from the stain she used on the totem. As she wiped at them with a rag dabbed in coal oil, they talked animatedly about how surprised Rebecca was going to be the next day. When the object of their conversation walked back through the door, they fell silent. Josie smiled at her warmly, and Charles gave her a wink. He rose and took the lamp from Rebecca's hand and darted out the door to relieve his bladder, which had begun to pain him after sitting for so long. He had been afraid to excuse himself while they were playing their game for fear she would go in search of Josie.

Pumping water into the sink, Josie washed her hands several times until she was satisfied that the smell of the coal oil was gone. She turned from the sink to find Rebecca standing virtually right behind her, a look of concern on her face. Josie blinked a few times in surprise to find that her self-defense mechanism had allowed the young girl to get so close without her even realizing she was there.

"What is it, Rebecca? What's wrong?" Josie reached out and brushed a strand of hair from Rebecca's forehead, then she lightly caressed her cheek. Running her hand down the adored face, she lightly touched Rebecca's lips with her fingertips. Rebecca trembled at the touch, and her eyes fluttered shut. Josie put her arms around Rebecca's waist, and the smaller woman allowed herself to be pulled into those strong arms. She laid her head on Josie's chest, listening to the sound of her heart thundering like an avalanche down a mountain.

Rebecca's plan to calmly talk to Josie dissolved as she blurted out, "Don't leave me here. Please take me with you; I c-couldn't s-stand it if you left me…." She burrowed into Josie's chest, her head resting just below the taller woman's chin.

"Whoa, whoa," Josie said, pulling back so she could see Rebecca's face. "What makes you think I'm going to leave you? I said you could stay with me as long as you wanted to, and I meant it. Of course you'll come with me." She tilted Rebecca's chin up so she could look into her eyes. "Rebecca, I'd be lost without you. Now come on, let me see a smile." Josie put her finger by the corner of Rebecca's mouth and gently pushed up, creating a lop-sided smile. "Kinda crooked but better than nothing," she said softly, which made Rebecca smile genuinely.

"All right, if you're not planning to leave me here, then what is it that you and Charles are cooking up that you both shut up every time I come into the room? I thought at first it was my imagination, but when it continued for days, I couldn't pretend it wasn't happening any more. I was scared, Josie."

"Oh, Sprite, it's... nothing to be scared about," she said quickly. She almost blurted out their plans for her birthday and bit the words back just in time. "In fact, I think you'll be pleased when you find out what it is." Rebecca still had a look of confusion on her face, but Josie shook her head and smiled. "I've said too much already. You'll find out everything soon enough. Be patient, and trust me, will you?"

"Yes of course, but...."

"No buts. It's time for bed. Come on." She grasped Rebecca's hand and led her toward the little bedroom they shared. Rebecca twined her fingers together with Josie's and followed willingly, still curious but no longer worried. She trusted Josie completely.

Josie cupped her hand behind the flame of the candle and leaned forward to blow it out so that Rebecca could get undressed in the dark, as was her habit. The gunslinger hoped that one day soon her precious young friend would no longer feel the shame and embarrassment she had carried for so long because of her abusive father and would allow Josie to see all of her.

"Wait," Rebecca said from behind her, and she turned to once again find the little blonde close enough to kill her, if that had been her plan. Josie's razor sharp instincts had been dulled by the safe life she had been living lately. Once they left this haven behind, she would need to hone them again for her own safety, as well as for Rebecca's. "I... want to talk awhile, and I want to see your face," Rebecca said softly.

"Fine with me," Josie said with a grin. "Do you mind if I get undressed while we talk?"

"Not at all," Rebecca replied softly, sinking down to the edge of the bed and watching as the gunslinger's fingers methodically unfastened the buttons of her black shirt. When she peeled it off to reveal her shoulders and her creamy breasts, Rebecca was unable to take her eyes away from the beautiful spectacle. Josie's breasts fairly glowed in the dancing candle flame, and Rebecca ached to reach out and touch them. Transfixed by the tantalizing beauty in front of her, Rebecca suddenly found herself tongue-tied and blushing. She could not even think of what it was she wanted to say, and she simply sat like a schoolgirl admiring her first real crush.

Josie could not help but notice where Rebecca's eyes were fastened, and she smiled at the mix of emotions revealed in that simple look. If she had ever wondered whether there was a chance the little blonde was attracted to her, she wondered no more. Blatant desire was written on Rebecca's young face, but there was uncertainty as well. Josie knew she must be patient with Rebecca and give her all the time she needed to sort out her feelings without her influence. Much as she wanted to take the smaller woman in her arms and smother her with kisses, she knew Rebecca was not ready for that. She would allow Rebecca to set the pace, taking her cues from her.

Rebecca suddenly realized that she was staring at Josie's breasts, and she had no concept of how much time had passed while she did so. She blushed as she wondered what Josie must be thinking. Reluctantly she dragged her eyes off Josie's glorious body and brought them to her beautiful face. Josie was watching her, a smile tipping up the corners of her mouth. Casually Josie turned away, pouring water from the pitcher on the washstand into the wash basin. She figured Rebecca would have time to compose herself while she washed up a little. She soaked a cloth in the cool water and scrubbed it over her face, gooseflesh rising on her skin at the contact with the water. She wished she had thought to warm up some water before retiring to the bedroom, but it was a bit late for that now.

The smooth planes of Josie's back were appealing to Rebecca, but were not the magnet for her eyes that her chest had been. Rebecca was able to remember what it was she wanted to talk to Josie about, and she cleared her throat and began. "Josie... I wanted to ask you about... I mean, I've been wondering if... that is, if you... did you love Genie? I mean, romantically love her. Like a man and a woman do?" She could feel her cheeks flaming, but once she started speaking, it suddenly became very important that she got her question out before she lost her nerve completely. Josie's back stiffened at the question, and she laid down her washcloth and turned around again to face the furiously blushing girl.

"Are you asking me if I was in love with Genie?" she asked, and Rebecca nodded mutely. "Yes. Yes, I was. But like a man and a woman?"

Josie shook her head and seemed to contemplate her answer. "It was very different. More intense, more... I don't know, fulfilling. I couldn't imagine having those kinds of feelings for a man. We didn't... make love. Perhaps we would have if she had lived... I don't know, but... we didn't even discuss it. I thought we had all the time in the world...." Her voice trailed off as she choked back a sob. This was not what she wanted to be doing, grieving for her lost love in front of the woman with whom she was now very much in love. She gulped a couple of times and took a deep breath to regain her composure.

"Have you ever made love with other women since then?" Rebecca asked breathlessly. Josie took a few moments to frame her answer, and Rebecca wished she could bite out her tongue for having even asked. In her mind she kicked herself for starting this train of thought, but she had to see it through. She needed to know if Josie was still attracted to women, or if that had been simply the crush of a teenaged girl.

"You ask hard questions," Josie said sincerely. She sat on the edge of the bed and began to pull her boots off while considering how to reply.

"Let me help," Rebecca said, dropping to the floor in front of the gunslinger. Lifting each foot in turn she pulled off her boots followed by the socks. She sat cross-legged on the floor and drawing Josie's right foot into her lap she began to massage it. Josie's eyes drifted shut and she gave a little sigh. "What's the answer?" Rebecca persisted.

"I've had sex with a few," Josie replied, and Rebecca looked at her questioningly with her eyebrow raised. "All right, more than a few," she amended with a wry smile. "But in my heart I never made love with any of them. It was just a pleasant way to relieve tension. Meant nothing to me… emotionally." Rebecca's thumbs pressed convulsively on the bridge of Josie's foot as she took in the meaning of her words.

"Easy, love," Josie said with a chuckle. "I have to walk on those feet, and that won't be easy if you crush my instep."

"Oh, sorry," Rebecca said, hastily letting go of Josie's foot. Her heart did a somersault in her chest at the word 'love' so lightly dropped from Josie's lips.

Josie laughed lightly. "Feast or famine with you, isn't it, Sprite? I didn't say you had to stop; just don't break my foot." Rebecca blushed again and averted her eyes, but she did pick up Josie's foot and begin massaging it again. "All right, now it's my turn. Why all the questions about making love with women?"

Once again Rebecca's gift with words deserted her, and she found herself unable to speak in coherent sentences. "It's the way you've been acting for the past few days, more attentive than usual… not that you're not attentive other times," she stammered. "I'm not saying this right… what I mean is, I thought you were just being nice to me because you were going to ditch me, but now I know you weren't, and I… it seemed like you were courting me. Like… well, like a man would. And I never thought about… that with a woman before, and I wasn't sure if I was right. Were you? Courting me, I mean?"

"Yes. But that wasn't fair; it was my turn to ask the questions. Now don't think about these questions, just answer from your heart. Do you love me?"

"Yes," she answered without hesitation.

"Are you in love with me?"

"I don't know... yes, I think so. How can I know? I was never in love before."

"Do you find yourself attracted to me sexually?"

Rebecca took a deep breath and then let it out in a shudder. "Oh God, yes. But Josie I'm afraid. I don't know what you want from me. What if I can't... what if I'm not... enough for you?"

"Oh, Rebecca... whatever you are, whatever you want to be, is enough for me. I want you to be happy. I would love nothing better than to make love with you for the rest of my life, but if all you want is to travel with me and be my friend, I can live with that. If anything happens between us, it will be because you say you want it to. I will never push you or try to make you do something you don't want to." She reached down and clasped Rebecca by her wrists and pulled her up to where she could place a kiss on her forehead. Then she whirled her around and sat her down on the edge of the bed facing the other side of the room, and at the same time she rose and unbuckled her belt and dropped her pants to the floor. "Don't turn around. I'm naked," she said as she grabbed her long johns from the back of a chair and quickly stepped into them. By the time Rebecca did turn around, Josie was slipping her arms into the sleeves and all but covered up. "I'm going to blow out this candle now so you can get undressed. Unless you want to tease me by getting naked in front of me," Josie said with a raised eyebrow and a sly smile.

"Blow it out," Rebecca said shyly. She really had wanted to see Josie strip, and the thought of taking off her clothes in front of the gunslinger excited her more than she could say. But it was too soon. Her mind was whirling like a cyclone, and what she wanted kept getting hopelessly tangled with what she thought she should do. "Can we sleep on this tonight and talk about it again tomorrow?" she asked hopefully.

Josie puffed out the candle and returned to the bed. "Of course we can. Tomorrow will be a perfect day to talk about it," she said, knowing what surprises the next day would bring to the pretty little blonde. She vowed to stay on her side of the bed as much as possible and to keep her hands to herself. When the time was right, she knew Rebecca would let her know.

39: A Birthday to Remember

Rebecca dreamed that she was a prisoner in the turret of a castle in a foreign land. She could not speak the language of the natives and had no idea why she was being held, but she sensed that days had passed since she had been captured. She watched from the parapet as the people came and went in the courtyard below, but was too far away for her voice to be heard if she cried out. Her strength was ebbing from lack of food and water; it seemed she had been forgotten in her lonely tower. When she thought she could hold on no longer, she saw a knight dressed in black ride into the courtyard on a golden steed. Her heart leapt with joy at the sight, as she knew this was her knight come to rescue her. With what little strength she had left, she called "Sir Knight!" and dropped her handkerchief over the parapet. The knight looked up as though he had heard her voice and saw the handkerchief fluttering in the wind. He vaulted from the back of his horse and drawing his sword he fought his way through the castle guard. She could no longer see him, but she knew he was making his way toward her and that rescue was at hand. Even as that thought flitted through her mind, she heard the sound of swords clashing outside her door and then silence. The bolt was thrown back, and the door was opened. The black knight stood outside the door as if await-ing her invitation to enter. She made a gesture to indicate he should enter, certain that he would not understand her language, and immedi-ately he strode into the room. His chain mail was red with the blood of her captors but he was unhurt. She watched as he crossed the room to where she stood, but before he got there, her legs gave out and she started to crumple. In an instant the knight was there, his strong arms around her, gathering her up and holding her against his chest. Rebecca reached up and grasped the helmet that covered his head and tugged it off. Long black hair tumbled free, and Josie's piercing blue eyes were fixed on her own. The knight bent to press her lips gently against Rebecca's. "Oh, Josie..." Rebecca murmured when Josie broke off the kiss, and her heart started to pound....

"Yes, Sprite, I'm here," Josie's voice said softly, but the dream knight's lips had not moved. Rebecca's dream self was still trying to figure out how the knight had accomplished that feat when Josie continued, "Wake up, Mary Sunshine. It's your birthday."

Rebecca tried to pull the voice into the dream, but the smell of cooked food contributed to the allure of the waking reality. She opened her eyes to see the gunslinger sitting on the side of the bed holding a tray laden down with food. There was a mountain of crisp bacon, fried eggs, biscuits, a cup of coffee, and a glass of orange juice. A vase full of bright flowers stood on a corner of the tray. Rebecca's mouth dropped open in surprise and she simply stared. She thought of pinching herself to see if she had just moved from one dream into another, when a very real Josie leaned over and kissed her forehead.

"Breakfast in bed for the birthday girl," she said brightly. "Now sit up higher so I can fit this tray over your lap." Rebecca did as she asked and Josie put the sumptuous breakfast in front of her. Rebecca just continued to stare first at the food and then at Josie, and the gunslinger laughed. The facial expressions alone made Josie determined to surprise the pretty blonde more often.

When Rebecca finally found her voice she asked incredulously, "You didn't make this, did you?"

"God, no. You don't think I'd do that to you on your birthday, do you? Charles and Horace made it."

"Horace?" Rebecca asked around a mouthful of food.

"Charles' brother. He got here this morning bright and early. We got tired of waiting for you to grace us with your presence, and I figured the smell of food would do the trick. Worked, too. Oh, by the way, what were you dreaming about when I came in? You called out my name and I thought for a moment you had seen me, but you were still sound asleep."

Rebecca's cheeks flushed a bright red as she remembered her dream about the dashing knight. "I don't remember," she lied softly, and Josie raised her eyebrow and looked at her questioningly. "All right, well... I was locked up in a castle and you were dressed as a knight and came to rescue me. Happy now?"

"Not as happy as that knight was, I think," she answered, causing Rebecca's checks to color again. "Mmm, that must have been some dream," Josie said with a wicked grin.

Rebecca slapped Josie playfully on the arm. "Stop it," she said.

"As you wish, m'lady," Josie said bowing from the waist. "Sorry," she said in response to the glare she got from Rebecca, who was too busy eating to take time for a verbal retort. Josie got up from the bed and pulled open the curtains to allow the morning sun to stream into the room. It was then that Rebecca noticed the bathtub in the corner. Josie followed her eyes and said, "I know how much you enjoy soaking in a hot tub. I've already got water heating, and you can stay in there until you turn into a human pickle. After that... well, we have plenty of surprises for you after that."

"But I have chores to do..." Rebecca started, and Josie cut her off.

"Not today, you don't. It's your birthday, and the only thing you have to do today is enjoy yourself." Tears brimmed in Rebecca's eyes and her lip trembled. Josie rushed to the side of the bed and took her hand. "Didn't anyone ever do anything special for you on your birthday?"

Rebecca shook her head. "Pa didn't believe in such foolishness, and Mother would never do anything against his wishes."

"Your father is one hard-hearted son-of-a-bitch," Josie hissed. She promised herself again that if she ever met up with the man she would make sure he got to experience a taste of the agony his daughter had suffered at his hands. But she smiled to lighten the mood and added, "Well, we'll just have to make it even more special to make up for it. How many birthdays will it be we're making up for?"

"Twenty."

Josie's eyes widened in surprise. "Really? I would have said you were maybe seventeen, eighteen. Why, you're practically an old maid," she said with a light laugh.

"Josie Hunter, if this is the way you make me feel special I have to say it needs work," Rebecca grumbled, but she was barely hiding a smile.

"Sorry, Sprite. I'll try harder. Now finish up your breakfast so we can get a start on the celebration." Rebecca sopped up the last of her egg-yolk with a bit of biscuit and popped it in her mouth. She gulped the coffee, which thankfully was no longer so hot that it would burn her mouth. She chased that down with the rest of the orange juice and then gave a satisfied burp.

"Excuse me," she said, covering her mouth with her hand. "Guess that was about the best breakfast I ever had in my life."

"You ain't seen nothin' yet. I'm going to go get the hot water; be right back." Rebecca nodded and, climbing out of bed, she began to unfasten the buttons of her nightgown.

Josie was back and forth several times with buckets full of steaming water until it seemed to Rebecca that the tub was full enough. Josie then pulled a vial out of her pocket, and poured the contents into the water, swirling it around with her hand. A light lavender scent filled the air and bubbles blossomed on top of the water. She inhaled the heady aroma and for a moment wished that it was she who would be climbing into the tub. But then she imagined the way Rebecca's skin would feel, warm from the bath and lavender-scented, and she was glad it was the other way around. "Your bath awaits you, m'lady."

Rebecca had removed her nightgown and stood with it demurely held in front of her body. "Turn around," she said softly, and Josie did. A light splash told the gunslinger that Rebecca was in the bath, and she turned back to see just her head and shoulders above the water. "Perfect," Rebecca said with a sigh. "Oh, Josie, thank you. This feels marvelous."

"I'm glad you're enjoying it. I've got a few more things I need to take care of, so you just sing out when you need some more hot water, or if you want me to wash your back." Reluctantly she pulled her eyes away from the vision floating in the water and started for the door. She would have loved to stay and just watch her bathe, but she knew it would embarrass Rebecca.

Josie was helping the two brothers drape colorful ribbon on the walls just beneath the ceiling when she heard Rebecca call out for her. "Be back shortly, boys," she said with a smile. Since neither of them could reach as high as she could, she suggested they go pick some more flowers until she was able to continue with the ribbon. They happily agreed, and the two men darted out the door like schoolboys when recess is called.

Josie knocked lightly on the bedroom door, and Rebecca said "Enter." When she walked in, Rebecca opened her eyes and looked up at her; she had been nearly dozing in the warm water. "Could you bring me more hot water, please? It's starting to cool off."

"Your wish is my command," she replied with a smile. "But I'll need to bail out some of this water first so there will be room." She picked up a bucket and dipped it in the tub and then did the same with the second bucket. The water level had dropped so that it was not quite covering Rebecca's breasts, and Josie's eyes were drawn to the creamy orbs. Josie's sharp intake of breath made Rebecca notice what she was looking at, and she almost responded by covering her chest with her washcloth. However, sometime between their conversation the previous night and that morning when she stepped into the tub, something had finally fallen into place in her mind. She realized that she wanted Josie to look at her and to desire her, in the same way that she desired Josie. Starting now, she thought to herself, no more covering up, no more undressing in the dark.

"And when you come back with the water, I'd love it if you'd wash my back," she said, blushing just a little despite her new resolve to stop hiding herself from Josie. A lifetime of modesty was not easily overcome.

"Water's on the stove. I'll be back in a few minutes." Josie retreated with the buckets and true to her word was back within five minutes with two steaming buckets of water. She carefully spread each bucketful evenly in the water to avoid burning Rebecca, and then took the washcloth from her hands and knelt behind the tub. "Lean forward a little," she said softly, and Rebecca complied, wrapping her arms around her knees. Josie soaped the cloth with the sweet-smelling French soap she had Horace buy for her in town, along with the bubble bath and a few other surprises Rebecca had not yet seen. She rubbed the cloth gently over the planes of Rebecca's back and shoulders, resisting the impulse to reach around and caress her breasts.

"You can scrub harder than that," Rebecca said, turning so that Josie could see her profile, "I'm not made of glass." Josie chuckled. She really had been treating Rebecca as if she were a priceless porcelain figurine, but now she bore down a bit harder with the cloth. "Ohhhh, that feels so good," Rebecca said with a sigh. "I could stay here all day."

"Ah, but then you'd miss all the other surprises we have for your birthday."

"Oh, Josie, this is too much already. I feel like a pampered princess."

"There's no such thing as too much, not on your birthday. Now, why don't you get up on your knees so I can reach the lower part of your back?" Rebecca hesitated only a moment before shifting around in the tub to get her knees under her and rising up. Her hips were completely out of the water, as well as the rounded globes of her behind. Josie's breath caught in her throat and she swallowed hard several times before she reached out to continue washing her beautiful friend. She ran the cloth over her hips and down both sides, and then over the soft mounds. Rebecca gasped slightly when the cloth parted the smooth cheeks. "Is this all right? Should I stop?" Josie asked in a husky voice.

"It's... fine. No, please don't stop." Josie did not fail to notice the expectant quiver in Rebecca's voice. She resumed her ministrations, paying special attention to the fleshy mounds. When it seemed that she must go further or go mad, she finally stopped and took a step back from the tub.

"Would you like me to wash your hair for you?"

"I... uh... yes," Rebecca answered, sinking back into the concealing bubbles. She tilted her head back as far as she could without totally immersing herself and then sat up. Josie remembered Rebecca's fear of putting her head underwater and determined to be especially careful this time. She worked the French soap into a lather with her hands and then applied it to the golden tresses. She kneaded her scalp with her strong fingers, and watched as Rebecca's eyes fluttered shut. Josie wanted to kiss her eyelids, her nose, her lips. Never in her life had she so desired anything as much as she desired this woman. The love she felt for Genie seemed almost sisterly by comparison, and she would never have believed that was possible.

"We need to rinse you off now," Josie said, and Rebecca nodded without opening her eyes. "I'm going to tip your head back and rinse off most of it in the tub. Then I'll get some fresh water to finish with. Ready?" Rebecca nodded again, and Josie lowered her head until just her face was out of the water. She rinsed as best she could and then sat her up in the tub. "All right, relax a minute. I'll be right back." Rebecca watched the tall woman walk out of the room, and the moment the door was closed she expelled the breath she did not realize she had been holding.

"Oh, God," she said through clenched teeth. "Josie, what you do to me..." she murmured just as Josie came back in the room.

"What was that? Did you want something?"

"Yes. No. Yes... but later." Josie smiled and raised her eyebrow in a way that Rebecca found completely disarming. The little blonde blushed, and Josie found herself thinking she would never get through this day without making love with her.

"Stand up now so I can pour this water over you." Rebecca did as she asked, fighting her natural impulse to shield her private parts from view. She could tell by the look on Josie's face that the tall woman was thoroughly enjoying the display of flesh before her. She stood for several seconds until her wet skin began to shiver in the morning chill.

"Uh, Josie. I'm freezing," she said through chattering teeth.

"Oh, baby, I'm sorry," Josie said as she snapped out of her reverie. "Shut your eyes," she ordered, and as soon as Rebecca did, she poured one bucket of warm water over her. "One more... don't move," she added as she upended the second bucket over her head, making sure all the soap was gone from her hair. "All right, I'm getting the towel now. You can open your eyes." Josie fetched the towel from the washstand and wrapped it around the slender body, rubbing against the towel to help dry her. "Let me help you out of the tub," she said, putting one hand behind her shoulders and the other against the back of her thighs and effortlessly scooping her out of the tub. She stood for a moment with Rebecca in her arms, just breathing in the exotic scent of her, then reluctantly she set her on her feet. "I almost forgot... I brought another towel for your hair." She fetched the second towel and wrapped it around the golden hair, twisting it up on top of Rebecca's head. The smaller woman was completely amazed; the extravagance of two towels for one bath was something of which she had never heard.

"Thank you, Josie. You're just... the sweetest person I've ever known."

"And so are you," Josie said sincerely. "I'm going to go help Charles and Horace finish up out there and let you get dressed. There's something hanging in the chifferobe for you to put on. Come on out when you're ready." She kissed Rebecca lightly on the lips and turned and strode from the room.

When Josie had gone, Rebecca crossed to the tall cabinet and opened the door. Hanging inside was a gingham dress the color of the summer sky, with white tatting around the collar and sleeves. The buttons looked like pearls, and a blue silk scarf peeked out of a pocket above the left breast. White shoes that looked like they were made of soft kidskin sat in the bottom of the closet. Rebecca's mouth dropped open as she looked at these beautiful items, and tears began to course down her cheeks. "Oh Josie..." she murmured as she gulped down her tears.

Josie inspected the room again just to make sure everything met with her approval. The walls were gaily draped in multicolored ribbons, and every available surface space had a vase or bowl full of flowers. In the center of the dining table was a cake, slightly off center from the trip from town, but Josie had put it back together so that it looked almost as good as new. It was covered with white butter frosting and decorated with pink flowers and green vines. "Happy Birthday Rebecca" was written in pink frosting across it. Horace had come through like a champ; he had fetched everything for which she had asked, and a little extra besides. It had not occurred to her to serve Rebecca breakfast in bed until Horace produced a rasher of fresh bacon and told her he could whip up a mean biscuit.

"Calm down, gal," Charles admonished her. "You're gonna wear a hole in my floor with all your pacin'. She'll be out directly."

"Oh, I know, I just...."

"Sit," he said sharply, cutting her off in mid-sentence. So shocked was she to be given an order from him that she simply sat. "Deal her in," he said to his brother who was shuffling the cards for a new hand of poker. She picked up the cards and arranged them without truly seeing what they were, and almost threw away a natural straight.

"How many do you want," Horace asked.

"I'll play these." At that moment the bedroom door opened and Rebecca emerged, her eyes taking in the transformation the room had undergone and growing wider by the second. She was a vision in the blue dress and all three people at the table gaped at her, none more than Josie. Embarrassed to be the object of so much attention, she shyly glanced toward the floor.

Josie tossed in her hand of cards and rose to greet her. Both men stood up also, as gentlemen should when a lady enters a room. Josie walked to her and took both of her hands in her own, and leaning forward she placed a kiss on each cheek. She paused for a moment before she straightened up and whispered in her ear, "You are breathtakingly beautiful, Rebecca. I hope you won't mind if I stare at you all day."

"Josie I... I don't know what to say...."

"Say that you love me," Josie whispered so softly only Rebecca could hear.

"I love you," she whispered back. Josie smiled from ear to ear and took Rebecca's hand to present her to Horace.

"Horace, this is my dearest friend, Rebecca."

Horace took Rebecca's hand in his and lightly kissed it. "Purely pleasured to meetcha, little gal. To hear these two talk, I was expecting to see wings and a halo on you. But you look plumb pretty even without 'em. Oh, and happy birthday," he added almost as an afterthought.

"Thank you, Horace," she said, dropping a little curtsy. "I heard so much about you from Charles, I feel like I know you already."

"Don't be hoggin' the pretty gal all to yourself, you old fool," Charles said jokingly as he elbowed past Horace to take Rebecca's hand and kiss it as well. Rebecca laughed as the two old men took good-natured pot shots at each other. She also noticed that Charles was wearing his Sunday-go-to-meeting clothes and had his hair neatly combed instead of flying off in all directions as usual.

"You're pretty spruced up yourself, Charles. You could sure turn a girl's head."

"Ain't I just? Your big, tall friend over there wouldn't have it but that we all had to get dressed up like the President hisself was coming to call." He winked at Josie, and Rebecca knew that it was at least as much his idea as hers. Clearly both brothers were enjoying having a woman to fuss over again. They pulled out a chair for her and had her sit at the table. It was then that she noticed the cake with her name on it, and her eyes widened in surprise and her mouth opened in a big "O."

"Hurry up and give her your... you know," Josie said, with a nod in the direction of the kitchen where Charles and Horace had stashed their gifts for her. "I want to see her open them, and I need to get cleaned up myself."

"Keep your drawers on," Charles muttered, but he did walk briskly to the kitchen and return a few moments later with two bundles wrapped in brown paper. "Sorry I didn't have no fancy wrappin' paper, but I guess it's what's inside that counts." He laid the two bundles in front of the astounded woman, who simply sat and stared at them. "Well, open 'em up, f'gosh sakes. They ain't gonna open themselves. This one first; it's from me."

Rebecca carefully peeled back the layer of brown paper on the first package and gasped in surprise when she saw "Little Women" by Louisa May Alcott. "Oh, Charles! I love it! I've wanted to read this book ever since I saw it in the mercantile in Chancetown!" She threw her arms around his neck and hugged him until his face turned bright red from embarrassment.

"Open the other one," Horace said brightly. Rebecca could scarcely believe what was happening to her that morning, and all because it was the anniversary of her birth. She untied the string holding the paper on the other package to reveal a small wooden box with an intricate design carved in the top. Imbedded between the designs were brightly colored pieces of mother-of-pearl. She lifted the lid on the box, and within she saw gears and springs. Even as she looked, the gears started to turn and she heard the strains of "Beautiful Dreamer" coming from the box.

"Horace, I... this is so beautiful. How can I thank you? I...."

"Oh, don't thank me. All I did was fetch it. Josie is the one who asked me to pick it up. This is from me." Horace reached into his pocket and pulled out a flat parcel and placed it in her hand. Rebecca unwrapped it without taking her eyes off Josie. It contained a handkerchief with an "R" daintily embroidered in one corner. The edges were scalloped with the same tatting that decorated the dress; clearly both items came from the same seamstress.

Rebecca hugged Horace and kissed him on the cheek. "This is beautiful, also. You have excellent taste in handkerchiefs as well as music boxes." Horace beamed at her and puffed out his chest like a little banty rooster. Rebecca tucked the handkerchief in her pocket and stood up. She walked to where Josie leaned against the bedroom doorjamb, her arms crossed over her chest, and came to a stop in front of her. A sheen of moisture glistened in Rebecca's eyes as she stood on tiptoe and placed a kiss on Josie's lips. The gunslinger's breath caught in her throat, and she felt a jolt that reached to the very core of her. "How did you..." Rebecca began, but Josie stopped her with a finger to her lips.

"I'll tell you everything later. Right now, just enjoy. Read your new book or play games with the old codgers."

"Hey, I heard that! Old codgers, indeed," Horace grumbled.

"Oh yes, and remember, Horace's hearing is much better than Charles's." She smiled at Charles, who stuck out his tongue at her. "I'm going to go clean up a bit myself. Be back soon. And no work – don't you lift a finger today, you understand me? We'll take care of everything."

"Yes, ma'am," Rebecca said, giving her a little salute. She walked back to the table with a huge grin on her face. "Get out the beans and deal the cards, boys. We're playing poker!"

Almost an hour later the door to the bedroom opened and Josie emerged. The trio at the table heard her splashing and even singing snatches from songs now and then, but they were so wrapped up in their playing they failed to notice how much time had passed. Rebecca looked up when the door opened, and did a double take when she saw the beautiful woman standing there. Her cards and the other people in the room forgotten, Rebecca stared openly at Josie. This was the first time she had seen her in anything but her long johns or her customary black shirt and pants. She wore a blue, satin-looking shirt with the top several snaps unfastened to reveal more cleavage than would be considered proper. Instead of her bandanna, she had a white silk scarf tied around her neck. Her pants were blue denim, tucked into her cleaned and polished boots. She wore her hair in a long braid down her back with a thong of leather braided into it. A hawk feather was attached to the leather and hung beside her right ear. Rebecca had never seen anyone more stunning. Her heart was hammering in her chest, and she found that she was holding her breath. She let it out in a rush.

"You clean up real good for a roofer," Charles said appreciatively. Horace nodded vigorously in agreement.

Josie laughed. "Thanks, old man. You sure know how to disguise a compliment. And you're awfully quiet there, Rebecca. What do you think? The duds suit me?"

"I-I… oh," she swallowed and took a deep breath and started again. "My God Josie, you-you take my breath away."

"Well, Horace, I'd say you did pretty damned well with what little I gave you to work with." She grasped his hand and shook it vigorously and then pulled him into her arms and gave him a solid hug. "Thank you… both of you, for making Rebecca's birthday so special. We'll never forget this day."

"Never," Rebecca agreed.

"Now if you boys can do without this pretty little gal for a while, I'd like to take her for a walk. Would you do me the honor, Rebecca?" She bowed and held out her hand, and Rebecca placed hers in it and allowed Josie to pull her to her feet.

"I'd be delighted," she said sincerely.

"Be back by noon time, ladies. Horace has a real special meal planned."

"We wouldn't miss it," Josie said breezily as they sailed out the door. It was a beautiful fall morning, the colors on the trees a hundred shades of red and orange and gold. Soon they would be dropping, but at that moment they were surrounded by a riot of fall colors. Hand in hand they walked past the flower garden, now nearly bare both from the shortening days and from the regular picking that had been going on for the past week. Josie led Rebecca into the work shed where she had been toiling on the totem, and sat her down on a stool. "Close your eyes," she said, and Rebecca did as she asked. "Now hold out your hands." When she did, Josie placed an object in her hands she could not identify by touch. "Open your eyes."

The object she held was a totem, but it was unlike any she had seen in books. Just over a foot long and about two inches around, at the base stood a bear and on its shoulders was a wolf. On the back of the wolf stood two women. They were entwined so that you could not readily see where one began and the other left off. One was considerably taller, her long hair flowing over her shoulders. The smaller one nestled against the tall one, but she did not appear to be diminutive despite her smaller size. Atop the totem was a phoenix, its wings spread to enclose the two women, keeping them safe. The piece was stained a rich red-brown and was sanded as smooth as glass. Rebecca did not realize she was crying until a tear splashed on the totem and brought her back to the moment. She put her arms around Josie's neck, still clutching the totem tightly in her hand, and for several moments she stayed that way, unable to speak, tears coursing down her cheeks.

"I love you," Josie whispered as she lowered her head and buried her face in the warm fragrance of Rebecca's hair.

"And I love you... with all my being." She pulled away from Josie so that she could look into her face, cradling the totem against her chest. "And this is the most beautiful thing anybody has ever done for me. I will cherish it for as long as I live." She raised up on her tiptoes and touched her lips lightly to Josie's and felt an unmistakable quiver in the lips that returned her soft kiss.

"Do you? I was afraid to hope."

"So was I. If only we had talked like this long ago."

Josie shrugged. "Things happen when they're meant to. We might have said the wrong things and ruined whatever chance we had." She wrapped her arms around Rebecca's waist and pulled the smaller woman close to her, their bodies tingling at each point of contact. "I want to make love with you," Josie said huskily. "I want to touch and taste you, to memorize every inch of you with my eyes."

Rebecca's breath caught in her throat and an intense stab of desire that pierced her center and radiated outward rocked her, causing her knees to threaten to buckle. She pressed her body even closer to Josie's and allowed the taller woman to hold her up, delighting in the feel of her warm flesh even through the layers of clothes that separated them. "I hope I don't...

disappoint you," she said softly, her lips only a breath removed from the tantalizing V of Josie's shirt. When Josie inhaled Rebecca felt the softness of her breast touch her lips and cheek, and she kissed the smooth flesh. She knew she had never felt anything more soft and at the same time exciting.

"Ohhh," Josie sighed, burying her fingers in the golden tresses and tilting Rebecca's head back until she was looking into her eyes. "You couldn't possibly disappoint me. The mere touch of your lips is enough to make me lightheaded. Anything more than that will be pure heaven."

Emboldened by those words, Rebecca put her hand on the back of Josie's head and brought Josie's lips down to where she could reach without standing on her toes. She kissed the gunslinger more passionately than she had the first time and felt Josie's lips parting slightly. Rebecca had never participated in such a kiss and was uncertain what to do next. The gunslinger, sensing her hesitation, took the lead and played her tongue along Rebecca's lips until they parted, which Josie took as an invitation to explore. Rebecca's tongue met her own, shyly at first and then more forcefully. Josie clasped the smaller woman's body tightly to her own and felt Rebecca's moan as a tremble against her lips.

Josie wanted nothing more than to tear the clothes from Rebecca's body and make love to her then and there, but common sense told her they were in a dirty work shed in the middle of a day of celebration. Not only did she not want their first time to be in such surroundings, but also there was the possibility that the brothers would come looking for them if they were gone too long, and she did not want to be interrupted. When they made love for the first time it had to be perfect... or as close to perfect as Josie had the power to make it. She broke off the kiss and pulled back slightly, reluctant to completely release the warm, soft body in her arms. "We have to stop...." Rebecca's look of disappointment pierced her and she paused momentarily, then continued, "Oh, please don't look at me like that. You must know that I'm dying inside from wanting you. It's just... this isn't the time or the place. Later tonight in our room I promise we'll make up for lost time." She kissed her again lightly on the lips and whispered into her ear, "It'll be worth waiting for... I guarantee it."

The sound of Josie's honeyed voice and the promise it carried made Rebecca weak. Never had she felt such emotional highs and physical stimulation. Her mind was on overload trying to sort all the new feelings. She knew only one thing with certainty; she had never wanted anything in her life as badly as she wanted Josie. Before reluctantly pulling her body away from Josie's, Rebecca kissed her again, briefly darting her tongue inside the outlaw's mouth, and then quickly backed away. Josie groaned when Rebecca said softly, "That's so you don't forget your promise." Hand in hand they emerged into the bright sunlight and returned to the house where their friends waited.

Rebecca sat in Charles' most comfortable chair. Her feet rested on a pillow that was placed on a stool. She was not allowed to do any work at all, but was told to sit and relax and read her book. The three other inhabitants of the house revolved around her as if she were the sun, her slightest fancy answered by one of the three without hesitation. Horace cooked and Josie and Charles cleaned up, and any offer to help from Rebecca was stifled with a menacing look. When they sat down to supper, the two women barely picked at the generous spread of food in front of them, so preoccupied were they with thoughts of what the end of the day would hold. Every time their eyes would meet across the table, they would quickly lower their gaze, certain the men would be able to tell what was in their minds from the looks on their faces.

When the meal was finally finished and the dishes washed and put away, the last of Rebecca's surprises was presented to her. Charles and Horace rummaged in a closet and brought out a fiddle and an accordion, and with Rebecca once again deposited in Charles' favorite chair, the two men began to play. Josie sat on the arm of the chair, her thigh touching Rebecca's arm, the graceful curve of her hip pressed against Rebecca's shoulder. Rebecca was thrilled by the touch and delighted by the music, unable to decide what gave her greater pleasure. The old men played a lot of old songs that neither of the women knew, but when a familiar melody started they both sang along at the top of their lungs. Rebecca had never heard Josie sing before, and her rich alto voice was like warm honey pouring over Rebecca, causing her to tingle all over.

"This here's dancin' music," Charles said as they began to play a lively tune. "You gals get on up and dance; shame to waste the music just because there ain't no fellers around."

Josie glanced down at Rebecca, who shook her head and shrugged. "I... never learned to dance," she admitted ruefully.

"Doesn't matter. I'll teach you," Josie said, standing up and holding out her hand for Rebecca. The younger woman shook her head again, but when Josie gave her an imploring look, she put her hand in Josie's and allowed herself to be pulled to her feet. Josie took Rebecca's left hand in hers and placed her own left hand in the small of Rebecca's back. "Put your other hand on my shoulder," she instructed, and Rebecca did as she asked. "Now when I press on your back like this," she demonstrated, "It means I'm going to turn you, like so." She executed a neat half turn, and Rebecca managed to stay with her. "Good. Now when I do this," and she pressed a different way on Rebecca's back, "It means I am going to lead off with my right foot, so you go back or forward with your left foot depending on which way I'm turning you. Got that?"

"No," Rebecca said with a laugh. "But I'll try to keep up."

"All right, here we go. One, two, three." The next thing Rebecca knew, they were whirling around the room, and to her utter amazement, she was able to follow the subtle motions Josie made with a minimum of toe stomping. By the end of the song she was following almost flawlessly, and Josie began to throw in a few new moves such as dipping Rebecca almost to the floor and then pulling her back into her arms. They were both breathless when the song ended, not entirely due to the exertion of the dance. Charles and Horace launched into a song with a similar beat, and without even catching their breath the women were whirling around the floor again, smiles wreathing their faces.

When that song ended, Josie gave Charles a little nod, and Charles tapped Horace with his bow. They began playing a slow ballad that Rebecca was not familiar with, and as Josie pulled her closer to her body she whispered in her ear, "I hope you like this song. I heard it somewhere along the line, and it makes me think of you." As she slowly moved Rebecca around the room in time to the music, she began to sing.

Believe me if all those endearing young charms
Which I gaze on so fondly today
Were to change by tomorrow and fleet in my arms
Like fairy gifts fading away
Thou would still be adored
As this moment thou art
Let thy loveliness fade as it will
And around the dear ruin each wish of my heart
Will entwine itself verdantly still.

It is not while beauty and youth are thine own
And thy cheeks unprofaned by a tear
That the fervor and faith of a soul shall be known
To which time has but made thee more dear
For the heart that has truly loved never forgets
But as truly loves on to the close
As the sunflower turns on her God when He sets
The same look that she gave when He rose.

As the music came to an end and Josie's voice grew silent, the two women came to a stop in the middle of the room. Josie's arms still held Rebecca tightly, for which the smaller woman was grateful, as she was not certain she could trust her legs to hold her up without assistance. She looked up at Josie and the sheen of tears that sparkled in her eyes tugged at the gunslinger's heart. Not trusting herself to speak, nor wishing to be overheard by the brothers, Rebecca mouthed the words "I love you," and then lightly touched her lips to Josie's cheek.

"And I love you," Josie whispered back, and then added conspiratorially, "Why don't we excuse ourselves from this party?" She did not need to add that the unfinished business of the afternoon had been on her mind so much that day, that she was not certain how she was able to get through the hours without dragging the little blonde away and ravishing her. That message was conveyed quite clearly in the ardent glow in her eyes. Rebecca nodded shyly and lowered her gaze; her cheeks suffused with a bright pink that left no misunderstanding as to her own desires.

Charles and Horace had already launched themselves into another spirited song and had not even noticed that the women did not start to dance. Josie waved to catch Charles' eye and he lifted his bow from the old fiddle and once again tapped his brother to get his attention. Josie smiled as she walked to where they sat, and then she thought perhaps a yawn might be in order so she stretched and yawned as she said, "We're pretty tuckered out after all the excitement today. Think we're going to turn in early."

"Shucks. We was just gettin' warmed up. Sure you can't do a few more jigs?"

Taking her cue from the gunslinger, Rebecca scrubbed at her eyes with her knuckles and tried her best to yawn. "You boys wore us out with all that dancing. I can hardly keep my eyes open."

"Well… we'd sure like to keep playing, unless you ladies think the noise will keep you awake," Horace said.

"We could go out on the porch and play," Charles added. "Shouldn't be too loud from out there."

"Oh, there's no need to…" Rebecca began, and Josie cut her off quickly.

"Out on the porch. That'd be good," she said emphatically. Rebecca looked at her quizzically, and Josie tried her best to convey that Rebecca should simply trust her, she knew what she was doing.

"Maybe that would be best. Josie hates to miss her sleep."

"Right, then," Charles said rising from his chair and tapping his brother on the shoulder. "Come on, old fool. Let's us leave these beautiful ladies to theirselves." The old men shuffled out, closing the door quietly behind them. A moment later the strains of "Tenting on the Old Camp Ground" wafted through the window. Satisfied they would be out there for some time and that the music would mask any unusual sounds that might come from their room, Josie took Rebecca by the elbow and together they walked toward their future.

Josie struck a match and lit the wicks on the candles on the bedside table and washstand. She turned around to find Rebecca standing by the bureau, her hands exploring the smooth contours of the totem she had placed there earlier in the day. The gunslinger walked up behind her and with a gentle nudge of her hands turned Rebecca around to face her, their bodies scant inches apart. With a slowness that was agonizing to both of them, she pulled the young woman's hips to her, the contact shocking each of them with its intensity. No words were spoken as the gunslinger lowered her mouth closer and closer to Rebecca's lips. They played a dance with each other over and over, lips moving forward, then pulling back in hesitancy.

"I love you so much," Josie whispered with a tremble in her voice. "God, I'm shaking like a leaf." The blood of desire rose within them, pushing their fears back bit by bit until at last there was no more doubt. They kissed again; their bodies pressed so closely together that each could feel the others heartbeat. Josie's tongue demanded entry to Rebecca's mouth as her grip around the young woman tightened. Rebecca gave up trying to focus and closed her eyes as the kiss deepened to a level never before experienced by the young woman. Only the outlaw's grip on her waist kept her up on her shaky legs. Each felt a pounding deep in her loins when they finally separated to catch their breath. Blue eyes locked with green as unspoken words were exchanged.

Rebecca placed her hands on top of Josie's and pulled them gently away from her waist. Maintaining eye contact, she knelt in front of Josie. She let go of the outlaw's hands and, with courage she did not even know she possessed, she ran her hands up and down the length of Josie's legs, following the cut of her britches. Josie groaned and placed her hands on Rebecca's shoulders when she felt the shy hands graze the inside of her thighs. Leaning in, the young woman nuzzled against Josie's right thigh while her hands were busy unbuckling Josie's leather belt. Rebecca leaned back and looked up in anticipation. A seductive smile played across Josie's lips as her hands moved to her belt.

"Is this what you want?" the gunslinger teased gently as she fingered the buckle, slowly pushing the leather through. Rebecca swallowed and nodded mutely, her mouth suddenly dry. Both women were completely focused on Josie's hands as they slowly removed the belt, letting it drop to the floor. There would be no rushing tonight, no sudden moves. This would be a night of softness and slowness, the giving of one's soul to another and receiving one in return. Josie reached for the button of her britches only to have smaller hands grasp her own.

"I'll do it." Rebecca's voice was barely a whisper as her hands moved in and took over the task. Her hands followed the path of the britches as they made their way down the gunslinger's legs. Desire feeding strength into her legs, she rose to capture Josie's mouth with her own. Tongues danced and explored as they exchanged soft sighs of pleasure at the long-awaited act. Josie's hands grasped at the young woman's dress, popping several buttons in her quest to pull her closer.

"Oh yes...this is so nice," Josie murmured, blazing a trail of kisses up Rebecca's jaw line before stopping just below the earlobe. "I love you, Sprite." Her warm breath tickled and excited as her hands moved between them to undo the remaining buttons on the disheveled dress. Rebecca could only groan helplessly as Josie's mouth moved down to capture her soft throat, marking it as her own.

Josie's mouth explored the newly revealed flesh as she lowered herself, undoing one button after another until the dress was open, loosely covering the young woman's breasts. Unable to take the anticipation, Rebecca removed her dress and camisole, exposing herself to the gunslinger's hungry gaze.

"Josie, I..."

"So beautiful," the older woman whispered. The cool autumn night and the blonde's own passions caused the coral nipples to contract and point in a most inviting way. Josie pressed her lips against Rebecca's firm abdomen, feeling her love quivering against her.

"Josie... please." The sound of womanly desire burst forth for the first time from her lips. She buried her fingers into the raven hair and guided her up for a kiss that left them both breathless and weak-kneed. Josie reached behind and cupped Rebecca's firm rear while equally busy fingers were trying to separate the gunslinger from her shirt and vest.

"I need you," Josie groaned, lifting the smaller woman into her arms and carrying her to the bed. Laying Rebecca down, she placed herself half over, half next to her, their breasts touching. Pulling Rebecca back into her arms, Josie rolled until she was on her back, the pleasurable weight of her blonde lover on top. They kissed deeply, tongues urging each other on as both women struggled to remove Rebecca's under drawers without breaking lip contact. As she moved her hips and Josie pushed down on the material, inch by inch of Rebecca's creamy flesh was revealed. Only when the outlaw could not reach down any further did they finally break their kiss, allowing her to finish pulling off the last of Rebecca's clothes. The orange candlelight reflected off the glistening moisture of her soft blond curls as Josie rolled her onto her back. A few quick movements and both women were completely naked against each other.

Josie's lips were inches away from the young blonde's ear when she whispered, "I want you." She quickly learned that the husky sound of her voice and her slow, gentle kisses made the young woman melt, and she planned on using every tool available to bring Rebecca pleasure. "You know," she whispered, drawing her lips across an exquisitely soft collarbone, "I could spend every day for the rest of my life right here beside you and never tire of looking at you, touching you. Loving you." A low moan escaped the blonde and Josie knew she had to continue. "Do you have any idea how hard it was not to touch you...to love you for so long?" She claimed Rebecca's lips with her own, sliding her leg between creamy thighs. She made no attempt to go further, concentrating on their kissing. After what seemed an eternity of searching and exploring the younger woman's mouth, Josie lifted her head. "Mm, I like that."

"L-like what?" Rebecca gasped.

"The way you moan when I'm kissing you," she whispered, bringing her lips down to touch her lover's briefly. "And this." Josie demonstrated by tilting her hips, smiling when she felt an answering rise from Rebecca.

"I...I can't help it. It feels so good."

Josie brought her trembling hand up to stroke Rebecca's cheek only to have it caught by a smaller one. The gunslinger swallowed hard as she felt her hand being guided to the fleshy mound. "Oh, Rebecca..." she sighed. Josie's voice was ragged as her fingertips explored the soft breast. "For so long... I've wanted this for so long." Rebecca arched into the loving touch and the words were lost in a sea of kisses. Josie's hand moved with more authority. She squeezed gently, rubbing her thumb across the pebbly flesh. She felt Rebecca's nipple hardening beneath her touch. Her kisses became more urgent, more demanding. Breaking the kiss, Josie gazed down at the breasts exposed to her. The hungry look in her eyes created a flood between Rebecca's legs. With great gentleness, the gunslinger lay on top of her, using her elbows to help support her weight. Like a hungry kitten, Josie licked and sucked, causing Rebecca to moan and murmur in pleasure. Instinctively, the young woman put her fingers in the raven hair and pressed Josie's head down. The gunslinger responded by nibbling and biting her sensitive breast, making Rebecca cry out and grind her pelvis against Josie's leg.

"Oh... Josie," Rebecca cried in response to the activity on her nipple.

Josie felt the passion building. Turning her attention to the right breast for a few moments, she lavished it with the same treatment the other had received, planting several soft kisses on it before continuing downward. She ran her tongue lightly over Rebecca's stomach, drawing more moans from the writhing blonde before returning to the creamy mounds of flesh. "Rebecca..." her voice was rough. "Tell me... tell me what you want." She suckled the other breast while her thigh continued to rub against damp curls.

"Ungh, oh Josie."

"You like that." She pressed firmly against Rebecca's mound and was rewarded with another moan from the younger woman. "Oh yes, my love. I know." Josie blazed a trail down Rebecca's body with her tongue, stopping to run the tip around an incredibly sensitive belly button before reaching the curly hair that covered the young woman's sex. Relishing the feeling, she nuzzled the soft curls. "I love you, Sprite." She wanted Rebecca, wanted her badly, and tonight she would have her. Tonight, Josie wanted to take this adored woman to new heights. The musky scent filled her nostrils as she slipped her tongue between the folds.

"Josie... please... I want you... I want to feel you... oh God, please," Rebecca said desperately as she arched her hips toward Josie. She had never felt this sensation before, never wanted to give herself completely to anyone. But, oh how she wanted this woman. She wanted everything her lover could give. "I need to feel you... inside me," she finally said, her green eyes locking with the blue of her friend, her mentor, and her lover. Josie stopped her oral assault and moved up until her lips were near Rebecca's ear. With exquisite slowness, Josie brought two fingers to rest just outside the coral opening.

"I love you." The words whispered into the young woman's ear could have been screamed for their intensity and force. With that, Josie's fingers found their mark, quickly entering her young lover. Rebecca gasped at the slight pain, then moaned at the feeling of having her lover inside her body. Her hips moved slowly at first, keeping pace with Josie's gentle stroking. It was not long before her body took over, increasing the tempo, demanding longer and deeper with each thrust. Her cries of passion flowed over Josie, intoxicating her with the power she held. There was no doubt in her mind that Rebecca wanted... no, needed... more.

"Yes... oh... Josie..." Rebecca's head was moving from side to side. She was completely lost in the throes of passion and did not know how to ask for what she needed. "More..." She was rewarded with a third finger sliding in and filling her up beyond words and feelings. She knew she could not last much longer. Josie felt it too. She slid her long body down and slipped her tongue between Rebecca's wet folds. She sucked, licked, and nibbled on the young woman's clitoris until she felt the rising crescendo approaching. She shoved her fingers hard into Rebecca, causing the younger woman to moan in her pleasure. Her focus was on what the gunslinger was doing between her legs, the soft tongue caressing her, the firm fingers thrusting in and out. Both women knew she was close to the edge.

"Rebecca... come for me." Josie's hand was a blur as it entered and exited Rebecca's womb. She felt the spasms start around her fingers.

Rebecca arched her back, forcing herself onto Josie's hand. Her hot tunnel gripped and released the fingers it held as she felt herself floating away on waves of ecstasy. "Oh God, Josie... Josie... OHHHHH!"

"Shh, it's all right, I've got you." The gunslinger gently withdrew her fingers and pulled the young woman into a gentle embrace. "I love you, Sprite. I've got you and I'm never letting go." Still overcome by the force of her orgasm, Rebecca found herself completely overwhelmed by the gentle words and tender touches. She clung to Josie, who patiently continued to murmur endearments of love and devotion.

Eventually Rebecca's pulse slowed back to a normal level and she focused on the warm, lean body pressed against her. Her left hand slowly moved down Josie's side, curving over the womanly flair of the gunslinger's hip and back up again. She felt the deep breath expelled and smiled in the darkness. Her touch did have an effect on the older woman. "You like that."

"Mmm, like doesn't begin to cover it." Josie replied, resisting the urge to guide the roaming hand to where she wanted it most. Rebecca repeated the motion, increasing her exploration until her fingers brushed against wiry curls soaked with desire. The touch was too much for the gunslinger to ignore. With a loud groan she pulled the young woman on top of her and brought their mouths together.

Rebecca slipped her tongue in and tasted herself in Josie's mouth. Passion fed boldness and she reached up between them to cup the gunslinger's left breast. "Ohh... you're so soft," she murmured. Although Rebecca was not experienced, she knew enough to know that what she liked her lover would enjoy as well. She brought her other hand in and had both of Josie's breasts under her control. "Am I too much for you?" she asked, knowing that all of her weight was on Josie. The gunslinger shook her head vigorously and wrapped her arms around Rebecca's back, holding her in place. The young woman rewarded her with another kiss as she rolled the nipples between her fingers, drawing growls of pleasure from the gunslinger's lips. They stayed like that for several minutes, throwing oil on the already out of control fire raging between them. Rebecca's leg slipped between Josie's thighs and the tall woman immediately tried to grind her sex against it.

"God, Rebecca, please..." Josie's eyes closed when she felt one of Rebecca's hands move down between her legs and press against the dark triangle of fur. She responded by pressing hard against it, soaking the young woman's hand with her desire.

"Yesss..." the gunslinger moaned huskily. "Oh, Rebecca, that's nice."

"Josie... I want to pleasure you," the young woman said in a raspy voice. Her finger slipped between the folds and felt exquisite wetness. A smile crept to her lips. "Hmm, I do believe you are quite excited." She moved her finger slowly in and out, unsure of how fast or hard to press. Her shy movements made Josie's knees weaken as she fought not to swim away with the feelings that were coursing through her.

"Yes... I am... rather... excited." The words came out in staccato bursts.

"So am I." With that, they interlocked their legs, rubbing against each other. Their hands moved over each other, searching, learning. "Josie...." Her voice was barely audible. She had never felt a passion like this. Rebecca continued her exploration, placing another finger inside the warmth of her lover. The gunslinger's back arched, giving Rebecca more access. Slowly she moved the fingers in and out, watching her lover's face as the excitement was building. Josie raised her hips, meeting each thrust.

"Rebecca... Oh... ahh... yes... yes... oh." Josie's words became incoherent as the passion consumed her. Rebecca placed her thumb on the swollen clitoris and rubbed hard, imitating what felt good to her. Her other hand was busy exploring the soft swell of Josie's breasts. The gunslinger's moans became louder as she lost control. Rebecca felt Josie's hot tunnel tightening around her fingers. She pinched the nipple and increased her pumping as the outlaw's moans gave way to screams of pleasure. Josie's body stiffened as a powerful orgasm ripped through her, and wave after wave of juice poured from the older woman. Rebecca stopped pumping and held her fingers still, waiting for Josie to return from ecstasy. Slowly, the body beneath her relaxed and she removed her fingers. They lay together for a time, not speaking. Josie's fingers drew lazy circles against Rebecca's back as their breathing slowed and reality once again intruded into their lives in the form of the music still drifting in from the porch. Rebecca's hand rested on Josie's breast and her head was snug on the tall woman's shoulder. Her mind still reeled from everything that had happened that day, and she sighed.

"This has been the most glorious day of my life," Rebecca said softly. "I wish it would never end."

"I'll do my best to make the rest of your days as glorious as this one," Josie replied. Rebecca mumbled something unintelligible against Josie's breast, cuddled against her side, and went to sleep.

40: Moving On

Josie was wakened by the sunlight streaming through the window. Rebecca's head was on Josie's shoulder, her arm was tossed over her chest, and her leg draped over her thigh, just like most mornings of late. The thing that made this morning different was that they were both naked. Josie cupped her hand around the soft globe of Rebecca's behind and pulled her even closer. Her skin tingled where Rebecca's naked flesh pressed against her own, and she shuddered involuntarily as she remembered the passion they had shared the previous night. She softly kissed the top of Rebecca's head, marveling at the depth of feeling the little blonde awakened in her. She might have lain there longer, but she heard the sounds of activity in the house and wanted to make sure she caught the brothers before they were out and about. The roof was finished and before she and Rebecca could move on they would need some help to get the axle put on their wagon.

"Rebecca. Wake up, Sprite. We need to get moving," she whispered, and received a mumbled response from the sleeping woman. "Hey, sleepyhead. Rise and shine," she said a bit louder, and was rewarded by a glimpse of sleepy green eyes.

"I'm up, I'm up," Rebecca said sourly, nuzzling her face into Josie's soft breast.

"Uh uh, none of that or we'll never get out of bed," Josie said as she reluctantly pulled herself away from Rebecca.

"Five minutes," Rebecca pleaded, clinging to the gunslinger.

"Sorry, baby. I hate to get up too, but we really do need to move on. Don't make it any harder on me... please." Josie extricated herself from Rebecca and slid off the edge of the bed before the blonde could grab hold of her again. She rummaged through her clothes and began pulling them on as Rebecca watched avidly.

"I sure hate to see you cover up all that beautiful skin," Rebecca said with a sigh.

Josie laughed. "Only one night and you're a sex maniac already," she said jokingly.

"You don't want me to be? A sex maniac, I mean? Because it's your fault if I am, you know. I was an innocent little girl when I met you."

"I want you to be exactly what you are. If that means you're a sex maniac, then I am truly blessed. You're my beautiful, sexy Sprite, and if you don't get out of that bed and put some clothes on, I am going to..." she paused and let Rebecca anticipate her words, and then surprised her with, "tickle you."

"No. Not that, please." Josie had tickled her once or twice in their time together, and she knew it made Rebecca laugh until she would cry. Rebecca threw the covers off and vaulted out of bed. Now it was Josie who admired the form before her, but not for long. "Brrr, it's cold in here," Rebecca complained, and she pulled her clothes on so fast her dress was wrong side out and she had to take it off and put it on again.

"C'mere, you. I'll warm you up," Josie said with a grin. Not needing to hear it twice, Rebecca scooted across the room and into Josie's arms. The outlaw rubbed briskly up and down the smaller woman's back several times before pulling her into a bear hug. "Ready to face those old men?" she asked playfully.

"If you won't come back to bed with me, I might as well," Rebecca pouted.

"Hold that thought until we get out on the prairie where nobody will be around to hear you scream when you come," Josie said huskily as she nibbled Rebecca's neck.

"Josie... you're terrible! You make me get out of bed and then you tease me with..." She broke off as she realized what Josie had said. "Scream? Did I scream? I didn't... realize."

"Oh, yes, you screamed all right. Just hearing it was enough to make me come with you." Rebecca's cheeks flushed, and she lowered her eyes in embarrassment. She wished she were half as worldly as the woman whom she loved so she did not find herself behaving like a school girl all the time. Ah well, all in good time, she told herself. She also found herself hoping that the old men had been playing their music nice and loud when she screamed. "Come on," Josie said dragging her out of her reverie, "they'll be sending out a posse for us pretty soon." She took Rebecca's hand and kissed it and then led her out of the bedroom.

Josie pushed back from the table and groaned. She had eaten more in the past couple days since Horace had been cooking than she had in the two weeks before that. Rebecca's cooking was far and away better than her own, but not near as good as Horace's. She would miss the old men and the quiet peaceful life out on the farm. Watching as Rebecca washed up the dishes from supper, she pictured her in a kitchen of their own on a nice little farm somewhere out west. With Rebecca by her side this was a lifestyle to which she could easily grow accustomed. But with a price on her head, she feared she would always be on the move. Now more than ever she did not want to find herself staring down the barrel of some sheriff's gun. She had Rebecca to take care of, and there was no way to do that if she were in jail, or worse. Her reputation as a fast gun could also earn her a bullet in the back from a cowardly bounty hunter more interested in the reward than concerned with whether he took her out in a fair fight. She shook her head to dispel such gloomy thoughts and stood up.

"Well, boys, I hate to leave such fine company, but we need to be moving on. I promised Rebecca I'd take her to learn from the Medicine Elders and I'd like to get there before the weather turns much colder." Rebecca draped the towel over the edge of the dishpan and came to stand beside her lover. She would also miss the idyllic life they had been leading, but she knew that as long as she and Josie were together it did not matter where they were, they would be home.

"We're gonna miss you gals," Charles said sincerely. "Havin' you here was like... well, almost like havin' Ruth and Lillian around. Made me want to take a bath on a Saturday night and get spruced up, and I ain't done that for a lotta years."

"Oh, Charles, we're going to miss you too. Both of you." She gave first Charles and then Horace a big hug and then turned and went to the bedroom to get their gear so the old men would not see the tears in her eyes. She could not help but think that if her own father had been half the man these gentle brothers were, she never would have left home. Never would have followed Josie and learned the true depth of love. As miserable as her youth may have been, she would not change a day of it if it meant she would not have met Josie. When she returned to the kitchen, Josie was shaking hands with Charles and promising that they would stop by again if ever they were anywhere close. She turned to see Rebecca coming toward her with their bags.

"Got everything?" she asked in a gravelly voice that almost betrayed her emotions.

"Yes." Josie took some of the bags from Rebecca and started for the door, determined not to cry. She and Horace had hauled the axle up to where her wagon had broken down and fixed it early that morning, and she had packed up all but their clothes and harnessed the horse right before supper. Now there was nothing to do but to get on the road. Josie stowed her bag beneath the canvas tarp after removing her gun belt and strapping it on. She had not worn a gun for almost two weeks, and the weight of it almost felt foreign to her. Rebecca came outside with the two brothers on her heels and Josie could hear her making the same promise to visit that she had made. She also knew that both of them would very much like to keep that promise.

Josie climbed into the seat and held out her hand to the little blonde. Rebecca placed her hand in Josie's and allowed herself to be drawn into the wagon. With a slap of the reins on Flossy's flanks and a sharp "gee up" the women pulled away.

The wagon moved slowly across the trail, the light clip-clop of Flossy's hooves against the hardened earth creating a hypnotic rhythm that threatened to put Rebecca to sleep. Josie looked over at her lover, shaded from the sun by her soft beige hat, the edges dog-eared from age and wear. She watched the way the soft blond hair cascaded out from under the hat to flow gracefully across her shoulders, the warm wind sending several strands whipping in the air. Her gaze fell on the soft earlobe—the soft, sensitive earlobe, she corrected herself. There was a moment the night before when the gunslinger swore she was going to send Rebecca over the mountain just by suckling that soft piece of flesh. Gone were the road, the fields, and the sky. All that was focused in Josie's eyes was the vision of her sprite. Her ears filled with the memories of their lovemaking, the moans, the sighs, the whimpers, and the gunslinger's favorite sound, the soft cry that Rebecca made just before her world exploded. It was a sound Josie knew she would never tire of and would always long to hear. Her visual inspection moved to Rebecca's lips. Those oh so soft lips that begged to be kissed. Those lips that parted ever so slightly when Rebecca was sailing under her touch. Those lips that sought to return the pleasure as often as possible. Those lips that covered her warm, inviting mouth. There was a place Josie never wished to leave, or have leave her. In a short time, Rebecca had mastered the art of lovemaking with her mouth. She had used her lips, tongue, and teeth in perfect harmony with each other to turn the gunslinger into a quivering mass of bones and flesh.

The wagon hit a small bump and Rebecca shifted position slightly, leaning back against the seat and drawing her hat down over her eyes to keep the sun off. Her arms were folded across her body below her breasts, which now had the gunslinger's complete attention. Josie licked her lips subconsciously as she undressed the blonde with her eyes. Her breasts - those full, soft, sensitive, and oh so responsive breasts. Those nipples that hardened with just a look, that sent palpable shock-waves through the young woman when they were licked, that never seemed to tire of being played with, much to the gunslinger's great joy. Josie felt the familiar stirring deep inside as her desire for Rebecca once again welled to the surface, threatening to take control. The gunslinger turned her attention reluctantly to the road, searching carefully for any sign of other people. The long, flat land stretched out for miles in all directions, satisfying her that they were completely alone.

Josie knew beyond a shadow of a doubt that she had to have Rebecca right then and right there, and she would. She tucked the reins under her leg, keeping them nearby just in case. Flossy was well mannered enough, or lazy enough, to follow the trail made by so many previous travelers. That task completed, Josie leaned over and, without warning, scooped her half-asleep lover up in her arms and deposited her on her lap. Before the startled woman could say a word, her mouth was claimed in a fierce kiss that spoke of the gunslinger's need and desire. "I love you, Sprite. I love you and I have to have you."

"Mmm," the blond replied as Josie thoroughly kissed her again. Sitting across the gunslinger's lap, Rebecca was completely helpless to her wandering hands, a fact that Josie exploited to her full benefit. Her left arm was supporting Rebecca's back while her right arm was roaming up and down Rebecca's body, squeezing firm thighs and buttocks, softly cupping her full breasts. Josie knew exactly where the blonde's nipples were and deliberately avoided them in her exploration, knowing that it would drive Rebecca even higher with desire. "Josie...." Although surprised by the sudden move onto the gunslinger's lap, Rebecca nonetheless willingly surrendered herself to whatever her love wanted. She moaned softly as a demanding tongue possessed her mouth, driving away all rational thought. Such was what the tall woman did to her. Her touch, the strength of her desire, the absolute wholeness of her love overpowered the younger woman's senses, leaving her weak-kneed and helpless, burning with an ache that only Josie could satisfy.

Tongues danced and dueled within the confines of the young woman's mouth while strong, nimble fingers deftly began to unbutton the top of Rebecca's dress. Small fingers dug deep into raven hair in a vain attempt to bring them closer. Josie's fingertip drew a slow, sensual line from just below Rebecca's ear to her navel, leaving a trail of goosebumps and excited nerves in its wake. Rebecca groaned in protest when the kiss ended, but gasped in pure pleasure when she felt those warm lips close around her earlobe. "J-Josie... mmm... don't you think we should... ooh... stop? For a while? Oh...." Every flicker of the gunslinger's tongue against her sensitive lobe sent jolts of pleasure through her body to pool between her legs.

"No," Josie replied as she pulled her lips away for a moment to whisper into Rebecca's ear, smiling when she saw and felt the younger woman shudder at the huskiness of her voice. "I don't want to stop... anything." Josie licked her ear to prove her point. "You really don't want me to stop, do you?" she said, grinning at the vigorous shake of the blond head. "Hmm, I didn't think so." She rewarded Rebecca's answer by continuing to unbutton the bodice of her dress and reaching inside to cup the left breast, her thumb lazily rubbing back and forth against the hardened nipple. "Very nice, Sprite... I love the way your body responds to my touch." She had no doubt that her young love was dripping with passion and the thought only served to increase the trickle between her own legs.

"Unngh... I love... your touch," Rebecca moaned as her hips started to rock.

"Hmm... so it would seem," Josie said before bringing her mouth down to taste the sweetness of Rebecca's lips again. The kiss turned from gentle to passionate, to searing, to completely out of control as the gunslinger's fingers squeezed and fondled Rebecca's painfully erect nipple. They came up for air and Josie leaned back in her seat, pulling the young woman's head against her chest as both fought to regain the senses the kiss had completely disseminated.

"Stand up," Josie said softly, stilling the movement of her hand on the younger woman's back.

"You've got to be kidding," Rebecca murmured, bringing her own hand from around the gunslinger's neck and cupping her right breast through the black shirt. "You don't really expect me to be able to move, do you?"

Josie let her play for a few moments, enjoying the feeling before her own desires for the young woman finally won out. "Up." She helped Rebecca to her feet, keeping her hands around the small waist for balance. The gunslinger turned her and pulled her back down, this time so that the smaller woman's legs were straddling her. Josie reached down and grabbed the backs of Rebecca's thighs, pulling her knees up onto the sheepskin covered seat, which in turn, brought the young woman closer until the crotch of her underwear was pressed up against the gunslinger's belly. "Much better," Josie said as she reached up and finished unbuttoning Rebecca's dress. She then pulled the top of the dress down off Rebecca's shoulders, baring her succulent breasts. The motion also caused the young woman's arms to be pinned by the sleeves, a situation that Josie did not want. She loved the feel of those arms around her, the fingers clasping and unclasping her hair as she drove Rebecca wild with passion. No, this just would not do. She reached back and helped free the young woman's arms, in the process claiming a soft breast for her mouth.

Rebecca cried out and did exactly what Josie wanted, burying her hands deep into the raven hair and pressing her body close. The constant jostling of the wagon made the familiar flicks of the gunslinger's tongue more pronounced, the sensations more intense. Josie kept both of her hands behind Rebecca's back, supporting her and keeping her close as she moved her mouth to give equal attention to the other breast. The rocking of the blonde's hips became more pronounced as her need grew. The gunslinger smiled and nipped the tender nipple with her lips, groaning herself when she heard Rebecca's moan. Josie reached down and cupped the firm buttocks with her hands, squeezing before allowing one hand to reach even further between the young woman's legs and press against her swollen sex. Rebecca cried out and pressed hard against the strong fingers, cursing the material that stood between her and the fingers she so desperately needed to feel.

"So ready," Josie murmured, pressing harder with her hand, the dampness of the cotton foretelling the flood that awaited her. She could not wait to remove Rebecca's underwear, the need to please as great as the young woman's need to be pleased. The gunslinger released her hold on Rebecca's breast and used the hand on Rebecca's rear to push the young woman against her, raising her slightly. The movement caused a certain amount of slack in the material, just as Josie had hoped for. Rebecca's head was buried in the crook of the gunslinger's neck, a position that the young woman quickly took advantage of, suckling and nibbling every piece of skin she could reach.

Josie closed her eyes at the delicious sensation of her love devouring her neck. The movements of her fingers between Rebecca's legs increased in pressure and speed in reaction to the young woman's movements against them. "Yes, Sprite," she murmured as a series of small cries escaped her lover's throat in rhythm to the firm strokes. The rough feel of her undergarments rubbing back and forth against her was enough to start the overheated blonde's body trembling. "Oh Rebecca... so nice... so very nice..." she murmured to her beloved as she continued the exquisite torture. The soft cries of passion mixed with deep, husky groans from Rebecca gave music to the motions of the gunslinger's fingers. Josie's own clitoris throbbed in rhythm to the activities taking place scant inches away. She spread her fingers out and pressed, trapping cloth and Rebecca's most sensitive spot between them. Josie captured the little woman's sensitive earlobe in her mouth and began sucking in synch with the squeezing together of her fingers.

"Josie... oh Josie ... unngh... oh." Each word came out at a slightly higher pitch than the previous one. The gunslinger's arm pressed Rebecca hard against her, breasts crushing against each other as she released the lobe and placed her lips softly against the blonde's ear. The young woman heard every passion filled breath caress her ear, matching the tempo between her legs.

"Oh, Sprite, I love you so much," Josie whispered softly, her own eyes shut tight as she lost herself to the feelings. "I love doing this, you know." The husky voice was having the desired effect on the treasure in her arms. Rebecca was doing more gulping than breathing as her thigh muscles clenched hard against the gunslinger's hips, unmindful of the gun strapped there. Josie pressed two fingers together and placed them squarely over the wet cotton that covered Rebecca's swollen clitoris and rubbed hard and quick. "Yes, Sprite... now."

The soft words spoken into her ear carried her over the edge. Rebecca's fingers clawed helplessly at the gunslinger's shoulders as she cried out, her whole body shaking with the force of her orgasm. Josie's hand stilled, enjoying the flood of wetness that seeped through the cotton. She shifted the limp woman until she was lying across her lap, holding her close. "I love you, Rebecca," she murmured as she placed gentle kisses on her lover's lips. "So beautiful."

Green eyes opened to slowly focus on deep blue ones so full of love for her. Beneath her ear, Rebecca felt the steady thumping of the gunslinger's heart. She raised her hand to stroke the bronzed cheek. "I just look at you and I melt," she murmured, slowly feeling her energy return along with her passion. She slid off Josie's lap, holding onto her arms for support and changed positions, mindful of the leather reins lying tucked under the gunslinger's strong leg. Rebecca pressed with her knee, forcing Josie's legs apart. She pressed her knee firmly against the older woman's sex while pressing her own down against the bounty hunter's strong thigh. Both women groaned into each other's mouths at the contact. Rebecca kept her knee still as Josie adjusted to just the right position. The blonde's hand gently fondled Josie's breast through the shirt as they started to rock against each other.

The road beneath became just a bit rougher at that point, adding a few extra jolts to their rocking. The constant pulsing between Josie's legs grew in intensity until she finally felt the release she so desperately needed - a small, sweet, gentle orgasm to take the edge off, to sate the need momentarily. She let out a long, deep groan and held Rebecca close, knowing that the younger woman could feel her sex still pulsing through the layers of cloth. Both knew they were not finished. Within seconds, Josie's hands were beginning to wander again and her mouth moved down to capture Rebecca's breast. "Josie... yessss," she hissed, arching her back and burying one hand into the raven hair, while the other held on to the gunslinger's shoulder for support. She thought she would go over the edge right then when she felt Josie's warm tongue flicking back and forth on the sensitive flesh. The gunslinger reached down and tried to separate Rebecca from her clothes while remaining affixed to her breast, and growled with frustration when the task proved to be impossible. They separated long enough for Rebecca to sit down on the seat next to her and try to remove her boot. Josie's desire overrode her patience as she reached down and yanked the boot off easily. "Thanks," the smaller woman said, leaning in for a kiss.

"Mmm, you are most welcome," she replied, deepening the kiss as her hand returned to one of its favorite places, namely her lover's breast. She leaned forward, pressing Rebecca back down against the sheepskin. The leather reins fell loosely to the ground, causing Flossy to stop, not that either woman noticed, nor did they notice when the mare spotted a nearby patch of grass that looked quite tasty and she and Phoenix left the trail and began to graze. All the women noticed was the exquisite passion and desire that flowed between them. As much as Josie needed to feel the velvet liquid of Rebecca, she needed to make love to her breasts and mouth at the same time and could not pull herself away. Rebecca, meanwhile, was completely under the gunslinger's spell and unable to do anything more than softly moan and gently caress the raven head lying on her breast. Neither woman was particularly comfortable, but they were reluctant to move and end the moment. Only when Josie's back screamed at her and Rebecca's leg threatened to cramp up did they finally separate. Josie looked at the fabric of Rebecca's dress pooled around her waist with the flowing skirt still covering the treasure she longed to possess. Her fingers moved to the belt that held the garment up and Rebecca noticed that, quite surprisingly, the normally strong and sure hands were trembling as she worked to loosen the buckle.

Josie knelt down in front of Rebecca, precariously balanced on the narrow floorboard. Somewhere in the back of her mind, Josie dimly noted that they were no longer moving, but filed it away such as one might the knowledge that apples were on sale at the trading post. Slower than she thought possible, her hands drew Rebecca's dress down over her hips, taking the under drawers with it. Josie swallowed and her eyes became hooded as her nostrils filled with the scent of her lover and soft blonde curls came into view, glistening with desire. "Oh, my little Sprite," she murmured, bringing her lips in to nuzzle against the soaked hairs. She shoved the under drawers down below Rebecca's knees and reluctantly pulled her mouth back, but not before snaking her tongue out to coat it with the sweetest of honey. Rebecca pulled one foot free of the confining underwear and then kicked them off with the other foot.

The gunslinger stood and quickly dropped her pants and drawers down to her ankles, the gun belt hitting the floorboard with a thud. She twisted and sat back down, holding her arms out for her willing lover to join her. Rebecca quickly straddled her leg; her soaked thighs resting just above equally wet ones. She put her hands on Josie's chest to stop her advances. "Wait." Rocking gently against her, the blonde unbuttoned the gunslinger's shirt, pushing it aside to reveal the full mounds, erect with need. Rebecca spread her knees apart, sliding down to cover Josie's nipple with her mouth. Instantly a firm hand grasped the back of her head, keeping her in place.

"Yes..." Josie hissed, throwing her head back, the raven hair falling loosely around her shoulders. Her eyes fluttered shut as Rebecca began to nibble and nip in addition to her suckling and licking. She pressed the young woman's mouth against her harder, not completely worried if she could breath or not, the need so overpowering. "Please...."

Rebecca knew the meaning behind the timbre of Josie's voice. She raked her teeth across the engorged nipple and moved to the other side, the gunslinger's hand still firmly planted against the back of her head. Her fingers quickly took up residence at the abandoned nipple, pinching and rolling it between them, while her lips, teeth, and tongue mercilessly attacked the other. Rebecca's soft moans of delight blended with the groans of the gunslinger as they remained lost in time to the rest of the world.

Josie's hands began a lazy descent down Rebecca's back until she could not resist the urge any longer. She reached down and slipped her index finger between the folds, groaning both at the amount of sweet nectar that awaited her and at the increased sucking on her breast, no doubt a direct result of her actions between Rebecca's legs. The gunslinger pulled her closer, causing the young woman to lose her hold on the bounty hunter's nipple. She quickly found Josie's mouth an acceptable substitute, driving her tongue in just as she felt the firm finger stroke against her clitoris. Rebecca wrapped her arms tightly around the gunslinger's neck and rocked hard against her hand. Josie slipped another finger in to join the first in her quest to take Rebecca. Once both were soaked to her satisfaction, she pulled them back and slowly circled her young love's entrance. "Oh God, please, Josie... please," Rebecca cried as she tried unsuccessfully to drive herself onto the strong fingers. She growled in frustration and dove against the gunslinger's neck, determined to convince her tall lover to give her what she needed.

"Rebecca..." Josie said with a moan, leaning her head back to allow better access, her fingers lightly brushing against the smaller woman's sensitive nub. Without warning, Josie entered her with one long, deep stroke. Rebecca cried out, slamming her hips down hard, trying to drive the gunslinger in deeper. Josie added a third finger, filling her lover while her other hand slid around to the front and joined the pleasure. She rubbed and circled Rebecca's sensitive clitoris in rhythm to her stokes in and out, both of which were picking up speed as the blonde's hips moved faster than they would ever have been able to do under any other circumstances. Her groans and cries grew louder and she reached for Josie's nipples, wanting her to share in the moment. "Yes... yes, my Sprite... so good...."

"It's... because... oh... of you...." Both women's voices were strained and panting from exertion.

"Rebecca...." Josie stopped the movements of her hands and waited until the young woman opened her eyes and looked at her. "Watch," Josie said softly as she moved her hand from the front of her love to reach between her own folds, letting out a deep groan as she touched the long denied nerve. She stroked Rebecca firmly, raising her off her lap with each upward stroke. The young woman's hands continued to fondle Josie's ample bosom while the gunslinger used her hands to pleasure them both. Rebecca looked down and watched as Josie's fingers moved back and forth rapidly against her own sex. She looked back up to watch the blue eyes flutter shut and the gunslinger's back arch. Josie's hand became a blur against herself as her other hand stilled within her lover. She threw her head back and gritted her teeth as she felt Rebecca's warm mouth claim her left breast, her right one being kneaded and pinched by knowing fingers. With a howl that barely resembled her lover's name, Josie's hips lurched off the seat and her legs slammed shut, trapping her left hand between them. Rebecca had the presence of mind to use her hands to grab on to the gunslinger's shoulders for balance. The bounty hunter remained motionless for a moment as the shocks pulsed through her body. Josie slowly lowered herself back on the damp seat with Rebecca tucked against her chest. With infinite slowness, she began to stroke her lover again, long, deep strokes that earned the gunslinger a hedonistic groan from the young woman. Within seconds, Josie felt the rush of renewed passion flowing from within Rebecca and she picked up the pace, bringing her left hand back through the golden curls to stroke the blonde's aching bundle of nerves.

"Josie... oh... yes, please... Josie...." Rebecca gave up on rational thought, digging her fingers into the gunslinger's upper arms. Her hips rocked back and forth wantonly as she forced her lover's strong fingers into her again and again. Her body quivered, then stilled, frozen in ecstasy. Josie expended her remaining energy, ignoring the ache in her forearm, as she tried to draw out Rebecca's orgasm as long as possible. The gunslinger's name was torn from the young woman's lips as she reached the pinnacle of pleasure and collapsed against Josie's chest.

The gunslinger immediately withdrew her hands, pulling Rebecca's center up to press against her lower belly in an attempt to maintain contact with the still quivering area. She wrapped her arms around her lover and murmured soft words of endearment to her. "Shh… I've got you. I love you… I'm right here, Sprite." Josie did not know if Rebecca heard the words or not, but she knew she understood the meaning and the tone as she felt the young woman relax against her. She felt the strong heartbeat slowing down to a more normal pace as she stroked the blonde hair and held her tight until she felt Rebecca try to move.

"You…" the young woman said, reaching up to stroke her finger down the length of the gunslinger's cheek, "…are wonderful."

"Mmm…" Josie took the wayward finger and kissed it before pulling Rebecca closer to her. "So are you, Sprite…so are you."

They sat together like that for several moments until a soft nicker from Phoenix reminded them of where they were. Rebecca picked her head up and looked around. "Seems like a good place to camp for the night."

"We still have at least three more hours of traveling to do before nightfall," Josie protested half-heartedly. The little woman looked at her thoughtfully for a moment before pulling herself up to whisper into the gunslinger's ear.

"Well… if we make camp now…" she flicked out her tongue to lightly touch Josie's ear, "perhaps I can arrange for a little something for both of us to eat, hmm?" Her husky-voiced whisper left little doubt as to what she had in mind for them to consume.

"An early camp, sure. What's a few hours one way or the other?" The gunslinger quickly agreed, pulling her lover in for a passionate kiss guaranteed to leave them both breathless.

41: Betrayal

Caleb Cameron sat at a table in the saloon by a window that commanded a view of the mercantile that also served as the post office for Tahlequah, Oklahoma. One hand tightly grasped the bottle of bourbon that had been his constant companion since his arrival in town three days ago, and the other methodically creased a piece of paper until it threatened to fall apart. It did not matter; he knew every word on that paper by heart. It was a letter that read:

Dear Katie
I wanted to write and let you know that I am well. I am traveling with Josie Hunter – yes, the outlaw we used to read books about. But believe me, she is nothing like those books make her out to be. She can be very kind and caring, and I have seen her risk her life many times to help others, including me. I can't tell you how many times she has saved my life, and I refuse to believe that such a person is guilty of all the crimes of which she has been accused. One day I hope to help her clear her name; it is the least I can do for all she has done for me.

She is taking me to Tahlequah, Oklahoma, to meet a real Medicine Elder. I want to learn the healing arts, and the

Cherokee, who are her father's people, are very skilled in that area. We hope to be there in another two weeks or so, and I would love it if you would write to let me know how you are doing - you know what I mean. I will check the general delivery when we arrive in town, and as often as possible after that until I hear from you. Please don't mention this letter to Ma, as I am afraid she will say something to Pa, and I don't want him to know I am with Josie. He would not understand, and I am afraid he might try to do something to get me back. And much as I love you and Ma, Katie, I can never live under a roof with him again. I just pray that he does not hurt you like he hurt me, and hope you find yourself a nice fellow that will treat you with the kindness and gentleness you deserve; like Josie treats me, even though she is a woman.

I love you, little sis. Be well
Rebecca

Caleb gritted his teeth and poured another slug of whiskey into his glass. He could just picture how that bitch was treating Rebecca with "kindness and gentleness," and the image made his blood boil. He had heard about women who kept after other women, and they were an abomination in the eyes of the lord. He planned to drag Rebecca back to Chancetown – bound and gagged, if need be, but not before he collected the reward on the head of Josie Hunter. He smiled at the good fortune that caused him to go into town to collect the letter that was intended for his daughter. Normally the girl would run errands in town while he sat in the bar drinking up what little profits he was able to eke out of running the farm. But both Katie and Sarah were down with the flu when Caleb ran out of liquor, which was about the only thing he went to town for these days. At Sarah's request he stopped in the mercantile to pick up a few items, and the proprietor had handed him the letter for Katie, knowing he was her father. From the moment he read it, he knew what he had to do. Within a couple of days he was on his way to Oklahoma, already planning how he would spend the thousand-dollar reward.

"Wait, wait, stop!" Rebecca called as their wagon rumbled almost past the mercantile. Josie reined in the horse thinking that Rebecca had seen something in the road that she was about to run over.

"What is it?" she asked, her eyes scouring the area in front of the wagon for the source of Rebecca's excitement.

"Oh, sorry... I didn't mean to make you think something was wrong. I just need to stop into the mercantile for something. Can you wait a minute?"

"Actually I need to pick up some grain at the feed store. You go ahead and shop, and I'll come back for you in a little while."

"All right," Rebecca said brightly, jumping down from the wagon and hurrying into the store. Josie gave the reins a jingle and Flossy trudged down the road.

Caleb almost did not recognize Rebecca; she seemed taller, healthier, and more robust than the girl he remembered. Living on the road seemed to suit her; or perhaps it was the attentions of the outlaw that caused her to look so content. His nostrils flared as he visualized the two women together, and despite his firm belief that what they were doing was a mortal sin, he could feel himself growing aroused at the mental image. He got unsteadily to his feet; he had been drinking almost steadily for several days, and even he had a limit. Holding his hat in front of the erection he could not quite will away, he lurched out the door and across the street, praying the outlaw would not show up too soon and spoil his plans.

Rebecca searched through the rack of store-bought shirts in hopes of finding... "There it is," she said excitedly. Holding the crisp black shirt in front of her she judged it to be the perfect size for Josie.. She walked to the counter, hoping for just one more thing to complete her business at the mercantile. "I'm looking for a letter addressed to Rebecca Cameron care of general delivery," she said to the gray-headed woman behind the counter. The woman smiled and turned toward a stack of mail behind her in a wooden box.

"I sure don't recall anything with that name on it," the woman said over her shoulder, "and I usually remember when I get something for a name that's not familiar."

"Don't waste your time," Caleb growled from behind Rebecca, causing the young woman to jump and turn toward him. Involuntarily she brought her hands up to shield her face before she realized he was not going to strike her. Not at that moment, anyway. "There ain't gonna be no mail there for little Rebecca, 'cause little Katie never got her letter." He wagged the grimy, creased paper in front of Rebecca's face.

"P-Pa," she stammered, "What are you doing...."

"Never mind," he said, cutting her off in mid-sentence. He grasped her arm with a grip like a steel band. "Buying a shirt fer your whore?" Jerking the dark cloth out of her hand he threw it down on the floor. "Damn bitch won't need that where she's going." The hapless clerk behind the counter looked on, uncertain what to do. Clearly this was a domestic quarrel of some kind and she would do well to keep her nose out of it, her husband would say. "There's gonna be a tall, half-breed, iron totin' woman coming in here looking for this little gal. When she does, tell her that Rebecca will meet her down to the sheriff's office. And don't mention that you seen anyone with her, or I'll make you right sorry you did."

"I... I..." The woman began, but before she could form a sentence, the pair were out the door.

Josie could not imagine what possible errand had taken Rebecca to the sheriff's office. The woman in the mercantile said only that she was to meet her there. She opened the door to the office and spotted Rebecca sitting in a chair with an older man beside her. His hands were placed possessively on Rebecca's shoulders, and Josie instinctively began to grab for her gun. At that same moment, Rebecca called out "Josie, don't..." and a gun butt caught her at the base of her skull, causing her to sink lifelessly to the floor.

When she regained consciousness she was lying in a cell on a cot that reeked of urine and God knew what else. Her head pounded, and her exploring fingers found a substantial goose egg on her head. The fingers came away sticky with blood, but at least the bleeding had stopped. Gingerly she sat up and tried to focus on what was going on in the outer office. She could not see anyone, but she could hear voices, one of them Rebecca's.

"... go of me! If you've hurt her, I swear..."

"Simmer down," said a male voice with a youthful tone to it, probably belonging to the sheriff. "I just knocked her out to keep her from killing your father. She'll be all right." Definitely the sheriff then. The man standing with Rebecca had not been wearing a star. Suddenly it registered on Josie that the sheriff had said the older man was Rebecca's father. The man who had beaten his daughter so bad she felt running away with a known outlaw was preferable to staying in his home. The man she had once vowed to kill if she ever found herself in the same place as him. Her face flushed with anger as she listened to the words that spewed forth from the abusive drunk.

"Shoulda killed her, Sheriff. Reward's good dead or alive, and dead is a lot safer with that one. Mean as a snake, she is. And corrupted my daughter to boot. She ain't hardly fitten fer marriage no more. I'll end up havin' to support the lazy...."

"Take your hands off me!" Rebecca's voice broke into her father's venomous diatribe. Josie's frustration at not being able to see what was taking place in the office and intervene doubled with each moment. She paced in her tiny cell, her eyes searching for a chink in the stone so she could dig her way out, or a loose bar that she could pry free and use to... *what*, she thought bitterly. *Bludgeon that snake to death?* Not likely he would get within arms reach of her, and certainly the sheriff would do more than hit her on the head if she did what she truly wanted to do. Killing for the sake of killing was not her way. She had killed countless men, but only those who would have killed her if she had not. Or those who threatened to do harm to someone she cared about. She knew she could kill Rebecca's father in a heartbeat and feel no remorse whatsoever. She was surprised to feel tears running down her face, tears that sprung from her fear of what would become of the woman she loved when they hung her. And she had no doubt at all that they would hang her, and this time there would be no bumbling lynch mob walking away without first making sure she was dead. Her thoughts were interrupted once again by the voices outside her range of vision.

"Mr. Cameron, I've got another empty cell right next to Miss Hunter I can put you in if you don't leave this young woman alone."

"She's my daughter. I have the right..."

"You have no rights!" Rebecca's voice rose in anger. "Whatever rights you had, you gave away when you beat me. A father should never hurt his children. A father..." Her voice trailed off, and Josie's heart broke as she heard Rebecca begin to sob. 'Oh, Sprite, don't let him hurt you anymore,' she prayed.

"All right, that's it, Mr. Cameron. You take yourself on out of here and sober up. If I catch you bothering your daughter again I promise I will lock you up. Those cells are pretty small and close together and I can't be watching Miss Hunter every minute, if you get my meaning." Josie found herself admiring this man who had clubbed her on the head. In other circumstances she was sure they could have been friends. But at least she did not need to worry quite so much about Rebecca while she was in Tahlequah. The sheriff would protect her.

"But my reward," Caleb whined, but the sheriff cut him off.

"You'll get your reward when they ship her back to the states," the sheriff replied. "I looked into it when you told me a few days ago she was coming to town, and Miss Hunter is not wanted for any crimes in Oklahoma Territory. Circuit judge will be here next week and will decide whether to send her back to the states or not, and you can whine at him about your reward. I'm sick of listening to you. Now move on." Josie could hear some mumbling which she assumed was Rebecca's father protesting, but a moment later she heard the door slam and it was quiet in the office. Josie heaved a sigh and sat back down on the sagging bunk.

"Thank you, Sheriff. I'm grateful for your help," Rebecca said sincerely. "Can I see Josie now?"

"Sure, Miss Cameron. Follow me." A few moments later the sheriff rounded the corner leading into the area where the cells were located with Rebecca a few paces behind him. Josie stood and walked to the front of the cell and extended her hands through the bars. Rebecca elbowed past the sheriff and ran to the cell, grasping both of Josie's hands and kissing her quickly on the cheek.

The sheriff turned to walk out of the room. "Sheriff, wait," Josie called to him and he turned around. "Thanks. For taking care of Rebecca." Now that she could see him, she understood why she had felt an affinity for the man. He had the look of a Cherokee. Unless she missed her guess he was a half-breed like herself. And the Cherokee's took care of their own.

"No problem," he said with a grin. "I'm just sorry I had to club you on the head when I did, but I was afraid you were going to shoot him. The man's an ass, but I couldn't let that happen. And you can believe that no harm will come to Miss Cameron while she's in my town."

"I believe you. And I'm sorry you had to club me, too. My head hurts like hell." He shrugged as if to say, "what could I do?" and she could not help but smile at him. "Do you suppose we could have some privacy here?" she asked, and he nodded.

"I'll be in the office if you need anything," he said, then he turned and left the room.

Both women stood there for several moments after he left, not speaking, their fingers twined together through the bars. Then both of them began to speak at the same instant.

"Let me see... "

"Rebecca, how..."

"... your head. Turn around and let me see." Josie did as she asked, and Rebecca gasped at the size of the bump on her head.

"I'll be all right," Josie said turning back around to see the look of horror on Rebecca's face. "It's stopped bleeding already. Don't worry. Rebecca, how did he find us?"

Rebecca's lip trembled and she looked as if she might burst into tears. Josie reached out through the bars and caressed her cheek, crooning softly as she did. "Shhh, baby, it's all right. Don't cry." Rather than comforting her, Josie's words seemed to push Rebecca over the edge. Tears began to course down her face, and when she tried to speak her voice came out in ragged gasps.

"I-I... wrote... to my s-sister," she sobbed. "I told her where we were g-going. I just wanted to know... she was all right and to let her know I was happy. Oh, Josie, I never thought he would pick up the mail. He never does. I'm so sorry, Josie..."

It had never occurred to Josie that Rebecca had betrayed her, however innocent her motives had been, and for a moment she was shocked into silence. The look of agony on Rebecca's face pierced straight into the outlaw's heart and pulled her from her silent contemplation. Once again she reached out to comfort the woman she loved, and Rebecca seized her hand. Josie smiled and kissed the back of Rebecca's hand.

"Don't blame yourself," Josie said softly. "You meant no harm."

"Oh, Josie, what are we going to do? If they send you back to the states, they'll hang you. I couldn't live with myself if that happened. I don't want to live without you."

"Don't talk like that," Josie said more harshly than she intended, and Rebecca fell silent and simply stared at her. "If something... if they do send me back, I want you to promise you'll go to Charles's place. You'll be safe there, and he and Horace love you."

"I'm not leaving you," Rebecca said firmly. "If they send you back, I'm going to be right beside you. You can't bully me, Josie Hunter. I'm in this till the end."

Josie could tell from the set of her jaw there would be no arguing with the younger woman. Her one hope for getting out of this mess without a pine box for a bed would be if they could convince the judge not to extra-dite her. Rebecca's gift with words might just be the thing that would do the trick. "You're a stubborn woman, Rebecca Cameron. And by God, that might be just what we need." She reached through the bars and put her hand behind Rebecca's head, pulling her in for a kiss.

It was several hours later when Rebecca emerged from the cellblock. Josie's headache had worsened while they were talking, and she thought if she could get some sleep it might help. Almost as soon as she laid her head down she was asleep. Rebecca watched her sleep for several minutes before she tore herself away, knowing there were many things to do before the judge arrived and nobody to do it but her.

The sheriff was not in the office when she came out and instead a deputy sat behind the desk. He barely glanced at her as he was busy cleaning guns. It reminded her of the evenings she and Josie spent while the outlaw did that same thing, and she felt a gripping in her chest like a vice around her heart.

"Excuse me," she said to the deputy, who finally looked up from his labors and blinked a couple of times to find a beautiful young woman standing before him. "I wonder if you can tell me where the sheriff has gone?"

"Uh, yes, ma'am," he said, tipping his hat in respect. "He's gone off to get himself a bite to eat. Should be back directly, or you can find him over to Miss Lucy's diner. He'll be bringing something back for your... for the prisoner to eat."

"Thanks," she said with a smile. "I better go help him with his food choices for Josie. She's... particular."

"Yes, ma'am," he said with a nod, and resumed cleaning the weapons.

The sheriff saw her walk through the door and, from the way her eyes were searching the crowd, he figured she was looking for him. He stood up and waved to catch her eye, and she smiled and walked toward him. He remained standing as she approached, pulling out the chair opposite his. "I'd be honored if you would join me," he said sincerely. Rebecca had been so concerned over Josie that she had not even realized how long it had been since she had eaten. She was indeed quite hungry, and her stomach growled loudly as he finished speaking.

"I... thank you again, Sheriff. You are very kind. I believe I will." She allowed him to scoot her chair under the table and then he went to fetch the waitress before resuming his seat.

"She'll be right here, Miss Cameron."

"Call me Rebecca, please. Just now I'm not so crazy about the name Cameron."

"All right, Miss... Rebecca," he said, catching himself and smiling sheepishly. "I'm John Kenwood. I'd be pleased if you'd call me John." The waitress appeared by Rebecca's side and ran down the list of specials available, adding that the roast beef was some of the best in the entire territory.

"That sounds good," Rebecca said with enthusiasm.

"And put together a plate of that for us to take with us," John added, then quickly turned to Rebecca and asked, "That is if you think that will meet with Josie's approval."

"Oh, it'll meet with her approval all right. We're used to eating what we can catch on the road, and beef is a rare treat." The waitress withdrew to give the orders to the cook, and for the first time Rebecca noticed that John's own plate of food was sitting, cooling, on the table in front of him. "Please, John, eat your food while it's still hot."

"Oh, I don't mind eating my food cold. Tell you the truth, I probably prefer it that way. I'll just wait until she brings your food. Maybe you can tell me a bit about how you came to be traveling with the notorious outlaw Josie Hunter while we wait."

Rebecca had sensed from her first meeting with the gentle sheriff that he was a man she could trust. She folded her hands on the table in front of her and began her story. "It all started when I was grabbed by three thugs intent on raping me. But they didn't reckon on Josie Hunter being within hearing range of my screams...."

Rebecca pushed her plate away and politely declined the waitress's offer of another cup of coffee. She felt as if she would burst if she took in another morsel. While they ate, she had summed up the high points of her life with Josie, highlighting the number of times the outlaw had saved her life. The only detail she left out was the fact that she and Josie had become lovers. She did not think such a personal detail had any bearing on their current problem, which was how to avoid letting Josie be extradited for trial in the states.

When Rebecca was through with her story, John sat there for a few moments deep in thought. Taking a deep breath, he said, "I sure wish it was up to me whether Josie were to stand trial or not. She'd be sitting here with us right now, laughing and drinking coffee." Rebecca glanced toward the empty chair on her right and felt a stab of pain that what the sheriff had just described was not the reality of the moment. "Josie is something of a... local legend, you might say," John continued. "The Cherokee will tell you that she is responsible for saving more lives than any other person they can name. The money she stole from the railroads she used to buy food and supplies for the Cherokee. According to legend, she never kept any of it for herself. She also helped the Chinamen and coloreds the railroads worked half to death for slave wages. To the white man she's a murdering thief, but to anyone with skin other than white she is something of a hero. To tell the truth, I was surprised to see her traveling with a white woman."

"I think you should wire the sheriff in Mason's Gulch and see if you can get him to send you a statement about how Josie saved that town from being sacked. That was an entire town full of white people Josie saved, and all she asked for in return was food for her horse and some salt pork."

"Hmm. Good idea. We're going to need all the help we can get with the judge that's coming through next week. His family was killed during an Indian raid, and he doesn't look too kindly on anyone with red skin, or even half-red skin like Josie's."

"Can't we request another judge?"

He shook his head and said, "I'm afraid not. We only have two judges in the area, and the other one is laid up with a broken leg."

Rebecca lowered her voice and looked intently into the sheriff's face. "I don't suppose you might... accidentally leave her cell unlocked one night."

"Oh, Miss Rebecca, I'd like nothing more than to see her free. But I'm sworn to uphold the law, and that means we have to find a way to get her out of there legally." He fell silent when the waitress materialized with a basket containing the food for Josie. Handing her several coins, he rose from his chair and picked up the basket.

"I'm sorry, John. Please forget I asked that. I'm just... desperate to get her out of there. But we'll do it your way... according to the law. Maybe we can go over the judge's head and find someone a little more sympathetic or at least willing to listen to reason."

The sheriff's face brightened, and he nodded vigorously. "You're right. That's exactly what we need to do, and I think I know just the man." Holding out his hand to assist Rebecca from her chair, he propelled her toward the door, all the while laying out his idea for the next steps to take.

"Josie." Rebecca's soft voice reached into the darkness that had enveloped the gunslinger, and was pulling her toward the light. The pain in her head had lessened, but she still squinted her eyes against the glare of the lantern outside the cell. "We brought you some food. And we have a plan." The enthusiasm in her voice made Josie open her eyes wider, and she was surprised to see that Rebecca was in the cell with her, kneeling on the floor by the cot. The sheriff was nowhere in evidence, but she noticed that the cell door was shut behind Rebecca and presumably locked. Her plan probably did not include making a break for it.

Josie sat up on the edge of the cot and peeked into the basket on the floor from which the enticing aroma emanated. "Ah, I see. We're going to blast our way out with... roast beef? Smells heavenly."

"We are not going to blast our way out. We are going to talk our way out, just as you suggested. At least that's what I am going to try to do. And if that fails, we're going to blast our way out."

"With roast beef," Josie finished for her. The light-hearted tone in Rebecca's voice was contagious, and Josie found herself thinking that perhaps the determined little woman could actually pull it off, whatever her clever plan was. "Who is it you're planning on charming on my behalf?" Josie removed the plate from the basket and began to eat as Rebecca told her about the judge and his hatred of Indians. As she listened, Josie's spirits dropped along with her appetite, and she set her food aside. "Doesn't sound like even you could charm a man with that much hatred in his heart," Josie said with a hint of bitterness in her voice.

"Oh, but it's not him I'm going after. John says the governor is very sympathetic to the cause of the Indians, and he can override anything the judge says as long as we can get him here before you're sent away. He's supposed to be a fair and honest man, and John thinks that if we tell him how you gave the money you stole to the people who should have had it in the first place that…"

"Wait, wait," she interrupted the little blonde, placing her hand on her lips to still her. "What's this I'm supposed to have done with the money, and who is this John who claims to know?"

"The sheriff's name is John. Didn't I tell you that? And he said it's common knowledge that you gave your cut of the robberies to the Indians. Why didn't you tell me? I always kind of wondered why you never seemed to have any money since you had stolen so much, but I never would have dreamed you…"

"Common knowledge, is it?" Josie said with a wry smile. "And I took great pains to try to make sure it was kept secret."

"Why? Why would you want to hide such a kind and generous act?"

"Think about it. Would you accept a gift from someone knowing that what they were giving you was bought with stolen money? Not to mention that the more people who knew, the more likely it was the railroad would find out what had become of their money. At the very least they would take it back and possibly even come in with guns blazing. I wouldn't want to be responsible for the death of any of my father's people. Besides, it suited me to have people think that I was no more than a ruthless outlaw. Most people pretty much leave me alone when they find out who I am and, all evidence to the contrary, I really don't enjoy being called out and having to kill people." She smiled a little sadly and shook her head before continuing, "It's almost funny. I've been given credit for so many robberies over the years that I would have to have been ten people to do them all. Some of them were in places I have never been. I never tried very hard to convince anyone that it wasn't me because it served my purposes. Now they'll use those crimes against me as well. Rebecca, even if you can get to the governor, there is nothing you will be able to tell him that will make a difference with that much evidence stacked up against me."

"I refuse to believe that," Rebecca said stubbornly. "I'll tell him about Mason's Gulch and Deadwood and all the people you saved there."

"Rebecca, a blind person could see that you love me. How much weight do you think your testimony is going to carry? They would figure you'd lie through your teeth to save me."

"Yes, I'd lie," Rebecca said through tight lips. "I'd do anything I had to if it meant you would go free. But Josie, it's the truth I'll be telling, and there are plenty of other people who know it too. We just have to get hold of them. Tomorrow we're sending out telegrams to everyone you've helped and asking them to send in a testimonial for you, if they can't come here themselves by next week. Then I'm going to New Hope where the governor will be dedicating the new City Hall on Thursday, and I'm going to talk to him. And if I can't convince him, I'll go higher. As high as I have to. Josie, I won't let them take you... I can't."

"The governor is as high as you can get out here in the Territories. And I know you will do as much as it's humanly possible to do. But please," she grasped Rebecca's hand and pulled her into an embrace, "don't get your hopes up too high. And promise me you'll do what I said... about going back to Charles' farm." Rebecca opened her mouth to say something but her reply was cut off by the sound of approaching footsteps. By the time John appeared in front of the cell they were sitting on opposite ends of the cot, both women looking grim but determined.

"I'm sorry, Miss Rebecca, but I need to lock down the prisoner for the night. I'll have to ask you to leave now." Faced with the prospect of separating from Josie, Rebecca's face looked stricken. Her feet seemed weighted down with lead as she rose and crossed the tiny cell.

Suddenly her eyes lit on the empty cell next to the one Josie occupied, and she said to the sheriff, "John, can I stay in the cell next to hers? I promise I won't be a bother."

"Oh, Rebecca, you don't want to spend the night in a cell," Josie protested. "It's damp and cold and..."

"If it's good enough for you, it's good enough for me," Rebecca said defiantly. She turned to the sheriff and added, "Besides, my father is still out there, and I'm afraid he might try to hurt me. I'd feel safer if I were in here."

"Miss Rebecca, it's really not..." The sheriff's refusal was dissipated like mist in the wind by the pleading look in the young woman's face. "All right," he said grudgingly, "but if I should have to lock somebody up I'd have to ask you to leave."

"I understand," she said. "Would it be all right if I get my things from the wagon? I'll only be a minute." Josie's face suddenly looked stricken.

"Rebecca, I forgot all about the horses! Flossy has been standing in harness for hours, and neither of them have had food or water since this morning. I expected to be coming right back to the wagon."

"Don't worry. I'll see that they're stabled and fed," Rebecca said reassuringly. John unlocked the cell and Rebecca hurried out. The sooner she attended to the horses the sooner she could be back with Josie. She turned and smiled at Josie before she rounded the corner into the outer office, blew the outlaw a quick kiss, and was out of sight. The brave smile Josie had been wearing to try to keep Rebecca's spirits up melted from her face, and she sank down onto the cot. With her foot she pushed the plate of barely touched food toward the cell door.

"Might as well take this away. I don't seem to have much of an appetite." John nodded and opened the door, his hand on his gun in case Josie should try something while he picked up the plate. She gave a bitter little laugh. "Don't worry, John. I'm not going to do anything. Just promise me you'll keep that sick bastard who calls himself her father away from her, or I'll get out of here – whatever it takes – and kill him."

42: New Hope

Rebecca stepped down from the stagecoach and groaned as her cramped muscles protested the long hours of inactivity that had brought her to New Hope, Oklahoma. She had taken a train from Tahlequah to Tulsa where she spent the night in the train depot. Early the following morning she caught the stagecoach, which, after a few other stops, would have her in New Hope by late that afternoon. At least for the past couple of hours she had the coach to herself and was able to stretch out and take a bit of a nap. But even so, her eyes felt gritty and she knew she must look a fright. As soon as the driver handed her bag down from the top of the coach she made her way to the saloon. A sign in the window boasted rooms to rent, bath included. A bath might make her feel human again. The dedication of the new city hall, whose clock tower was visible from where she stood, was to take place the following day. She did not know if the governor was in town already and would not be able to recognize him even if he were, so she planned to approach him immediately after the dedication. There was nothing for her to do until then, so she decided a bath and a good night's sleep would be the best thing in the world next to freeing Josie.

There was a festival attitude in the air the next morning when Rebecca made her way toward the new City Hall. Flags and streamers of colorful paper garlanded every building on Main Street leading up to the impressive new building. It was still several hours until the official dedication, and she decided to get something to eat to stop the rumbling in her stomach. The smells from the café drew her across the street a block away from the City Hall. There was not an empty table to be had, but as she searched the room she saw a table for two with a lone occupant. It was a well-dressed woman perhaps 10 years older than she was, and she was engrossed in reading a newspaper. Rebecca wound through the tables until she was standing near the woman's shoulder.

"Excuse me, I wonder if you would mind letting me share your table? There doesn't seem to be another empty seat in the place." The woman looked up and smiled, and Rebecca found herself smiling back. The woman's eyes were as green as springtime grass, with laugh lines creasing the corners. She had dimples that crinkled when she smiled and a scattering of freckles across her cheeks.

"Please do. My husband has eaten and gone off to get ready for the ceremony, and I'd be glad for the company."

"Thank you," Rebecca said, dropping her bag on the floor and sliding it under the table. She held out her hand to shake the other woman's, as she sat down. "I'm Rebecca."

"Eugenia," the woman said. She looked around until she spotted the waitress and motioned for her to come over. "Would you clear away these plates please and bring a menu for Rebecca. Oh, and a little more coffee for me, please."

"Oh, me too. Coffee. Please." The waitress smiled and returned a moment later with a menu, a cup, and a pot of coffee. Rebecca wrapped her hands around the steaming mug to warm them up and regarded her companion in silence for a moment. Something about her struck a familiar chord, yet she was almost certain they had never met. "This place is certainly doing a brisk business for this hour of the day. Is it always like this?"

"I wouldn't know. I've never been here before; we're in town for the dedication. Is that what brought you here?" Eugenia poured some milk into her coffee and stirred in a spoonful of sugar then sipped the steaming brew.

"No. Well, yes, sort of. Actually I came to talk to the governor, but since he is here for the dedication I guess you could say that's why I'm here too. I don't suppose you know what he looks like? I'd like to talk to him before the ceremony, if I can."

Eugenia laughed and the sound reminded Rebecca of the ringing of a bright clear bell. "I guess I know what he looks like. He's my husband." Rebecca nearly spilled her coffee as she banged her cup on the table.

"You're joking."

"There have been times when I thought our marriage was a joke, but…." Her voice trailed off, and after a moment she smiled again at Rebecca and asked, "What business do you have with my husband, if you don't mind my asking?" Rebecca decided to tell the entire story to Eugenia and see if she could get her to speak to her husband for her. What incredible luck to find herself with just the person she needed to arrange an introduction to the governor!

"My...." She stopped a second to contemplate how to refer to Josie. Friend just did not cover it any more. "My partner is in jail. She's supposed to go before the circuit judge next week, and he's going to decide whether to send her back to the states to stand trial for train robbery, among other things. But she didn't do all those crimes, and she never killed anybody that didn't need killing. And she gave the money back to the Cherokee', and..." Eugenia's face drained of color and her eyes widened as she listened to the young woman plead for her partner. The moment she heard the word "Cherokee'" the face across from her at the table faded away, and she was back in a barn beside her best friend as bullets flew through the air around them.

"Eugenia, are you all right?" Rebecca's voice pierced through her trance and brought her back to the moment. The young woman was holding her hand and lightly rubbing her wrist. "You looked like you might faint there for a moment."

"No, I'm all right. Rebecca, your... partner, what's her name?"

"Josie Hunter." Eugenia leaned back in her chair and closed her eyes. She gasped in a few shallow breaths and then expelled them before she opened her eyes to once again regard her young companion.

"You know her." It was not a question. Eugenia nodded.

Josie had never mentioned a Eugenia from her past, but then she was pretty closed mouthed about the life she led before they met. Suddenly she knew what was familiar about this woman – Josie had described her so perfectly. She was the one with the dancing green eyes and the infectious smile that had captured the heart of a teen-aged Josie. Even as the thought was forming in Rebecca's head she realized the impossibility of it, but the words tumbled out of her mouth. "You're Genie," she said simply.

"Yes."

She stared at Genie, her thoughts miles ahead of her ability to put words together rationally. Finally she managed to stammer, "But how... they told her you were dead."

A small sob escaped from Genie's mouth before she could stop herself, and a tear coursed down her cheek. "They told me she was dead, too, but not until months after I had recovered from the gunshot wound. So that's why she... I never understood why she didn't make an effort to contact me." She scrubbed the tear off her face with the napkin she was holding, and her fingers continued to twist the fabric until it was in a tight knot in her hand. She seemed not to notice even as her hands turned white from the effort, and it was not until Rebecca reached across and lightly touched her hand that she realized what she was doing. She smiled at Rebecca and continued. "I told my father what had really happened that night, and he told me she had run away. I think he was afraid I would have a relapse if he told me the truth then, and later... well later he just didn't want me to know what a coward he was, I think. Anyway, I made sure her name was cleared, and they arrested the men who were actually responsible for the thefts. I was sure she would read about it in the papers and come back. One of the ranch hands finally told me that they - my father - had hanged Josie."

Tears ran down her face again as she relived the horror of the night she learned the truth. She had been so blinded by anger that she had taken a gun from her father's collection, stormed into the barn where he was working, pointed it at his head, and pulled the trigger. There was a hollow click as the hammer fell on an empty chamber. Before she could try to fire again the gun was wrenched from her hand by one of the men working with her father. Without a word of explanation she had turned and run from the barn, going straight to her room to pack up her clothes. She refused to speak to her father when he pounded on her door. He pled with her to tell him what was wrong, but she said nothing until she had her suitcases in hand and was ready to leave. She opened the door to see his shocked face as his eyes took in her obvious preparation for leaving.

"I know what you did," she hissed through clenched teeth.

"Genie, I..."

"Don't bother to try to deny it! You had to know she was trying to help me catch the rustlers. She was my best friend in the world. She would never have done anything to hurt me. And she was not a thief! You killed her because she was an Indian. She was the most decent person I ever knew. I have half a mind to tell the sheriff..."

"Now don't be hasty, honey, let me ex..." She cut him off and shouldered past him.

"I'm leaving. I'm going to stay with Aunt Stell until fall and then you are going to pay for me to go to school back east. And if I never see you again that'll be far too soon for me."

Genie took another sip of her now cold coffee. She pushed the cup aside and took a deep breath and continued. "I met William while I was at Vassar. He was a bright young man with a lot of ambition and I knew he was going to be a success. There was never any... great romance between us but he loved me and was at least willing to marry me without a dowry, which I refused to ask my father for. It was after we married that I read about Josie being arrested for robbing a train. I told William I was going to visit a sick cousin in Pennsylvania but I actually went to try to see Josie in jail. By the time I got there she had escaped, and I was never able to track her down. I always thought... if I could find her and tell her she wasn't wanted for the rustling at my father's ranch that I might be able to turn her away from the path she had chosen. I blamed myself for her turning to a life of crime. If I hadn't talked her into trying to fight a bunch of murdering horse thieves..."

"Don't blame yourself, Genie. She went after the railroads because of what they did to her father and her father's people, not because of what happened to you. There was nothing you could have done about it."

"I could have talked her out of it. She listened to me; she believed in me."

"She loved you." Rebecca's heart lurched in her chest as she spoke those words. For the first time it truly sunk in that the woman across from her was Josie's first true love. The jealousy she had successfully conquered when she believed Genie to be dead reappeared and caught her off guard. She had to force herself not to bite off her next words. "She never stopped loving you."

Genie's expression changed from one of sorrow for the past she could no longer effect to determination for the future, which she could. She did not notice the bitterness in Rebecca's voice, or if she did she gave no sign of it. "She's still the best friend I've ever had," Genie said sincerely, "and I promise I will help you convince my husband not to let them send her back to the states." The clock in the new City Hall pealed the hour of eleven o'clock. The ceremony was due to start at noon exactly. "We have an hour for you to fill me in on the current situation, and as soon as William is finished with his speech I'll introduce you to him." She reached over and patted Rebecca on the hand and smiled. "Don't worry, Rebecca. I won't let her down this time."

Rebecca and Genie separated a half-hour later so that Genie could freshen up before taking her seat on the platform with her husband. Rebecca went to the telegraph office to send a wire to John and let him know she had succeeded in her mission. The fact that she had not yet spoken to the governor himself did not worry her. She had no doubt that Genie could talk him into pardoning Josie if she had him wrapped half as tightly around her finger as she once had Josie.

She waited in the telegraph office for a reply to her telegram, which read:

JOHN: FOUND THE GOVERNOR STOP
TELL JOSIE NOT TO WORRY STOP

BACK IN THREE DAYS STOP ANY PROBLEMS?
STOP
WAITING FOR YOUR REPLY STOP
SIGNED: REBECCA CAMERON

The clock struck twelve and Rebecca was about to walk out the door when the machine began to clatter and the clerk called out to her to stop. Excited, she rushed back to the desk while the rest of the message was received, and the clerk handed her a piece of paper.

REBECCA: JUDGE IS EARLY STOP THREE DAYS
MAY BE TOO LATE STOP
HAVE GOVERNOR SEND WIRE TO JUDGE STOP
URGENT STOP
SIGNED: JOHN KENWOOD

Rebecca had to read the message twice before the meaning truly sunk in. The paper fluttered from her fingers as she raced out the door and toward her now more important than ever meeting with the governor.

The morning sun streaming through the bars of her cell wakened Josie. As she swung her legs over the edge of the bed her eyes lit on the scraps of paper she had thrown on the floor the night before. One was a wire addressed to the sheriff from Judge Fellowes saying that his schedule had changed and he would be stopping in Tahlequah possibly as early as the next day. The other was from Rebecca saying that she had found the governor and Josie was not to worry. John had promised he would do what he could to delay the proceedings long enough for Rebecca to return with something written in the governor's own hand saying that Josie was not to be extradited. Or even better, if the governor himself would come. She paused in her ruminations and chided herself. According to John, Judge Fellowes was known to be one of the most mule-headed men he knew, and it was not likely he would accept anything less than the governor face to face before he would admit that his authority could be overridden. And that he would swiftly decide in favor of her return to the states and make arrangements for her transportation was a foregone conclusion in John's opinion.

The sound of the door leading to the cells opening and slamming shut resounded through the small area in which she was confined and was followed by footsteps coming down the hall. She had to smile; the sheriff invariably made a good deal of noise before entering the room to allow his prisoner time to "get decent" in case she was using the chamber pot.

"You awake, Miss Josie?" he called before he actually came into view.

"Yes," she grumbled. "Me and everybody within a mile of this place, with all the noise you're making."

"Sorry," he mumbled, "but I figured you'd want to see this." He stood in front of her door with another wire held in his hand. By the look on his face she could tell the news was not good. She took the paper from his hand and glanced at it, then dropped it to the floor with the rest. The judge was arriving that afternoon and wanted to get the hearing under way immediately.

"Nothing from Rebecca or the governor?"

He shook his head. "No, but I did find out that the school is staging a pageant this afternoon. Since we use the schoolhouse as a courthouse it won't be possible to have a hearing there. That buys us one more day anyway."

"It's just postponing the inevitable, John. Tomorrow's Saturday, which means no school, and no conflict with the hearing. Rebecca won't be here before Sunday, and by then I'll be on a train heading east."

Rebecca gazed out the window of the stagecoach where a dust devil gathered a collection of leaves and pieces of tumbleweeds only to scatter them again and move on. Since Josie had been jailed, she felt as scattered as those tumbleweeds. She lowered the flap once again and settled back on her seat. Across from her Genie sat with her head resting against the side of the coach, her eyes closed. Up until a short while before she had been knitting while the two women sat in silence, but the rocking motion of the coach had apparently lulled her to sleep. Rebecca took the opportunity to study Genie as she slept. It was easy to see why Josie had fallen for her. If anything, she was prettier than Josie had described. Rebecca's emotions warred within her. She knew that Josie would be pleased beyond words to find that her friend had survived, and she would not begrudge her that happiness. But at the same time she could not help fearing that Josie might prefer this mature, sophisticated woman who once meant everything to her. She felt like a country bumpkin compared to Genie, and she wanted to hate her. But when the coach hit a rough patch of road and Genie woke up and flashed those dimples at her, she could not help but like her. She smiled back.

"Penny for your thoughts," Genie said as she resumed her knitting. So skilled was she that her eyes never left Rebecca's face, yet her fingers flew as she worked, never dropping a stitch. Genie could tell something was bothering the younger woman more than Josie's current plight, and from the occasional looks she saw on her face, she surmised that it had something to do with herself. She wished there was something she could say or do that would allay her fears, but she did not want to assume anything until Rebecca confirmed her suspicions.

"Wouldn't be money very well spent, I'm afraid. My thoughts are kind of... muddled right now."

"Can I help?" The look of concern on her face and the sincerity in her voice brought tears to Rebecca's eyes. Genie set aside her knitting and moved from her side of the coach to sit beside Rebecca, grateful that her husband had been able to arrange for a private coach to transport them to the train depot. She put her arm around Rebecca's shoulders and gently pulled the young woman's head down to rest on her shoulder. The act of kindness only seemed to make Rebecca cry harder, and she began to sob outright. Genie stroked her cheek with her free hand and lightly kissed her hair as she murmured softly, "Shhh, its going to be all right. Everything will be fine. We'll get there in time; don't worry." She continued to stroke Rebecca's face and hold her until the sobbing stopped and Rebecca pulled away.

"I-I don't know what I'd do if I... lost her."

"She's not going anywhere, Rebecca. William will be there as soon as he finishes his business, and he promised he wouldn't let them extradite her before he has a chance to hear her case himself."

"That's not... the only way to lose her," Rebecca said so softly Genie almost did not hear her.

"You love her very much, don't you?" Rebecca nodded, unable to trust herself to speak without bursting into tears again. Genie took Rebecca's hand in both of hers, lightly caressing it as she spoke. "I love her too, Rebecca. She was the first person to ever make me believe that I could be and do anything I wanted to be. Remembering her strength was what allowed me to pack up and leave my father; I knew Josie would have wanted me to stand up for myself, and I did. Any time I found myself in a tough spot in my life I asked myself, what would Josie do in this situation? And I think I made some very good choices. Marrying William was one choice I was not so certain about when I did it. In my heart I was grieving for Josie, and I almost felt I was being unfaithful without even truly recognizing the feeling for what it was. But as the years went by I grew to love him, even more so after our children were born. He's such a kind and gentle father. The girls adore him, and so do I. I am where I belong, Rebecca. I will always love Josie, but not the way you do. And if she loves you half as much as I can tell you love her, I'd say the two of you are where you belong also."

"Oh, Genie... you.... I don't know what to say. Thank you. I feel like such a baby, but I couldn't... stop thinking about how she looked when she told me about you. She loved you more than anything else in the world. I got jealous just listening to her, and I didn't even know you were alive. Then I meet you and find that you're the perfect woman...."

Genie threw back her head and laughed. She laughed so hard tears came to her eyes. "Perfect woman? Oh darlin', I am so far from perfect I can't even see it from here. But thanks for the compliment. And the laugh. Thought I was going to bust a gut." Genie's laughter was infectious and Rebecca found herself joining in. Soon they both had tears of laughter streaming down their faces, and a bond of friendship had been welded that would last through their lifetimes.

Josie formed a mental picture of the judge as she listened to him sputter and argue with the sheriff in the outer office. She pegged him for one of those balding, banty roosters with a beer belly and a drooping mustache. He was the type who would cross the street to avoid passing too close to an Indian, and when forced to deal with them as human beings he would look down his long pointy nose with an attitude of superiority. She had known dozens just like that in her lifetime; Genie's father was a prime example of the breed. The shame of it was that these little petty tyrants frequently rose to positions of authority and power where they could impose their will over people whose only crime was that their skin was not white.

"And I don't know why you didn't tell the teacher to cancel that damned recital when you knew I had to be out of town by Sunday," the judge thundered.

"It's not a recital. It's the Autumn Festival, and the children have been looking forward to it since school started. Besides, the wire from the governor says we are not supposed to...."

"To hell with that wire, man! For all I know it was sent by that half-breed's friend." The wire from the governor had shown up no more than 15 minutes before the judge himself. It said that no action was to be taken in the case of Josie Hunter, and that he would review it upon his arrival Sunday or Monday. The judge had planned to be on his way to his next appointment by Sunday, and the thought of being held up by that Indian-loving pantywaist just stuck in his craw. Although he truly believed the wire had indeed come from William Howe as the sheriff claimed, he was not about to admit it. And since he had taken the wire from the sheriff, it was his word against that half-breed's that it even existed. With luck he could be gone before the governor arrived, after making sure that Josie Hunter was on board the same eastbound train. "You just have the schoolhouse ready for me by 9AM tomorrow, and the first case I'll be hearing will be Josie Hunter's."

Josie heard the sound of the street door slamming followed by John's footsteps approaching her cell. He did not even bother to make the noise he usually did to warn her of his approach; she could not have missed the loud exchange between himself and the judge unless she was deaf as a post. He knew she would be expecting him. Sure enough she stood leaning against the bars, her face an unreadable mask.

"You heard?" She nodded. "He's a real prince of a fellow, no doubt about it."

"I can tell. John, it doesn't look much like the cavalry is going to come riding over the hill at the last moment, so I think we need to come up with some alternate plans." She paused and looked into his eyes for a moment and continued, "That is, if you still want to keep me from getting my neck stretched."

"As long as it's within the law, I am up for anything," he responded emphatically.

"Well then, let's put our heads together and see if we can come up with something."

In her dream she was standing in the pouring rain watching as a group of men constructed a gallows with which to hang her. She was not bound or restrained in any way, yet she knew that running would be pointless. On the top of the platform a stout, balding man pulled a lever to release a trap door, and a large sack of grain dropped through the opening and swung from the end of the rope, creaking as it moved in the buffeting wind. The bald man turned and looked at her with a malevolent gleam in his eye and said, "We're almost ready for you, half-breed." She had not seen him in years, but there was no question as to who he was - Genie's father.

"I was only trying to help," she protested, knowing he would not listen. He had never listened.

The man took his eyes off her and glanced toward someone she could not make out in the heavy rain, and he beckoned to the person to come to the platform. "She's going to swing for what she did to you," he said to the distant figure. "Come and watch." As the figure drew closer she could tell that it was a woman, but she wore a heavy cloak with a hood and her face was completely in shadow. Instead of approaching the platform, the woman turned and walked toward Josie, and the closer she got the more familiar she seemed. When she was almost within Josie's reach she stopped and took the hood off her head. Light brown curls tumbled out from under the hood, and green eyes crinkled at the corners as she smiled at the outlaw.

"Josie," the woman said softly as she reached out her hand.

"Genie," she answered tremulously, reaching out her own hand, only to see the landscape and the beautiful vision within it dissolve into the dirty stone walls of her jail cell. The sound of rain persisted even as the dream faded and she realized that she had incorporated the actual rain into her dream, even as she had conjured Genie from her past. But the voice had seemed so real, and she could not shake the feeling that if she had been able to hold on to the dream for a few seconds more she would have been able to touch her....

"I'm here, Josie."

Josie twisted frantically around on her cot and saw the woman standing outside the bars of her cell. She wore a hooded cape much as the vision from her dream had worn and her face was obscured, but there was no mistaking that lilting voice. But of course that was impossible. Certainly she must still be asleep, even though she could swear she was wide-awake. She swung her legs off the cot and stood up, taking the few steps required to bring her close to the bars and the specter that waited for her on the other side of them. She was in no hurry to wake up from this dream.

"I didn't have any dinner, so you couldn't possibly be a bit of undigested beef."

Genie laughed and pulled the hood from her head. " A Christmas Carol," she said as she removed the cape and draped it over her arm. "We took turns reading aloud from that book, remember? Your English accent was terrible."

"And yours was..." Josie's voice trailed off and her eyes widened. She studied the face of the woman before her, and it was Genie as she would have looked today if she had lived. "You... you're... I'm not dreaming, am I?"

"No," she said with a shake of her head, her face wreathed in a smile.

"Genie!" Josie cried, reaching through the bars to grasp Genie's shoulders. She pulled her as close as she could with the iron in the way and, when she realized she was probably crushing her, she let go of her shoulders and placed her hands on either side of her face. Without even thinking, she brought her lips to Genie's and kissed her softly. "Oh, Genie, I missed you so much." Tears welled up in her eyes and ran unchecked down her cheeks. Genie produced a handkerchief from her pocketbook and gently wiped the tears away.

"I wanted to die when they told me you were dead. I almost gave up the struggle when I was dangling from that rope, but I knew you would want me to live, so I fought to free myself. I can't believe you're really here. And now... how did you... find me?"

Rebecca watched the reunion of the two friends from the doorway leading into the cell area. She wanted to give them some time alone, even though she ached to take Josie in her arms and make her forget that there was anyone else in the world but themselves. Watching Josie kiss Genie was one of the hardest things she had ever done, but she reminded herself of what Genie had said and forced a smile to her face as she walked into the room.

"I found her. Josie, meet Mrs. William Howe, wife of the governor of the Territory of Oklahoma."

Josie turned toward the source of the voice she knew so well and her smile left no doubt in Rebecca's mind that, even though she may love Genie, her heart was committed only to herself. Josie reached through the bars and said in a husky voice, "Come here."

Rebecca grasped Josie's fingers and the outlaw pulled her toward the bars. When her face was within reach, Josie put her hand behind Rebecca's head and pulled her in for a kiss. The kiss she gave Rebecca made the one she gave Genie seem like the kind one might give to a visiting elderly aunt. After several moments, Genie cleared her throat and the lovers reluctantly separated.

"I hate to… interrupt, but 9 o'clock isn't that far away, and I think we need to discuss our strategy."

"The hell with that," Josie replied. "I want to hear all about you." She raised her voice and called to the outer office, "John, how about some chairs for my guests? We should get comfortable, ladies. It's going to be a long night."

The judge was working on his third whiskey and was just about to call it a night when the farmer approached his table. The man looked to have had more than his share of liquor, and the judge was about to brush him off as a drunken barfly when the man spoke.

"S'cuse me, sir. Th' bartender tole me you're the judge that's gonna be decidin' whether to send Josie Hunter back to the states. Izzat true?"

"True enough," the judge allowed. No point in mentioning the governor had effectively taken the decision out of his hands. If he could get that half-breed out of town before the governor arrived he would deal with the consequences of his actions later. "What's your interest in the matter?"

Without waiting for an invitation, Caleb pulled out a chair and sat down across from the judge. "Well, sir, my daughter has fallen under the spell of that she-devil, and I reckon the only way to get her away from her is ta make sure that bitch is locked up good an tight. Until they hang her, that is. And I'm the one tole the sheriff she was coming to town and got him to arrest her, so I reckon the reward is mine." He held out his hand, which the judge grasped reluctantly; the man looked as though he had not bathed in months. "Name's Caleb Cameron."

"Sounds as if you and I have a common goal, Mr. Cameron. I have no use for Indians, even the so-called "peaceful" ones. And this one is anything but peaceful." The judge twisted the strands of his long moustache as he contemplated how he might use this man to his advantage. "Suppose your daughter is the one Josie sent off to find the governor and try to get him to override my decision. If she shows up in town before I get a chance to rule, I think we need to get her out of the picture."

"'S no problem," he slurred, " 's long as I know I don't have ta stick around here ta get my reward, I'll juss grab the girl and head on home."

"You do that, Mr. Cameron. Leave Josie Hunter to me."

When Rebecca woke to find her body spooned around a soft female form she instinctively cuddled closer, wrapping her arm tightly around her partner's waist and pulling her toward her. Her nose was buried in the fragrant curls of her hair... and her eyes flew open when she realized the smell was not Josie, but Genie. When they had left the jail in the wee hours of the morning there was only one room available in the tavern, so they had to share. Hoping the other woman would not awaken, she gently eased her body to the side of the bed and dropped her feet to the floor. She dressed as noiselessly as possible and, after leaving a note to let Genie know she had left for the jail already, she let herself out of the room.

John was speaking to two men in a language Rebecca could not understand when she walked into his office. By the look of their clothes and the language, Rebecca assumed they were Cherokee. She smiled in greeting to them and then sat to wait for John to finish so he could unlock the door to the cells.

"Help yourself to coffee, Miss Rebecca," John said with a nod toward the pot on top of the iron stove. "I'll only be a few minutes." Gratefully Rebecca poured herself a cup, which she held in her hands to keep the morning chill away. The rain had finally let up some time during the night, but the temperature was unseasonably cold. She stood by the stove and reveled in its warmth. John had to have been here since before dawn to get the stove going and warm up the room as much as he had. Perhaps he had not even gone home after seeing the women safely to the tavern, but had returned to the jail. She was grateful once again for the kindness of this gentle man, without whom she would not have had a prayer of getting Josie out of this mess.

After the men left, John came to join her beside the stove and refill his own coffee mug.

"Don't worry, Miss Rebecca," he said confidently. "I have a feeling things will work out all right."

Rebecca put her hand on his forearm and gave a gentle squeeze. "Thank you for everything, John. I don't know what we would have done without your help. If there's anything Josie or I can do for you, I hope you'll let us know."

He looked slightly embarrassed when she leaned in and kissed him on the cheek, and his eyes seemed to be glued to a spot on the floor. Rebecca poured a second cup of coffee to take in to Josie and began to walk toward the cells when John's voice stopped her.

"Miss Rebecca, I wonder if you'd consider... that is, when this is all over, would you allow me to... call on you?"

Rebecca could not believe she had not seen this coming. Her preoccupation with Josie's problems had blinded her to the look on his face that was so obvious now. John was such a sweet and kind man and Rebecca could not bear the thought of hurting him.

"Oh, John, that's very sweet, and I'm honored that you would want to court me. But I'm not... free to see other people. My heart is committed to another."

He had been so taken with the lovely young woman and felt so badly for her when her father made the remark about being stuck with her because she was tainted by the company she kept. He had assumed there was no man in her life – mistakenly, it would seem.

"I'm sorry, I didn't realize. I... you never mentioned having a beau, so...."

"That's because I don't." She looked at him and said pointedly, "But I do have a lover."

His brow furrowed for a moment as he considered her words, and then comprehension showed on his face. "Oh, of course. I should have realized. I'm not the brightest candle on the tree, I reckon."

"Don't sell yourself short. If I were in the market for a man, you are exactly the type I would be interested in. And I'm sure there are plenty of women out there who would be proud to walk on your arm."

He simply nodded and walked to the door leading into the cells and unlocked it. He swung the door open for her and stood aside to let her pass.

"I'll be going to get some breakfast now for Miss Josie. Can I fetch you something as well?"

"I'm not really hungry," she said, surprised to note that it was true. It was rare for her to be so keyed up she could not think about eating, but the upcoming court appearance had her stomach tied up in knots.

"Deputy won't be on duty for another hour or so. I'd be obliged if you would come fetch me over at Rudy's if something comes up while I'm gone."

"Of course I will. Thanks again, John."

43: Abduction

Caleb watched as the sheriff walked down the street and into the little diner. He had seen Rebecca go into the office some twenty minutes earlier and a short time later had seen the two Indians come out. He was reasonably certain there was nobody left inside but his daughter and the halfbreed, and she was behind lock and key. He figured he did not have much time before the sheriff returned, so if he was going to act, it had to be now. He would not be able to get Rebecca out of town until the late afternoon train, but he had already found an abandoned house right on the edge of town where he could hide her until departure time. A grin spread over his face as he walked quickly across the street and stepped through the door behind which his reward was waiting.

"Sound's like John's back," Josie said when she heard the sound of the outer door.

"He hasn't had time to get your breakfast. I wonder if something's wrong? I'd better go check." She had been sitting on a stool right outside Josie's cell, and she rose and walked to the door. Josie listened to the sounds of the footfalls in the other room and furrowed her brow. It did not sound like John's tread.

"Wait a minute, Rebecca. Don't go out there…" she began, but Rebecca had already stepped through the door. Josie heard a muffled yelp and the sound of the tin cup with Rebecca's coffee hitting the floor. "Rebecca!" Her heart clutched in her chest as she listened to the sound of a scuffle. She grabbed the bars and screamed again at the top of her lungs, "Rebecca!" but the footfalls had already receded toward the back door of the jail. She heard that door open and slam and then all was silent.

When John came back fifteen minutes later he was greeted by the sound of Josie banging on the bars of her cell with the tin cup that had held her coffee.

"Keep your shirt on! I've got your breakfast," he called with a smile on his face. Then he saw the other cup lying on the floor in a puddle of coffee, and he dumped the plate of food on his desk, drew his gun, and ran to the cells. Other than the drunk in the cell next to Josie's, who had not stirred once all morning despite the din, there was only Josie back there.

"John! He's taken Rebecca!"

"Who has?" he asked, putting his gun back in his holster.

"I don't know; I didn't see him. But there was only one person's footsteps out there."

"It's almost certainly her father."

"Of course," she said bitterly striking her fist against the wall. "With everything going on I had almost forgotten about him. John, you've got to let me go after him."

"You know I can't do that, Miss Josie. I'll go after him." She shook her head vigorously.

"You said you had to get the schoolhouse ready before court could begin, John. Let me go. I can track him and get her and come to the schoolhouse by nine. Please – I swear I won't try to run away; I just have to make sure she's safe before I go into that courtroom."

"I shouldn't be doing this," John muttered as he pulled the key ring off his belt and walked toward her cell. "I'll lose my job – or worse – if you don't show up in court by nine, Miss Josie." He unlocked the door and she sprang out like a cat freed from a cage.

She paused long enough to grasp his hand and pump it a few times. "You have my word, John. I'll be there by nine; I'll wait outside while Rebecca comes in to get you, and we'll act as if you just brought me over from the jail."

"Promise me you won't kill him."

"I won't kill him," she said over her shoulder as she stepped out the back door. Under her breath she muttered, "but he'll wish to hell he was dead when I'm through with him."

A child would have had no difficulty following the tracks of the two people from the jail to a tumbledown cabin on the outskirts of town. Clearly she had resisted him the entire way, and as often as not beside the odd indentation left by his unevenly worn boot were the drag marks from Rebecca's heels. Josie's anger grew with every step she took, and she was glad she did not have a gun or it would be very difficult to keep her promise to John.

There were no windows in the little one room cabin. One opening in the wall was covered with oilcloth, so even though she could not see she could hear every sound from within. She crouched silently outside trying to determine from which part of the room the voices were coming so that she could decide whether to go through the door or the empty window frame.

"...knew you were hatchin' up some scheme with that damned Injun sheriff, and I ain't gonna run the risk of ya doin' something to free that bitch. I don't give a damn what ya do after she's safely back in the states and I've got my money. Now you stop wigglin' and keep yer hands behind yer back so I can tie 'em."

"Pa, please don't do this. If it's money you want I can raise enough to equal the reward, or even more if you'll just leave us alone. They'll kill her if they get her back there, and she doesn't deserve...."

"She deserves every damned punishment they want to heap on her, and more! She's a murderin' thief and a defiler of innocent young women. And you," his voice was full of venom as he spoke, and Josie had to force herself to stay where she was. She wanted so badly to rush in there and choke the life out of him. She could almost see the hatred in his eyes as he continued to berate his daughter. "Yer a disgrace to yer family and an abomination in the eyes of the Lord. You probably egged her on like ya done them poor fools she killed back there to home. Oh yeah, they found the bodies. Figure yer girlfriend did 'em in fer their horses and the silver in their pockets."

"They were trying to rape me." Rebecca's voice was a hiss. Clearly she no longer believed she had a chance of reasoning with the man and she held nothing back. "You'd rather a gang of men rape me than one woman love me, wouldn't you? What kind of father...."

"I'm not yer father!" he said sharply cutting her off in mid sentence. "Yer Ma had a roll in the hay with that music teacher right before he up and left town. I reckon I ain't the smartest man in the world, but I know how to count to nine, and I sure as hell weren't there when she got pregnant with you. She finally admitted it to me when you were a little girl, after we...."

Well, it don't matter, I ain't yer Pa. And since we ain't blood relations it wouldn't be a sin if I was to get a little taste of what ya been handin' out to that Injun, now would it?"

That was as much as Josie could take. She quickly walked several paces away from the building and then turned and ran toward the oilcloth, diving through with her arms straight out in front of her as if she were plunging into water. The oilcloth tore free of the window frame and landed on Caleb who was just beginning to wonder what the commotion was all about. An instant later Josie landed on top of him as well, propelling him to the far wall, which he hit with a loud thump. The air was knocked out of him and he slowly crumpled to the floor still not knowing what hit him. She gave him a solid kick to the crotch just to keep him down, and he screamed like a pig being slaughtered. She lifted up the oilcloth covering his head just enough to see if he was truly out and, satisfied that he was not going anywhere for a while, she turned to Rebecca, who was tied to a chair.

"Josie, thank God! How did you...."

"No time to explain now. We have to get your fath... I mean him," she said with a sneer, "tied up and gagged before he comes around. I'd just as soon he didn't know it was me that took him out." Her hands worked at the knots around Rebecca's ankles as she spoke, and as soon as she was free she began trussing up Caleb's feet. "Tie his bandanna around his mouth for a gag and help me tie his hands and feet together."

Rebecca did as she asked and within minutes he was lying on his side with his hands and feet bound together behind his back. He would not be able to do much more than turn over onto his stomach. Josie covered him with the oilcloth so that someone casually glancing through the open window frame would not see anything but a heap of fabric in the corner. That should do until the sheriff could come and free him. She took Rebecca's hand and pulled her in for a quick kiss.

"Follow me," Josie said taking Rebecca's hand once again and leading her out of the cabin. She skirted behind the buildings when they arrived in town until she was behind the church, which was the closest building to the schoolhouse. She crouched behind a large bush and whispered to Rebecca, "Go tell John where I am. He should be in there waiting for you. Hurry. It's almost nine."

"Josie, why are you doing this? You're free; you could run. I could meet up with you somewhere...."

"No. I'm not running any more. I made a promise to John, and I'm going to keep it. Go now... please. I'll see you again inside. I love you."

"I love you, too." She leaned down and kissed the top of Josie's head and then walked away without looking back.

Rebecca threaded her way through the people on the steps of the schoolhouse, some of whom looked at her as if to question why she thought she should be allowed in the building, but she carefully avoided looking into any of their faces and simply pressed on. Every seat in the schoolhouse was taken, and people stood against the walls and in the cloakroom. Those who were not lucky enough to find a space on the wall sat on the steps of the small building, or stood talking in small groups on the school grounds.

John was just inside the door, watching intently for Rebecca to appear. When he last looked at his watch he saw that it was ten minutes until nine and with every minute that passed his anxiety level rose until he felt certain he was going to collapse from sheer worry. The sight of the little blonde making her way up the steps made him almost want to cheer, and he stepped outside to intercept her.

"There's a seat for you up front; some friends of yours are saving it for you. I'm going to go get the prisoner now." He deliberately spoke loud enough for those in the vicinity to hear.

"Thank you, Sheriff. Lord knows we need a friend right about now." She emphasized the words "lord" and "friend," and cut her eyes in the direction of the church. John nodded imperceptibly to show that he got the message, and he hurried off in the direction of the jail. He passed by the church on the way, and as soon as he was out of sight of the school, he doubled back and went down the side yard between two buildings and came up behind the church.

At first he thought he must have misunderstood after all because he saw no sign of the outlaw, but he softly said, "Miss Josie, are you here?" There was a rustling in the bushes and the black-clad woman emerged. Relieved, he walked to where she stood brushing off leaves and dirt and a smile lit up his face. "You'll never know how happy I am to see you," he said sincerely.

"Been kicking yourself ever since you unlocked that cell, have you?" Her tone was light, but the slight flush that appeared on his face told her she was on the mark. She laughed softly. "You've been good to us, John. There's no way I'd put your livelihood on the line, even if I thought I could have made a break for it. The running ends here. One way or another."

He held up a pair of handcuffs and she extended her hands. "Sorry to have to do this, Miss Josie." The teeth on the cuffs clicked into place, but he stopped when they were still comfortable. "Let's go in the back door of the jail and come out the front," he said. "Try to keep out of sight in the meantime."

"No problem. Let's go."

44: Judgement Day

As Rebecca walked down the center aisle of the schoolhouse she could feel every eye in the place follow her steps. She kept her eyes on the floor, uncertain what reception she would get from the local populace.

"That's her friend," a voice whispered from a seat as she passed. "Come to town with the outlaw, she did."

"More than friends is what I heard," a male voice hissed.

"What of it?" A woman spoke loudly, and something familiar in the voice made Rebecca turn toward her. Victoria, Stacey, and Elaine sat together, and it was Victoria's voice that Rebecca had recognized.

"Victoria! Oh God, it's good to see you!" The women were on their feet, each one hugging Rebecca in turn.

"Couldn't let you face this alone, could we?" Victoria said with a grin. "You'd best go sit down. Almost time to start this circus. We'll talk later."

As she finished the short walk down the aisle she scanned the crowd wondering if any of the other people she had sent telegrams to had shown up. She caught the eye of Martha Jane who winked and gave her a thumbs up. A few seats away the mayor of Mason's Gulch sat talking with Belle Shirley. And in the front row, Horace and Charles sat on either side of Genie. When she reached them, the trio moved apart to make room for the little blonde. She gave Horace and Charles each a quick hug and then sat down. She opened her mouth to speak to her friends but before she could utter a word the room erupted in whispers once again as the outlaw was ushered in.

Josie ignored the stares and whispers and walked proudly across the room with her head high. The shackles on her wrists did nothing to diminish her regal bearing. Rebecca's heart swelled with love and pride as she watched her beautiful lover pass her by and take a seat at a small table in front of the teacher's desk that would serve as the judge's bench. John sat on one side of her and a short man in a suit and tie sat on the other side. He leaned over and whispered something to Josie, and she nodded. This must be the lawyer Belle said she would contact. She swore that if anyone could get Josie out of this mess, it would be Ira Greenspan. Josie twisted slightly in her seat until she was able to see Rebecca, and she gave her a reassuring smile. Rebecca mouthed the words "I love you," and Josie nodded to show she understood.

"All rise! This session of the Circuit Court of the Territory of Oklahoma is now in session. The honorable Judge Lucas Fellowes presiding." Chairs scraped the floor as the people got to their feet, and the Judge made his way to the front of the room with his clerk trailing behind. The Judge was a tall, imposing man with a thick head of steel gray hair. He took his place behind the desk and sat, and the clerk turned toward the assemblage and said, "Be seated." While waiting for the hubbub to die down, Josie studied the clerk and noticed that his mannerisms were effeminate, as was the sound of his voice. She would be surprised if he was not a kindred spirit, and she smiled at him. His face registered shock to have a defendant act friendly toward him, but he recovered his composure and handed a stack of papers to the Judge.

"The first matter before this court is the extradition to the United States of Josephine Hunter, known as the outlaw Josie Hunter," the clerk intoned. "Will the defendant please rise?" Josie and her lawyer stood up. The Judge glared openly at the outlaw making no effort to disguise his dislike of her.

"Sit down," the Judge growled. "This isn't a trial and there is no reason for the defendant to enter a plea." Resuming their seats, Josie continued to maintain eye contact with the Judge who was finally forced to look away. "I will listen to qualified petitioners with reasonable arguments as to why this person should not be returned to the States to stand trial for her crimes there, and at the conclusion of these proceedings I will make my ruling. Because this is not a trial, there is no prosecuting attorney. I will ask questions on behalf of the people. Is that clear?"

"Yes, your Honor," Mr. Greenspan replied.

"Very well. You may proceed with your argument, Mr. Greenspan. But I caution you; I have no tolerance for theatrics in my courtroom. If your client or any of your witnesses try to turn this into a sideshow I promise it will not help your case any. Do you get my point?"

"Yes I do, your Honor. There will be no theatrics."

"All right. Get on with it."

"Thank you. May I stand, your Honor?" The Judge simply nodded, and Mr. Greenspan rose and turned toward the townsfolk and visitors. "Ladies and gentlemen, I'm sure there is not a one of you who hasn't heard of...."

"There is no jury here, Mr. Greenspan. You will address your comments to me and me alone."

"I'm sorry, your Honor." Ira looked down at his notes on the table before him, cleared his throat and looked up at the Judge. "Your Honor, my client is not wanted for any crimes whatsoever in the Oklahoma Territory. Furthermore, she has selflessly assisted many people present in this room today – placed her own life at grave risk – in order to preserve the life and liberty of those and other people. The money that she obtained as a result of her career as a train robber was all given to the people displaced by the railroads. She kept none of it for herself. She is not a ruthless cold-hearted killer as the dime novels portray her, but a friend to the less fortunate and defender of the weak. Her actions over the past months show that she is trying to atone for the wrongs she has done, and she should be allowed to continue on the road to salvage her soul."

He paused and the Judge inserted into the silence, "That didn't make Robin Hood an upstanding citizen any more than it does your client, Mr. Greenspan. I doubt she could redeem her soul if she were allowed to live for a hundred years. If you have no more compelling arguments than that, this hearing is a waste of my time and the taxpayer's money. I suggest you produce your witnesses so we can bring this farce to a close."

The lawyer had expected the Judge to be unsympathetic to his client based on his discussion with the sheriff, but he had not anticipated this complete unwillingness to be fair-minded. He had hoped that the stories of his witnesses might be able to produce a spark of humanity in the Judge, but it seemed his human kindness was reserved for the fair of skin. "I call Martha Jane Canary."

"...managed to bring in enough medicine to save most of the people who would surely have died without it. She worked day and night to save them too, with nary a thought to herself. Deadwood would have been a ghost town if it warn't for Josie Hunter." She smiled at Josie as she finished her testimony, and the outlaw mouthed 'thank you' in return.

"And where did she get the medicine?" the Judge asked.

"Why, she got it from a snake oil peddler or some such. I'm not rightly sure."

"And was the snake oil peddler outside the quarantine area when she got the medicine from him?"

"I believe he was, but…."

"So she disregarded the quarantine and put an innocent person at risk for smallpox. Thank you, Miss Canary. That will be all. Next witness."

"Well, actually it was the other one… uh, Miss Cameron over there, who volunteered Miss Hunter's services," Mayor McGregor from Mason's Gulch explained. "We didn't see Josie… that is, Miss Hunter, until after I agreed to give her immunity in return for her help in stopping the Karam gang from looting our town."

"If not for your promise of immunity she would have ridden on by and left your town for the vultures, is that it?" the Judge asked with a sneer.

"Oh, I don't think so. Miss Cameron was quite sure she could get Miss Hunter to help even without the immunity."

"I'm sure Miss Cameron can be very persuasive," the Judge said with a hint of sarcasm. "You can step down, Mr. McGregor. I think I know what was behind Miss Hunter's heroic behavior in Mason's Gulch."

"But your Honor, I…."

"Step down, sir. I'll find you in contempt if I have to ask you again."

One after another the witnesses came forward to tell of the selfless acts and heroic deeds Josie had done, and one after another the Judge found reason to belittle the witnesses and downplay the good things she had done. The Judge refused to allow Rebecca to testify on the grounds that she was not an impartial witness. The lawyer had no choice but to pull his ace from the hole. "I call Missus William Howe, wife of the Governor of the Territory of Oklahoma." The Judge's eyebrows pulled together in a frown as he watched the finely dressed woman make her way to the witness' chair. He had never met the Governor or his wife, and he would not have recognized her. The daguerreotypes in the paper did not do her justice. He was not pleased to know she was prepared to speak on behalf of the half-breed. It was one thing to know the Governor wanted to hear the case to rule on a request for asylum. It was another thing entirely to have his wife speak up for the outlaw.

"I fail to see how Missus Howe can provide a character reference for Miss Hunter since she has not personally witnessed any of the so-called heroic acts this parade of witnesses have described."

"On the contrary, your Honor. Missus Howe has known the defendant since she was a youth. And she has a very moving tale to tell of how Miss Hunter tried to help her catch some rustlers."

"And I'm certain it's a real tear-jerker, Mr. Greenspan. Unfortunately, it has no bearing on this case since it happened before Miss Hunter decided to switch sides of the law. Take your seat, Missus Howe."

"With all due respect, your Honor, the events Missus Howe wishes to relate to this court were a turning point in the life of this young woman. She was falsely accused of rustling and was hanged for it…."

"Are you hard of hearing, Mr. Greenspan? Missus Howe's testimony is irrelevant. Don't try my patience any further or I will find you in contempt." The icy glint in the Judge's eye made it clear that he would do exactly that.

Ira was stumped. He shuffled through his notes again and studied the people in the room to see if there was any tactic or witness he had overlooked that might help to delay what was now clearly inevitable. As his eyes passed over Josie he noticed that, though she appeared to be calm and stoic, the muscles of her jaw clenched and unclenched in silent rage as she stared at the Judge whose prejudice threatened to end her life. His only hope was that she still had an ace up her sleeve he could use. "Your honor, I request a recess to confer with my client."

The Judge pulled his watch from his pocket and glanced at it before answering the lawyer's request. It was nearly noon, and since it did not seem likely they would be able to finish before lunch, he decided to grant the request. He rapped his gavel on the desk before him and said, "This court will stand in recess until two o'clock. Sheriff, remove the prisoner to her cell until then."

"All rise," the clerk lisped. As the spectators shuffled to their feet and began to leave, the sheriff removed the handcuffs from his belt and showed them to Josie with an apologetic look on his face. Wordlessly, she held out her hands and he snapped them in place. With the lawyer on one side and the sheriff on the other, Josie was escorted to the jail, a procession of concerned friends with Rebecca in the lead following in their wake.

Despite the seriousness of the circumstances, the mood in the jailhouse was almost festive. John removed the handcuffs as soon as they were inside the building, and he did not bother to put Josie in a cell. The friends who had come to support her were clustered around her, hugging her and slapping her on the back. Jane and Belle exchanged a glance as they watched their usually untouchable friend not only allow herself to be touched, but actually seem to enjoy it. Belle shrugged and Jane smiled as they both got in line to collect their share of hugs from the enigmatic outlaw.

Josie had no idea she had so many friends until they were all assembled in one room. She glanced down at the little blonde who never left her side, and realized that if it were not for her most of the people would not be there. Rebecca had peeled away the layers of armor that had shielded Josie from harm, but had kept love away in the bargain.

"Thank you. All of you… for coming here to help me," Josie said. The quiver in her voice betrayed her emotions as she continued, "If I don't get out of this mess it won't be because you didn't try. And I love you for it." Her arm was around Rebecca's waist and she gave her a squeeze to show that she loved her more than all the rest. The gesture was not lost on Genie, who felt a stab of jealousy to see such closeness between the two women. If not for her father, she knew that it could have been she who earned such adoring looks from the tall gunslinger. She was not unhappy with her life, and in fact loved her husband dearly, but she could not help but wonder how her life might have been if not for that fateful night in the barn. She sighed and then smiled as Josie's gaze caught her eye. Josie held out her hand to Genie, and she placed her own hand in it. Josie gently pulled Genie until she was against her other side, and put that arm around her waist. Flanked by the two diminutive women, Josie looked like a book between two bookends.

"I hate to take you away from your friends, but I think we need to discuss our strategy," Ira said. "I suggest you folks go get some lunch before court resumes this afternoon, and give us a chance to talk." One by one the people filed to the door after giving Josie words of encouragement. When Genie and Rebecca made a move to separate themselves from Josie, the outlaw pulled them back to her sides.

"These women are my family. They stay with me."

"Suit yourself," the lawyer said with a shrug. He motioned for the women to take a seat on the bench that flanked the sheriff's desk, and he sat in a chair facing them. "I don't have to tell you this is not looking good," he said solemnly. Josie raised one eyebrow and regarded him silently. He swallowed hard at the cold glint in the gunslinger's eyes and averted his gaze, then went on, "Truthfully, I did not expect him to completely ignore the telegram from the governor. The man is committing political suicide and doesn't even seem to care. He must have a huge axe to grind with you, Miss Hunter."

"Not with me in particular. I just seem to be the only Indian handy for him to take out his revenge on. A man with such hate in his heart for an entire people should not be allowed to hold a position that wields authority over those people." Her voice was tinged with bitterness as she turned to Genie and continued, "I hope you make sure your husband disbars that bastard, no matter how this turns out."

"Count on it. But we can't give up hope. I already wired William and told him he had to be here by tomorrow. I haven't heard back from him yet, but I know he will be here on the afternoon train. We just have to keep the Judge from taking you out on the morning train."

Josie shifted nervously in her seat in the schoolhouse as the lawyer checked his watch for the third time since they had been seated. She raised her eyebrows and he mouthed the words "two-thirty." Knowing the Judge's eagerness to have this hearing at an end and Josie on her way to the gallows, the outlaw could not help but feel his lateness did not bode well for her life expectancy. A murmur from the back of the room announced the arrival of someone, and Josie turned in her seat to see the Judge making his way down the center aisle, followed by his clerk… and Caleb Cameron. As the trio made their way past her she could have sworn she was in a brewery, so strong was the smell emanating from their pores. Josie glared openly at the man who had pretended to be Rebecca's father, and made a tiny motion across her neck with her hand that only he could see, and which left no doubt in the man's mind that he would be dead if he allowed himself to be caught once again by the outlaw. He gave her a wide berth and sat down in a chair on the far side of the room toward the front.

"All rise," the clerk announced. "This court is now in session, his Honor…."

"Never mind. They know all that," the Judge growled. His speech was somewhat slurred, and his eyes were red rimmed. The clerk opened his mouth to say something, then thought better of it and sat down. The rest of the people took that as their cue and resumed their seats. The Judge continued with a baleful glare at the defense table, "Do you have anything more to say before I render my decision?"

"I do, your Honor."

"Be quick about it then."

"Your Honor, I wish to say for the record that this hearing is premature in view of the injunction from the Governor to delay until his arrival. Even if you will not allow Missus Howe to testify in regard to Miss Hunter's past, I request that she be allowed to testify to the validity of the telegram from her husband. And I further…."

"Enough!" He turned his baleful glare on Genie and bellowed, " Madam, were you with your husband at the moment that he supposedly sent the telegram to which defense counsel refers?"

Genie was caught off guard, and her reply was a stammered, "No, I was not actually with him...."

"Then you cannot swear with absolute certainty that he did in fact send a telegram. It could just as easily have been sent by Miss Cameron, isn't that true?"

"Your Honor, he told me he sent the telegram. We discussed it at length before he did, and I knew exactly what he was going to say." Genie's cheeks flushed with anger at the effrontery of this pompous ass. She opened her mouth to tell him just what she thought of him when he cut her off.

"Hearsay; inadmissible. Mr. Greenspan, unless you have some new evidence to present, this court would very much like to begin the conclusion of this hearing."

"Your Honor, I protest this mockery of a hearing and believe that you should disqualify yourself from this case owing to your prejudice toward Indians. If Miss Hunter were not a half-breed we would not be sitting here today." The look the Judge bestowed on Ira left little doubt that he held Jews in much the same esteem as he did Indians.

"Your protest is noted." The Judge leaned on his desk and glared first at Josie then at Ira. Josie did not flinch, but the lawyer shrunk down in his seat under the unrelenting hatred coming from the man. With a feral grin, the Judge continued, "And now it's my turn. I think these good people should hear what Josie Hunter is really like, from Caleb Cameron, the man who was her most recent victim." He turned to Caleb who had alternated between the desire to flee from the room, lest Josie somehow managed to get free, and his wish to see the look on Josie's face when the Judge told her she had a one-way ticket to hell. Since it seemed the Judge had things well in hand and Josie did not appear to be going anywhere, he had stayed. He looked at the outlaw with utter contempt as the Judge motioned him forward.

"Mr. Cameron, will you tell the people how you came to be acquainted with Josie Hunter?"

Caleb cleared his throat several times before he could speak loudly enough to be heard past the first few rows of people. "Uh, she ambushed some poor cowpokes that was trying to court my daughter, and shot 'em dead. Then she kidnapped my daughter and drug her to hell and gone all over the country. And when I tried to get my little girl back to take her home to her Ma, that Injun beat me to within an inch of my life."

He made sure to turn his head to both sides of the room so that everyone could clearly see the black eye and the cut on his cheek, both courtesy of the outlaw. Josie was certain that the little weasel had not seen her, but she could not be sure he had not heard her voice before falling into unconsciousness. Josie shot a glance at John to try to convey to him that she would not allow him to be implicated for her release if the Judge delved into that. The look he gave her in return showed that he was not as confident as she appeared to be. But then he shrugged; he had known when he let her out of the cell that this could happen and had been willing to take the risk. Both of them turned their attention to the front of the room once more, where Caleb had finished showing off his wounds to the audience and had continued to speak.

"But the worst of it is that this... this... sick and twisted pervert has taken my innocent little girl and turned her into an abomination in the eyes of the Lord, just like herself." Josie grit her teeth to avoid saying something that would not serve any purpose but to worsen her case. She thought if she had to listen to that sanctimonious hypocrite use the phrase "abomination in the eyes of the Lord" one more time, she would rip his tongue from his mouth and shove it up the flap of his long johns. Caleb's eyes skirted over Josie's as he spouted his well-practiced, venomous diatribe, and quickly moved away as the look in her eyes made his heart clunk in his chest like the last hard apple in the bottom of the barrel. His voice was not quite so strong as he continued, "Won't be no decent, God-fearing man want to have nothin' to do with the likes of Rebecca now that she's been tainted by that outlaw. She should pay for what she done to my family. And I aim to see that I get the reward that is due me for havin' to take care of this worthless girl for the rest of her unnatural life."

The Judge scowled at Caleb for the embellishments he had added to the rehearsed script they had discussed in the saloon while sharing a drink... or four. Nevertheless, he felt that the exposure of the outlaw for her crimes against nature itself should help to sway public opinion away from her, and prevent the Indian-lovers in the community from doing anything to prevent him from carrying out his plan. He could tell that morning as he looked over the crowd that the prevailing opinion was that she had redeemed herself and should not be forced to go back and stand trial for her crimes. He hoped they were not so quick to overlook her unnatural behavior as they were her crimes. To get Caleb back on track, he asked, "And when did Miss Hunter inflict these injuries on you, Mr. Cameron?"

"Why, today. This mornin'...."

Ira shot to his feet and spoke without waiting to be recognized by the Judge. "That's absurd, your Honor. Miss Hunter has been behind bars for five days. She could not possibly have done what this man claims she did." In truth, he believed Josie capable of nearly anything, including getting in and out of jail without anyone knowing it, but he kept that opinion to himself.

Before the Judge could reprimand Ira for his outburst, Rebecca had also leapt to her feet. Turning toward the crowd instead of the Judge she said quickly, "It wasn't Josie that hit him; it was a man from town, a stranger to me. The man heard me screaming for help when he," she pointed at Caleb accusingly and then continued, "was trying to rape me...." The lie came effortlessly to Rebecca's lips, even though lying was as foreign to her as breathing water would be. She knew then what Josie meant when she said the Judge would assume Rebecca would lie to protect her. But the man whom she had called Pa for all her life knew Rebecca for an honest person, and the look on his face clearly showed that he had not seen Josie, but had merely assumed that it had been she who had come to Rebecca's rescue. That look was not lost on the Judge either, as he watched the credibility of his only witness crumble into the chalk dust on the floor.

"You're out of order!" the Judge bellowed, but Rebecca went on.

"I left with Josie because she was kind to me. She protected me. That man never had a kind word for me and beat me for every imagined wrong...."

"I'll cite you for contempt if you don't sit down and be quiet, Miss Cameron."

"These people deserve to know the truth! You can cite me, but you can't make me stop talking!" Once again she turned her face to the people who stared at her, hanging on her every word. "Don't let their hatred and bigotry cause the death of... my best friend." She gestured with her hand to include both Caleb and the Judge, who at that point seemed to be the only people present in favor of extraditing the outlaw. Even the court clerk had tears pooling in the bottom of his eyes as he listened to Rebecca's impassioned plea.

All of Josie's friends present began rising to their feet, and one of them started to chant "Free Josie." Within moments, the voices had swelled to include the townspeople as well, and the Judge banged his gavel repeatedly on the desk but was unable to get the crowd to quiet down. Caleb scuttled around behind the Judge as if seeking his protection. The Judge was beginning to wish that he had someone to hide behind, but then he realized that the people were only chanting. They were doing nothing to show they intended to do violence. The Judge reached into his boot and took out a derringer that he kept hidden there for emergencies, and he fired the gun into the ceiling, causing a shower of wood splinters to rain down on the spectators. It had the desired effect, as the chanting lost volume and then stopped altogether, and the Judge bellowed into the near silence.

"I'll clear this room if you don't all shut up and take your seats NOW!" His face was so red with anger that it looked as if he might have a stroke at any moment. "You," he aimed his gavel at Rebecca as if it were a gun, "are in contempt of court. I sentence you to a night in jail. And you," his gaze swiveled to Josie who met his eyes unflinchingly, "are to be transported by train to Missouri tomorrow where you will stand trial for your crimes against the United States. Sheriff, take both of these women into custody. Have Josie Hunter ready to travel at ten o'clock tomorrow morning, at which time you will hand her over to Caleb Cameron who I am deputizing to transport the prisoner. This court is adjourned!" He rapped his gavel sharply and got to his feet.

John had no choice but to do as the Judge ordered. He slipped one of the bracelets of the handcuffs on each woman, and motioned for them to precede him from the room. Once again a procession of people followed the women from the schoolhouse to the jail, only now it was a much larger crowd.

As the last of the spectators trickled out the Judge sent the clerk ahead, and grabbed Caleb by the sleeve when he started to leave as well. The farmer would just as soon take their conversation to the saloon, but the Judge did not look to be in a very convivial mood. Caleb was not sure just what he had done to make the Judge so angry but it was not long before he found out.

"Why in hell did you tell me that damned Indian was the one who knocked you around, you worthless sot? Now this entire herd of yokels thinks you're a liar and I'm an idiot. Not to mention they're ready to nominate that bitch for sainthood."

"I-I thought it was her," Caleb whined. "Who else would come flying through a window like the hounds of hell were after them?"

"Who? How about any good Samaritan that heard your daughter screaming for help." Caleb lowered his eyes and scuffed his toe in the drifts of chalk dust on the floor. He was not used to being the one on the receiving end of a tongue lashing, and he did not much like it. Not for the first time he began to wonder whether the reward for the outlaw was worth the abuse he had been forced to take. And the gunslinger was still a far cry from the states.

"Why did you say I would take her back to the states?" he asked in an effort to shift the conversation off the fiasco with Rebecca. "That woman scares me... she'd kill me as soon as look at me."

"She'd probably have to stand in a rather long line for that privilege," the Judge said under his breath.

"What did you say?"

"Just don't worry about it. She'll be handcuffed, and you'll have the gun. You shouldn't have any problems taking care of a woman who can't fight back... what with all your experience." The sneer in his voice told Caleb that while he had no use for Indians and Jews, he nevertheless took a dim view of men who were heavy-handed with women. "And you can hand her over to the Federal Marshals in Kansas City, so you'll only have her for less than a day on the train."

"Well, I don't like it. Why can't the sheriff take her?"

"You really are a dunce. The two of them are thick as thieves! The sheriff is a half-breed also; we may as well set her free as put her in his custody for the trip. He knows better than to let her go while I'm here, but there would be nothing to stop him once he got her on the train. No, if you want that reward, you're going to have to earn it."

45: A Night to Last Forever

The sound of the tumblers turning in the lock of their cell rang with the finality of a nail being pounded into a coffin. John had allowed their friends to stay until he absolutely had to lock down the prisoners for the night. He apologized repeatedly for having to imprison these women whom he had come to think of as friends himself, but they both reassured him that they bore no ill will toward him for doing the job he had been hired to do. Intuiting that they would prefer to share the same cell, he had moved the bunk from the empty cell into the one Josie had called home for the past several days.

Rebecca watched as John walked through the door at the end of the hall, pulling it shut behind him with a click. Once again the sound of a key in a lock reminded her that this time she was not free to exit the cell if she chose to; she was as much a prisoner as Josie. The outlaw stepped up behind Rebecca where she stood looking out through the iron bars and, placing her hands on Rebecca's shoulders, she gently turned the smaller woman around to face her. Rebecca's face was pale and drawn as if she had already spent years in confinement. The indomitable spirit Josie had grown to love and depend on seemed to have fled, leaving a hollow ghost of itself behind in the fragile woman who stood before her.

"I'm so sorry, Sprite," she said softly, drawing Rebecca to her and wrapping her arms around her tiny waist. She could feel her heart fluttering in her chest like the wings of a bird as it always did at the nearness of this woman. A caged bird, she thought wryly. Josie would gladly have sold her soul to the devil to spare this gentle creature from the pain and indignity through which she was going, but she had made such a bargain years ago in return for a pair of six guns and had nothing left with which to barter.

"You have nothing to be sorry for, Josie. This is my fault! It's all my fault!" Rebecca's chin was trembling and her eyes welled with tears.

"No, it isn't, Rebecca, you…."

"Yes it is!" Rebecca wailed, unable to check the tears that poured down her face. "I handed you over to my fa… to Caleb just as surely as Judas gave Jesus to the soldiers. And he won't be satisfied until he knows you're d-dead!" She buried her face in Josie's chest and sobbed uncontrollably while the outlaw stroked her hair and gently crooned into her ear.

"Shhh, baby, don't cry. I'm not dead yet. They'll give me a fair trial in the states, not like this kangaroo court. Don't give up, please. I need your strength." Her own voice quavered when she realized the truth of that statement. Rebecca was her anchor, her foundation. The naive blonde who constantly needed rescuing had grown into the most important person in her life. Rebecca was the reason she wanted to live; to protect her and to love her. If she stopped believing, Josie would be without hope.

"Oh, Josie. I love you so much. I can't… bear the thought of… going on without you…."

"Then don't think about it. There's still some time before that train leaves. Who knows what might happen. We can't give up on William. I need you to help me be strong, Rebecca. Please…."

Rebecca looked up into cerulean eyes that begged for her to be the one to pull them both out of this predicament. She took a deep breath and gently touched her lips to Josie's, and when she pulled away she smiled up at the outlaw and said softly, "You're right. There is time before that train comes. And we can't allow ourselves to waste it by wallowing in tears."

Josie smiled back. "And how would you like to spend all that time, Sprite?"

"Oh, I can think of something I'd much rather wallow in than tears," she answered huskily, her fingers moving to the buttons of Josie's shirt. Slowly she unfastened each button, her fingers brushing against the gradually exposed flesh of Josie's breasts. Josie gasped and inhaled sharply as Rebecca pulled the tails of her shirt free and in the process inserted her fingers down the front of her pants to touch the crisp hair on the top of her mound. Rebecca put her hands under the fabric of the shirt and rolled it off Josie's shoulders, her eyes feasting on the flesh she loved so well as it was slowly revealed. The hungry look in her eyes was enough in itself to make Josie's nipples stiffen with anticipation.

Rebecca leaned forward and touched her lips lightly to the valley between Josie's breasts, her nose delighting in the musky scent of her lover. "You are the most beautiful woman on earth," she whispered as she tilted her head back to look into Josie's face. With gentle pressure of her hand on the back of Josie's head she brought their lips to within a breath of each other and then said softly, "I want you more than I have ever wanted anything in my life, Josie Hunter." Her lips met Josie's and her tongue gently begged entrance to her mouth. With a groan, Josie parted her lips to allow the caress and met the inquisitive tongue with her own. She pulled the smaller woman closer and deepened the kiss, causing Rebecca to moan softly deep in her throat.

When at last they separated Josie replied, "And I want nothing more than to spend the rest of my life loving you, Rebecca Cameron." Neither woman would allow herself to dwell on how brief that might be. "I've missed having you beside me these past nights. I can't tell you how many times I reached out to touch you and found only empty space. I want to see you... touch you... feel you... taste you." Her fingers began to work the buttons of Rebecca's dress, and while she was careful to avoid pulling them off, she did not take her time to remove the garment, so eager was she to behold what she had craved all those lonely nights.

Josie slid the dress down Rebecca's arms and released the garment to settle on the floor at her feet. Reaching down she grasped the hem of her slip and in one quick movement she pulled it over her head, leaving Rebecca wearing only her panties and shoes. Josie dropped to her knees in front of Rebecca to untie the cord that held her panties in place, and that garment joined the rest on the floor. The sight of the red-gold curls and the warm scent so near to her made her want to bury herself between Rebecca's legs right that moment, but she was determined to take as much time as she could. She wanted to tease and excite the younger woman before she finally brought her hands and mouth to the spot that so captured her attention. She ran her hand down Rebecca's calf and put slight pressure on her ankle to indicate she should lift her foot. When Rebecca complied she removed the shoe. She performed the same move on the other foot and then stood up to take in the sight of all of Rebecca. For a moment she could not breathe. Nothing she had beheld in her life gave her as much pleasure as the sight of this woman.

"My turn," Rebecca growled. Her hands found the buttons that clasped the familiar black pants over Josie's sensuous hips and pulled them apart.

Josie trembled as Rebecca's fingers once again brushed over her abdomen. The mere suggestion of a touch from this beloved woman was enough to make her heart race and her knees grow watery. Rebecca peeled the pants off Josie's hips, taking her underwear with them. The clothes pooled at her calves, held up by her boots. "Sit down," Rebecca ordered, arching her brow. Without hesitation Josie dropped to the edge of the cot and Rebecca knelt in front of her. The little blonde grasped the heel and toe of first one boot and then the other, pulling them off quickly and tossing them aside. She ran her fingers over Josie's well-muscled calves and shivered in anticipation of feeling those legs wrapped around her body. She drew the pants and underwear off, and they joined the growing pile of clothes occupying a large part of their small space. Fortunately they did not need much space, as they planned to be as close together as if they were one.

Rebecca trailed her fingers up the inside of Josie's thighs and delighted in watching the eruption of gooseflesh trailing her fingers. She avoided touching the soft curls that covered Josie's mound, as she wanted to make the tall woman frantic with desire before giving her what she craved.

"Something you want?" she asked in response to the soft moan Josie could not suppress. Rebecca's lips covered the same trail her hand had blazed moments before, her chin just grazing the curls as she brought her lips to Josie's belly.

Josie was half reclining, supported by her hands held out to her sides. She sat up when Rebecca began to run her tongue around her navel and, putting her hand under the younger woman's chin, she lifted her face so she could see her sparkling green eyes. "Ahhhh, yesss, there is. But first...." She put her hands on Rebecca's waist and picked her up as if she weighed nothing. "Put your legs around me," she said in a commanding voice, and Rebecca obligingly parted her legs as the outlaw lifted her onto her lap. Josie had parted her own legs so that Rebecca's mound was pressing against her own damp curls. Rebecca molded her body against the tall gunslinger, her breasts just reaching Josie's ribcage. The feel of Josie's breasts on top of her own and the warmth of her moist center commingling with that of her lover made Rebecca writhe and moan.

Josie bent down to capture Rebecca's lips. Her kiss was soft and slow at first, but soon both women were frantic in their need to feel and taste even more of each other. They broke apart, gasping, hearts racing at the same tempo.

"Rebecca, I have to taste you... now."

"Oh, but I...."

"Please... let me...." Her voice was a husky growl, and it made Rebecca shiver to hear the need in it.

"Yes, yes... you may, but I want to taste you too. Both of us, together."

"Yes." Josie lay on her back and, cupping the soft globes of Rebecca's behind, she urged the younger woman to move up her body. As she did, the moist trail left by her lips made Josie even more frantic to run her tongue over those folds. Rebecca paused in her ascent and lowered her body onto Josie's breast, effectively coating the tip with her juices. She could feel the nipple hardening against her nether lips, and she whimpered softly.

"God, you excite me, Josie!" she said through clenched teeth as she continued to rub against Josie's breast. Rebecca's words and the warm wetness of her sliding over Josie's body caused the outlaw to gasp. "I never thought...never imagined it could be this good." She rocked her hips, her groan joining that of her lover. "I love you, Josie."

"You make me crazy, Rebecca.... Please, give yourself to me."

Rebecca moved further up until her mound was scant inches from Josie's face. Josie wrapped her arms around Rebecca's thighs and gently pulled downward until her knees spread far enough on either side of Josie's head for her to reach the treasure she sought so desperately. The first touch of her tongue on the outer folds struck like lightning to the core of the smaller woman.

"Oh, oh..." Rebecca groaned, nearly forgetting her resolve to taste Josie at the same time. She let Josie get enough of a taste to whet her appetite for more, then abruptly rose up on her knees and shifted around so that she was facing toward Josie's feet.

The move was so quick it caught Josie off guard, something only Rebecca could do. By the time she realized Rebecca had withdrawn she was already back, her velvety folds once again tickling Josie's lips and nose. Rebecca was lowering herself slowly onto the outlaw's body, hungry for the taste of her center, but not wanting to miss any of the delights along the way. She tongued the underside of Josie's breasts, which was all she could reach from that angle, but she vowed to come back and suckle them as soon as the raging desire to sip from her nectar had been quenched. She trailed her tongue over Josie's abdomen and then dipped it into her navel. Josie's stomach muscles tensed and Rebecca caressed the flesh there with one hand while holding herself up with the other. Her fingers slipped into the crease between Josie's thigh and her mound, the warm scent intoxicating and pulling her further down. Lying full out on top of the outlaw Rebecca could only just touch the top of Josie's mound of curls. Never having made love to her in this fashion, she did not realize that her shorter stature would not allow her to reach her intended goal without some assistance from Josie. She cupped her hands around Josie's bottom and tried to lift, but the result only brought her a bit closer to where she wanted to be.

"I can't reach," she said petulantly, her frustration obvious in her voice. Josie chuckled, the sound muffled by the warm folds where her mouth was buried.

She let Rebecca try reaching a few more times before she finally said, "I can fix that." Grasping Rebecca around her buttocks, Josie lifted them both up and then she maneuvered them on the narrow cot until they were side by side. One more shift put Rebecca on her back beneath the taller woman, whose mouth had never ceased its exploration the entire time they were moving.

"Ohhhh," Rebecca moaned as the object of her desire was now tantalizingly in reach. She kissed the flesh of Josie's inner thighs before running her tongue over each one in turn. Her tongue got closer and closer to her goal each time she moved from one leg to the other until finally she allowed herself to touch the rose-colored lips lightly with her mouth. Josie shuddered at the contact and burrowed her face even deeper into Rebecca's center.

Rebecca was determined not to rush; she wanted to take her time and tease her lover until she begged for release. But even as she thought 'take it slow,' her mouth was taking its tempo from the woman above her, and Josie was building up speed. Rebecca pulled her mouth away from Josie's lips for just a few moments, and when she touched her again with her tongue she consciously slowed her movements. It was enough to send a message to the outlaw.

Josie had not realized what a pace she was setting until Rebecca subtly reminded her. She too had vowed to make this night's lovemaking last until both of them were taut as piano wire, but her resolve melted away with a touch of Rebecca's tongue. Never in her life had she been so taken with another human being, and she nearly wept with joy that she had been given the past several months with this beautiful woman. Whatever the outcome of the trial in the states, she would not have traded one moment of the time they had spent together. Josie slowly and carefully parted Rebecca's lips with her tongue, and then she ran it up one side and down the other, occasionally dipping inside to pull out some of the accumulating moisture there. She brushed over the knob that she knew would send Rebecca hurtling over the edge, but was careful not to apply too much pressure too soon. She could not resist lightly grazing her teeth over the nub before she moved away and she could feel it harden with the tip of her tongue.

Rebecca wanted to grind herself against Josie but fought the impulse, knowing the signal that would send would put an end to this exquisite exchange. Instead she brought one arm from behind Josie's thighs and placed her fingers against the folds of skin. She separated the folds to give her tongue greater access and, even as she lovingly caressed the soft lips, she slid two fingers inside the moist cavern. Her other hand roamed over the soft contours of Josie's buttock, delighting in the way Josie responded to her touch.

Now it was Josie who wanted to thrust against Rebecca, and involuntarily she began to pick up the pace to match what her inner core wanted to receive from the little blonde. Rebecca picked up the tempo, ready to feel the explosion that was building inside her, and to pull the same from the woman she loved. She also sucked the hardening nub of flesh into her mouth as she built up momentum with her fingers, and she was rewarded by a gasp from Josie as the gunslinger stiffened her body and began to rise up off Rebecca's body. The smaller woman clung to her, holding her within reach to prolong the delicious sensations.

Josie could not have delayed her climax any longer if she had wanted to. Her one goal was to bring Rebecca to the edge at the same time so that they could plunge together. She tongued the bud that had risen from its hiding place and begged for attention. Faster she moved until she heard Rebecca cry out with the beginning of her orgasm. They both rose so high it seemed they must be hovering just under the ceiling, each sucking every bit of moisture from the other until they finally collapsed back onto the cot. Their breath came in labored gasps, and neither could move from where she lay, faces pillowed on each other's thighs.

When at last their hearts had slowed and they felt they could once again command their muscles to obey them, they rearranged themselves so that Rebecca was lying full length on top of the gunslinger, her mouth inches away from a tantalizing nipple. She cupped the soft breast in her hand, pulling it toward her mouth as she stretched out to meet it. She circled the brown ring with her tongue and felt it contract, the nipple hardening once again into a bullet. She tasted the essence of herself on Josie's breast.

"Rebecca…."

"Hmmm?" The breast in her mouth muffled her response.

"We need to… make a decision about what you should do while I'm gone, in case William does not show up in time." She tried to make it sound as if her being gone was only a temporary thing instead of the final chapter of her life. "I still think you should take the horses and wagon, and go stay with Charles and Horace. They love you like a daughter, and God knows that place needs a woman's touch."

Rebecca raised her head to look into Josie's eyes before she answered. "We've been over this. I already asked Charles to take the horses and wagon and he said he would, unless you try to prevent me from going with you on the train, in which case I'll need the wagon to follow you. I am going with you. One way or another. You can't shut me out of your life now, Josie. I'm your strength, remember?" A sheen of tears made her eyes sparkle like diamonds as she lightly traced the shape of Josie's face with her fingers. She wanted to memorize every part of the woman she loved... with her eyes, her body, and her hands. If this were to be their last night, she would be able to recall every detail of it for the rest of her life.

Josie could not help but see the tears glistening in Rebecca's eyes. She pulled the smaller woman close to her breast and stroked her hair. Tears traced their way down the slope of her breast as they lay there for several minutes in silence. Finally Josie took a deep breath and said, her voice ragged with emotion, "Rebecca, there is nothing more I want than to have you with me. Always. If I could marry you, I would. I have dreamed of you and me together in our old age, the days quietly passing as we rocked on the porch and watched the sunset. That kind of life never appealed to me before I knew you. And now...." her voice broke and the words were almost inaudible when at last she continued, "I can't bear the idea of your being there watching me hang. Please, stay with Charles."

"I'm not going to let them hang you," Rebecca said with grim determination. "And I am not going to let them separate us. Where you go, I go. I don't want to argue about it any more." She put her head back down on Josie's breast, cupping its softness in her hand. Josie lay there in silence for several minutes listening to Rebecca cry softly. She knew there was no point in arguing. She hoped that once again the little blonde would be right. If determination alone could stop the hanging, Rebecca would find a way to pull it off.

46: Another Rescue

A flash of lightning lit up the window, followed almost immediately by a clap of thunder that rattled the pane and shot Josie into instant wakefulness. Rebecca still lay with her head on the gunslinger's chest, but she had slid down and was now curled up against her side. Josie had pulled the blanket off the cot they had not needed during the night and spread it over them to keep off the chill. She was glad she had because the temperature had dropped considerably during the night, and Rebecca was shivering slightly even with the blanket.

A hard rain began to pound the building with a force that shook the window yet again. Josie was not certain she heard the knock on the outer door until she heard John's voice call out, "Miss Josie, Miss Rebecca. I'm going to go fetch you some breakfast. I should be back in fifteen minutes or so."

Josie smiled to think how kind this man had been to her and Rebecca. He could easily have locked them in separate cells for their last night, and undoubtedly would be in trouble if it were to get out that he had not. "Thanks, John," she called back in acknowledgment. She wrapped her arms around the sleeping blonde and hugged her tightly. It was inconceivable that this could be the last time she would hold Rebecca, feel her precious body against her own. She kissed Rebecca's forehead and whispered into her hair, "Sprite... wake up. We have to get dressed."

"In a minute," Rebecca mumbled, nuzzling her face into Josie's soft breast. Josie settled back and pulled Rebecca close; a minute was about all they had, and it was little enough to give to the woman she loved. Without warning, she felt wetness sliding down the side of her breast and realized Rebecca was crying.

"Oh, Rebecca, please don't cry. It kills me to see you so unhappy." Poor choice of words; the little blonde began to cry aloud. "Shhh, baby. Where is that strength you promised me? We aren't giving up, remember?"

"I can't do it, Josie," she sobbed. "I'll kill them before I let them take you!"

"Don't even joke about that. You'd be in the same boat I am."

"That's where I want to be."

"No you don't. Listen to me." She put her hand under Rebecca's chin and lifted her head. The soft green eyes were red and swollen, her cheeks splotchy and red. "If you did something like that, you would be arrested and tried here. It would not prevent them from sending me back; it would just end your life early. If I felt I was responsible for that I would spend eternity in hell."

Rebecca edged her way to the side of the cot and sat up. She took a few deep breaths and then turned back to face Josie. "I know that. It's the only reason I wouldn't kill them. But I don't know how I can bear this…."

"It's not over till it's over." She put on a brave face and shifted to sit beside Rebecca on the edge of the cot. "We have to get dressed. John will be back soon."

"Yes," Rebecca replied dully. She began to stand up to gather the clothes that had been scattered the night before, but at the last moment she turned and threw herself into Josie's arms. "I love you so much, Josie. I pray we still have our whole lives ahead of us, but if this is all we are allowed to have, you should know that being with you has been the best thing that ever happened to me."

Josie swallowed hard to try to keep the tears from forming in her eyes as she softly replied, "You must be reading my mind. I was just…." Knocking on the outer door interrupted her thought and she called out, "Just a few minutes, please, John." Kissing Rebecca lightly on the forehead, she rose and began to pull her clothes on. Rebecca did the same, the two of them managing to dress within a few feet of each other without getting in the way, their motions practiced many a night when they could not bear to be so far away from each other that they could not touch.

"All right, we're decent," Josie said loudly enough for John to hear. Despite that, he took his time opening the door and coming down the hall, allowing the women a few more moments alone.

None of them did more than pick at the breakfast John had laid out on the desk in the outer office. When the rain finally began to slow down, the sounds of utensils scraping plates were the only ones to be heard... until the far off wail of a train whistle pierced the silence.

"It's time," John said softly. He reached to his belt to pull off the handcuffs that hung there, and Josie held her hands out in front of her without a word. She rose from her chair and walked to where her hat hung on a rack by the door.

"May I have my hat?"

"I'll get it," Rebecca said, shouldering her way past John who was already reaching for the hat. She removed the black Stetson from the rack and placed it lovingly on Josie's head after brushing back the dark tresses as Josie always did.

"Thank you," Josie said, putting every bit of love she felt into those two words. Rebecca smiled at her, but did not trust herself to speak without crying.

John shuffled for a moment as if uncertain what to do, and then he cleared his throat. "I took the liberty of getting your bags from the boarding house," he said, thinking to himself that it was a boarding house they never had the chance to use. He picked up the bags from where they lay behind his desk and, handing the lightest one to Rebecca, he shouldered the heavier one himself. "If you'll open the door and go first, Miss Rebecca, then you, Miss Josie...."

As the little procession made its way toward the train station, the townspeople came out to watch. The rain had stopped completely shortly before they began their walk, but the bruised-looking clouds in the distance told of more rain to come. As they walked they gathered people as a snowball down a mountain picks up snow. Genie fell in beside Rebecca and Jane took up a place on the other side of Josie. The rest of their friends flanked John who walked behind Josie.

A small knot of people waited on the platform for the train to arrive, among them the Judge and his clerk, as well as Caleb Cameron. Caleb wore a gun, which looked as out of place on his hip as a sunbonnet would have looked on his head. He nervously fingered the grip as he watched the approaching crowd. He had not bargained on being the one to haul the outlaw back, and he was not certain he would be able to handle things if she decided she did not want to go. For now she seemed to have accepted her fate; he hoped she would not change her mind. The Judge wore a smile, which did nothing to cover up the hate that radiated from his eyes and danced around his body like ball lightning. It made Josie shudder to see such unbridled evil aimed at her, and her step faltered as she realized that she might once have been accused of putting out such a vicious aura. Suddenly, she realized that the Judge was simply a man who had lost something precious in his life, allowing the pain of his loss to turn him into a bitter and lonely person. Unfortunately, the power of his position allowed him to use that bitterness to exact his revenge. Josie straightened her shoulders and with her head high she climbed the steps onto the platform, most of her entourage remaining on the ground, only Rebecca and Genie remaining by her side.

It started to rain again and, in an effort to keep them dry, John suggested they take a seat on the train even though departure was still twenty minutes away. He needed to handcuff Josie to a seat anyway so that he could go get tickets for the two women to Kansas City. There was no way he was going to leave her in Caleb's charge for any longer than he absolutely had to. He asked the conductor to show them to the car with the fewest number of people in it, and the man pointed to a car at the middle of the platform.

John placed Josie's bag in a rack at one end of the car, and when Rebecca started to put her bag beside it, he stopped her with his hand. "Keep it with you. You might need it." She could not imagine what use her spare clothes and a few books would be on the train, but she did not think it worth arguing with him. She nodded and picked the bag up again. John addressed the few people who were sitting at one end of the car and asked them to move to the other end. He had to show his badge to one surly, older matron, and finally with a loud 'hrumph' to show her annoyance, she rose from her seat and flounced to the other end of the car.

"Sit here please, Miss Josie," he asked, indicating a seat by the window facing forward in the car. When she did, he unlocked the handcuffs and passed one bracelet between the armrests on the seat, pulling it up and refastening it around her wrist. There was very little room for her to move her arms, and she had to turn her torso sideways to get comfortable. John's expression told her how sorry he was that he had to leave her like that, and she smiled at him.

"I don't blame you for any of this, John. Please don't look so guilty; this was my own doing."

"I know that, Miss Josie. I just hate to hand you over to those two, even for a little while."

The two in question had stepped into the car, and the Judge overheard the comment and chuckled to himself. Not only did he have the murdering Indian where he wanted her, but also he had outwitted the sheriff and all of his delaying tactics. By that evening Josie would be in a jail in Kansas City, and he hoped to use his influence to make sure she got a speedy trial. He wanted to see her dead before he himself succumbed to the cancer that was ravaging his body. He actually looked forward to seeing his wife and children in the hereafter, but if he was going, he wanted to take one more redskin with him. Josie Hunter was probably his last chance.

"Give that handcuff key to Caleb," the Judge ordered. With a sigh, John did just that, moving out of the way so that Rebecca could take a seat beside Josie. As she was sitting, Rebecca dropped her bag on the floor beside her seat, and the catch popped open. When she reached down to close it, her eye was caught by the polished gleam of the barrel of one of Josie's Colt Peacemakers. Quickly glancing up to make sure neither Caleb nor the Judge had seen it, she fastened the catch on the bag and lifted it up to hold in her lap. She knew the gun was not in there when she left the bag at the boarding house, intending to come back and sleep there. Clearly John had put the gun, which he had confiscated from Josie when she was arrested, in there for a reason. It made no sense that John would have given it to her thinking she would use it to try to help Josie escape; he was too honest a lawman to contemplate such an act. As Caleb took a seat opposite Josie, with the gun John had reluctantly issued to him resting awkwardly in his lap, Rebecca began to suspect that the purpose of the gun was not to free Josie, but rather to protect herself from the man she could no longer even remember thinking of as her father. The Judge settled into the seat opposite Rebecca, his eyes flicking over her quickly and dismissing her as unimportant. He turned his gaze to Josie and gave a twisted smile.

"Enjoy the ride," he said venomously. "With any luck, your next trip you'll be lying flat out in a pine box."

Josie said nothing for a few moments, merely contemplated him with her face an unreadable mask. The look on his face reminded her of what she had seen reflected back at herself from the mirror during the years she allowed her hatred for the railroads and her desire for vengeance to poison every part of her life. Until Rebecca showed her that it was possible to love and to forgive... herself as well as others... she realized that she had been just the same as the man who sat across from her. At last she said, "I feel sorry for you, Judge. Your wife would hate that you have wasted so much of your life nursing a hatred for an entire people because of a few bad ones. I hope you can sort it all out with your God before...." The Judge's hand lashed out to slap her across the face, but Rebecca was faster. She seized his wrist and held it tightly in her hand.

"Don't you touch her," she hissed through clenched teeth. The Judge turned toward this little woman whom he had so easily dismissed and took a harder look. She had strength, and a fierce determination to keep the outlaw from harm. The Judge decided to pick his moments, and it was too early in the day to provoke a conflict with either woman. Once the train was out of the half-breed sheriff's jurisdiction, he could do as he liked, with no one to tell him otherwise. Without comment, he withdrew his hand and placed it in his lap. Rebecca rested her hand on top of the bag in her lap, feeling her heart rate decelerate and hoping her shaking was not visible to the man across from her. She would shoot him before she would let him hurt Josie, and she wanted her hand close to the bag just in case.

John came back into the car and saw the silent tableau in the end seats. He stopped beside Rebecca and held out two tickets to her. She glanced at them; they read one way to from Tahlequah to... nowhere. The space for destination was left blank. She furrowed her brow as she looked at them, but John shook his head imperceptibly as if to say, this is right, don't worry about it.

"Thank you, John. I appreciate everything you've done for us. We'll come back through here when all this is over."

"I'll look forward to that, Miss Rebecca." He cocked his head at the sound of the conductor calling "all abooard," and then turned to Josie. "Good luck to you, Miss Josie. The Cherokee will not be forgetting you anytime soon." Josie just nodded and smiled, unable to trust her voice. The train whistle sounded, and John made his way to the door, jumping out just before the train began to move. On the platform Genie, Charles, Horace, Jane, and Belle stood silently watching as the cars pulled through, looking through the windows until they saw Rebecca and Josie. Genie had told Josie as they walked to the station that she would wait for her husband and follow as soon as they could. She still believed that he could do something to free Josie even if she were already in the states. Josie was once again grateful for the two women who were determined to stand by her through this ordeal.

Rebecca nodded to Josie to turn her head toward the window, and when she did, she was able to see her little group of supporters one last time before the train left the station. Dimly she noted that the rain had stopped once again and was glad that she would not have to make this trip in a downpour. Rain depressed her, and she wanted to at least try to put on a brave front for Rebecca. She turned back to Rebecca and looked into her sparkling green eyes. Oddly enough, Rebecca seemed very calm compared to the way she was when they first boarded the train. Perhaps her success in thwarting the Judge's attempt to strike her had given her confidence a boost. Whatever it was, it lifted Josie's heart to see her lover relaxed, as she had not been since they first woke up that morning.

The train had only been gone from the station for a few minutes and had not yet reached full speed, when it was obvious that it was beginning to slow down again. The whistle shrieked several times as if the engineer were trying to warn someone away from the tracks, but despite the warning the speed still decreased until the train finally came to a complete stop. The conductor made his way down the aisle reassuring the passengers that it was probably just a minor problem and they would soon be under way. The Judge was not mollified by that explanation and insisted that he make his way to the front of the train and find out what the problem was. After trying in vain to convince him, the conductor finally gave up and left the car, promising to return within a few minutes.

Josie's gaze drifted to the window and she blinked several times as her eyes tried to make sense of what she thought she saw. At first it appeared to be a river stretching out in front of the train, with morning mist rolling on top of the water. But upon looking closer, she saw that it was not water, but people, and the mist was steam rising off of them as the rain evaporated from their clothes. As far as the eye could see, the track was covered with people: women, children, men, all ages and sizes… and all Cherokee. They were on the move, flowing around the train to surround it on all sides, and yet it did not seem as if any of them had moved off the tracks. The Judge had yet to look out the window and thus had no idea what was causing the delay, but Rebecca saw the crowd begin to gather three and four deep outside the window and she could not keep the smile from her face. Upon seeing that, the Judge swiveled in his seat to look past Caleb and his face whitened at the sight of this sea of Indians.

"Nooooo," he bellowed in rage as he realized the intent of those savages. They made no move to board the train, but they formed a solid wall of humanity that would be impossible to move through, either with the train or on foot, should he decide to take his prisoner off the train and strike out by horseback. He turned to his clerk who was sitting on the opposite side of the aisle from him and shrieked at him, "Go to the front of the train and tell the engineer to plow through those people! They'll have no choice but to move if he starts up the train!" When the clerk made no move to get up, the Judge stood up himself and grabbed the smaller man by his lapels and pulled him to his feet. "I said go tell him to move this Goddamned train!" The Judge's face was almost purple with anger, but even though he trembled at each word that fell from the Judge's mouth, the clerk shook his head no.

"I'm not going to do it," the younger man finally squeaked out. "If you want him to do that, you have to tell him yourself. I quit." The Judge released the man as if the very thought of touching him was repugnant. He stumbled away from the Judge and sat with the other passengers at the opposite end of the train, but not before giving Rebecca a small thumbs up sign.

Irate, the Judge turned to Caleb, who was the only person he had left on his side and said, "Keep that gun on her. If she moves, shoot her. I'm going to get this train moving again." Caleb fumbled with the weapon and trained it on the outlaw across from him. The Judge made his way up the aisle and disappeared into the next car.

Knowing that a man with Caleb's limited experience with a gun was as likely to shoot by mistake as on purpose, Rebecca wanted to talk him into lowering the gun. "Pa, you don't have to point the gun at her. She isn't doing anything. She can't hurt you. Please, lower that gun before you hurt someone."

Caleb wanted a drink. He wanted to be doing something... anything... besides sitting here in the middle of nowhere surrounded by Indians with a vicious murderer. The fact that he was the one with the gun was a very small consolation. He needed a drink.

"I'll lower the gun if you'll get me a bottle," he finally managed to say around his parched lips. Rebecca turned to Josie with a question on her face, and the outlaw gave a small nod. It would buy them some time if he were to have a few drinks, not to mention it would slow down his responses and make him less likely to pull the trigger. She hoped. At least it would take the gun away for as long as it took him to finish a bottle and that might be enough.

"Sure. All right, I will, but please lower the gun now. I'll be right back." Caleb lowered the gun, but kept it on his thigh with the muzzle still pointing at Josie's midsection. His finger was no longer on the trigger, however, so Josie relaxed somewhat. Rebecca got to her feet and went to where the small group of passengers was huddled together, fearing there could be gunfire at any moment. "It's going to be all right," she told them softly. "Just stay back here and you'll be fine. Do any of you have a bottle of alcohol you can let me have? I need to distract the man with the gun." One by one they shook their heads no until she looked at the matron who had refused to budge from her seat earlier.

The woman nodded to indicate she did indeed have a bottle. "It's a fine French wine for my son who just got married," she said haughtily. "I would hate to see it wasted on a lout like that." She jerked her head in Caleb's direction with scorn.

"Please. I'll pay you for it. I'll pay twice what you paid for it, but I need that bottle now." The woman looked into Rebecca's desperate face and it reminded her of her own daughter. How could she say no? With a grumble Rebecca could not quite hear, the woman reached into a satchel on the seat beside her and pulled out a green bottle wrapped in shiny paper.

"Oh, thank you, thank you so much." Rebecca gave the woman a brief hug before returning to her seat and handing the bottle to Caleb.

Caleb could not unwrap the bottle and keep his hand on the gun, so he stuck the weapon in the waistband of his pants. When the paper was removed he saw that the bottle cork was flush with the top of the bottle, and he scowled. "How'm I supposed to open this damned thing?" he grumbled. The words were scarcely out of his mouth before the matron was standing beside Rebecca holding out a corkscrew. Wordlessly, she took it from her and handed the tool to Caleb. His hands shook quite a bit as he tried to remove the cork, and in the end it was broken to pieces. He finally pushed the remaining bits into the bottle figuring he could strain them out with his teeth. In fact, he did not much care if he drank the whole damned cork... he just needed a drink. Tipping the bottle to his lips, he took several long swallows until at last his hand seemed to steady itself and he began to feel in control of himself. He sat back in his seat and smiled at Rebecca, and for a moment she was reminded of the father she once had. After only a few moments however, his gaze traveled from Rebecca's face to the front of her dress and he leered. She knew that she would never make the mistake of thinking of him as a father again.

Caleb seemed to retreat into himself a few minutes later, the bottle the only reality he knew. Rebecca leaned toward Josie and was about to tell her about the gun in her bag when the Judge's voice once again filled the train car.

"I told you to keep that gun on her!" he bellowed. Caleb blinked a few times, tipped up the bottle and took another swallow before pulling the gun from his waistband.

"She ain't goin' nowhere," he mumbled. Nevertheless he pointed the gun at her with one hand, while clutching the bottle with the other. His finger was loosely on the trigger but it would not take more than a nudge to send a bullet hurtling into Josie. From that distance there was no way he could miss.

The Judge paced up and down the aisle of the train; his anger building with every moment that passed. The engineer had flatly refused to attempt to move the train with all those people on the tracks. He had tried to talk them into moving and was met with nothing but silence. Turning to the Judge, he simply shrugged as if to say they were there until something changed. And the something that would undoubtedly change would be the afternoon train bearing the Governor's car arriving right on schedule in just a few hours. If he had a deputy he could trust, the Judge might have tried to shoot his way out with the outlaw and take her by stagecoach or horseback. But the drunken sot with the bottle to his lips was less than worthless and he knew they would not get a foot away from the train before those savages separated him from his prisoner. It had become personal for him now. To begin with, she was just another redskin to be taught a lesson, but now she was a thorn in his side, and worse: she might just be allowed to wiggle out of this if he could not come up with something.

The Judge stopped his pacing and walked back to stand over Caleb. "Looks as if that reward is going to slip through your fingers," he said in a sympathetic tone. Caleb dropped the now empty bottle to the floor and turned his bleary gaze to the Judge.

"Huh? Whyizzat? I got her, ain't I?"

"You've got her, but not for long if these savages have anything to do with it." Caleb turned toward the window and scowled at the people there. The muzzle of the gun followed his eyes, and Josie's heart lurched at the thought of him opening fire on the unarmed people outside the window. "They'll never let us take her out of here alive," the Judge continued, drawing Caleb's attention back to him and away from the window. Josie visibly relaxed as the gun was once again lowered to rest on Caleb's thigh. The Judge leaned down closer so that his words would not be audible to the people at the other end of the car. "Kill her. Her dead body is worth nothing to them, but the reward is good, dead or alive. You can say she got loose and tried to take the gun from you. You struggled over it, and it went off."

Caleb blinked again as if trying to digest this suggestion. Josie and Rebecca had only caught a word or two of what the Judge whispered to Caleb, but it was enough to know the man did not intend to let her live to tell her story to the Governor. As Caleb's mind registered what he had to do, he slowly began to raise the gun, stopping when it was pointed squarely at Josie's heart.

"Pa, don't!" Rebecca said loudly to draw his attention away from Josie. In that same instant, Josie scooted down in her seat as far as she could, kicking up and connecting with the hand that held the gun and sending it flying to the far end of the car. Even as that was happening, Rebecca was pulling the gun from her bag and before the Judge had even registered what had happened, Rebecca had the gun trained on him. "You do anything to hurt her in any way and I'll kill you," she said evenly. The tone of her voice left no doubt that she meant exactly what she said.

"Ow," Caleb said, shaking his wrist and rubbing it with his hand. It looked as if he had already forgotten that a moment before he had held a gun ready to take a woman's life. Now he simply wondered why his hand hurt.

"Give me the key to the handcuffs," Rebecca said to Caleb. He looked at her blankly for a moment, and she said again, "The key. In your watch pocket." She took her eyes off the Judge while she was talking to Caleb, but out of the corner of one eye she could see that he was edging down the aisle. As soon as Caleb figured out which of his pockets was the watch pocket and handed the key to Rebecca, she turned back to the Judge. "Stop where you are and sit down. Now!" The click of the hammer pulling back on the gun was like a cannon volley in the quiet car. He dropped into an empty seat and glared at her silently while Rebecca unlocked the handcuffs. Josie's wrists were red and chafed in spots and she rubbed them to bring back the circulation. Rebecca held the gun out to Josie while keeping the barrel pointed at the Judge, but Josie pushed her hand away.

"I can't take that," she said seriously. "I haven't broken any laws here, and I'm not starting now. I think possessing a gun while in custody would not look very good to the Governor. Besides, you're doing fine without me." She grinned at Rebecca who smiled back broadly. Josie looked to the front of the car where the small group of people was finally beginning to relax and said, "Will one of you pick up that gun please and help my friend here keep an eye on him?" She jerked her head in the direction of the Judge. Without hesitation, his former clerk got up from his seat and fished the weapon out from under the seat where it had landed. He walked back up the aisle and sat far enough away so the Judge could not reach him with his foot, and pointed the gun at him.

"You'll never work in another court of law, you pathetic little worm," the Judge said venomously.

"That's certainly true of one of us," the younger man replied calmly. The Judge merely sank back into his seat and glared at each of them in turn, as if unable to believe the tables had been so completely turned. He was already planning how he would contact a friend who was a general in the army and make sure that all these savages paid for what they had done to assist in Josie's release.

Josie turned to the window and held up her free hands with the hand-cuffs clutched in her fingers to show the crowd that she was no longer a captive. The cheer that rose from the people made tears spring to her eyes, and she quickly turned away.

"Listen," Rebecca said excitedly. "Did you hear that?" It was now late afternoon and she was beginning to wonder if the Governor's train would indeed be arriving.

"No, what did you...." the far off wail of the train whistle cut her off, and she grinned as she took Rebecca's hand in hers. Now the only thing to worry about was whether he was able to connect with that train, but that concern would be resolved one way or another very soon.

Even before the train itself was visible, Josie could see the Cherokees begin to shift to the back of the train so that if the incoming train did not stop in town, it would be forced to slow down.

There was no need for that precaution; with a final blast of the steam horn, the incoming train came to a stop at the platform.

Genie craned her neck to see if her husband's car was hooked up in the back, and when she saw the crest of the Governor's office on the side, she let out a very unladylike whoop and began to run to his car. The sheriff had told her the train with Josie aboard had been stopped a couple miles out of town and that it would be held there until the Governor arrived. She prayed the Judge had not taken matters into his own hands, having figured out that he could no longer hope to succeed in getting Josie extradited.

The Governor's footman opened the door of his car and extended the step so the Governor could step down. When he did, he was nearly bowled over by Genie as she launched herself into his arms.

"William, thank God you're here! He took her already. But the Cherokees have stopped the train and they're waiting for you to come. You have to hurry..."

"Wait a minute, slow down. Let me get my land legs under me." His tone was light, but as he looked at her he realized how very worried she was. "Where is she? How do I get there?"

"I'll take you to her," John stepped forward and extended his hand, which the Governor grasped. "I'm John Kenwood, sheriff of Tahlequah."

"Rebecca spoke highly of you," William said, acknowledging that he knew the sheriff was an ally of Josie's.

"I'm afraid the train she's on was stopped a few miles down the track by some of her supporters who believed – as I do – that it was not right to extradite her without a fair hearing. Judge Fellowes was anything but fair;

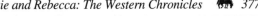

he refused to listen to her witnesses, and he made sure to get her out of here before you could get here."

"Well, let's go hear her side of things, shall we?"

"I have a horse saddled and ready to go. Your wife and some of Josie's friends will follow in wagons, if that's all right with you. I think they want to see for themselves that Miss Josie is all right."

"I have very little luck in keeping my wife from doing exactly what she wants to do, Sheriff. If she's determined to go, I sure don't want to try and stop her. Let's go." Indeed, Genie and the rest of Josie's friends were already piling into two wagons that were tied up outside the station house.

"What in the world?" The Governor's mouth dropped open at the sight of so many people surrounding the stilled train. The sea began to part as he and the sheriff rode up, making a path that led to the car that housed the outlaw and her lover.

"She has a lot of supporters," the sheriff said, as if that explained how so many people had known to be on the tracks at the time the train was due to leave.

"I see," the Governor said, leveling his gaze not at the assembled multitude but at John. The sheriff shrugged; he counted himself among her staunchest supporters, and he did not care if the Governor knew it. The two men dismounted and hands materialized out of the crowd to take the reins of their horses. When they reached the door of the car, a man stepped out of the crowd with a wooden box, which he placed in front of the door for a step. He climbed up on the box and wrenched the door open, then jumped down and stood aside for the Governor to enter. The people were eerily quiet; even the children stood silently watching as he mounted the step and entered the car.

The occupants of the car were aware that something was happening even before the door opened. The Judge had made a move to rise from his seat, but his former clerk pulled back the hammer on the gun that was pointed unswervingly at his head, and he fell back into his seat without a word. Rebecca had put Josie's gun back in her bag. There was no need to keep Caleb covered; he had passed out shortly after finishing the bottle of wine. The clerk had the Judge well in hand.

Rebecca turned when the door was flung open, and when she saw William step into the car, followed by John, she was on her feet and moving toward them. She threw her arms around William's neck and kissed his cheek. "Am I ever glad to see you," she enthused. Then she stepped to where John stood and hugged and kissed him as well. The blush that suffused his cheeks was clear to anyone who looked. "John... I don't even know what to say. She owes her life to you. How can we ever repay you?"

"Just... live a long and happy life. That's all I want."

"Thank you. We will."

The conductor tapped John on the shoulder, and the sheriff turned to see a very angry looking man.

"You the one responsible for keeping my train here?"

"Yes."

"Then I'll thank you to take your business elsewhere and let us get underway."

"Yes, of course. I'm sorry. Give me a few minutes to get the people off the tracks and we'll let you go on your way." John stepped outside to talk to the Cherokee, and before he even returned the tracks were free of people. The sound of the steam engine firing up brought a cheer from the passengers who had been sitting for the better part of the day. But Josie knew they would all have a story to tell about Josie Hunter and the Cherokees who stopped the train. It was probably the most excitement many of them had seen in their lives.

Rebecca led the Governor to where Josie still sat, and she introduced them. "Funny. You don't look like a cold-blooded killer," he said lightly as he shook her hand.

Josie laughed. "And you don't look much like a Greek God, but you must be because that's what Genie said she married." William threw back his head and laughed.

"You should hear what she said about you," he quipped.

"Will you please get these people off my train!" the conductor snapped at John, who in turn tapped the Governor on the shoulder.

"We need to get off the train, sir. I'll take Miss Josie's bag if you will get Miss Rebecca's."

"All right. There's just one thing I have to do first." He walked to where the Judge sat glowering and fuming. John had filled him in completely on the way to the train, and there was no doubt in his mind that this man had completely lost his objectivity – if indeed he had ever had any – and had no business sitting in judgment of his fellow man. "Mr. Fellowes, you are disbarred. Your license to practice law in the Territory of Oklahoma is revoked, and I suggest that if you hope to continue in the legal field at all that you do so as far away from here as you can get. I plan to make sure our neighboring states get an earful about you. Is that perfectly clear?"

The Judge said nothing; he knew he was hopelessly outnumbered. The Governor turned back to Josie and offered her his arm. "Miss Hunter, I believe we need to vacate these premises before Attila the Hun over there tosses us out on our ears." The conductor scowled as Josie stood and took William's arm.

"That's the best invitation I've had all day," she quipped. William collected Rebecca's bag and the three of them made their way from the train. John paused to get the gun from the clerk and was on his way back when Rebecca poked her head in the door.

"Can you arrest Caleb for something and bring him with you, John? I need time to contact my sister and get her out of that house before he gets back there."

"Well, he's drunk in a public place. I suppose I can hold him for a day or so on that." He pushed Caleb forward in his seat and put his arms under the sleeping man's arms and around his chest. With a heave he pulled him up and dragged him to the door. Caleb never stirred even as he was handed out to several of the Cherokee who were still milling around beside the train. John grabbed Josie's bag from the rack and jumped out of the car just as the whistle blew and the wheels began to move.

The parlor in the boarding house was completely packed with friends and wellwishers who came out to say good-bye to Josie and Rebecca. It had taken no time at all for the Governor to decide against extradition for Josie, and the celebration had begun shortly after the decision was announced. Rebecca sent a telegram to Katie telling her to come to Oklahoma where Genie had said she could stay indefinitely until Josie and Rebecca settled out west, at which time Katie would join them.

Charles and Horace were playing song after song, and everyone was either singing along or dancing. Josie and Rebecca were both constantly being whisked away to dance with someone besides each other, but knowing that this may be the last time they would see these friends, they whirled and danced with everyone who asked. No one seemed to notice that most of the dancers were women, or if they noticed, they did not care.

Josie turned to a tap on the shoulder to find Genie standing behind her, her hands outstretched. "I think it's about my turn," Genie said with a smile. Josie nodded and pulled the smaller woman into her arms. They were playing a slow tune, and Genie's head naturally rested on Josie's shoulder, her body moving in perfect rhythm with the tall gunslinger. Josie felt a soft inhalation and a sigh before Genie pulled herself a bit farther away so she could look into the blue pools that were Josie's eyes. "Sometimes," Genie said softly, "I wish we had… taken that next step in our relationship. I knew you wanted to. I could tell by the way you looked at me. I wanted it too, but I was afraid. Can you forgive me for being such a coward?"

"There's nothing to forgive. I knew you loved me, too. I always thought that if we had not been so tragically separated we would have become lovers. But that's so long ago now. You have William and I have Rebecca, and we're both happy. But you'll always be the first woman that I loved, and the place you own in my heart no one can ever share." As the music ended, she kissed Genie on the forehead before allowing herself to be turned by yet another hand on her shoulder. This one belonged to Rebecca.

"I heard that," the little blonde said softly. "And I know there is a part of you that will always belong to her." Josie opened her mouth to speak, but Rebecca touched her lips with her fingers to silence her. "No, it's all right. I accept it. I could never ask you to let go of something so precious to you. All I ask is that you remember who loves you now, and tell me if there is ever anything I should be worried about. Promise me?"

"You have nothing to worry about…."

"Promise?"

"I promise." The soft notes of "Beautiful Dreamer" began to play, and Josie held out her hand to Rebecca. "May I have this dance?"

"Yes. And all the dances of my life." She stepped into her arms and they whirled into their future.

THE END

JUSTICE HOUSE PUBLISHING
PROUDLY PRESENTS

A preview of...

GUN SHY

LORI L. LAKE

The gold and white squad car swung around the corner onto Como Boulevard, no headlights and little sound but tires squeaking on hot pavement. To the left, in the heart of the city of St. Paul, was Como Lake, a small body of water only half a mile in diameter. The street ran parallel to a walking and biking path that ringed the lake. To the right sat a row of darkened homes up on a slight slope, which were heavily shaded by huge elm and oak trees.

The police car paused four houses away from a white, two-story stucco house. Officer Desiree "Dez" Reilly turned off the air conditioning and powered her window halfway down, staring intently at the stucco house. With a weary sigh, she let herself listen for the nighttime noises over the engine of the car. The neighborhood was silent, almost too quiet. She should hear crickets, but all was still. She cut the engine, picked up her flashlight, and stepped out of the car, shutting the door so it clicked quietly. As she strolled along the sidewalk, the hum of nighttime insects started up, and she stood in front of the stucco house, waiting, listening. Somewhere down the street came a faint bass thump of music as a car passed through the intersection and faded off into the distance. Otherwise, no one was out.

Her eyes scanned the street and the houses with practiced speed. Nothing seemed out of place, but someone had reported the sound of a woman screaming and had pinpointed the noise as coming from the house in front of her. A string of residential break-ins had occurred over the last two months, all centered in this area. Even more disturbing was that, in three of the seven cases, a woman had been raped. Cops at roll call were beginning to toss around the words "serial rapist". It was enough to make Dez take notice, living as she did within a mile of the lake."

Outside the air-conditioned car, the August humidity seeped into her pores through the short-sleeved blue uniform shirt, through the bullet-proof vest, and through the white cotton t-shirt she wore, adding to her fatigue more than she thought possible. She took a deep breath of the dank air and felt herself sweating. August in St. Paul was no fun, but at least the mosquitoes weren't after her. Yet.

She was tall, lean-hipped, and broad-shouldered with long black hair caught up in a French braid. She walked with a confident stride across a strip of grass, over the sidewalk, and up the cracked walkway to the house, pausing periodically to listen. There were six stairs to the porch, and the first floor windowsills were slightly above her eye level. The front windows were dark, but a shaft of golden light shone from an open second floor window around the corner of the house. Leaving her flashlight off, she strode around to the south side and paused for a moment. Now she could hear angry muttering, the sound of an urgent, high-pitched voice, and then a frantic scream quickly muffled.

Dez heard a ripping sound, and then deep-throated laughter. A male voice growled, "Stop it! Stop fighting or…"

"No, you stop it. Get out of here!" shouted a woman's voice.

"Oh, shit!" said the man. "You move, I cut her throat. Got it?" In a different tone, he hollered, "Get her!"

That was all Dez needed to hear. She touched her shoulder mike and called for backup as she ran toward the back of the house and around to the other side, visually checking the doors and windows until she found what she suspected: a sliced window screen leading into what she thought would be the dining room.

Hearing another scream, she flicked on her shoulder mike again and advised the dispatcher to hurry the backup team. In a hoarse whisper she reported, "This sounds bad. I think there are at least two male suspects and one, maybe two, female victims." In the background she heard faroff sirens, and as her skin crawled, she felt an uncharacteristic compulsion to do something and do it now. A loud crash startled her, and she hit the shoulder mike again. "I'm going in. Tell 'em to follow quick as possible—north side window."

Hooking her flashlight on her belt, she hoisted herself up over the windowsill headfirst and tumbled into the darkened house as quietly as she could. Scuttling across the floor on her hands and knees, she moved toward the faint light of the doorway and peeked around the corner. *Stairs, where are the stairs?* She rose and silently inched around the corner out of the dining room. She grabbed the flashlight off her belt, feeling the metal warm against her palm, then clicked it on and unholstered her gun.

Jaylynn Savage realized she was tired when her watch chimed eleven. She had spent the entire evening in the air-conditioned college library cramming for her summer term finals, and visions of Constitutional Law danced in her head. She persisted for another ten minutes, then gave up when her vision kept blurring. Running hands through short white-blonde hair, she hoped the political theory exam would go well in the morning, but she just couldn't study one more minute. Going over and over the material was no longer productive. Since the library closed at midnight anyway, Jaylynn decided to head home. She packed up her books, said hello to friends on the way out, and exited into the humid summer air.

Jaylynn liked to say she was five-and-a-half feet tall, but that was only if she was wearing shoes with an inch heel. A slender build, lightly tanned skin, and sun-bleached blonde hair were evidence of time spent outdoors. Her face, framing warm hazel eyes, was full of youthful innocence and of something else perhaps best described as contentment.

As she strolled away from the library, her legs felt strong, but fatigued, from the five mile run she'd taken earlier in the day. She walked slowly from the library to the bus stop, going over first amendment issues. *That's one area of the exam that I'll ace. I know that cold.* She thought about how glad she would be to finish this final class. Perhaps she'd have time to write poetry again.

The bus deposited her half a block from the rented house she shared with two friends. Cutting up the alley, she let herself in through the kitchen door. Jaylynn loved the old house she and Tim and Sara lived in. Not only was it situated right across the street from Como Lake, but it was also enormous. Every room was spacious with tall ceilings, ornate woodwork, and walk-in closets. She shut and locked the door quietly so as not to awaken Sara. Her other roommate, Tim, wasn't home yet. She could tell because his beat-up red Corolla wasn't parked out back. She tossed her keys on the table and crept up the stairs.

Sara must still be up, she thought as she turned the corner on the landing. The lamp in her roommate's room cast a faint patch of light that slightly illuminated the top stairs. She thought of her friend sitting on the couch, studying in the spacious master bedroom and she smiled, but then an acrid smell, like body odor, assaulted her senses causing Jaylynn to squinch her face up and frown. When she heard a thud and a ripping noise, she paused on the stairwell, heart beating fast for reasons she didn't understand. She eased up the last two stairs and peered silently around the doorway into her friend's room.

Sara lay twisting on the floor in the wide space between the twin beds, her hands taped together. A huge figure in a dark gray sweatshirt and black pants straddled her waist, muttering and threatening. He held a knife in one hand and a silver strip in the other. Sara screamed as he tried to put the duct tape over her mouth. She shook her head furiously, whipping around her long brown hair and causing it to stick to the tape. Her assailant slapped the side of her face and she screamed again and struggled, tears running down her cheeks, as he forced the strip of tape over her mouth.

He said, "Stop it! Stop fighting or I'll…"

Without a thought, Jaylynn pushed into the room. "No, you stop it. Get out of here!"

"Oh, shit!" He rolled aside and spun around, grabbing the girl on the ground by the neck. "You move; I cut her throat. Got it?"

He wore a tan nylon stocking over his head, obscuring his face and making his features looked distorted and diabolical. He glanced towards the shadowy area behind the door and said, "Get her!"

Jaylynn turned to see a smaller man, dressed like the first and also wearing a nylon mask. She screamed, a loud, throaty bellow. He was no taller than she, but was much stockier and held a wooden bat in one hand. As she screamed again and backed toward the door, the smaller man grabbed her by the shoulder and arm. He dragged her onto the twin bed near the door and shoved her so hard that she bounced when she hit the mattress. She saw the baseball bat coming at her face and rolled to the side to avoid it. It hit the wall with a resounding crash. As he dove toward her, Jaylynn got her feet up, knees to her chest, and kicked him in the torso, sending him sprawling against the opposite wall and to the floor. Before she could roll off the bed, he was up. He dove on her again, the bat in one hand and a hank of her hair in the other.

Jaylynn shrieked and growled, kicking at him and swinging wildly, some of her blows connecting solidly. He stumbled back from the bed, panting. Getting a better grip on the bat, he advanced on her again. "I'll kill you, bitch!"

Footsteps pounded on the stairs, then a husky voice shouted, "Police!" A flashlight beam shone down the hall. Jaylynn's attacker turned toward the doorway and she saw him swing the bat. It struck an arm coming low through the doorway and she heard a clatter. Jaylynn rolled off the bed. She yelped when her knees hit the floor and then she looked up to see a blue-clad figure dive into the room and roll. Instantly the cop was back up.

Dez winced when she saw the bat descending, but it was too late to pull back. She felt an explosion of pain when the bat connected, and her hand involuntarily turned and opened. Her Glock flew from her grasp and skittered behind her. She knew she didn't have time to find it in the hallway and instead burst into the room shouting in rage.

The beefy man with the knife let go of Sara and pulled himself to his feet. His partner, wielding the bat, rushed Dez, only to be met by her right elbow slamming a solid blow to his face. He dropped the bat and staggered back, cradling his face. Jaylynn took the opportunity to kick him behind the knee and he screamed in pain and fell. She looked for Sara, caught her eye, and saw her friend's look of terror. Jaylynn gestured, pointing toward the closet, but when Sara tried to rise, the big man shoved her, knocking he back to the floor. The bound woman made a high-pitched noise as she squirmed away and slid halfway under one of the twin beds on the far side of the large room.

The man with the knife came at Dez in a rush, but out of control. She got the flashlight up to block the downward lunge of the blade, then kicked at his groin with her steel-toed service boot. Enraged, he yowled but kept on coming, managing to slice downward through her shirt to imbed the knife in her vest. She knocked aside his knife arm and gave him a right elbow to the chin, sending him off balance, then punched him in the side of the head with the flashlight. As he went down, the other man regained his footing and picked up the bat. He swung high and Dez ducked to a squat, then launched herself to head-butt him across the room. He hit the bedside table and smashed the lamp to the ground. Sara squeezed further under the bed to avoid being landed on.

Dez extricated herself from the little man's grip as Jaylynn sprang across the room and wrenched the bat from his hand. She whacked at his head. Though he raised his arms in defense, the blonde woman nailed him solidly on the collarbone, feeling a surge of adrenaline when he roared in pain. She stepped back, tripping over the big man's leg as he rose, cradling his bleeding head. Scrambling on all fours, Jaylynn crawled across the carpet, up and over the twin bed near the door, and dove into the hall. *I've got to find the gun. Find the gun. Find the gun.* It repeated like a chant in her head. She spotted it on the landing three stairs below and picked it up, surprised to find it much lighter than she expected. She realized she didn't know how it worked. Was there a safety?

As Jaylynn came back through the doorway, she saw the woman in blue whirl, graceful and deadly in the same motion. Every time an attacker came at her, she used quick left jabs and kicks to flatten one, then the other. The larger man wailed in a high-pitched voice and tried to get up. The cop nailed him in the side of the head with a vicious roundhouse, then kicked him in the chest.

"Stay down," she shouted. The smaller man lay on his side, heaving with exertion. The officer handcuffed his wrist to the bigger man's ankle, then jumped clear of them and, with her left hand, dragged Sara out from under the bed and toward the closet across the room.

Jaylynn stood in the doorway holding the bat and the black gun. "Here," she said, offering the weapon to the police officer. She kept the bat for herself.

The tall, dark woman turned, her face white despite the exertion. She seemed enormous to Jaylynn—not fat, just solid and very powerful. Later, Jaylynn would remember the feral smile of satisfaction on the cop's face and consider that she might be a very dangerous woman. But at that moment, as she looked into steel blue eyes for a heartbeat, she felt as though she knew her. A thrill of recognition coursed through the blonde. The blue eyes narrowed as they met her own, and for a brief moment, Jaylynn wondered if the woman recognized her. But of course she couldn't know her. The cop hurried across the room and snatched the gun from Jaylynn.

Sara whimpered, and Jaylynn moved further into the room. "Sara! Sara, are you all right?"

"Wait," said Dez. She held the Glock in her left hand and stood over the two panting men. "Don't move. I'd be so *very* happy to shoot your fuckin' heads off if you move a single muscle." Dez could hear the sirens coming, their whining becoming more insistent as her backup drew nearer. She glanced at Sara and made a quick motion with her head toward Jaylynn. "Get her outta here," she growled. "Now! Into the hall. And be sure to stay clear of these two jokers. Wouldn't wanna have to blow their brains out, now would we?"

Jaylynn wanted to tell her it was perfectly all right with her if the cop emptied her gun into their sorry carcasses. Instead, she leapt to Sara's side and helped her to her feet. She pulled her out into the hall where her friend sank to the floor sobbing. Jaylynn slowly pulled the duct tape off her mouth. She was still trying to loosen the twisted tape from Sara's hands when the backup officers burst into the house.

The house was surrounded with spotlights and curious onlookers. Police ran in and out of the stucco home as a tremendous commotion, both inside and outside, engulfed the neighborhood with noise and light. After a few tense moments, Dez relinquished her guard role and let the backup cops take charge. Once the suspects were properly cuffed, she stepped over and pulled the nylon masks off their heads. Two white males, in their early twenties, neither very handsome—especially in light of the damage she was glad she'd inflicted. The bigger man was bruised and bleeding from three gashes in his brows. His ear bled a trail down his neck. The slimmer man bled profusely from a cut below his left eye. At the moment, they were both sullen and angry as they sat on the floor muttering and cursing her. The backup cops read the two men their rights before dragging them out of the room and down the stairs.

Dez's right arm throbbed painfully as she eased down the steps, passing the emergency medical team coming up the stairs for the injured young woman. A stream of cops crowded through the front door to take a look at the two suspects, both of whom Dez suspected were responsible for the neighborhood's recent rapes.

The living room, now flooded with light and activity, was furnished with overstuffed chairs, a fluffy sofa, an upright piano, and a futon couch. Four oak bookcases full of neatly ordered books stood along one wall. Movie posters covered most of the other walls: a black-clad Schwartzenegger from *The Terminator*, Jackie Chan in a flying kick, Geena Davis pointing a gun, and Stallone hanging from a cliff. The dark-haired cop walked through the room, past a Bruce Willis *Die Hard* poster, and out the front door. As she stepped wearily down the front stairs, a thin man dressed in khaki slacks and a tan t-shirt ran up the walkway.

"Where's Jay and Sara?" he asked her breathlessly, running his hand through his red hair.

"Inside." Two paramedics maneuvering a stretcher came up the walk towards her, and she navigated the last two stairs and stepped over onto the grass, gesturing to the young man to do the same. "Who are you, sir?"

"Tim Donovan—I live here." He started to push past, looking back at her, his face pale and stricken. . "Are they...uh...okay?" he asked.

"Yup, I think so." Dez continued down the walk, suddenly feeling a bit sick to her stomach. As she moved along, she tried to flex her forearm, but it hurt too much. She looked at her watch: 11:58. In two minutes her shift would be over. Good timing. She headed over to the ambulance to have her arm looked at.

Tim took the stairs two at a time and blasted into the house just in time to nearly mow over the EMTs and his two roommates.

"Sara! Jay! What happened?"

"Oh, Tim!" Sara cried as she fell into his arms weeping.

"Excuse me, sir," said the EMT as he gently grasped Tim's shoulder. "Please...we need to transport her." The medic turned back to Sara. "Come along, Miss. Let's take you in for a little look-see and make sure you're okay." He helped Sara onto the stretcher and covered her with a blanket.

"I'll go with her," said Jaylynn.

"Only room for one, ma'am," said the EMT. He strapped Sara down and nodded toward his fellow medic, and they moved the stretcher toward the stairs.

Jaylynn turned to Tim. "One of us needs to go with her, but we need to close up the house, too." She pointed at the open window at the top of the stairs.

"Here, Jay," said Tim. He shot a hasty look toward the stairs as the EMTs rounded the corner and disappeared. Digging in his pocket he pulled out his car keys. "Take these. You drive over, and I'll go with Sara now." He turned and took the stairs down two at a time.

"Wait, which hospital?" Jaylynn called after his departing back. He paused, looking back at her impatiently as she said, "How do I know where to go?"

A patrolman standing behind her in the hall touched her arm. "I'm Officer Milton. I've got a lot of questions for the report. Why don't you follow me over to the hospital?"

"There you go," said Tim. "I'll see you over there." He disappeared down the stairs.

"I have to lock up the house," said Jaylynn.

"Good idea," said Officer Milton. "I'll help you with the windows."

Jaylynn collected her things and locked all the doors.   As Officer Milton escorted her through the yard, a white van pulled up and two men piled out of the vehicle. One shone a bright light in her face while the other man held a microphone and shouted questions at her.

The reporters did double-steps on the lawn next to Jaylynn and the officer as he tried to hurry them down the walk. "Can you tell us what happened?" asked one reporter in a breathless voice.

Jaylynn said, "I came home to find two men in our house attacking my roommate. They tried to get me too, but before they could, a cop..." She stopped and looked around the yard, letting her eyes come to rest on the various police cruisers. "It was a woman cop. I don't know who she is, but she nailed both of them even without her gun. It was incredible, a sight to behold!" She looked up at Milton. "Who was she, Officer? Where'd she go?"

"Reilly," Milton muttered.

"Who?" said Jaylynn, but the reporters had already heard.

"Reilly? Desiree Reilly?" one of the men repeated excitedly. "Reilly was the officer? Oh, this is going to be a *great* story! What else can you tell us?"

"That's it, folks," said Milton as he pushed past them. "You know the channels to go through." He took hold of Jaylynn's elbow and rushed her down the walk. Wordlessly, he helped her into Tim's Toyota, then got in his cruiser and slammed the door. He turned on his lights, but not his siren, and pulled around the other police cars parked haphazardly along the street, slowing to wait for Jaylynn to catch up with him. Jaylynn looked back at the scene. Neighbors stood in tight little bunches watching from the front stoops of their houses. She waved as she passed the couple on the corner and they hesitantly waved back, not quite sure who she was.

Dez's forearm swelled so quickly that, before she even arrived at the hospital, the paramedic had to immobilize the forearm with an inflatable splint. "It's likely broken, you know," he said.

"That's what I'm afraid of."

At the emergency room they led her through the crowded waiting area and toward an examining room. She didn't want to look around, but she couldn't help herself. The last time she had been here was for Ryan...even now her eyes filled with bitter tears, and she bit her lip to try control her thoughts. She hated this place, didn't want to be here. She considered turning around to leave, but before she could, the nurse on duty was at her heels ushering her into the ER and onto a table. The nurse helped her unbutton and remove the bloodied and tattered blue shirt, and Dez pulled at the Velcro on the bullet-proof vest. The nurse picked up a pair of trauma shears.

Dez said, "Hey, no! These things are expensive."

"Do you keep them if they're sliced open like that?" The nurse pointed to the big cop's left breast. Dez looked down, surprised to see an 8-inch gash.

"It's easier to cut it away. Otherwise I might hurt you," the nurse said, a question in her voice.

Dez shrugged her shoulders. "Don't worry."

The nurse put down the shears and ripped away at the Velcro straps on the vest as Dez looked around.

The emergency room wasn't all that big, with six bays, three on either side of an aisle that ran up the middle of the area. Her overall impression of the room was that it was filled with a lot of pipes and tubes and contraptions, and the dominant colors were white or dull silver. She thought it smelled like some sort of cleaning fluid. Dez sat on the exam table closest to the door. In the back corner, furthest from the door, an elderly woman lay hooked up to oxygen and strands of other tubes. With eyes closed, her hands fluttered across the chest of her pink robe as a technician fussed over her. *Heart attack*, thought Dez. *That's what that looks like.*

The nurse managed to get the vest loosened and off. She pulled at Dez's t-shirt.

"It's just my arm. No need to strip naked is there?"

"I need to be sure you're not hurt anywhere else." The nurse pulled the curtain around the bay.

Dez frowned. It occurred to her that if she hadn't realized her vest was shredded, then the nurse probably thought she might not know about other injuries. "Here, check me over." Dez lifted her shirt with her left arm and the nurse ran her hand across her back, down her abdomen. "I think I'm fine. Really. I'd tell you if I was hurt anywhere else."

The nurse nodded as she helped pull the t-shirt back down. "Can't help it, Officer. They'd have my head if I missed anything." She leaned down and untied Dez's black oxfords and slipped them off. "Step out of the slacks, too. Stand up...here, I'll help you." She laid the blue pants over the exam table and checked the big cop over, then handed her a nearly translucent sheet to put over her bare legs. "Just sit back up there." Once she was situated, the nurse got out a blood pressure cuff and strapped it on Dez's arm, checked her pulse and heartbeat, and shone a light in her eyes. The big cop bore the exam patiently.

"Okay, you're doing fine," she said as she removed the cuff. "Let's go ahead and get you dressed again, and I'll have the doctor come in as soon as possible." They worked together to get her redressed as Dez cautiously held her right arm.

The nurse whipped open the curtain around the area and tried to catch the attending physician's eye. When that failed, she sighed and her brown eyes looked tired.

Dez said, "Been a long shift, huh?"

"Yes, and I've only been here four hours. It's been quite a night. As soon as he checks you over, we'll get you across the hall to radiology."

From outside the tiny box of a room where the x-ray machine was kept, Dez sat on a bench and observed the arrival of the victims of the evening's melee. Paramedics rolled a weeping Sara into the E.R., followed closely by the red-haired man who stutter-stepped alongside the gurney in order to hold the hand of the young woman. Moments later, Jaylynn came running in, Officer Milton at her heels. Not long after that, a middle-aged woman appeared in the doorway and was ushered over to the partly curtained area.

When the x-rays were done, the nurse gave Dez an ice pack for her forearm, and she was led back into the emergency room where she eased herself back up on the exam table.

"Hey, Milton," Dez called out at her fellow officer as he finished talking to the young woman on the gurney and flipped his notebook closed.

He looked up and nodded, then strode toward her and smiled. "Reilly. You're hurt, huh?"

"Arm. Guy hit me here." She lifted the ice bag and gestured toward the middle of her forearm. "Think it's busted—maybe I'll get lucky and it'll just be a bad bruise, but I have a hunch it's broken."

"Tough luck, but hey...you did good tonight."

"Yeah, I'm glad for them."

Their backs were to Dez, but she could see the red-haired man with his arm around the feisty blonde. Dez's face took on a puzzled look as she stared at the young woman. *Where have I seen her before?* She surveyed the lean legs and khaki shorts, the hot pink tank top and the well-rounded hips and shoulders. Short white-blonde hair topped a long, regal neck. Dez wished the woman would turn around so she could study her more closely.

She couldn't see the girl who had been attacked, though she could see an older woman she assumed to be the young woman's mother leaning over her. Dez could hear a soft murmur of reassuring words being spoken to the girl. The doctor and another nurse swept past Milton and headed for the bay where the brown-haired girl lay. The nurse stopped for a brief moment and waved the two onlookers away. It was clear that the blonde tried to protest, but the doctor reached up and pulled a curtain around the bay to shut them out. They stepped back and Milton called out, "C'mon, people. Let her mom handle this for a bit. They'll take good care of her. Come out and wait with me."

Jaylynn and Tim looked disappointed, but they headed toward the door, both focusing on Milton. The blonde glanced briefly at Dez and did a doubletake. "You! It's you!" She stopped in front of Dez, close enough to put her hand on the big cop's knee. "What happened to you?" Behind her the red-haired man stepped up to peer over his friend's shoulder.

Dez shrugged as she felt herself start to blush. She lifted the ice bag again to display her swollen arm, which was also beginning to show the pale outline of a wide bruise.

Puzzled, Jaylynn said, "How did you...how did that happen?"

"Little guy hit me with the bat when I first came in the room."

"But—but, how did you do that—stop them, I mean—with your arm like that?"

Dez shrugged again and knew her face was fully crimson.

Jaylynn said, "Well, that was totally exhilarating! It was amazing to see! You were incredible."

Dez mumbled, "Not really...actually, you did half of it. If you hadn't kicked them a few times, I would've been in worse trouble."

Dez's nurse returned just then. "All right, all right," she said. "Enough with the visiting. I've got work to do. Out. Out into the waiting area." She shooed them out, waving at Milton too.

Dez put her hand on Milton's sleeve to hold him back. "Before you go, what are their names?"

"Don't know the young man yet, but I'm gonna question them now," he said. He flipped open his memo book and thumbed down a few pages. "Her name's Jaylynn Savage, and that one over there," he nodded toward the bay in the corner, "she's Sara Wright."

"Thanks," she said, and then the nurse demanded her attention to tell her the doctor would be in shortly to set her arm and have it casted. *It's broken,* Dez thought. *That's just great. Three or four weeks of desk duty. Just what I need. Shit.*

Jaylynn and Tim settled into the waiting room among a conglomeration of sickly and unhappy people either waiting to be seen or waiting for some loved one.

"She didn't look so good, did she, Tim?" said Jaylynn.

He fidgeted and said, more sharply than he meant, "Well, she just survived a beating and a near rape. What do you expect?"

"No, I don't mean Sara...the cop. I meant the cop."

"Oh yeah, her too." He reached into his back pocket and pulled out a comb to nervously style his hair.

Jaylynn winced, remembering the dark-haired cop's battered arm. *And to think I didn't even notice what happened! How could I have been so blind? I remember him hitting her with the bat...but now that I think about it, of course she wouldn't escape unscathed. In bat versus arm, the bat always wins.*

Tim put his comb back in his pocket. "I don't know what would have happened if I had come home and found you both being raped. Oh god!" Shaking, he took a deep breath and put his head between his knees, messing up his hair.

Jaylynn draped her arm across his back and leaned down to speak in his ear. "That didn't happen, so don't even think about it. It's all right, Tim."

He sat back up and shivered. "Keep reminding me, okay?" He got his comb back out and repeated the styling, his hands shaking.

It took almost an hour before they learned the hospital would keep Sara overnight for observation. Until then, they sat in the waiting room watching wounded people being hauled in and scores of cops coming and going through the ER entrance. Jaylynn wondered if every cop in St. Paul had stopped by the hospital to check on Officer Reilly.

She turned the events of the night over and over in her head. What if she hadn't come home when she did? What if Sara had been killed? She shuddered. What if *both* of them had been killed? What if the cop hadn't shown up when she did? Too many "what-ifs." Jaylynn looked over at Tim. His head was tipped back against the wall and he was asleep, his hand in hers. Just then the glass door leading to the exam rooms opened and the woman cop emerged, followed by a nurse. She carried her blue uniform shirt and a gray vest in her good hand. In the thin tank t-shirt, her broad shoulders were nearly as white as the cast that covered her right arm from knuckles to elbow. She and the nurse went to the main desk and spoke briefly with the clerk who handed her a white prescription bag. Jaylynn watched her as the dark-haired woman tried to sign something with her right hand, then gave up and switched to her left hand, which she held awkwardly above the paper on the high counter.

Two patrol officers rose from the uncomfortable waiting room chairs on the other side of the room and strolled toward the woman cop. The male officer was young, his bleached white hair in a buzz cut, and he wore golden wire-rimmed glasses. He swaggered over, his bow-legged stride confident and sure. Taking shorter paces next to him was a smaller, wide-shouldered Latino woman. Her short-cropped hair was jet-black and she was probably in her late thirties. The male cop came up behind the wounded woman and gave her a mock blow to the lower back, and she turned. A slow smile crossed her face and she smacked him in the stomach with the back of her good hand as the shorter black-haired woman slid her arm around Reilly's waist. She said something in the injured woman's ear, which must have been serious because the dark-haired cop looked down at her cast and nodded grimly.

That Reilly sure is tall, thought Jaylynn. She towered a good foot over the nurse and was maybe six inches taller than the other woman cop. Without the bulk of the vest she looked slimmer than she had during the fight. Jaylynn admired her lean hips and very wide shoulders. From behind she was as broad-shouldered as a man, except that, with her brunette hair French-braided so beautifully, it wasn't likely she'd be mistaken for one. The big officer slung his arm across her shoulders, and as the three moved to leave, Jaylynn could see how tired the injured cop looked.

"Hey," said Jaylynn over the low din in the room. She almost didn't expect to be heard, but Dez looked at her and gave her a quick nod.

"Wait a minute," Jaylynn heard her say to the two cops, then she strolled toward Jaylynn and the sleeping man. The blonde stared at the dark woman's angular, high cheekboned face and was captivated again by the bluest, steeliest eyes she'd ever seen, eyes that bored right through her. Her heart beat faster and she choked in a short intake of breath, tilting her head slightly to the side to try to take in the strange, almost disturbing glimpse of something familiar yet forgotten. Jaylynn extricated herself from Tim and rose to face the woman in blue. She reached out for Dez's left hand saying, "Thanks for what you did," and squeezed the bigger woman's hand, then reluctantly let go.

"No problem. It's my job."

Jaylynn smiled and gazed up into tired but warm blue eyes. "I hardly think getting your arm broken is in the job description."

Dez shook her head. "Not usually." She took a deep breath and turned to go. "Good luck to your friend in there, Ms. Savage. She's going to need a lot of support."

"We'll take care of her," said Jaylynn. "Thanks again."

"Yup. See ya around." Dez turned and made her way out the door as Jaylynn peered after her thoughtfully. *Nice looking woman.*

Jaylynn and Tim finally got home after two in the morning. The house was a little spooky to her, but she was so tired that she fell into bed, taking only enough time to set her clock for her nine a.m. final. If her professor asked any questions about arrests or searches and seizure, she was sure she'd have some good examples from tonight.

Dez stirred awake the next morning to the thump-thump sound of her downstairs neighbor, Luella Williams, beating a broom handle on the ceiling. She looked at her bedside clock: 6:40 a.m. She didn't think three hours of sleep was going to cut it but her landlady had given the signal, and from the warning, Dez knew she'd be on her way up the stairs. Luella lived downstairs in the two-story house, and she and Dez had grown close over the nine years Dez had lived there. Groggy from the pain pill she had taken in the middle of the night, she rolled out of bed, barefoot, still wearing her duty slacks and a t-shirt. Her arm throbbed mercilessly.

She opened the apartment door just as Luella, in all her plump, elderly blackness, rounded the newel post with newspaper in hand, and Dez turned to face her.

"Good lord, Dez!" she said. "Sorry if I woke you, but you're on the news again. What have you done to yourself now?" She shuffled in, her pink bedroom slippers skiffing on the hardwood hallway floor, her flowered robe swirling around her, and her silver hair in wild disarray. What Dez liked best about her landlady was the indomitable spirit that animated her deep brown eyes. Luella had a good-hearted smile always full of love and compassion for her moody tenant.

Dez looked at her casted arm and shrugged. She pulled the door open wide and Luella entered, dropping the folded newspaper on the table. She stood looking at Dez with a frown on her face. The injured cop sank down into a seat at the dinette table as Luella reached over to smooth dark hair off her forehead and let her hand rest there for a moment. "You feel like you've got a fever, gal."

Dez did not respond, so Luella moved over to open a cupboard.

"What are they saying on the news?" Dez said as she watched Luella set the tea kettle in the sink and fill it with water, then put it on the stove to heat. Dez stood, reaching with her good arm, and took down a wicker basket of various teas from the top of the cupboard and set them on the table. Both women sat down and gazed at one another.

As Luella fingered the packets of tea, she said, "Channel 5 is calling you a hero. Channel 4 asks why the police didn't catch the criminals sooner. Channel 11, as usual, did a more in-depth story. They say you caught two rapists—in the act, too."

"Not exactly. I got 'em before that happened." Dez shifted in her chair, not sure what to do with her casted arm. She set it on the table, but that felt awkward and made it throb. She moved it to her lap. It still throbbed. Oh well. She was going to have to get used to that.

Luella picked up the newspaper and unfolded it to the bottom of page one. "Check this out. One of them stinkers has welched on his buddy already, even told the cops that they'd done four other rapes, so it looks like this is a good collar for you. It's a pretty decent story—see?" She handed the paper to Dez, who winced immediately upon seeing the headline: *The Life of Reilly: Tragedy and Triumph.*"

"Geez, what a stupid headline."" Dez dropped the paper onto the table and looked away.

"You might not want to read it right now, Dez. They go into detail about...you know...about Ryan's death and everything." The older woman hesitated when she saw the pain in Dez's eyes. "But according to the paper, this was a great collar. You captured two very nasty guys, and since they gave each other up already, I think it's safe to congratulate you."

Dez was relieved. From what she'd seen, she knew they had enough evidence to convict the two men of assault, but if they didn't have criminal records, which she suspected might be the case, they could have gotten off easily. Of course there was always DNA evidence from the other attacks, but sometimes that didn't work out in court either. Much better that they'd turned against each other.

Luella gestured toward Dez's arm. "Is that broken?"

Dez nodded. "One of the jerks hit me with a bat. I can't believe I didn't really feel it until later." Which was actually a lie. She had known immediately that something was wrong because she had no grip in her hand, but she decided Luella didn't need to hear about that. "It'll be a good three or four weeks, I guess, before I can go back on regular duty." She shook her head in exasperation. "Just what I need now."

Luella reached over and covered Dez's good hand with her soft fingers and patted her. "A little bit of rest might be just what you need after what you've been through lately. You look exhausted, and you've been pushing yourself like there's no tomorrow. Ever since Ryan...."

"Yeah, I know," Dez said abruptly as she stood up to check the tea kettle, which was hardly warm yet. She leaned back against the counter and tried to cross her arms, but that sent a shooting pain up her arm, and she suddenly felt nauseated. She moved back to the chair and sat, allowing Luella to reach out again and stroke her pale arm with her soft, mahogany-colored hand and pink fingers.

Dez said, "I'm sorry, but I don't think I can take you over to Vanita's house today."

"Big deal. She can get off her fat butt and take a cab. You're always running us around."

"That's no way to talk about your sister," Dez said in mock seriousness. "Look at the bright side though; you won't have to iron for me for a couple weeks."

"No more chores for you for the rest of the summer either."

"Not much summer left. Wish I'd mowed yesterday."

"Oh, don't even worry about it. I can hire out the lawn," Luella said.

With a sudden fierceness Dez said, "For crap sake! I suppose I won't be able to play guitar for weeks."

Luella gazed at her grumpy friend and nodded. "Could be. You heal fast, though." Then she clucked and frowned. "But right now you don't look so good, little missy." An understatement. Dark circles under Dez's eyes paired up with lines of pain across her forehead. "You look beat. And *when* was the last time you ate?" Luella accused.

Dez gave her a half smile and a shrug, then got up to take the tea kettle off the hot burner with her good hand. She took down two mugs one at a time and set them on the counter.

"Here. Let me do that," said Luella. "You sit down there." In the absence of protest from Dez, Luella got the two mugs of tea ready and shuffled back over to the table where she added three spoons of sugar to hers. She lowered herself into the dinette chair, took a big sip, and said, "You're nothing but skin and bones, Desiree Reilly. You need decent food to recuperate. I'll be making up some good stuff for you today. It's not like you'll be able to cook. And besides, that so-called healthy stuff you eat isn't enough to nourish a squirrel." She reached for the sugar bowl and proceeded to heap another teaspoon of sugar into her lemon tea.

Dez had to smile. Luella was from the old school of red meat and potatoes, rich desserts, and three squares a day. Dez had long ago ceased to eat fatty foods, beef, or pork, but she didn't skimp. She ate plenty of grains, poultry, eggs, fish, vegetables, and fruit. She certainly ate enough to keep 175 pounds on her muscular six-foot frame.

"You're going to let me help whether you want to or not," Luella was saying. "I'm not going to stand by this time while you waste away. For once you've got to…"

"Okay."

"…take better care of your—what?"

"I said okay. Whaddya got for breakfast?"

The speed at which Luella rose belied her 74 years. As she hustled toward the door she said, "Fresh made jam and toast, pancakes, fruit. You want a little bacon or ham?"

"Everything but the meat sounds great."

As Luella made her way down the hallway, Dez could hear her: "I'll let you off this time, but you need good meat to heal. I think we'll be having roast beef tonight...." Skiff, skiff, skiff. Luella's arthritic knees navigated the stairs. "...and some nice roasted potatoes to go along with it...and fresh juicy corn...."

Dez stood up and got out some protein powder and a shaker cup. She drizzled water into the cup with the powder and shook it vigorously with her good hand, then sat down to drink it. She knew she couldn't ask for a better landlady. She and Luella had an arrangement that worked for both of them. Dez kept up the yard and lawn, fixed anything mechanical that she could, and helped with heavy spring cleaning. In return, Luella did her wash and ironed her uniforms, looked out for Dez, and served as a loving mother. The arrangement had evolved over the last nine years until Dez was as fond of Luella now as she would be her own mother; that is, if her own mother were still speaking to her.

Good as her word, Luella brought a tray of breakfast treats up. She sat drinking tea at the dinette table while Dez tried to eat. The food was excellent, but she had no appetite. After she ate what she could, Luella cleared everything away. She smoothed the hair off Dez's brow and brushed her warm lips across her forehead. "You go get some rest, honey," she said. "I know you haven't had much sleep. Call me if you need anything." She shuffled to the door balancing the tray carefully.

"I'll get the door, Luella." Dez stood and saw her out, then shut the door and turned to face the empty apartment. She was so terribly tired, but when she went to lie down, sleep would not come. She lay on her back, light slicing in through the small window high above the bed. Her mind raced, and she couldn't help thinking about all the violence she had witnessed lately. She had been a cop for over eight years, and she'd only been in minor altercations, usually just scuffles with people who didn't want to be arrested. Those periodic chances to flex her muscles she had actually enjoyed, not minding busting a few heads if it was needed. But she had never broken a bone, never been seriously injured.

Then all of a sudden, in the last fourteen months, there had been a rash of attacks on cops. Two officers had been shot to death by a crazy man who wasn't even going to trial, but instead went straight to the mental hospital. Murders of civilians in the city had doubled, and she'd been to far too many bloody crime scenes lately. Worst of all, her partner, Ryan Michaelson, had died, and now she'd been wounded by last night's attackers.

The department shrink had told her after Ryan's death that it was normal to be upset about these things, and Dez had eventually admitted she wasn't sleeping well. The shrink gave her instructions: don't go to bed until sleepy; if sleep doesn't come within about twenty minutes of lying down, get up and do something else until sleepy; get up on time, regardless of whether she'd had enough sleep. She'd tried all these things with no success. When she mentioned it to the counselor, the word depression came up, setting off major alarm bells. The doctor spent time talking about it and the types of medication that could help, which scared off Dez completely. She resolved not to be depressed and, the next time the topic came up, she told the shrink she'd finally started getting good sleep again. She attended the mandatory six sessions with the department psychologist, and that was it. She never went back.

But here it was, nearly three months since Ryan's death, and still, no good sleep. Instead, her mind busily spun through traumatic events, tried to rewrite what actually happened, though she knew it was futile. The only good thing about last night was that she had enjoyed subduing the two rapists, had enjoyed the solid sound of her fist and feet on flesh. At least after this altercation she felt a sense of grateful relief—nothing at all like the feeling of helplessness she had experienced after shooting Ryan's killer. She would have liked to have beaten that man to death, make him pay for what he'd done, but she didn't get the satisfaction. Ryan was dead, and that man was still alive. It made her angry to think about it.

She banished thoughts of Ryan from her mind, tried to breathe deeply, to let her thoughts float away. Instead, her monkey mind took a few more twists and turns and brought other painful images to mind: a tall, willowy, red-haired woman with laughing eyes and a deep tan standing on a rock in front of the water of Lake Superior; sitting in the low light of a banked campfire in the Boundary Waters Canoe Area; lying here in this very bed. The eyes, the smile, the presence: Karin. She put her out of her mind as best she could and turned over on her side, annoyed and restless. She tried to settle her cast somewhere comfortable and ended up placing it on a pillow, her arm tucked close to her side. She tried not to think of Karin, but the more Dez willed her from her memories, the more stubbornly the redhead stayed.

It was the oldest story in the book: older woman woos the younger, treats her special, gets her in the sack a few times, has fun for about three months, and then when commitment was at hand, it was "so long, been nice knowing ya." Dez was totally smitten, ready to plan a life, move in together, spend the rest of her days at Karin's side. The Day Of The Dumping, as she had come to think of it, she showed up at Karin's place as planned. They had made plans to go out to dinner, but as usual, they skipped the plans and wound up in bed, a trail of clothing dotting the hallway from the front room to the bedroom. Karin was inventive, passionate, and beautiful.

Dez couldn't get close enough to her. They lay in the brass bed after making love, and the phone rang.

"No, don't go," said Dez. "Just let it ring." She wrapped her arms tightly around Karin, laughing and teasing her.

Her lover struggled. "Let me go," she said coldly. She pushed Dez away and struggled out of the bed, pausing to grab her robe, but before she could get down the hall, the answering machine clicked in. A woman's voice, a husky, trash-talking woman's voice, filled Dez's ears. In the middle of the message, Karin picked up, and Dez didn't hear the rest. She lay wide-eyed in the bed trying to understand why a woman was calling her lover, her Karin, and begging to come over for sex and shrimp cocktail.

Dez was shocked at the change in Karin when she returned to the room. She held a handful of clothes and tossed them on the bed. "It's been fun," she said, "but it's over, Dez."

"What?" The black haired woman sat up in the bed, pulling the covers around her to try to stave off the ice-cold shock invading her body.

Karin began pulling on her own clothes. As she slipped on jeans she said, "You had to know this wasn't going to last forever."

"But—but—I don't understand. Why?"

Karin sighed and squeezed her eyes shut. "Dez, please don't tell me you're going to make this difficult. Get up and get dressed. Go home. The party's over." She pulled a sweater over her head and smoothed it down, then stood with one hand on her shapely hip, a look of disinterest on her face.

Dez was shaking too hard to get up. She reached over for her t-shirt and slipped it on over her head. "This was all a game for you?" She couldn't keep the disbelief from her voice.

"No, no, it wasn't a game. It was just—good fun. Like sports. A little action here, some fun times there." She gave a jaded laugh. "Don't tell me you ever thought this was something meaningful?" She laughed uncomfortably.

Dez fought back tears as she untangled her clothes and tried to make her fingers work to put them on. She stood and slipped on her jeans, then turned to face Karin. In a low voice she said, "Yeah, I thought we had something good going here." With an aching plea she couldn't hide she said, "Are you seeing someone else, that other woman?"

Karin let out a deep breath. "Of course," she sighed. "I thought you knew. Never stopped seeing her. *She's* not the jealous type."

"How would I have known?"

Karin shrugged. "Just thought maybe someone from around the department would have said something. I may have a bit of a reputation."

"No. No one said," she whispered.

And how could anyone tell her anything? She had done all she could to distance herself from Karin, to hide from others the fact that she was a lesbian. Perhaps people might wonder, but she didn't think so. It was a secret she kept to herself, and no one in the department would have known, except that Karin seemed to have had very effective radar. She'd played the seduction game to the hilt and Dez had fallen for it completely. A wave of anger washed over her, then a feeling of physical revulsion. She grabbed her things and stalked out of the house.

The next six weeks were nearly unbearable. After a week, she didn't care about Karin's other lover. She went to Karin and told her she would look the other way, but Karin had laughed at her, said the break was final and that it was over. Every day at work, Dez had to see Karin at roll call. Every day was a misery.

Then two things happened. First, Ryan asked her to partner with him in a two-man car, and second, Karin accepted a position with the Bureau of Criminal Apprehension. Out of sight, out of mind. With the woman gone, Dez could finally begin the process of sorting out her feelings. She had never considered herself a particularly violent person, but in this case, she found herself wanting to hurt or maim Karin. The images came to her in dreams: Karin, beaten and bloody, begging for forgiveness, falling off bridges to the rocks below, shot repeatedly. Dez was filled with a hatred so strong she felt sick to her stomach at times. But slowly it abated. As the winter days grew longer and spring beckoned, the injury that had felt like a death wound began to heal. After nearly seven years, she still bore the invisible scars, but she wasn't dead. She had survived, and never again would she let that happen to her.

Ryan had brought light into her life, his laughing presence a balm to her pained soul. Without even knowing the kind of medicine he was dispensing, he had taken her into his heart and made her a friend. With Karin assigned across town at the BCA, the constant reminder of her smile, of her shapely legs, of the passion they'd shared faded into the background. Dez had dated a few other women since then, but no one that stuck, nobody who was particularly special. In the past year, even before Ryan's death, she hadn't wanted to go out with anyone at all. It didn't seem worth the effort, and she tried hard not to think about there being an emptiness in her life. At one time she had wanted a lover, a life partner, but she was younger and naïve then. These days she no longer thought about it.

Now Dez was left with those old images and memories only when she slowed down long enough that they could intrude, uninvited, upon her. Nothing like what occurred with Karin would ever happen again. Never again would she have to face her coworkers feigning good humor and pleasantness when, deep inside, a pain festered and burned. A wall went up, a rule was made: all cops are off limits.

...To be continued in
GUN SHY
by Lori L. Lake
Available from Justice House Publishing
wherever fine books are sold